Also by ROBERT CONROY

1901

1862

1945

Red Inferno: 1945

1942

1942

A Novel

ROBERT CONROY

BALLANTINE BOOKS

NEW YORK

A Ballantine Books Trade Paperback Original

Copyright © 2009 by Robert Conroy

Published in the United States by Ballantine Books, an imprint of The Random House Publishing Group, a division of Random House, Inc., New York.

BALLANTINE and colophon are registered trademarks of Random House, Inc.

Library of Congress Cataloging-in-Publication Data
Conroy, Robert (Joseph Robert)
1942: a novel / Robert Conroy.
p. cm.
ISBN 978-0-345-50607-8
1. Pearl Harbor (Hawaii), Attack on, 1941—Fiction.
I. Title. II. Title: Nineteen forty-two.
PS3553.O51986A616 2009
813'.54—dc22   2008053825

Printed in the United States of America

www.ballantinebooks.com

4 6 8 9 7 5 3

INTRODUCTION

The attack on Pearl Harbor has resulted in vast amounts of speculative literature, much of it seen through the clear light of hindsight and, therefore, quite useless. Some have focused on the possibility of a plot on the part of President Roosevelt to get us into war with Japan. Not only has this been unproven but the rationale defies logic. Simply put, there was no motive. Roosevelt wanted us to go to war with Germany, not Japan.

Still, others feel that we had ample warning because we had broken the Japanese codes, which is partly true. We had broken the diplomatic codes but not the military codes, and the Japanese diplomats in Washington were totally out of the loop. They did not know that the attack on Pearl Harbor was coming.

However, there are items of fact that, had they occurred as they were expected to, would have changed the course of the war in the Pacific. The planned final strike on Pearl Harbor by Admiral Nagumo's fleet is one such item. Admiral Yamamoto had counted on it, and the Japanese pilots wished it, but Admiral Nagumo flinched in the face of success and denied it. He was happy with a partial victory and afraid of losing both precious pilots and his ships should the missing American carriers suddenly show up. In effect, Nagumo stole defeat from the jaws of victory.

1942 is the story of what would quite likely have occurred if Nagumo had been persuaded to let his pilots attack the oil storage facilities, machine shops, and dry docks at Pearl Harbor. Such a seemingly innocuous event and such prosaic targets, involving only a few score planes and resulting in a few hundred additional casualties at most, could have changed the course of the war in the Pacific.

Indeed, many of the changes could have been permanent and vastly to the advantage of the Japanese.

Initially, the changes to history resulting from the final strike would have been small. For instance, I have Admiral Nimitz replacing Admiral Kimmel at a slightly earlier date, as well as Admiral King superseding Admiral Stark in Washington as the extent and implications of the revised disaster become known. Other changes evolve as they would have logically developed as history begins to change.

To simplify matters and make the reader comfortable, I have used the American way of giving the names of the Japanese participants, rather than the Japanese way. Also, I have largely ignored the ramifications of the International Date Line.

And whether what I refer to as the final strike would have been the second or third strike depends on whether one counts the attacks on Pearl Harbor as one or two events.

Everything I've written and all the facts, right or wrong, are products of my own research and imagination.

1942

Admiral Chuichi Nagumo clasped his hands behind him and glowered as he looked down and across the flight deck of his flagship, the carrier *Akagi*. The ship's crew lined the deck and lustily cheered each returning hero, and it was both astonishing and exhilarating to see how many of the brave young eagles were home from their morning of triumph.

Why then was he so disturbed? The surprise attack on Pearl Harbor had been an overwhelming success that had exceeded virtually all expectations. He had accomplished everything he reasonably felt that he could. Why then did he have this feeling of uneasiness at what should have been the most glorious moment in his life?

Nagumo felt that he knew the answer, and it disturbed him. He was fifty-five, not too old for active command, but he was a man whose career had been without combat experience and bridged several developing technologies. By training and inclination, he was a big-gun man, a battleship man, a believer in traditional surface fighting. Nagumo had served on destroyers and cruisers, and commanded the battleship *Yamashiro* before his promotion to rear admiral and appointment to preside over the Naval Staff College. He was not a pilot and had never before served on an aircraft carrier.

But in April 1941, Nagumo had been promoted to command the First Air Fleet, which consisted of six carriers and more than four hundred planes. He had then been tasked to command the surprise attack on Pearl Harbor, which would launch Japan into a war with the United States. Because of America's naval might, total surprise was essential to the attack's success. Nagumo had thought it too risky and had protested. His superior, Admiral Isoroku Yamamoto, had overruled him, and he had done as ordered to the best of his abilities.

Kido Butai was the name of the task force that included the six carriers, along with two battleships and attending cruisers and destroyers. When it sailed from northern Japan in late November, Nagumo had been cut off from the rest of the world.

To ensure secrecy, his ships kept total radio silence, and the enforced loneliness preyed on his doubts, causing him moments of near despair. Despite maintaining a stoic exterior, Nagumo was terrified that the *Kido Butai* would be located and either forced to withdraw in shame or defeated by the angered Americans, who had many more battleships than he.

While he commanded six carriers, Nagumo was still convinced that the battleship, and not the upstart and unproven carrier, was the queen of battle. No modern Japanese fleet had ever been defeated, and Nagumo had a deathly fear that his would be the first.

With luck and skill, they had made it to the launch point without detection. Incredibly, they caught the Americans by surprise and quickly eliminated the American battle line. The American battleship force in the Pacific was destroyed in an overwhelming victory for the Empire of Japan.

So why then was he still in turmoil?

Again, he knew the answer to his own dilemma. Along with some of his senior admirals, the young Turks in his command wanted more. They did not agree with him that the battleships were their main objective; they weren't satisfied with what he considered a total victory, and Nagumo was afraid that their greed would ruin him.

However, Nagumo felt compelled to listen to two of the most vocal of his critics. Commander Minoru Genda had planned the attack and was a protégé of Yamamoto's. Genda had fervently argued that the next war, the one Nagumo had just started, would be fought with carriers, and not battleships, as the main protagonists. Genda had been ill; otherwise, he would have been in a plane observing the battle. The thirty-seven-year-old commander was fearless as well as brilliant.

Nagumo thought Genda's idea was preposterous, but then he reminded himself that he commanded six carriers whose planes had just destroyed at least that many battleships. It was very disturbing, and he acknowledged the irony that he now worried about the American carriers, and not their battleships.

The second voice that had to be listened to belonged to Lieutenant

Commander Mitsuo Fuchida. Fuchida was thirty-nine, flight commander of the *Akagi*, and had commanded the first wave over Pearl Harbor. His excited voice had signaled that the surprise had been absolute. Fuchida's uniform was dirty and strain showed on his face, but his eyes were bright, and Nagumo knew the younger man was like a tiger yearning to be unleashed.

Nagumo shook his head. "We have overstayed our welcome. We must depart before the Americans locate us and attack. Our carriers are precious and cannot be squandered. Had the American carriers been in Pearl Harbor and had they been destroyed, there would be no question about launching another attack. As it is, Halsey's carriers could be approaching us as we speak and could be preparing a devastating attack. Even a thief," he added with a grim smile, "knows not to return to the scene of the crime."

"We are warriors, not thieves," Genda said softly, in a voice that was nearly a hiss. It was important that others in the vicinity not hear their argument. "We have six carriers to their two, and, more important, we are operating as a unit while they departed Pearl Harbor singly. Any American attack would be piecemeal and easily contained. Also, the Americans have no battleships to protect them while we have two. Let the American carriers find us and we will destroy them as completely as we destroyed their battle fleet."

Nagumo reluctantly agreed with Genda's math. Along with the *Akagi*, the other five Japanese carriers were the *Kaga, Shokaku, Zuikaku, Hiryu,* and *Soryu,* and they carried a total of 423 combat planes in a deadly mix of fighters, bombers, and torpedo bombers. The two battleships were the *Hiei* and the *Kirishima,* and they would easily outgun any other surface warship the Americans now possessed. America's big-gun ships lay in the muck of Pearl Harbor.

The missing American carriers were the *Lexington* and the *Enterprise,* which had only recently departed Pearl Harbor. Japanese intelligence, as provided by spies from their Honolulu consulate, had proven excellent.

Genda was correct that the two American carriers had only a third of what his six carried and that they were at sea in two separate commands. The Americans had not yet learned the principle of unity. Divide and be conquered appeared to be their strategy.

Genda declined to mention that a third carrier, the *Saratoga,* might also be in the area, although it was more likely she was still off California. Such information might have further upset his surprisingly timid admiral.

"Admiral," Genda continued in a whisper, "with utmost respect, may I speak freely?"

The comment broke the tension, and Nagumo smiled at the intense young man, whom he genuinely liked. "Has it ever been otherwise, Genda? You have always spoken your mind."

"Then please let me remind you of our objectives, which were threefold. First, we were to destroy the American battleships and, second, the carriers along with their heavy cruiser escorts." Genda felt that the order of precedence was reversed but discreetly said otherwise.

"Our third and final task was to destroy the oil storage and maintenance facilities at Pearl, thus eliminating its usefulness as a base. We have accomplished only one of those three goals, in that the battleships are destroyed. Fuchida says at least four are sunk and three others badly damaged.

"As to the carriers and cruisers, it is simply bad luck that they are at sea. They are gone, and there is nothing we can do about it. But if we destroy Pearl Harbor as a base, neither the missing carriers nor the replacement battleships the Americans are sure to send from the Atlantic will have a home to return to. All of Hawaii will be useless to the Americans, until and if they replace what they will lose if you will only permit us to attack once more."

Nagumo wavered. The attack was indeed part of the plans, and the oil and dock facilities were extremely important targets. Again, Genda was correct. The Americans had lost badly, but they had other battleships in the Atlantic, and, since they were not yet at war with Germany, they would likely transfer some of those to fight Japan. It occurred to him that they might even transfer other carriers. The United States had been hurt, but far from fatally or even permanently.

He agonized. Perhaps he was being too cautious, too shocked by the ease of victory.

"We will suffer heavily," Nagumo said. He hated the thought of losing the brave young men under his command. In the earlier attacks, he had lost an astoundingly low number considering the risks entailed. However, most of those lost had been from the second wave. By that time, the Americans were alert and outraged, and had fought like furies with what weapons remained at their disposal. This meant that a final attack would be against an aroused and infuriated enemy.

"We have all trained to fight," Genda answered, "and fighting involves dying. Fuchida has a plan, and I am confident that an attack focused solely on the oil storage and dry dock facilities can be an overwhelming success with minimal losses."

"Then you would not need a large force?"

Genda and Fuchida exulted. Their admiral was coming around to their way of thinking. Nagumo had extended a straw, and they would grasp it.

Fuchida spoke for the first time. "That is correct, Admiral, a large force would not be necessary. We can change our plans and attack with a greatly reduced number. I would wish a screen of forty or so Zero fighters and a main force of sixty Kate bombers. Torpedo planes would be useless against land targets, and the remainder of the aircraft would be kept with the fleet for defensive purposes.

"My plan is simple. The storage tanks and docks are located just to the east of the narrow entrance to the harbor itself. We will approach from the south in a thin line of planes. As if they were a spear point, Zeros will precede the bombers and attack any antiaircraft positions protecting the target areas. They will attack low and fast, and then take on any American planes that rise to challenge us. The shaft of the spear, the Kates, will come in higher and then either dive-bomb or level-bomb first the dry dock facilities behind the oil storage tanks and then the oil tanks themselves. That priority ensures that smoke from burning oil does not interfere with the attack on the dry docks. A smaller group will veer off and attack the storage tanks behind the submarine pens. The smoke from the burning warships was a hindrance during the latter part of the second attack."

Fuchida's voice rose as his enthusiasm increased. "Our pilots will escape by flying over Ford Island and across other fleet maintenance areas at Pearl City, which they will attack if there are bombs remaining. At that point the planes will turn west and fly away from the island. As you are aware, the targets are very close together. It will take but a few minutes to accomplish their destruction."

Fuchida knew it would not be that simple. In order to hit the oil facilities, they would first have to fly over Hickam Field, which was sure to be well defended by American antiaircraft guns. Nor could the planes turn and head west without placing themselves between Wheeler Field and the Marine air base at Ewa. If the Americans reacted quickly, the casualties would be severe.

However, most of the American planes had already been destroyed on the ground, and it was unlikely that the few that got in the air against the attack would be able to coordinate their efforts. Both Fuchida and Genda thought it was a risk well worth taking.

Fuchida smiled. "Admiral, the battleship *Pennsylvania* is in one of the dry docks, as are the cruisers *San Francisco* and *Honolulu,* and we do not believe either is badly damaged. Therefore, when we get the docks, we will sink the *Pennsylvania* and the other ships, adding another battleship to the tally."

Nagumo was in turmoil. Genda was right about the desirability of destroying the oil tanks and the dry docks, and the virtually unharmed *Pennsylvania* was a truly tempting target. Fuchida was right about utilizing only a small number of planes in a localized attack on a target that was tantalizingly close to the safety of the ocean. Japanese planes would be able to attack directly from the sea and not overfly much of Oahu at all. They would not be subject to antiaircraft until the very last moment. It was brilliant. It would save lives.

"Admiral," Genda said, "the planes are fueled and armed, and the pilots are ready to go. This entire event can be over and done with in little more than three hours. At that time, the fleet can steam northward and be many miles away from here before nightfall."

"How will you select the pilots?"

Genda chuckled, and Nagumo smiled at the foolishness of his own question. "Admiral, if I ask for volunteers, everyone will step forward. No, I will select only those I consider the best and bravest from among the best and bravest men in the world."

The first attack had been launched at six in the morning, while the carriers pitched in the deep swells. There had been no mishaps, and the second wave had followed forty-five minutes later. By eight o'clock, the assaults had commenced and war with the United States had begun with a tremendous Japanese victory. Two hours later, it was over and almost all the planes had returned. Only twenty-nine had been shot down, and another seventy damaged.

Nagumo again fretted and regretted the loneliness of command.

He wondered what Yamamoto would do and heard himself answer that his intimidating superior was a predator who would go for the throat. Yamamoto would not let the opportunity to further hurt the American navy pass by. If Pearl Harbor could be denied to America as a base for her reinforcement fleet, the final attack could easily be as great a victory as the destruction of the battleships in the first two.

If he gave in to Genda and Fuchida, it would mean turning the fleet southward, as it was already heading northwest on a course that would take it back to Japan. Such a turn might place the *Kido Butai* in the path of the two American carriers. However, there was nothing to indicate that the Americans had any idea he was to the north of the islands. Planning back in Tokyo had presumed that the Americans would think the attack had come from the west or south; thus permitting an easy withdrawal. So far, nothing had happened to indicate otherwise.

Nagumo knew that he had recourse by radio to Yamamoto himself. The senior admiral commanding the Combined Fleet had already received notice of the victory. It would be a small matter to ask for advice.

No, Nagumo thought angrily. He would not ask for advice. Yamamoto had entrusted him with command and he would command. He, and not Yamamoto, was the man in charge of the battle, and he, not Yamamoto, would make the right decision.

Then Nagumo smiled. Genda was right. What if the carriers did find him? He outnumbered them three to one, and, even if attacked while Fuchida's planes were away, he still had the firepower to destroy any American attackers and achieve their third goal, the destruction of the carriers.

"Go," he ordered simply.

CHAPTER 1

•

*T*he day threatened to be pleasantly uneventful for U.S. Army Captain Jake Novacek as he dressed and got ready for another Sunday in paradise. After a hard week's work, he thought he might go to Waikiki, lie in the sun, and stare at the attractive young women in their bathing suits.

His only concern was that he still ached from Saturday's Army-Navy touch football game with other officers. They were ex-athletes like himself, but unfortunately, they were several years younger than Jake's thirty-six and had nearly run him into the ground. Jake was larger than most at just under six feet and almost two hundred pounds, which somewhat compensated for the age disparity when he managed to catch up with one of the young navy pups. It may have been touch football, but some of the touches were damned hard.

Jake grimaced from a stiffness in his shoulder as he finished shaving. He was in his overnight quarters at Hickam Field's officers' club instead of the small apartment he had in Honolulu, and admitted he had no one but himself to blame for the situation. But then he grinned. Touch football or not, it was fun to knock a sailor-boy officer on his ass every now and then. He checked his thick black mustache—which pushed the limits permitted by the army—and trimmed a couple of errant hairs.

Jake had just put on his trousers and was deciding whether to eat breakfast in town or at the officers' club when he thought he heard thunder. At first, he ignored it, but it was sunny out; why the thunder?

As he pondered this, the sounds got closer. "Oh, shit," he muttered. Somebody was going to get in a whole lot of trouble for scheduling gunnery practice on a Sunday morning in December.

Then he was on the floor and gasping for breath while his ears rang from the shock of an explosion. His small room was full of dust, and something cut his arm.

Jake got up and ran down the stairs and outside, where other officers were gathering, shock and disbelief on their faces.

"What the hell's going on?" Jake yelled, and no one answered. Had some asshole dropped a bomb or plunked a shell down on the wrong spot? He felt a twinge of sorrow for the poor bastard. Then a plane flew overhead, and he saw the rising sun on its wing.

"Japs!" someone yelled. "We're being attacked by the Japs!"

Another bomb landed nearby, and he felt the concussion. Jake ran in the general direction of the airfield, dreading what he would see when he got there. He knew that the planes on the ground were vulnerable. Nobody was prepared for an attack.

He arrived just in time to see a Jap plane peeling off from a strafing run. It passed over his head by no more than a hundred feet, and he saw the pilot's face. It looked like the monkey-faced bastard was grinning.

Jake wrenched his eyes back to the runways, where so many planes had been parked nearly wingtip to wingtip in anticipation of a saboteur's attempt to sabotage them, which General Short feared in these tense times. Jake had said it was a bad idea, and now, as he watched them burn and explode by the dozens, he knew he had been vindicated and hated the fact.

Across the runway, a pair of 37 mm antiaircraft guns pointed uselessly at the sky while their crews watched the destruction. Angered, he ran across the field to the guns, dropping to the ground when another Jap plane streaked overhead. He comforted himself with the thought that a single man foolish enough to dash across a runway wasn't much of a target for a Jap in an airplane.

He reached the guns, where a sergeant saluted him quickly. "Sergeant, who are you and why the hell aren't you shooting at them?" Jake yelled, his voice shaking in anger.

The sergeant shrugged in utter disgust. "I'm Sergeant Steinmetz and I've got no ammo and no one will give me any." He pointed to a storage shed. "Our ammo's in there, and the asshole in charge will only give it to officers. I guess he thinks it's his and not the army's."

"Then where is your officer?"

"Sir, I have absolutely no idea where Lieutenant Simpkins is." The look on Sergeant Steinmetz's face told Jake that Simpkins was not sorely missed. It occurred to both men that the Japanese attack had stopped, and there was a dreadful silence punctuated by periodic explosions and the distant wail of sirens.

Jake wiped a dirty handkerchief across his sweaty brow and then over his close-cut dark hair as he turned and looked out over the ocean. From where he stood, the sea to the south looked marvelously tranquil, even normal. He turned again and saw the ruins of Pearl Harbor and the smoking, burning death of America's military strength in Hawaii. Jake was an intelligence officer and, like others, had pondered the meaning of the "war warning" they'd recently received from General Marshall in Washington. He wondered if the Japs had attacked other areas on Oahu. Logic said they had.

Jake was angry at the total stupidity of it. He gathered the sergeant, commandeered a truck, and drove to the storage shed, where Jake bullied a poor supply sergeant into releasing some ammunition to them. Just for the hell of it, he also grabbed a .45 automatic and a couple of clips of ammunition. Having a weapon on his hip just made him feel better.

But by the time they'd returned and loaded their guns, it looked like the fighting was over. The close-packed planes on Hickam's runways were charred ruins, and some of the hangars and other buildings were burning. The dead and wounded lay on the ground, and other soldiers had begun to tend to them. Behind their position, they saw numerous churning clouds of black smoke that came from the warships in the harbor itself. A lot of good people had died this December 7, many of them his friends. Many of them guys he'd played football with the day before.

A staff car pulled up behind his guns, and a neatly dressed young lieutenant jumped out and ran over. On seeing the bars on Jake's collar, he stopped and saluted.

Jake returned it briskly. "Are you supposed to be in charge here?"

"Yes, sir. I'm Lieutenant Simpkins."

Jake didn't recognize him. Pearl was a large base, and he'd been back for only a couple of months. "Where the hell've you been?"

Simpkins grimaced. "I was off base, sir, and the bombing woke me up. It took some time for me to get here."

That made sense, Jake thought. If he hadn't stayed late at the club the night before, he'd have been several miles away in his own apartment. Sunday was a sleep-in and goof-off day, unless it was your turn to draw duty at a base located in the most beautiful spot on the earth. It was only luck that he'd been on base this awful morning. Then he noticed something and drew Simpkins away from the group, where they could talk in private.

"Lieutenant, you shaved after you got up, didn't you?"

"Yes, sir," he muttered.

"Shower?"

Simpkins was puzzled. "Yes, sir."

"And then you had breakfast, right?"

"Coffee and a doughnut, sir," he said reluctantly. "Why?"

Jake rubbed his eyes in weary disbelief. No wonder the sergeant wasn't concerned about Simpkins's absence. "You're telling me it was more important to complete your personal ablutions and feed yourself than it was to get to the battle and defend your country? You saw that the Japanese were attacking. Why didn't you just throw your clothes on and rush over? Or did you think they'd hold up the war until you got here?"

"Sir," Simpkins replied weakly, "I would have been out of uniform." Then he realized the inanity of what he was saying. "My God."

Jake shook his head. There was no way he could blame Simpkins or the supply sergeant who'd hoarded the priceless ammo during the battle. They just didn't understand what was happening. Hell, did he? He'd already shaved and showered when the bombs started dropping, so he too had arrived clean for the battle. But would he have continued if the bombs had fallen only a few minutes earlier? Jake didn't think so, but he wasn't absolutely certain. Being at war was something totally new to everyone.

"Don't worry, Lieutenant, there'll be a lot of recriminations for this among the higher-ups, and not a whole lot of concern about how one lieutenant might or might not have fucked up. I'm not so sure I'm doing the right thing myself, but at least we're here and doing something."

Simpkins looked relieved. He was about to say something when air-raid sirens went off again.

"Jesus," said Jake and looked around for an enemy. Was this a new attack, or was somebody finally getting around to sounding the alarm for an earlier one? By his count there'd been two distinct assaults on the Hickam Field area, with the last one several hours earlier.

Simpkins yelled and pointed out to sea. A long line of dots was low in the sky and approaching from the south. "My God," Simpkins said. "They're coming right over us."

Jake told the gunners to hold their fire. The 37-millimeters had a range of about ten thousand feet, which wasn't very much. The lead Japs were coming in low and fast, with other planes in long lines higher up and behind them.

"Now," he yelled, and both guns opened up with a roar that was extremely satisfying. They were fighting back, and it felt good, damned good.

"What're they going for?" Simpkins asked through the din. "Hickam's pretty well shot over already."

Jake agreed that it didn't make sense unless they were going to make an additional strike on the ships in the harbor. However, if the smoke from the Ford Island area was any indication, they'd been pretty well shot up also. So what was the target?

Then he remembered the large cluster of oil storage tanks behind him. They were the target, not Hickam, and not the ships.

A Jap fighter peeled off the main group and lined up on them, daring Jake's guns to shoot him down. The plane couldn't have been twenty feet off the ground as it streaked toward them. Lights twinkled on the plane's wings, and seconds later the ground around Jake's guns was churned up by a storm of bullets.

Jake ducked and tried to claw into the earth while dust and debris covered him. In all his years in the army, today was the first time anyone had shot at him, and he didn't like it at all. He whimpered and heard others crying and screaming. Then he heard a voice a lot like his own moaning in fear.

The plane was gone. He raised himself and looked around. One of his guns was destroyed, although the sergeant continued to fire the second at Jap bombers who were high overhead and out of range. They passed, and he saw their ghastly bomb loads tumble down onto the fuel tanks.

For a second there was silence, and he hoped they'd missed, but then the tanks began to explode in fiery bursts of oil that rolled into the sky. They were a couple of miles away, and he could still feel the heat. God help anyone near that inferno, he thought.

Again Jake scanned the skies. No more planes were approaching him, and there were smoking streaks across the blue that might indicate a plane had been shot down. He hoped so. Somebody had to punish the bastards. This attack was over, but was it the last? He prayed it was. How many more could Pearl Harbor take?

"Casualties," he called out.

"Everyone's okay," Steinmetz answered, "except for the lieutenant."

"Where is he?"

"Over here," the sergeant answered grimly, "and over there."

Jake looked where the sergeant pointed and gagged. Simpkins had been cut in half by the Jap fighter's guns, and the two parts of his body were about twenty feet apart, connected only by a bloody trail.

Jake wrenched his eyes away from the awful sight and looked skyward. Far up, he saw a couple of planes. Japs, he thought, checking on the damage they'd done.

"Fuck you," he screamed at them. "Fuck you!"

ALEXA SANDERSON HAD AWAKENED well before seven. It gave her plenty of time to put on the coffee and awaken her husband, Tim. He grumped when she tickled him, and that made her laugh. It was a shame Tim had duty this wonderful Sunday morning, but that was the life of a naval officer. At least they'd had a marvelous Saturday night, attending a concert consisting of a battle among several of the battleships' bands. The consensus was that the *Arizona*'s band was the best.

After that, they'd gone home, made marvelously noisy and athletic love, and then fallen asleep.

Tim left with plenty of time to make it from their small but expensive rented house on the outskirts of Honolulu to duty on the battleship *Oklahoma*. While she hated his leaving her, she was thankful that they were able to spend so much time together. So many other wives simply couldn't afford to follow their husbands to their duty stations. Alexa didn't consider having money a curse, although she took great pains not to flaunt it.

Alexa was also thankful that she and Tim had married. She didn't think of herself as terribly pretty, and at twenty-eight, she was five foot nine and nearly one hundred and forty pounds. By contemporary standards, she was too tall, too athletic, too muscular, and, to compound problems, too intelligent, articulate, and outspoken for most men's tastes. She had light brown hair, brown eyes, even features, and she thanked God that Tim had been attracted enough by the package to marry her three years earlier.

At least she knew he hadn't married her for her money. He had even more than she did. There were those who thought Tim was dull, but she knew otherwise. He was quiet and sincere, and, better, would be out of the navy in a few months. Then they could go back home to Virginia and start the family they'd talked about so much.

She turned at the sound of a pounding on her kitchen door.

Melissa Wilson burst in, with her infant son in her arms and concern on her face. "Do you hear it?"

Melissa was Alexa's neighbor. Short and pretty, she was the type of buxom princess other men always seemed to lust after. Melissa, Missy to her friends, was also very excitable.

"Hear what?" Alexa asked.

"The explosions."

Alexa strained and realized there were rumblings off in the distance. She'd been so wrapped up in her thoughts that she hadn't heard a thing. She grabbed her friend, and they ran outside. Located near the hills that overlooked Honolulu, her little bungalow was on higher ground than most of the area, but she still couldn't quite see the harbor or where the sounds were coming from.

What she could see was smoke starting to rise from the area where the ships were anchored. Planes circled the smoke like bees, and she wondered if they were somehow trying to put out the fire. There were tiny puffs of black smoke in the air that looked like antiaircraft fire, but that just couldn't be. Evidently it was a bad accident, but nothing that would involve antiaircraft fire.

Whatever it was, Alexa hoped it didn't involve the *Oklahoma*. Tim had told her that a battleship was the safest place in the world to be, but she didn't want that theory tested. She didn't worry about Melissa's husband, who was at sea on the carrier *Lexington*.

People had begun to gather on the dirt road that led to the city.

Everyone was puzzled and concerned. Whatever the accident was, it was beginning to look serious. Then another neighbor burst out of his house.

"Japs! I just heard it on the radio. Japs have attacked the battleships!"

Alexa was first incredulous, then stunned. She grabbed Melissa. "I have to get down there. Tim's on his ship."

Tim had taken their car, so Melissa said she'd drive and gave the baby to a neighbor to watch. Then Melissa got behind the wheel of her Chevrolet and drove toward the base. It was slow going as people filled the streets and stared at the growing conflagration. The closer they got, the more damage they saw, including homes and buildings burning fiercely. The Japs weren't attacking just the base.

They looked in horror at a car that was up on a lawn. A line of bullets had stitched holes in its top, and at least two people were slumped over inside, dead.

At the base, a grim-faced guard stopped them. "Sorry, but you can't go in."

"My husband's on the *Oklahoma*," Alexa pleaded.

The guard's expression softened, but he didn't relent. "Look, ma'am, I'd like to help, but I can't. There's just too much happening and you'd be in danger. Go back home and wait. I'm sure everything'll be okay."

Reluctantly, she saw the sense of it. Like it or not, there suddenly was a war on, and Tim had more important things to do at this moment. But dark clouds of smoke were growing overhead like a malevolent and terrifying thundercloud. Something awful was happening in the harbor.

At Melissa's suggestion, they drove slowly from the base and to a rise that overlooked the harbor. It was a favorite spot for those who wanted a good view of what was referred to as Battleship Row, and also served as a place where kids went to make out. Both women discounted the dangers from Japanese planes, which seemed to have flown off.

Hundreds of other people had had the same idea, and they had to park a ways off. Finally, they made it to where they could see the battleships. The great clouds of smoke, however, made viewing difficult.

"Oh my God," Melissa said. "I never dreamed it could be so awful."

Alexa didn't answer. She was busy trying to figure out where the *Oklahoma* was. Normally, she had no problem spotting Tim's ship, but everything seemed strangely out of kilter. Something was terribly, horribly wrong.

First, the *Nevada* was missing, and behind where she had been lay the *Arizona*. Or, she realized grimly, what had once been the *Arizona*. The battleship was a mass of flames and was sinking. She wondered how something made of metal could burn so brightly.

Behind the *Arizona* was the *West Virginia*, which was also on fire. The *Tennessee*, anchored between the *West Virginia* and Ford Island, seemed to be okay.

But where the devil was the *Oklahoma*? Could she have escaped, as the *Nevada* appeared to have done? Something large, metal, and cylindrical was where the *Oklahoma* should have been. Alexa doubled over in nausea and sudden agony as she realized that the strange and obscene shape was Tim's ship. The massive battleship lay far on its side, with nothing of its superstructure showing. Anyone inside had to be trapped in what was now a grotesque parody of a warship.

"Tim," she groaned.

Melissa saw and hugged her. "He'll be all right," she tried to reassure her friend through her own tears. "Let's get out of here. We can't just stay here and stare."

Alexa looked around and saw many others were weeping. She wasn't the only one with a loved one in danger. "Drive around," she said.

"Why?"

"We've got to find a place where they're taking the injured and volunteer to help. Missy, I've got to do something. If I just go home and wait, I'll go crazy."

Alexa took a deep breath and tried to calm herself. Even if he was okay, it would be hours at best before Tim had a chance to call her. At least she would be able to stay active and put her first aid training to use. At least she would be able to do something. Anything.

COMMANDER FUCHIDA IGNORED the steady drone of the Nakajima B5N2's engine and looked down on Pearl Harbor. He would rather be piloting the three-man bomber instead of observing, but it was more important for him to be a spectator at this time. Let the others fly the plane and be on the lookout for American fighters.

It was difficult to see because of the height at which he was flying and the blankets of dark smoke that obscured much of the target area below. He considered flying lower, but that would only invite antiaircraft fire, and might even attract one of the few fighters the Americans had left.

From what he could tell, the final attack had been extremely successful. First, he had led somewhat more than the hundred planes he'd told Nagumo he wanted. It had proven impossible to stop all of the eager young pilots from joining him, and several of the more aggressive carrier captains had conspired in letting them join the attack.

Second, he'd been right in his tactics. The lead Zeros had quickly overwhelmed and obliterated the antiaircraft defenses that shielded both Hickam Field and the now burning oil storage tanks. He wasn't certain about the extent of damage to the *Pennsylvania* and the adjacent cruisers, but he could see fires on the battleship. The *Pennsylvania* might not have been sunk, but she was damaged. More important, the dry docks appeared to be a burning shambles.

A handful of American fighters had tried to intercept the attack and been beaten off with substantial losses. As predicted, their attacks were uncoordinated and offered more proof that neither their pilots nor their tactics were up to Japanese standards. Most of the Americans had been shot down, with only a few losses to the Japanese air fleet. Fuchida now concluded the American planes were also inferior to the Japanese Zero. So much for the myth of American technology, he thought.

Predictably, Admiral Nagumo had lost his nerve and tried to cancel the attack. When Fuchida received the radio message, he'd first ignored it and then said it was too late—the attack had already begun. It had been a small lie but an effective one. The planes were only minutes away from Pearl and had doubtless been sighted.

As they flew over the burning harbor, the rear gunner took pictures, and Fuchida thought it was a shame they weren't in color. The harshness of the contrast between the loveliness of the harbor and the cruelty of the fires would make a marvelous picture if only someone could capture the vivid colors.

Japanese losses had been even lighter than he'd hoped, with only a few planes falling from antiaircraft fire as they flew over Ford Island and turned westward. Fuchida genuinely felt the loss of American lives as well as those of his own men. He had planned and fought for Japan and would again, but the devastation upset him. The carnage below should not have happened. Why hadn't America seen reason and avoided war?

Enough, he thought. Perhaps someday he'd know the answer. Fuchida promised himself that, when the war was over, he'd learn more about the United States and the beliefs of her people. What little he knew fascinated him. Perhaps he would even visit there.

But that was for later. He tapped the pilot on the shoulder and ordered a return to the fleet.

CHAPTER 2

.

Admiral Isoroku Yamamoto was the hero of the moment and had decided to take advantage of it. His was the dominant personality within the navy, despite the fact that he was merely the first among several equals. As admiral of the Combined Fleet, he had by far the largest portion of the seagoing navy, but he was supposed to coordinate with entities within the naval hierarchy, many of whom seemed to have their own agendas. Yamamoto also reported directly to the naval chief of staff, Admiral Osami Nagano. So far, Nagano had proven easy for Yamamoto to dominate.

More than once Yamamoto had thought Japan was as likely to be defeated in the new war by her own byzantine bureaucratic mazes as by American industry and military strength. Japan was run by the military, but cooperation between the army and the navy was almost nonexistent.

For that reason, Admiral Yamamoto had asked for a private audience with the prime minister, General Hideki Tojo. If he could convince Tojo of the rightness of his idea, then Tojo would convince the others. It was irregular, but he felt the circumstances required it. As the hero of the moment, he knew he could bend protocol to the extent of having a private discussion with the prime minister, who was also the army minister. He had, of course, informed Admiral Nagano, who had given his discreet blessing to the mission. If Yamamoto was turned down, Nagano could then plausibly deny having encouraged him.

Yamamoto had managed to make the appointment within hours of hearing of the totality of the victory at Pearl Harbor. His dreams of victory had always been tempered by the realistic assessment that he would lose two of their priceless carriers and much of his airpower in destroying the American fleet at Pearl Harbor. When that did not happen, he realized that a new door had opened for Japan. At fifty-seven, Isoroku Yamamoto also knew that he personally had only a few remaining opportunities to influence the course of Japan's history.

Leaving his aides with a whirlwind of tasks, Yamamoto had flown from the naval base at Hiroshima to Tokyo and arrived early the morning after the attack. He was alone and incognito. This was not the time to draw attention to himself. As a further concession, Tojo had agreed to meet with him at the prime minister's residence.

Tojo greeted Yamamoto warmly, even exuberantly. After all, hadn't the admiral given Japan the greatest naval victory since the victory over the Russians at Tsushima in 1905? Perhaps Pearl Harbor was even greater than that now legendary victory. Coincidentally, a very young Yamamoto had been present at Tsushima and lost two fingers from a shell fragment.

"General," Yamamoto began, "I have requested this meeting because I wish to make a substantial change in our strategy regarding the Americans."

Tojo turned serious. "Let me guess. You now wish to invade Hawaii."

"Correct."

"But why? You were against both that and the attack on Pearl Harbor. So was I until I recognized the need for it."

"General, I based my opposition to attacking the American fleet on the fact that it would arouse a sleeping giant, the United States. We have no way of countering her industrial might. Remember, please, that I have been to America and toured her factories in Pittsburgh and Detroit, and we have nothing to compare with them.

"I said that we would run wild for six months to a year, and then I said I could not guarantee what would happen thereafter. The Americans have been constructing a vast fleet that could overwhelm us in a year or two at the most if peace is not arrived at."

"I know," Tojo said grimly. "Our strategy subsequent to attacking the United States was to be so solid defensively that any attempt at conquering us would be too expensive for them. It was also decided that Hawaii was outside the limits of our defensive perimeter, because it would be too expensive for us to conquer and hold. Admiral, what has changed your mind?"

"Simply put, the defenses at Pearl Harbor and the rest of Hawaii were far weaker than we believed and are now nonexistent. We can take and hold Hawaii, and the United States will not be able to use it as a forward staging area for assaults on Japan. Any attacks will have to come from California or Australia. I'm also sure that, as prime minister, you can see any number of diplomatic reasons for our holding Hawaii."

"Of course. But the Americans will immediately bring reinforcements to Hawaii, won't they?"

"They can't," Yamamoto said simply.

"What?"

"They have no fuel. They cannot bring ships or planes to Pearl Harbor because they cannot resupply them with fuel. The final attack on Pearl destroyed the American oil reserves. These cannot be made up, at least not for quite some time. In my opinion, they will have to send their fleet, including the carriers that escaped us, to either Australia or California."

"I don't understand. Ships and planes go to Hawaii all the time."

"Certainly," Yamamoto conceded, "but many of the ships need oil to get back, and all of the planes need to refuel. Under the current circumstances, any attempt by the United States Navy to reinforce Pearl would result in a graveyard of fuel-starved ships. Few, if any, major ships have the ability to travel such distances and return without refueling. Please recall that Nagumo's fleet required midocean refueling in order to attack Pearl Harbor."

"Can't they use tankers, as we did?"

"Yes, but not until they accumulate a sufficient number to make an impact. I am convinced they will begin to repair the facilities at Pearl fairly quickly, so haste is of the essence."

Tojo was intrigued. He leaned back and smiled. "Then won't they reinforce their army? If we believe both their propaganda and our intelligence, they have more than thirty thousand soldiers on Oahu."

"General, many of that number will be useless mouths in the event of an assault. Thousands are tied up in coastal batteries, administration, and, of course, maintaining an air force that no longer exists, and the remainder are simply not combat ready, despite their claims to the contrary. When we attack, we will totally dominate the air and the sea. American numbers will be irrelevant. As to their reinforcing the army, it will not happen for the same reason that the navy will not make the attempt. The lack of oil will deter them. I am convinced that the United States will not make any attempt to strengthen or enlarge their defenses on Oahu until they have the capability to store fuel for their planes and ships."

Tojo rubbed his chin. "And when will they be able to do that?"

"My engineers feel it will take them at least three months to repair the depot, and several months after that to accumulate a sufficient quantity of oil to support a fleet."

Tojo leaned forward. "And why will we be able to succeed in using Pearl as a base when the Americans cannot?"

"General, both mentally and physically we are prepared for war and they are not. We have the necessary tankers and they do not. And, finally, we can make the repairs much more quickly because we will be able to pour engineers into the area and use indigenous labor, even prisoners, to hasten the reconstruction."

"It is intriguing," Tojo said with a smile. "Yet so much is happening now. The Philippines have been attacked, as have Malaya and Hong Kong. Other campaigns are beginning or about to begin all over the Pacific. There is a timetable of conquest in place, and you are asking for it to be changed. It could result in chaos."

"Yes," Yamamoto replied solemnly. "But I would not request it if I didn't think it was so very important. Remember when I said we would run wild for six months to a year? Well, the conquest of Hawaii could extend that estimate to years, perhaps decades. Perhaps"—he smiled grimly—"forever."

"Do you have plans?" Tojo asked, and then he threw back his head and laughed heartily. "Of course you do."

Yamamoto grinned back. "Nothing final, of course, but enough to show that it is more than feasible. It is an enormous opportunity to en-sure the security of Japan."

Tojo nodded. It was indeed intriguing, but there were other com-plications that could preclude such an operation. For one thing, the United States was at war only with Japan. While he had been assured that Germany would support Japan by declaring war on America, this had not yet happened. If the full force of American might was thrown against Japan, Yamamoto's navy would be on the defensive far sooner than anticipated, whether Japan held Hawaii or not. Germany had to declare war so that the Americans would be compelled to fight a two-front war.

Additionally, he would have to deal with the fear that Japan's generals had of Russia. The Soviets were considered to be the far greater threat to Japan's security and had massed forces along the Siberian-Manchukuo border. However, everything indicated that the Russians were totally preoccupied with keeping Hitler out of Moscow. If the Germans declared war on America, and if the Soviets stayed out of it, then the seizure of Hawaii was indeed feasible.

"I will meet with my generals," Tojo said. "If forces are to be made available, they will probably have to come from those in reserve in Japan, or from other areas, such as China or Manchukuo. We cannot jeopardize ongoing operations to facilitate your endeavor."

Yamamoto nodded. "I am confident that no more than one reinforced division or its equivalent will be necessary, and the navy will provide both shipping and marines to lead the assault. It is not a great requirement at all. Our total domination of the air will eliminate any need for overwhelming ground strength. Add to that the fact that many of Oahu's targets are within the range of naval gunfire, and we will be able to obliterate their defenses."

Tojo was impressed and found himself exhilarated at the prospect. "We will meet in a day or two," he said.

AT THE REQUEST of his superiors in army intelligence, Captain Jake Novacek had completed a tour of the damage to the naval facilities and had also been on the lookout for any evidence of possible sabotage. There was none, of course. All damage had come from the skies. He did not think it unusual that he would be asked to confirm what the navy might say about the damage to the fleet. That one service might evade, or even lie, in dealing with another was a given. In situations like this, it was human nature to try to gloss over failure, and the army needed an accurate report to enable it to commence its own plans. That the army would lie to the navy about the extent of its own losses was another given.

Jake was stunned and sickened by the devastation. Which horror was worse? The sunken and shattered ships settling in the harbor or the long rows of casualties, most of whom lay in uncomplaining silence despite their horrible burns and wounds? Saddest of all were the bodies that had been sewn into mattress covers. Many of them were burned or shattered beyond recognition and would never be identified.

As a result, Jake was physically and mentally exhausted by the time he was done. It was the evening of December 8, and he'd barely been able to grab an hour's sleep since the fateful morning of the day before.

He had stopped to talk with the guards at the gates to the naval base and was just about to drive through them and down the road to his apartment in Honolulu and a long overdue shower when he heard his name.

"Captain Novacek, may I talk to you?"

A woman was standing in the shadows outside the gate, where he couldn't quite recognize her. "Ma'am?"

"Captain," one of the guards said, "it's Mrs. Sanderson. She's been out there for a couple of hours."

Sanderson? Did he know anyone named Sanderson? His groggy mind refused to kick in for a moment. Of course. He'd played touch with Tim Sanderson just a couple of days earlier and had met his wife at a party following the Army-Navy Game of November 29. God, he was more tired than he thought if he couldn't recall meeting someone like Tim's wife only a week earlier.

Jake parked his car and walked over to the woman. She was distraught, although she was doing an admirable job of keeping herself under control.

"I'm sorry, Mrs. Sanderson, I didn't recognize you right away."

"That's all right," she said with a forced calmness. "I need a favor from you."

"What is it?" he asked warily.

"I want to see the *Oklahoma*."

Jake sagged. He recalled that Tim was on the ship that lay virtually upside down alongside Ford Island.

"Captain, Tim has not come home, and there's been no word of him. I've seen the ship from the hill, and I've heard horrible things about what's happening. I want to see if they're true, Captain. I want to see where Tim might be."

"Mrs. Sanderson, I will not take you there for the simple reason that the navy will not allow me there either. Yes, it is true there are people trapped in the ship, but the navy is moving heaven and earth to get them out."

Jake saw the woman bite her lower lip and turn her head away. He hadn't the heart to tell her that he had been by the devastated battleship, and it was a nightmare. Sailors were trapped in the ship, and the sounds of their clanging against the armored hull served as beacons for those who were desperately trying to drill through and rescue them. He couldn't begin to imagine the nightmarish conditions in the pitch black of an overturned battleship.

Several sounds from within the hull had already ceased as air must have run out of the pockets in which men were trapped. Farther away, other sailors and workers played their radios loudly in order to drown out the agonies of the incessant pounding. If Tim Sanderson was trapped in the *Oklahoma,* then God help him.

Jake had been truthful when he'd said the navy was trying desperately to save the trapped men. As the hours dragged on, however, it was becoming a losing battle.

Jake asked where she lived, and she told him. She added that a neighbor had dropped her off. When he offered to drive her home, she almost pathetically said not to bother.

"It's okay, Mrs. Sanderson, your place is on the way to Shafter and pretty near mine."

With that, she demurred, and they drove in silence to her home. When they arrived, Missy Wilson walked up with her young child sleeping in her arms.

"I'll take care of her," Missy said after hearing that nothing had come of Alexa's vigil by the base. She took Alexa by the arm and led her into the house. Alexa neither resisted nor complained. To Jake it seemed that she was beyond feeling.

Jake shook his head in sadness. He had met Tim's wife only once before and been struck by her poise and patrician good looks. She was the type of woman he would never have otherwise met if it hadn't been for the weekly football games.

Football? God, he thought, was the world ever that innocent? As he headed back to his car, another vehicle pulled up and a grim-faced naval lieutenant emerged.

The two men introduced themselves. The naval officer was Jamie Priest, and he was from the *Pennsylvania.* Like dogs sniffing, the two

men checked each other's rank and academy rings. Priest was a lieutenant in the navy, which was equivalent to a captain in the army. He
looked several years younger than Jake, a fact that Jake had found
more and more frustrating lately. Jamie Priest was also much smaller,
wiry, and, when he removed his hat, showed thinning straw-colored
hair.

"I've got to talk to her," Jamie said. "They found her husband's
body in the harbor."

"Christ," Jake said.

What a waste of a decent young guy, Jake thought, and what a hell
of a way to destroy a young woman. But at least that meant Tim
hadn't been trapped in the *Oklahoma*, spending a day and a half going
mad in the claustrophobic blackness. Should she be thankful for small
favors?

Missy emerged from the house, the sleeping child still on her shoulder. She had heard the conversation. "You won't be talking to her
tonight. I gave her some pills my doctor gave me after Killer here was
born. Let her sleep. I'll break the news to her when she wakes up."
Then she looked puzzled. "Shouldn't there be a chaplain with you?"

Jamie shrugged. "Too many dead and not enough chaplains. Since
I knew Tim, I volunteered."

Jake made a mental note to find out when the funeral was and to
check up on Tim's wife. No, he corrected himself, Tim's widow. The
grief on Mrs. Sanderson's face as she waited in vain for word of her
husband's fate had touched him deeply.

As he drove away, he realized that Alexa Sanderson's innocent
plight had brought the war home to him in a way that was far different
from what the rows of wounded, the anonymous dead, the planes
shooting at him by Hickam, and the sight of Lieutenant Simpkins's
shredded body after the Zero had strafed them had done. At least
Tim's widow and her blond friend were far enough away from the carnage that they didn't have to smell it, or watch as the last of the flames
were put out.

ADMIRAL HUSBAND KIMMEL TOUCHED his chest and felt the
bruise where a spent Japanese bullet had struck him during the height
of the attack. At the time he had lamented that it would have been bet-

ter had the bullet killed him instead of dropping harmlessly onto the floor. Since then, nothing had happened to change his mind. The spent piece of lead was now in his pocket.

"I just received a telegram saying I've been relieved," Kimmel said. "I guess no one's surprised, although I think it's without justification. The war-warning message from Washington was manifestly ambiguous. They did not tell me to beware of an attack on Pearl."

To the contrary, Kimmel thought. No one felt that any navy had the capability to do what Japan had done. And, in particular, no one felt that a semibarbaric country full of nearsighted little yellow men with buck teeth would even attempt such an enterprise.

"No one even informed me that the Jap fleet was at sea."

General Walter Short nodded politely. He wondered if he too would be relieved and thought it was quite possible, although unlikely. After all, he'd lost only a few score planes, while Kimmel had lost almost the whole damned Pacific Fleet.

Short was confident that what he'd done would hold up under the inevitable scrutiny, although he understood the navy's screaming need for a scapegoat. Sadly, Kimmel would be it. Hell, you don't lose a fleet without blaming someone.

The navy had been horribly unprepared for anything remotely resembling war on the morning of December 7, 1941. The army, by contrast, had been prepared for the only type of assault deemed possible—sabotage by untrustworthy elements among the very large Japanese population on Oahu. The fact that the attack had been from the sea had been the navy's fault, not the army's.

"They name a replacement for you yet?" Short asked. He scarcely knew Kimmel. Neither the two men nor their underlings met frequently. Each had his own responsibilities. Now Short wondered if they shouldn't have coordinated their efforts more closely. It would be something to take up with Kimmel's replacement.

"Chester Nimitz is replacing me. He's anticipated out here in a few days. He's a good man. You will work well together."

Short smiled. Time would tell on that.

"I'm to leave Hawaii as soon as possible," Kimmel continued. "That means Admiral Pye will be in charge until Nimitz gets here. Along with defending Hawaii with what we have left, he will be sending his damaged ships to California for repair."

Short was surprised. Admiral William Pye commanded the battle line, most of which was at the bottom of Pearl Harbor. "I didn't know any could travel."

"*Maryland* and *Tennessee* are relatively undamaged and will depart as soon as possible. The engineers say we may have to dynamite *West Virginia* to free up the *Tennessee*, but that's acceptable since the *West Virginia* is so badly damaged she may not be salvageable. As to the others, only the *Pennsylvania* is capable of departing anytime soon. She survived the first two assaults fairly unscathed, but bombs from the last attack destroyed her forward turrets. Burning oil from the storage depot flowed down and around her in dry dock and caused additional damage, although not to her power plant. She will leave as soon as we can make certain she's seaworthy."

The departure of the remnants of the battle fleet disturbed Short. Even though Halsey had returned with the carriers *Enterprise* and *York-town*, Short was not comfortable that their protective shield would be long term. Halsey wanted to cruise the Pacific and search for Japanese ships, and not use the fleet to protect Pearl Harbor, which Short felt was imperative.

This was something else to take up with Kimmel's replacement.

General Short was thankful he had the Hawaiian Division to protect the island from invaders. So what if he had lost most of his airplanes? The invasion, if it came, would be fought on the ground, wouldn't it? After all, the Japs couldn't take Hawaii without landing on it, and he longed to come to grips with the little yellow bastards.

Even though it hadn't materialized, he was still concerned with the possibility of sabotage and, as military governor, had begun rounding up some of the more radical among the Japanese community. He couldn't imprison them all, as General DeWitt was going to do in California. That wasn't practicable, since the Japanese represented almost half the population of the islands, but he could defang any rebels among the Japs in Hawaii by arresting the leaders of any potential revolution.

Hell, even if he were to intern all the Japs in Hawaii, he wouldn't have enough men to guard them all.

"Tell me, Admiral, have you uncovered any evidence of sabotage or espionage, other than the spying done by the Japs from their consulate?"

"No," Kimmel said. "And that's quite a surprise, isn't it?"

Damn, Short thought. His intelligence people hadn't found any either. General Marshall, the army's chief of staff in Washington, would be second-guessing him like a son of a bitch for having focused on potential sabotage that hadn't occurred. In hindsight, he thought he knew why nothing had happened. In order to keep the attack a secret, the Japs in Tokyo hadn't told their cohorts in Honolulu about it. That made sense and told him that sabotage could still occur, although what was left to destroy? The fleet was gone, as were the planes, and the Hawaiian Division was armed and on guard. Hell, the soldiers almost hoped some local Jap would try something. One sergeant had said exactly that to Short and added that he'd blast the Jap's ass back to Mount Fuji.

Marshall would understand that he'd done his duty, wouldn't he? Short swore silently as he agreed with Kimmel's comment about the war warning messages being so damned ambiguous. Who would have thought the Japs, or anyone else for that matter, were capable of sailing a fleet across the Pacific and striking without any warning at all, and without anyone even noticing them? Since then he had ordered additional patrols by his remaining planes and had begun working with Kimmel on coordinating those patrols with naval planes and then sharing the information. Should they have done that sooner? Probably, he thought.

"You got enough oil for your ships?" Short asked. He was well aware of the extent of the fuel loss and what it implied. He was, however, curious as to what Kimmel would admit.

Kimmel sighed. "We're gonna need help, and fast. Halsey's ships are guzzling it like there's no tomorrow, and the three movable battleships will need to have their tanks topped off before they can depart. Frankly, General, we're suspending all but the most essential patrol operations until we get resupplied. As much as I'd like to humor Halsey, we just can't afford to have him running around chasing Japs and burning oil at this time. Christ, we lost four and a half million gallons of it that morning, and we have no way of replacing it, or storing it even if it was replaced."

This confirmed to Short what his own intelligence people had found out. It did not strike him as unusual that he had used army personnel to spy on navy operations. He was disturbed because the events of Sunday had conclusively proven that a fleet anchored in Pearl Harbor wasn't much use to anyone. Someone had better get some oil to Pearl Harbor so the navy could get out and do some fighting.

Short considered himself fortunate that he had sufficient aviation gas for the planes he had remaining. He also had the eight B-17s that had flown in on December 7, although several had been damaged in the fighting. If the Japs came again, he would use these superweapons, the so-called Flying Fortresses. Time would tell if they were as effective as they were supposed to be.

At least, he reminded himself, he hadn't lost a fleet, only a few planes. Planes could be replaced fairly quickly, but battleships took years to build. Poor Kimmel. Poor bastard.

CHAPTER 3

There was silence in the War Room of the White House as the litany of disasters was enumerated. Guam had fallen, and it was only a matter of time before isolated and outnumbered Wake Island would be conquered. The Japanese had landed in the Philippines, and the combined American and Filipino forces were falling back in disorder in the face of the Japanese onslaught.

Nor were the Americans alone in their agonies. The British in Malaya had been invaded, and the Japanese were driving through what had been considered impassable jungles to the city of Singapore. Hong Kong was surrounded and besieged, and, like that of Wake, its fall was inevitable. The British, in their haste to shore up the defenses of Singapore, had suffered a naval defeat almost on a level with the disaster at Pearl Harbor when the battleships *Repulse* and *Prince of Wales* were sunk by Japanese planes.

As a result, there were no Allied capital ships in the Pacific Ocean west of Hawaii. The Japanese had at least ten carriers in that area to America's two, although a third carrier was en route. The Japanese had a dozen battleships operating in the Pacific, while the Americans had only four, and these were in West Coast waters, nowhere near the scene of the action.

For the time being at least, the Japanese possessed overwhelming naval strength in the western Pacific.

To further complicate matters and drain America's still limited resources, the Nazis had declared war on the United States and had commenced U-boat operations along America's eastern shore. Shocked American civilians now saw oil tankers burning off the shores of New Jersey, and U-boats were rumored to be moving up the St. Lawrence and Mississippi rivers.

That the Chinese had followed with a declaration against Japan and Germany was considered a mixed blessing at best. While China had been fighting Japan for years, her army was considered corrupt and inept. Numerous other countries had followed America's lead and declared war against the Axis, but they were small nations and would have little impact in the coming struggle.

Franklin Delano Roosevelt swiveled his wheelchair and looked at Admiral Ernest King. King, irascible and blunt, had just been named chief of naval operations. He replaced Admiral Harold Stark, who had been the navy's senior officer at the time of Pearl Harbor. Stark's reputation was in decline as some of the blame for Pearl Harbor had fallen on him.

King paced angrily, like a bear in a cage. Roosevelt smiled slightly. "I envy you."

King stopped and blinked in surprise. "Envy me what, sir?"

"Your ability to pace like that. It must help you relieve your frustrations. Me? All I can do is rock back and forth in this confounded chair. If I feel really energetic, I can sort of sway a little."

King flushed and sat down. "Sorry, sir."

Two of the three others in the room chuckled. The exception was the army chief of staff, General George C. Marshall, who made it a personal point never to laugh at Roosevelt's jokes. Secretary of War Henry L. Stimson and Secretary of the Navy Frank Knox were the others in attendance. This was a war meeting, and there was likely to be little input from the two civilian secretaries.

"Well," Roosevelt said to King, "give us your opinion."

"Mr. President, if the Japs have any idea how weak we are in the Pacific, they will attack Hawaii. Until the fuel situation is resolved, there is very little we can do to stop them should they wish to invade. Very simply, our ships in the Pacific do not have enough fuel for combat patrols or to mount an effective campaign against the Japs. Further, the ships we now have on the Pacific coast can cruise to Hawaii and back but would also have very little in reserve for any combat patrols or other actions."

"I don't understand," said Marshall. "I thought that many of our warships had cruising ranges in excess of ten thousand miles, and Hawaii is only twenty-three hundred miles from San Francisco."

"That's correct," King answered. "But our ships must keep enough in reserve to return for more fuel, and that's California until our Hawaiian facilities are repaired. Thus, almost half a ship's fuel is going to be used just coming and going. Also, that ten-thousand-mile range is at a ship's most effective speed, which is usually far below a combat speed. Under even the best of circumstances, a ship cannot count on its range as being a real indicator. Other variables, such as weather, can affect it adversely."

King smiled slightly as he warmed to his lecture. It wasn't often he got a chance to educate his army counterpart, and he relished it. "And, last, while on patrol, the larger warships, like the battleships and carriers, often act as tankers for the smaller ships, such as the destroyers, which further erodes any range figures."

"Well then, what about sending tankers with the fleet?" Marshall asked.

King had been promoted from commanding the Atlantic Fleet, where he had been primarily concerned with running the undeclared war against Nazi Germany that had just become a fully declared war with Japan. As a result, he had to pause and recall before he answered.

"A simple answer, General. We do not have enough tankers to support major fleet operations. That can and will be rectified by requisitioning tankers from the merchant fleet, but it will still take months before we have enough to make a difference."

"Are you suggesting the fleet should abandon Pearl?" Roosevelt asked.

"I've told Nimitz it's his call. I will support whatever he recommends. But yes, I do think he will recommend that we pull what's left of the fleet back to California, where it was until last summer, and lick our wounds. If the oil depot can be repaired and replenished without Jap interference, then we can move back fairly quickly. Until then, we are just too vulnerable at Pearl Harbor.

"Let's face it," King added. "Without the ability to mount effective patrols, the navy is almost as blind as it was on December 7. If the Japs launch a force and hold to radio silence, any warning would be counted in hours, not days. Even our Magic intercepts were useless, remember."

The mention of Magic intercepts referred to the fact that the United States had been deciphering Japan's diplomatic code for some time, and had been making progress in unlocking the secrets of the military codes. Even so, those abilities had not helped to prevent the attack on Pearl Harbor. The Japanese diplomatic codes had made no reference to any specific action, and the Japanese fleet had kept remarkably tight radio silence as it steamed toward Hawaii. There were times when technology was ineffective and old-fashioned methods proved best.

Marshall nodded grimly. "Then I will make no effort to reinforce General Short until the situation is resolved. Until we can establish naval and air parity, it won't matter how many soldiers I ship over. Short will have to make do with the resources he has."

Marshall paused and then added, "I've also directed Short to put on hold the reorganization of the Hawaiian Division into the 24th and 25th Infantry Divisions."

The general briefly explained that the Hawaiian Division was a large World War I–type division that had been organized for trench warfare in Europe in 1917. He had been reorganizing all the army's divisions into smaller and more mobile units, and the Hawaiian Division was one of the few left to make over.

"It also makes no sense," Marshall continued, "to have the division in the middle of a reorganization should the Japs invade. Let them keep their current structure and leaders for the time being."

There was no argument from Roosevelt or the others. "There's another reason for deferring the change," Marshall said grimly, "and it's a psychological one. If the Japs invade and are successful, the American public won't be too distressed if something called the Hawaiian Division is lost. Let's face it, it sounds like a bunch of people in flowered shirts and sarongs. But if the 24th and 25th Infantry Divisions are forced to surrender, the scope of the loss will be apparent."

The president looked at him in astonishment. Admiral King's jaw dropped and it took him a moment to find his voice. "Jesus Christ, General, that's just about the most coldhearted and devious thing I've ever heard of."

Marshall eyed him with apparent dispassion. Only he knew the internal agony he was feeling at the thought of losing any of his soldiers. "Do you approve?"

King nodded. "Yes, General, I do."

·

ALEXA SANDERSON STOOD by the edge of the newly dug grave and half listened to the chaplain intone some prayer or other. From what she was able to gather, she should be overjoyed that Tim was in heaven with the angels, instead of lying in a wooden box that was about to be covered with dirt. She did not accept that assessment. She missed Tim terribly, and her whole body ached with the loss.

However, she'd had some time to think over the fact of Tim's death and accepted both it and the fact that she had nothing to regret. She didn't even resent the fact that the coffin had been sealed. Perhaps it was a blessing. She would be able to remember him as he was in life and not in death. Alexa fully understood that he had died violently and had been in the oil-soaked water for more than a day. The remains in the box would in no way resemble the man she'd made love to the night before he left for duty that morning.

They had loved each other, but it was over. She would revere and honor his memory, but she would also move on with her life. She could even use the word *death,* which surprised some people. It amused her how others used terms like *gone away,* or *departed,* as if the dead person was coming back. Tim was dead. Nothing would change that.

Alexa even found a moment to wonder if she would marry again. To her surprise, she didn't find the thought repugnant, not even at this early stage of her widowhood and in the depth of sorrow. Their lives had been happy, so why wouldn't a future life be as well? She was twenty-eight and, despite her grief, knew that she would someday recover.

When the service ended, she would thank the chaplain for his nice prayers, although she was far from certain that he had any idea who he was burying. She didn't blame him. Thousands had been killed by the Japs with additional thousands wounded. Even as they mourned, other interments were taking place around them. The area in Punch-bowl crater was rapidly becoming a national cemetery for the dead of the young war. Alexa stared at the chaplain, who faltered over a prayer. The poor man looked exhausted, but at least he was alive.

Finally it was over. A couple of her neighbors and a handful of the students she taught at the church-run school drifted away. With the exception of Melissa's husband and the rapidly departing chaplain, only one man in uniform had been present, and she walked over to him. "Thank you for coming, Captain."

Jake Novacek nodded. He was determined not to embarrass himself by saying something banal or stupid, as he had managed to do at other funerals. He was surprised at the lack of attendance by naval personnel but said nothing.

"Tim spoke kindly of you on a number of occasions. He said you didn't hit him too hard."

Jake smiled slightly. "We generally played on opposite sides, but he was always a good guy. I'll miss him." And a helluva lot of others, he didn't add.

Alexa took the compliment. She was a little surprised by the burly Novacek. At first glance, it would be easy to mistake him for a Neanderthal who had stolen an officer's uniform. But a few words with him had convinced her the impression was wrong. There was depth to the man, as well as compassion.

"I'm not surprised that no one else came," she said. "So many of his friends are dead or wounded themselves, particularly those from the *Oklahoma,* and everyone is so busy with the living that it's easy to forget the dead. Then there's the fact, of course, that I'm not very popular with the other officers and their wives."

"Oh?" What the hell had she done to be disliked, he wondered, and did he really want to know?

"My political views are anathema to them. I'm a pacifist, and I hate war in all its forms. Does that bother you? If it wasn't for the fact that my uncle's a congressman, I think Tim and I would have been totally ignored."

A pacifist? Was that all? But it would have been enough to result in ostracization in the close-knit family of military officers. However, he understood the deference she would have received with a political relative. "What bothers me, Mrs. Sanderson, is that I cannot recall the last time I used the word *anathema* in an intelligent conversation."

The comment brought a wide and unexpected grin from her, and he continued. "I have no argument with anyone's political or moral views. Somehow I've always felt that part of my job was to protect them. Maybe I'm a little naïve, but I have no problem with pacifists. After this war is over," he added drily, "I may become one myself."

"Well then, Captain, I'm even more glad you came." Melissa Wilson and her recently arrived husband stepped behind them as they walked to their cars. "I presume you will have to return to duty."

He grinned sheepishly. "Uh, I told my bosses that's where I was now."

Alexa laughed out loud. It felt good. "Well, get back to them and don't get in trouble for playing hooky. You were Tim's friend, and now you're my friend. Please don't hesitate to stop by when you're in the area."

Alexa meant the invitation. Even though she barely knew Jake Novacek, she found herself trusting and liking him. She needed strong friends at this time in her life, and Captain Jake Novacek looked like he would more than fill the bill.

"I will do that, Mrs. Sanderson," Jake said, wondering if she meant it or was just being polite.

"My name is Alexa, Captain, and my friends call me Lexy for some ungodly reason."

"Mine is Jake," he said, grinning. She did mean it. Lexy? What a lousy nickname for an elegant lady. He decided that he would never call her Lexy. They shook hands as if meeting for the first time, which, in a way, they were. Her grip was strong and firm, which was interesting; most women had no idea how to shake hands. "And I am honored to be your friend, Alexa."

Behind them, neither saw Melissa nudge her husband in the ribs.

ADMIRAL ISOROKU YAMAMOTO again entered the residence of Prime Minister Tojo. He was pleasantly surprised to find that Tojo was not alone. Present with him was Lieutenant General Sakai Takashi, who commanded the 23d Area Army, based near Canton, China. Yamamoto took Takashi's presence as a good omen, although the army general looked grim and unpleasant.

As was proper, Tojo took the lead. "As you may have surmised by General Takashi's presence, we have decided to give conditional approval to the invasion of Hawaii. The fact that Hitler has declared war on the United States means there will be no major reinforcements available for their Pacific Fleet for some time."

Yamamoto bowed from a seated position. "I am honored. However, you said 'conditional approval.' May I ask what the conditions are?"

Takashi answered. "I'll be blunt, Admiral. I agree that it is a marvelous opportunity to further injure the United States and thus further ensure Japan's victory. But it will necessitate changes to plans and events that are already taking place. I am also concerned by the size of the American army contingent on Oahu. Therefore, I insist that the navy provide total superiority of sea and air."

Takashi's comments verged on rude, but Yamamoto ignored it. Too much was at stake to let interservice pride get in the way. "When the army steps ashore," he replied firmly, "there will be no opposition from American planes or ships. Additionally, I will provide a full brigade of marines to lead the amphibious part of the assault."

Takashi blinked in surprise. He hadn't expected that.

Yamamoto continued. "I will provide a diversion that will confuse the Americans and cause them to split their forces. Right now, they expect that any landing will occur on the northern shore of Oahu, farthest from Honolulu. In that regard they are correct; however, we will make them think otherwise."

Takashi almost smiled but caught himself. "Good. For my part, the army will provide the 38th Infantry Division. It is now involved in mopping-up operations in Hong Kong and is not scheduled for further action for a couple of months. It will be resupplied and will be the focus of the invasion."

Yamamoto was delighted. The 38th was a crack, class A division, instead of the second-tier force he'd planned on, and it consisted of nearly thirty thousand men. Takashi, however, was not quite telling the truth. The British were putting up a stout defense, and it was estimated that they would fight on for another week or so.

"Additionally," Tojo said, "the 38th will be reinforced by one infantry regiment each from the 52nd, 53rd, and 54th divisions, which are stationed in Japan. They are class C divisions but will give a good account of themselves under the circumstances."

Yamamoto nodded. The additional regiments, regardless of quality, would bring the 38th up to a total of nearly forty thousand men, and, when the marine brigade was added, the Japanese ground forces would truly be formidable.

"However," Tojo said, "you may have these forces for only sixty

days after landing on Oahu and the landing must take place within a
month. If the island isn't conquered by that time, we will have to eval-
uate the situation. We must not unduly delay our activities around
Borneo and elsewhere. Those other lands contain the oil the navy said
it so desperately needed."

Yamamoto smiled at the transparent gibe. "It will not take sixty
days. By the time of the landing, the Americans will be confused and
disoriented."

Tojo nodded appreciatively. "You mentioned a diversion, what is
it?"

"It will occur in two phases," Yamamoto answered. "In the first
phase, which is commencing as we speak, I have ordered our submarines back into Hawaiian waters. They will strike at any shipping
that attempts to leave or enter the islands.

"As to the second phase, the First Air Fleet is refueling and resup-
plying and will return to Hawaii with additional planes and a regiment
of marines. They will then land on the island of Molokai, perhaps
Lanai afterward, and establish air bases there that will be operational
within a few days. That will place the Japanese air forces permanently
within a hundred miles of most of the targets on Oahu, particularly
those around Pearl Harbor. I am confident the Americans will find it
extremely difficult to justify moving their forces to the north of Oahu
when we are so close to them in the south."

Takashi did smile this time. Yamamoto thought it looked like a
monkey grinning. Tojo recognized that a deal had been struck and ordered sake brought out.

"Excellent," he said. "But restrict your efforts to a plan and nothing
more at this time. Do not land on Molokai or elsewhere until the army
is completely ready to support you. Should there be a delay in taking
Hong Kong, or should other factors arise, we might yet have to recon-
sider Hawaiian operations."

"I fully understand," Yamamoto answered.

Tojo raised his cup, and the others followed suit. "Let us drink to
the success of the operation and the confusion of our enemies."

CHAPTER 4

.

In Jake Novacek's opinion, the office on the second floor of a nondescript Honolulu building was better suited for a small-time lawyer than for one of the most powerful men in Hawaii's Japanese community. As the one receptionist-secretary recognized and greeted him, Jake knew that security personnel were just across the hall and were watching him carefully. He was in civilian clothes in an attempt to avoid undue notice. Many military personnel dealt with Toyoza Kaga, but few in an official capacity. If anyone was watching, he would be noted as just another soldier who owed Kaga money, wanted to borrow some, or maybe needed a compliant doctor for a girlfriend's abortion.

After a moment, Kaga welcomed him warmly and by shaking hands, an unusual gesture for a Japanese. Most preferred to avoid physical contact with others. Kaga was average height for a Japanese, five four, thin, bald, and in his early sixties. He was one of the richest men in Honolulu, although he lived simply, without ostentation or extravagance.

"Captain," Kaga said cheerfully, "have a seat. Coffee?"

"No, thank you. How is your empire prospering?"

"Mine or Imperial Japan's?"

Jake laughed. "Yours."

It was little known, but Toyoza Kaga had his hand in scores of businesses throughout the islands. Many he owned outright, and others he simply influenced and prospered from by dealing with them. Not all Kaga's businesses were totally legal. There were gambling operations, minor bootlegging, and, of course, prostitution. By keeping tight control on the operations, he avoided the wrath of either the civilian or the military police, who all knew that soldiers and sailors had to have their ashes hauled every now and then. Kaga's places were clean, nonviolent, and discreet, and therefore easy to ignore.

"This is the first time we've spoken since the attack," Kaga said. "I hope it will not be the last."

"Nor I," said Jake. "I used the information you gave me about the unlikelihood of sabotage and gave it to my boss, who gave it to General Short. Unfortunately, Short or his staff chose to ignore it."

"A shame," Kaga said and meant it. He was firmly convinced that a Japanese victory in the war would be a disaster for both himself and the Japanese living in Hawaii. "At least there have been only a few incidents against my people by American military personnel."

"Do you object to the internment of the radicals?"

Kaga laughed. The Japanese population of Hawaii was 160,000 people, more than a third of the total population of the islands, and 120,000 of them lived on Oahu. Of these, about 1,500 of the most radical supporters of Japan had been rounded up and interned. These were all people who had visited Japan, sent sons to fight in her army, and made bellicose speeches on behalf of Japan's right to conquer Asia. There were many others who had cheered on Japan's earlier conquests, but both the FBI and the military government considered them nuisances and not dangerous. Toyoza Kaga's eldest son was an officer in the Japanese army, but that was a well-kept secret and a fact that deeply disturbed Kaga.

Some of the fifteen hundred radical Japanese might have been enlisted as saboteurs for Japan, but none had known of the timing of the attack. Japan had not trusted them with the information, which both men thought was an interesting fact in itself. With weapons reasonably scarce on the islands, they were also unarmed. Now, with emotions running high and tens of thousands of armed U.S. military personnel looking out in all directions for enemies, anyone contemplating sabotage would have to be a complete fool or insane, especially if they had a yellow skin. There would be no attacks from the Japanese community on Oahu.

"No, Captain, I do not object at all. However, I would suggest that you move the internees from Sand Island and elsewhere and ship them off to the mainland. That way they cannot be used to establish a sympathetic puppet government when Japan attacks and conquers these islands. Even with them gone, there will be many who will collaborate with the Japanese, but they will lack the venom and enthusiasm of those your army has imprisoned."

Jake's eyebrows arched at the declaration. "You think that's definite? The Japanese will attack?"

"Absolutely. And it will come sooner rather than later."

"And your people?"

"The first-generation issei and the second-generation nisei differ fundamentally," Kaga said. "Most of the issei have their homes here but are sympathetic toward Japan, and they are confused now that their two homelands are at war. They revere Japan and love her memory, but, after all, they left for good reasons. The nisei, however, by and large have no great love for a distant land most have never seen or care to see. Nisei, remember, are American citizens as well as holding Japanese citizenship according to Japanese law."

It was a bitter point. The older generation, like Kaga, had been denied citizenship because of the race quota laws, and many resented it. Ironically, the children of the issei had automatically become American citizens by virtue of being born on American territory. To many people, Jake included, it made no sense whatsoever. However, the nisei had been declared Japanese citizens by the Japanese government and, technically at least, were subject to Japan's military draft. A small but unknown number had traveled to Japan to make themselves available for conscription, but the overwhelming majority wanted no part of the Japanese armed forces. On the contrary, almost fifteen hundred nisei had volunteered for the Hawaiian Territory's two national guard regiments.

"The vast majority of my people," Kaga continued, "will do nothing but try to survive the conflict as best they can. I doubt there will be any acts of sabotage, even random ones. The fear of retribution is too great."

"And what will happen if the Japanese do invade?" Jake asked. "Where will loyalties lie then?"

Kaga shrugged. "Like I said, get rid of the radicals and the rest will play a waiting game. When—not if—the Japanese invade, there will be confusion regarding their long-term aims. If Hawaii is to be a bargaining chip for a future treaty in which we will be returned to American control, then my people will be cooperative but quiescent. If the occupation is going to be long term, or permanent, then people will adjust to the new realities in order to survive."

Jake agreed. It fit what he had learned about the Japanese-

American community. Beleaguered, picked on, insulted, and discriminated against, most of them still thought there were more advantages in being American than in being part of the militaristic Japanese empire. He would report this to General Short and the rest of the Hawaiian command. This time perhaps they'd listen to him.

THE JAPANESE SUBMARINE *I-74* lay on the swells of the Pacific, rolling gently and using only enough power to maintain seaway. She was shielded by the night and the fact of her low silhouette. A panther, she lay in wait for her prey.

The *I-74* was only a couple of years old. She'd been constructed at the shipyards in Kobe and was armed with eight torpedo tubes and a 4.7-inch deck gun, and could cruise for sixteen thousand miles.

Like most submariners, her captain preferred to attack while on the surface. Doing so meant more torpedo accuracy, as well as the ability to travel at more than twice her speed when submerged. The *I-74* could move at twenty knots on the surface but only nine submerged. Underwater movement was saved for special situations, such as hiding from an enemy warship, stalking a dangerous or elusive target, or traversing dangerous waters. Submerged, a sub could last only a dozen or so hours before the batteries that drove her needed charging, or before the air became so foul that sailors started to pass out and die.

But who needed to stalk or hide when the enemy was being so cooperative? Commander Jiro Boshiro could not believe his good fortune and the stupidity of the Americans. The four freighters must have discounted the existence of the war; they still had their navigation lights on. They were more afraid of collision than of him. He did not think they had traveled together. It was more likely an unintended clustering, of the kind that frequently occurred near a major port, and they were less than fifty miles from Honolulu. Why they were together didn't matter. The result was a fairly neat line of enemy freighters close up and inviting him to kill them.

Under normal circumstances, it was an enemy he would have ignored. Japanese naval doctrine called for submarines to strike only at warships and, preferably, capital ships. This doctrine was in keeping with the code of *bushido* and the way of the samurai warrior. Orders were so specific that submariners were told how many torpedoes could be launched against each target. Freighters and transports were considered unworthy for samurai to attack, and demeaned the spirit of the offensive.

Orders, however, had been changed. In the absence of major targets and accepting that Hawaii was under a sort of siege, submarines of the Imperial Japanese Navy had been instructed to attack supply ships heading toward the islands. Those leaving would only be taking wounded and civilians and should be left alone, thus conserving precious torpedoes. But those approaching the islands would be carrying war materials that would enable the United States to recover from Japan's glorious victory of December 7. They must be destroyed.

It galled Commander Boshiro to obey the orders, but they came from the revered Admiral Yamamoto and, therefore, must be right. He chuckled silently in the darkness. As if Yamamoto had ever been wrong.

At a thousand yards from the nearest ship, Boshiro ordered the first pair of Type 95 oxygen-propelled torpedoes hurled at the lead ship. Seconds later, another pair was fired at the next freighter. The forward tubes were quickly reloaded and the firing repeated.

The first torpedoes hit and exploded. Flashes of light were followed by plumes of white water and the crash of explosions as the four ships were hit and staggered in turn before they could flee. Two of them started to burn immediately, and the others quickly followed suit. All four began to settle as the sea rushed in to claim them.

Boshiro was slightly disappointed when none of the four burned in a way that would signify they carried either ammunition or fuel. Regardless, these were four ships that would never again carry cargo for the Americans.

The ships rumbled and creaked as they began to break apart and plunged to the bottom. Boshiro wondered if any sailors were trapped and screaming in their metal coffins. He shuddered. It was the submariner's nightmare.

The deck crew of the *I-74* saw lifeboats lowered and the surviving crew members scramble to safety. Brief thought was given to killing them, but Boshiro dismissed the option. Surely they'd had time to radio for help, which meant that either airplanes or destroyers would be on them in a short while. All the time the sub had been on the surface, lookouts had ignored the one-sided battle and strained instead

for the sight of a warship or an airplane. The Americans were now patrolling the approaches to Pearl Harbor and, even though badly hurt,
were still a dangerous enemy. They would delight in wreaking vengeance on a Japanese sub.

Commander Boshiro made a decision. He ordered the sub submerged. He would stay underwater until certain that his boat was safe,
then he would head east, toward California. He would travel back
along the route the four ships had taken from America and see if any
other plums were ready to fall from the tree.

Perhaps next time he'd get a chance to sink something truly important.

HALSEY AND NIMITZ HAD TOURED the harbor area and been
brought up to speed on the damage to the ships. Admiral Chester W.
Nimitz was fifty-six, white-haired, and robust. He had an affable, easygoing personality, which hid a degree of toughness that often surprised others when it came to the surface. At first, Nimitz was not
going to relieve the disgraced Admiral Kimmel until the end of the
year, but realization of the scope of the fuel crisis, which threatened to
cripple the Pacific Fleet, had accelerated his takeover.

Although three years older, Admiral William "Bull" Halsey was
subordinate to Nimitz. Halsey was colorful, aggressive, energetic, and
he made good press copy. Upon receipt of the pre–Pearl Harbor war
warning, Halsey had not dallied. He had ordered his ships and planes
to shoot any nearby Japanese and the hell with the consequences.
While he wished nothing more than to have his two carriers unleashed against the Japanese, he accepted the logic that it was not possible until the supply situation was resolved and the fleet beefed up by
reinforcements from the Atlantic.

It was for this reason that the two admirals met in Kimmel's old office, overlooking the submarine pens. General Short had been invited
to attend, and he was expected momentarily. In the meantime, the
two admirals reviewed the catastrophe.

Of the eight battleships so neatly anchored off Ford Island at the
time of the attack, two, perhaps three, would be of use by the end of
1942. For the others, it would take longer, perhaps forever.

The *Arizona* and the *Utah* were sunk and likely unsalvageable. The *Arizona*, in particular, was a charred hulk in which more than a thousand men were entombed, while the *Utah* had partially capsized.

The *Oklahoma* had also capsized and had been prevented from rolling completely over only when her masts snagged themselves in the harbor's muddy bottom. The *Oklahoma* would be out of commission for years at best. It was very likely she would never be salvaged.

The *California* had also been sunk, but engineers had declared it was possible that she could be refloated by spring and sent to the mainland for repairs. So too would the heroic *Nevada*, the only battleship that had tried to escape the carnage at Pearl.

The *West Virginia* had sustained extensive damage and, like the *Arizona*, was a burned-out hulk. However, engineers were confident they could raise her in about a year and send her back for refitting. Nimitz and Halsey wondered if they would have a year to work with.

Not all the news was bad. The *Tennessee* had sustained damage to her number 2 and number 3 turrets but was otherwise unhurt. She had already departed for California. The *Maryland*, even though hulled by a bomb, had also departed for the States. During the attack, she'd had the ghoulish good fortune to be protected from Japanese attackers by the corpse of the *Oklahoma*, just as the *Tennessee* had been covered by the *West Virginia*.

That left the *Pennsylvania*. The battleship had been in dry dock and not anchored off Ford Island; thus, she had emerged relatively unscathed from the first attacks. The last one, however, had hurt her badly. Bombs had knocked out her forward fourteen-inch turrets, and a near miss had sprung her hull. Flames from the burning oil and fuel cascading from the storage tanks had caused additional damage, but her engineering plant was still intact and she could make headway.

"Get her the hell out of here," snapped Halsey. "If the Japs come, they'd get the present of a nearly usable battleship. Send her to California just as fast as she can get there."

Nimitz agreed and gave the orders for the *Pennsylvania* to depart as soon as she was minimally ready. With the departures of the *Tennessee* and the *Maryland*, along with escorting destroyers, the fleet anchorage was beginning to look empty and forlorn. Many other ships had been sunk or damaged, but they were replaceable, while battleships were not. The *Colorado* was on the West Coast, and additional help was arriving there in the form of the *New Mexico*, the *Mississippi*, and the *Idaho* from the Atlantic Fleet.

More important, in both admirals' estimation, was the arrival in the Pacific of the carrier *Yorktown*. Nimitz and Halsey were convinced that the day of the battleship had passed and that the carrier was the new queen of the seas.

Until the damaged ships were repaired and new ones delivered, the balance of power in the Pacific still lay with the Japanese: ten carriers to three; and maybe a dozen Jap battleships to America's four. The United States still had a number of cruisers, destroyers, and subs in the area, but these were more than matched by the Japanese. With the war raging in the Atlantic as well, it was unlikely that very many more reinforcements would be forthcoming from that arena.

General Walter Short entered the room and sat down. "I hear you've routed ships back to the States after yesterday's attack on those freighters."

"Yes," said Nimitz while Halsey glared at the general, who, in his opinion, had been as negligent as Kimmel during the December 7 attack. Both admirals considered it hideously unfair that Kimmel had been sacked while Short retained his position. "Six civilian ships were sunk yesterday, and we believe four of them by the same sub. We have to prepare for convoy and escort duty just like we are doing in the Atlantic against Nazi U-boats. I decided that any ship that could be sent back to the mainland should be returned there. In the future, priority will be given to escorting ships carrying material that can repair the ships and the fuel depot. Anything else will have to wait."

"You don't understand," said Short. "Those ships contained more than supplies. They contained food."

"Food?" Halsey asked harshly. "Who the hell cares about food on a tropical island?"

Short met Halsey's anger with his own. "You will in a little while, Admiral. This place may be tropical, but it grows everything except food. Much of what we eat is imported. No food ships and the people of Hawaii starve. Maybe you boys on your floating palaces have enough to eat, but the people of Honolulu are going to be hurting in a couple of weeks if the food ships stop coming in."

Nimitz rubbed his eyes. It was another unexpected problem. "How many shiploads do you need?"

"Maybe fifty a month, depending on the size," Short said. "More, of course, if the place is going to be reinforced. More construction workers and more soldiers mean more mouths to feed. It's just that simple, gentlemen. And don't forget that everything from razor blades to toilet paper has to come from the mainland. Counting military personnel, there are about half a million people who need the navy to keep them fed, clothed, and their asses wiped."

Nimitz accepted the obvious. Precious resources would have to be allocated to feed and sustain the military and civilian population of the islands.

Short managed a tight smile. "Contrary to what's being said about me, I am taking steps to alleviate the situation. As military governor, I am ordering the confiscation of all foodstuffs from stores and warehouses, and will institute a food rationing program within a couple of days. We'll stretch what we have for as long as we can, but the civilians aren't going to like it one bit. For one thing, I am going to give priority to my soldiers and the men working to repair the facilities."

"I understand," Nimitz said. "We'll do what we can."

"I'm also gathering all the gas and oil I can to keep my trucks and what planes I have left operational. We'll be rationing civilian gas, and a lot of people are going to be walking or riding bikes. Without shipping, these islands are a goddamned mess. Look, I can't even replace the planes I've lost without ships. Not a fighter in my air force or your navy has the range to fly from California to here. They all have to be ferried, along with the fuel to get them in the air when they finally do get here."

With that, an angry Short left as abruptly as he had arrived.

"Now what?" Halsey asked. He still strained to go after the Japanese, although he would have loved to have vented his frustrations on General Short.

When Nimitz responded, it was in a voice filled with gloom. "You will take the *Lexington* and *Enterprise* to Australia."

"Australia?" Halsey was incredulous. "The Japs are coming here!"

"You're probably right."

Nimitz knew that Halsey was more than right. As a recipient of Magic information that was denied Halsey, Nimitz had been told of troop movements in and around Japan, as well as another gathering of the Japanese fleet. Logic said that Hawaii was a possible destination. Under the circumstances, Nimitz had reluctantly concluded that the situation in the islands was temporarily hopeless.

"Oh my God," Halsey said. "You're abandoning Pearl, aren't you?"

"Not entirely. But I cannot justify attempting to defend the place at this time. If the Japs don't come and the repairs are made, we can return just as quickly as we left. The remainder of the fleet will protect our West Coast, while your carriers protect Australia. You might not like that directive, but it comes directly from Roosevelt."

"But if the Japs do come here, the army'll be overwhelmed."

Nimitz nodded sadly. "The way things are, that'll happen even if we stay. I'm returning to San Francisco by air and taking Kimmel's staff with me. From there we'll plot our next steps."

"Chester," Halsey said softly, "what about the dependents? There are thousands of wives and children of army and navy personnel here, not to mention ordinary civilians. Should we try to take some of them with us?"

Nimitz took a deep breath. It was the most agonizing decision he would ever have to make. "No. I have authorized the removal of the sick, the very old, and the very young, and that's it. We cannot take them all, and I am not in a mood to play Solomon over who stays and who goes. Further, any attempt to evacuate other civilians will cause a panic. No, we'll simply say that our actions in moving our ships from here are being taken to fight the Japanese, which is true. We'll leave enough smaller ships to placate the civilians, and just maybe deter the Japanese, but the heart of the fleet must leave."

"I hope it works," said Halsey.

"So do I," Nimitz answered in a voice that was almost a groan. "So do I."

JAKE NOVACEK DROVE his '38 Buick carefully down the darkened streets of Honolulu. There were very few cars on the road as a strict curfew was in effect. He'd been stopped several times, and only the fact that he was an armed army officer in uniform had kept the local police or Military Police from taking him in.

His apartment was across the street from a couple of stores. One was a grocery owned by an old Japanese man who also owned Jake's apartment building. Jake wondered just how he'd fare with the nation at war with Japan. To his chagrin, Jake realized that, even though he'd shopped there often enough, he didn't know whether the old man was a citizen or not. Jake just bought food and beer, and paid his rent. The old man was named Matsuo, and Jake didn't know if that was his first or last name.

Jake was dirty, bloody, and exhausted. A bed, he thought, my kingdom for a bed. Oh, yeah, and a shower. He'd seen so much death and so much grief. He just wanted to get the hell away from anything military, if only for a few hours. His apartment was his oasis.

He was haunted by the faces of the families who'd lost loved ones, in particular the pain shown on the face of Alexa Sanderson. Such a beautiful lady in so much agony, he thought, and no possible way for him to help her, or all the others whose loved ones were still being pulled from the dirty waters of Pearl Harbor. He wondered if the funeral had provided any solace for her.

He pulled into his parking spot and wondered just how much longer he'd be able to drive his car, since gas rationing was inevitable. He made a mental note to get a lock for his gas cap. He wondered if somebody might someday steal his tires and what the hell he could do about it. Then he'd be reduced to riding a bicycle. He'd been reliably informed that he looked stupid on a bike. Of course, he'd been drunk the last time he'd attempted to ride.

Food rationing was inevitable too. Thank God nobody'd thought to ration beer. He had a dozen bottles of Budweiser in the fridge that he would cherish after drinking two of them tonight. Then another thought hit him. What would he do if the power went out? He disliked warm beer, but, he thought with a chuckle, he would drink it in the service of his country.

"Get out, you bums!"

"Fucking Jap!"

Jake turned quickly at the sounds. They came from Mr. Matsuo's store across the street. Three young white men spilled out of the store, followed by an outraged Matsuo. The men were carrying food and beer.

"You pay, you pay," yelled Matsuo. "Thieves, you thieves!"

The leader of the three, a tall, rangy man in his thirties, stopped and kicked the old man in the gut, dropping him to the ground, where he groaned and writhed.

Shit, Jake thought as he trotted across the street. His sidearm, a venerable but reliable .45 automatic, was already in his hand. "Enough, children," he snarled. "Drop everything and get your hands up."

"What the fuck?" said the leader. "Hey, you're a soldier. You should be on our side. This is a fucking Jap, just like the bastards who killed our men."

Jake held the pistol steady. The three were drunk. No surprise. "Yeah, and what branch of the service are you in?"

"Registered civilian," said the leader, smirking. "Now, what are you going to do? You can't arrest us. You ain't no cop."

"Don't have to be," Jake said. "There's a curfew on, you're robbing this guy, you're drunk, you assaulted him, and, if you haven't noticed, I've got a gun pointed right at your empty heads."

Sirens could be heard in the distance, and they were approaching. Somebody had called the real cops. The would-be thieves heard them too.

"You ain't gonna shoot us and you know it. We're all white men and this is a yellow-skinned, slanty-eyed Jap," the tall one said. "And we're leaving right now."

"No," Jake said and pointed the weapon at the leader's chest. "What you're going to do is lie down on the ground and wait."

"Bullshit," the leader said. "Take him, boys."

The three men lunged forward. Jake quickly reversed the pistol and smashed the leader in the face with the butt, turning his nose into a bloody mess and knocking out several teeth. He then wheeled on the second man and hit him alongside the head with the pistol. The man screamed and dropped to his knees. Jake kicked him in the ribs, and he fell over. The third man stopped and lay down on the ground, his eyes wide with terror.

"I'm dying," said the leader, his voice distorted by his smashed face and the blood running from his mouth.

A squad car with one cop arrived seconds later, and the store owner, now shakily on his feet, quickly explained the situation. Equally quickly, Jake had wiped any blood off his pistol and put it back in its holster.

He recognized the officer as one of the good guys, a cop named

Malone, who wasn't stick-happy when it came to arresting drunken military types. Mr. Matsuo told Malone that the three louts had tried to rob him and that Jake had saved him.

Officer Malone looked at the three men and then at Jake. "They're pretty messed up, Captain. Any idea what happened to them?"

Jake shrugged. "They may have run into each other while trying to run out of the store."

"Yeah," the cop said solemnly. "They look like clumsy types."

Air-raid sirens went off again. Japs or another false alarm? Odds were a false alarm. There'd been scores of them since the attack. Malone swore, pushed the three drunks into his squad car, and sped off down the road, his own siren wailing. Jake looked around. It all had happened so quickly. He shook his head. Now more than ever he needed to clean up and rest.

Mr. Matsuo ran up to Jake and shoved a bag in his arms. "Thank you, Captain. And here."

Jake grinned. He now had another six bottles of Budweiser.

THE NORTHERN PACIFIC WAS BLEAK and windswept, but this was no deterrent to the men who loaded their precious cargo onto the decks of the Imperial Navy's carriers. Victory was a fever, and the crews were flush with it.

Standing on the dock and looking at the ships a half-mile away, Commander Fuchida thought that the carriers looked top-heavy with the extra planes they carried and that they would capsize in the first strong wind or wave. He knew better, but the sight was unsettling.

Unseen, but even more congested, were the lower decks, where spare parts, ammunition, and additional fuel had been jammed into every available space. The men of the Imperial Japanese Navy would be damned uncomfortable for this crossing, but Fuchida was certain they'd all applaud the results. Japan was again going to punish the arrogant Americans, and Uncle Sam's white beard would be singed by flames.

As strong as the task force that had destroyed the American battle fleet, this new incarnation of the *Kido Butai* was again commanded by Admiral Nagumo, and this was one of Fuchida's few worries. Although Nagumo was again protected by two battleships along with numerous other cruisers and destroyers, Fuchida feared that the admiral might flee in the event the Americans were sighted before they reached their target, the island of Molokai.

Fuchida feared that the bold stroke might be too bold for Nagumo, but he dared not voice the complaint. He was too junior to take the risk, although the outspoken Commander Genda had sent whispers through the corridors of the high command.

The plan was marvelous in its simplicity. The fleet also included a regiment of Imperial marines, a battalion of engineers, and sufficient supplies to build and sustain airfields on Molokai.

Molokai had been chosen because it had a number of private airstrips that could be utilized until larger fields were constructed. Thus, immediately after the marines secured the area, the extra planes could be flown in from the carriers and operations against Oahu begun immediately.

Little resistance was expected; intelligence said there were no military units on Molokai, and any civilian opposition could be brushed aside. Molokai was large, but the marines could hold it and protect the air arm. When the planes landed, Fuchida was proud that he would command them and the subsequent softening-up assaults against the Americans. The carriers would linger only as long as necessary. They would depart and leave a handful of smaller ships to protect the new Japanese base. It was clearly understood that the Americans did not have the ability to launch a naval counterattack from Oahu, although Fuchida and most of the other officers wished they'd try. It was presumed, however, that air assaults would commence quickly, thus the need for the carriers to stay in the area until the base was fully operational.

Molokai had been chosen instead of Lanai for two additional reasons. First, Molokai was less rugged than Lanai, which meant more fields could be constructed, and, second, Lanai was considered entirely too close to Oahu. Even though the Americans had very few planes, any American counterattack against Lanai would be overhead before a warning could be made and countermeasures taken. No, Molokai was the perfect distance, although no one ruled out occupying Lanai at a later time.

Fuchida saw Admiral Yamamoto approach as he stood on the dock. He snapped to attention. Yamamoto greeted him warmly. "I am very pleased with your plans and your efforts," he told Fuchida.

Fuchida bowed. "Thank you, sir."

"Yours will be a brave endeavor, and one that will be instrumental in the conquest of Hawaii. Everyone is thoroughly aware of the importance of this mission. Everyone will support it to the utmost."

Fuchida's heart surged. Yamamoto would never criticize Nagumo in the presence of a junior officer, but he had just told Fuchida that Nagumo had been forcefully informed that he had better succeed or face dire consequences.

Yamamoto chuckled. "So many planes. Are you sure there's room on the flight decks to get them airborne?"

Fuchida smiled, glad to change the topic. "Just barely, sir. Thank God we won't have to land them back on the carriers."

"Just remember," Yamamoto said sternly, "pilots are more important than planes. We can replace planes from our warehouses and factories, but our brave pilots are irreplaceable."

Fuchida understood. In the unlikely event that major American forces were located and did attack, the extra planes would simply be pushed into the sea to enable the others to return safely. It would be more necessary that the carrier pilots be preserved than that a landing be effected on Molokai. Many officers wished such an American attack would occur. It would give the navy an opportunity to smash the Americans again.

Japanese strategy called for such a battle, even planned on it. The navy's ultimate goal was to lure large American forces away from their bases and toward Japan, where they would be ambushed by the overwhelming might of the Combined Fleet. It was for this reason that Nagumo had been given a strong force but not an overwhelming one. If the Americans took the bait, he was to inflict damage and withdraw in apparent retreat toward Japan, where Yamamoto waited with a force that included the secret superbattleship *Yamato*. The *Yamato* was twice the size of any other battleship, had eighteen-inch guns, and had been plucked from her sea trials to join the fleet. Yamamoto would keep his flag on the *Yamishiro*, but the *Yamato* would be the iron fist of the supporting fleet.

If the Americans did not rise to the temptation, then Molokai was secured. Either way, Japan won. But, as Fuchida had been reminded, winning could not come at too great a price.

The war was only a few weeks old, but a potentially serious problem was beginning to emerge. Japanese planes were superb and could be manufactured in sufficient numbers by Japan's factories, but not so the pilots. Japanese naval pilots were considered the elite of the elite, the bravest of the brave, the fittest of the fit. In short, the standards for a carrier pilot were so high that they were almost impossible to fulfill and sustain.

Fuchida was a product of the system, and he had seen the vast majority of apparently highly qualified applicants fail to make the grade. Now he and others were wondering whether the standards were too high. For the moment, there were more than enough pilots to man the planes and enough replacements on hand for those lost, but the downward trend of the curve was inexorable and already unmistakable. If the coming air battles became ones of attrition, the quality of the Japanese air arm would suffer as incompletely trained pilots replaced the skilled ones.

America's pilot standards were nowhere near as high as Japan's, and this had already proven itself as American air-to-air casualties had been far higher than Japan's. But the battles had not been totally one-sided. Japan had also lost planes and pilots. The Americans, with a larger population base to draw from, could simply replace their losses much more easily. Even if Japan shot down two planes for each one of her own lost, the Americans might prevail through the sheer weight of numbers.

Fuchida had a heavy responsibility. He must fight, but he must also preserve his forces. He must help defeat the Americans in Hawaii, which would bring the Americans to the conference table for a negotiated peace.

Yamamoto had walked a distance away. Fuchida had a wild urge to call after him and tell him that he understood, and that the mission would be a success. The commander laughed. After all, didn't Admiral Yamamoto already know that?

The fleet would sail in the morning. There was time for a farewell dinner with Commander Genda, who would later be on the flagship at Nagumo's side. Once again they would reenact the roles they had played at Pearl Harbor. Once again he was confident that there would be both surprise and overwhelming victory.

CHAPTER 5

.

One of the most endearing facts about Hawaii was that winter was nonexistent. It was late December, and the warm sun had driven the temperature into the low eighties with only moderate humidity. It was a perfect time to relax with friends and a cold drink, and that was precisely what Captain Jake Novacek found himself doing.

The invitation to attend a cookout-picnic-potluck dinner and wake for Tim Sanderson had been a surprise. He'd managed a phone call to the widow's neighbor, the little blonde, and been told that the occasion was informal and if he could bring something to share it would be marvelous, as food rationing was making events like this difficult.

No problem. Dressed in a flower print shirt and civilian slacks, he'd been welcomed warmly, even more so when Alexa and Missy realized he'd brought several pounds of ground beef that he'd caused to disappear from the officers' club.

In different times, such a party would have been unseemly or in bad taste, but the fact of the war made for new values. "Enjoy life while you can" was the new motto. The Japanese navy and army could be just over the horizon.

Regardless, the *Lexington* would be departing and, with it, Missy Wilson's husband. The *Pennsylvania* was just about ready to head east to California, and Jamie Priest would be on her. Thus, the get-together was as much a going-away party as it was a wake, and one that could not be delayed for a more traditional time. That it brought a brief period of normalcy and happiness was not lost on anyone either. War was on the horizon, on everyone's minds, and the evidence of it lay in charred abundance around Oahu.

With all the ships departing, it looked like the entire navy was bailing out and leaving the army on its own. It was disturbing and, according to Jake's own sources, very true.

Jamie had brought a local girl named Sally. She was a little loud and had gotten drunk quickly, which caused Jamie some embarrassment. A Father Monroe was there, and he seemed to think that Jake's Polish last name made him a fellow Catholic. Jake was too polite to refute this assumption. Although he had been baptized and confirmed a Catholic, it had been a long time since he'd been in a church for other than a wedding or a funeral.

However, Father Monroe had brought some excellent sacramental wine that, when chilled, went well over ice and eaten with hamburger. He'd also brought some of the older children from the school for poor native Hawaiians that he ran, where Alexa taught. Jake thought it was an interesting and unexpected perspective on Alexa. He also thought that one of the girls, a fourteen-year-old named Kami Ogawa, was an absolute stunner who would soon be breaking all the young male hearts in Hawaii if she wasn't doing so already. The girl looked Hawaiian, Japanese, and God knew what else, and she and Alexa seemed to be good friends.

"Comfy?" Alexa asked as she sat down in the folding chair beside him. She was dressed in a sleeveless blouse that was drawn in a knot just below her breasts and a flowered skirt that stopped well before her knees. In any place other than Hawaii, it would have been inappropriate. In Hawaii, it was delightful. She had marvelously athletic legs, and he had a hard time not staring at them. They were lightly tanned, as was the small expanse of bare midriff that appeared above her waist.

"Everything's just perfect," he answered.

"This is the smartest thing I've ever done," she said as she swept an arm to encompass the gathering. For a minute Jake thought she was drunk, but the look in her eyes told him different. She was excited and pleased; a little brittle perhaps, but otherwise under control, and he admired her inner strength.

"There may never be another chance for something like this," she said. "Everyone's leaving but you. Both Missy and I are trying to get on a plane or ship back to the States, where it'll be safer."

"Good idea," Jake said.

If the islands were a war zone, then civilians should be out of it. But he would miss his new friends and the chance of seeing Alexa

Sanderson again. God, he thought, how could I even think that? Tim was just dead and Alexa was wealthy and so much more sophisticated than he, which meant he could never be more than a casual friend to her. It was nice that she considered him part of her military and Hawaiian family, but she would move on with her life and so would he.

"Where's home?" Jake asked.

"Virginia. A horse farm about fifty miles outside Washington. We used to go to town on weekend trips to see how our money was being spent. Can you believe they're actually talking about deducting income tax from people's pay? Tim's family came from Massachusetts. When this is over, he'll be sent back and reburied there, along with his ancestors. Where's home for you?"

Jake laughed. "Anywhere and everywhere. My parents went where the jobs were. Sometimes we worked farms, and sometimes the mines. I was born in Pennsylvania and spent a few years in West Virginia. I think we gave new meaning to the word *poor*. We were so broke we didn't even notice when the Depression hit. If you have nothing to lose, nobody can take it from you."

Alexa was puzzled. "But you went to West Point?"

"That's right. And counting academy time, I've been in the army for twenty-two years."

Alexa did the mental math. "But that would make you older than Tim thought."

"Alexa, I enlisted when I was fourteen."

"Fourteen? You were just a child!"

"At fourteen I weighed a hundred and seventy pounds and ate more than anyone could afford to feed me. My father had died in a mine accident, and my mother had tuberculosis. She'd been sent to a sanitarium, so I had the choice of enlisting, running away, or working in the mines. A friend of mine was an army recruiter, and he made a few discreet mistakes on my application to get me in. After that, I found that military life fit me. More important, I found that I could play football and played for several posts before someone decided that maybe I could play for the academy, where they were always short of big, dumb linemen. I was tutored, strings were pulled, and I wound up at West Point. I don't think anyone thought I'd actually graduate, but I did, and now I'm an officer and a gentleman, although one who's without connections, family, or influence."

This was something Alexa understood quite well. Tim's family had been navy for generations, and, with her uncle as a New Deal Democrat from Ohio who'd arrived in Washington in 1933 with Roosevelt, Tim's future had been assured. Connections and ability were an unbeatable combination, and factors she and Tim had taken for granted.

Alexa was visibly impressed with what Jake had made of himself. "Good for you," she said warmly. "And now you're a captain. And won't the war give you further opportunities for advancement, even without influence?"

Jake sighed. "I had hoped so, but I may have screwed up badly. You see, I wrote an honest report that got General Short and some others really teed off at me."

Alexa was incredulous. "How could honesty get you in trouble?"

"Simple. About a month before the attack, Short asked my boss, Lieutenant Colonel Fielder, for a study on the likelihood of the Japanese on Oahu attempting to sabotage our war effort by doing things such as blowing up our airplanes on the ground. Since I speak a little Japanese and have contacts in the community, I got the assignment. When I submitted a report saying that sabotage was extremely unlikely, I was informed that it wasn't what General Short, or his chief of staff, Colonel Phillips, were after. They wanted a report saying that sabotage would occur, not an analysis that it wouldn't. They were afraid of the Japs on Hawaii and wanted to justify their plans, which were to bunch all the planes together to prevent sabotage. Later, when the Jap air force destroyed them, they wanted some evidence that they'd acted in good faith on an analysis from their intelligence department. Unfortunately, my already submitted report said just the opposite."

"In other words, they wanted to save their skins."

"Right. And I would have been the scapegoat. No way I could win this one."

Alexa had to admit he was right. She'd heard of such things before. She decided to change the subject. "How well do you speak Japanese?"

"I won't hurt myself, or get something awful in a restaurant. Actually, I seem to have a bit of a flair for languages. I speak some Spanish and a little French as well. I got into the habit of immersing myself in the culture of wherever I was stationed, and that sort of led to my getting involved in military intelligence."

Interesting, Alexa thought. The big bear of a man really was deeper than she had first thought. "I am very glad you came today," she told him.

"Me too," Jake said and grinned. "Although the circumstances aren't all that pleasant, this is one of the nicest holidays I've ever had. Uh, you said you and Missy were leaving here. Any idea when?"

Alexa shrugged. "Actually, nobody knows. All the outgoing planes are reserved for the wounded and important military people, and there are no ships available for civilians, not even dependents. While it could happen very shortly, I'll probably be here for the next several months, perhaps longer."

Jake nodded and sipped his wine. His emotions were mixed. On the one hand, he was delighted that Alexa Sanderson would be around for a while, but, on the other hand, he was concerned about what might occur should the Japs make a move toward Oahu. He was getting information about the things the Japs were doing to civilians in Hong Kong and elsewhere. The thought that barbarism could descend on the people of Hawaii was both chilling and terrifying.

PRIME MINISTER TOJO SMILED with genuine pleasure. The war was going well for Japan. "Admiral, I am pleased to inform you that final permission to seize Hawaii has been granted."

"Thank you," Admiral Yamamoto responded warily. He wondered just how much the prime minister and head of the army had known of his plans to go ahead, with or without permission.

Had permission been refused, the attack would have been categorized as a raid, or a reconnaissance in force, and, assuming its success, the existence of a Japanese base on Molokai would have been a means of exerting pressure on Tojo's government to take the obvious step of attacking Oahu.

"The 38th Division suffered about fifteen hundred casualties in taking Hong Kong," Tojo said. "A small number. These will be replaced, and the division will be ready to depart China in a matter of days. The other regiments that will fill it out are already at ports and ready to embark. I trust you have found enough transports to support this operation?"

Yamamoto smiled. "Just barely, Prime Minister. Quarters will be cramped and living conditions miserable, but that will only serve to make the soldiers more fierce."

Tojo laughed. The idea of a commanding officer being concerned about the comfort of his soldiers was ludicrous. Japanese soldiers were trained with extreme harshness and expected to live in conditions of privation that would cause lesser men to collapse.

"Admiral, I have addressed your concerns about civilians with General Tadoyashi. To the extent that it is possible, there will be no repeat of what occurred in Hong Kong. I agree that it would be counterproductive for there to be wholesale massacres and rapes of those people whom we would wish to utilize as hostages, or even allies. It could be a political and diplomatic disaster."

Yamamoto was relieved. Although the bulk of the terror in Hong Kong had been directed at the indigenous and despised Chinese population, it would be too easy for the troops of the 38th to run amok. Anything resembling a massacre would polarize resentment and make the conquest and occupation more difficult.

"However," Tojo continued, "there is always the possibility of incidents occurring during the heat of battle, and the army always has permission to utilize terror against the military population to induce surrender."

This time Yamamoto's concurrence was more reluctant. Tadoyashi's troops had butchered British prisoners, then raped and murdered the female military nurses they'd captured and threatened the entire garrison with death if they didn't surrender. The horrified, outnumbered, and outgunned British had immediately pulled down the Union Jack. After that had come the reign of terror against the civilian population.

"I can only trust in the army's best efforts," the admiral said warily.

"Indeed," Tojo responded. "On another matter, it now appears that we could have given you one of the better trained divisions from the Siberian border. Our embassy in Moscow is quite convinced that the Soviets will make no move toward Manchukuo. They are far too involved in their counterthrust against the Nazis to entertain any thought of opening a second front against us."

Yamamoto shrugged it off. "No matter. Between what the army is providing and the brigade of marines under Admiral Iwabachi, the forces will be more than sufficient."

"Very good. And Iwabachi will be the military governor of Hawaii?"

"Yes."

"Again a good decision. Iwabachi is a very stern man who will maintain tight discipline and brook no interference from the Americans under his control. There will be a *kempetei* field detachment under Colonel Omori to support him."

The *kempetei* were the Japanese version of a secret police. They had wide jurisdiction and powers, and Yamamoto acknowledged that Admiral Iwabachi would be controlled in significant matters by Omori. It was not unusual. The governor would govern the islands, while police and security matters fell under the jurisdiction of the *kempetei*.

"Does Colonel Omori speak English?" Yamamoto asked.

"Fluently. Even more important, he understands the need to pacify the three races that exist in Hawaii. The white Americans will be tightly controlled, while the native Hawaiians will be given every opportunity to support us. The Japanese in Hawaii will be expected to be loyal to us from the first moment."

When Yamamoto raised an eyebrow in a silent query, Tojo continued. "We acknowledge and respect that many Japanese in Hawaii have been away from pure Japanese culture for years, even generations, and that some of them might have to be reeducated. We are confident that, with Colonel Omori's wise assistance, the overwhelming majority of the Japanese in Hawaii will see the wisdom of rediscovering the worth of being Japanese."

The meeting ended. When Yamamoto had departed, Tojo yawned. He was tired and under a great deal of strain. Yamamoto was a brave and wise man, and one he greatly respected. Tojo, of course, had his own spies in the navy's camp and was well aware of the continuing plans for a landing on Molokai. If it succeeded, then more glory would come to Japan and the government headed by Hideki Tojo.

If it failed, then it was on Yamamoto's head, and it would be Yamamoto, along with the rest of the naval coterie, who would lose face.

Tojo chuckled. There were those who thought the lack of cooperation between the army and navy a deplorable state of affairs. But that was not true. Divide and conquer was a fundamental rule of war, whether the enemies were foreign or domestic.

Tojo was confident the attacks on Hawaii would succeed. Along with Yamamoto and others, he shared concern over what the future might bring to Japan. In a brief while, the Philippines would fall, and they would be followed by the myriad of islands of the southern Pacific. Australia might be intimidated and coerced into a surrender, or at least a peace treaty that would be most favorable to Japan. The future of Japan was bright.

THE STINK of the Philippine jungle was almost as bad as the stench of defeat. The crew of the submarine *Monkfish* thought they could smell both jungle rot and defeat as she cruised slowly eastward from the doomed Philippines. They were incorrect, of course; the fetid land smell was overwhelmed by the combined odors of diesel, sweat, and urine as the cramped sub progressed underwater. The odor of defeat, however, was pervasive.

Only a few weeks earlier, the naval base near Manila had been home to more than a score of American submarines. It had been the largest concentration of submarines anywhere, and it had been presumed that the subs, along with General MacArthur's American-Philippine army, would be able to take on anything the Japs had thrown at them.

It hadn't worked out that way.

First, the American army's air arm in the Philippines had been wiped out a few hours after the attack on Pearl Harbor, despite having had warning of the attacks on Pearl several hours earlier. For reasons that might forever be unknown, the news had paralyzed the American command, and they did nothing. Thus, when the Japanese planes finally did attack, they found a situation much like that at Pearl. The vast majority of American planes had been destroyed on the ground, where the Jap fighters had found them parked in neat rows.

This total aerial superiority enabled the Japanese to attack other American army and naval facilities with impunity. It also meant that the numerous subsequent Japanese landings on the Philippines were largely unopposed.

Admiral Thomas C. Hart, the senior naval officer and commander of the United States Asiatic Fleet, had been appalled. The Japanese army quickly pushed the small American army and the larger, but poorly trained, Philippine army backward.

MacArthur's defenses had proven to be without substance. Manila would fall shortly, and the American presence on Luzon now mainly consisted of the peninsula of Bataan and the fortified island of Corregidor.

Earlier, Admiral Hart had evacuated all major surface ships from Philippine waters, and only the subs and their support craft had remained. Now, even they had departed, and it was conceded that the Philippines were doomed unless a relief force came from the United States. While some believed that an American fleet was always just over the horizon, the clearer thinkers realized that the islands were going to be conquered by the Japanese.

Commander Frank Griddle despised himself for being in the position of retreating and for being so relieved that he would not be in the Philippines when the Japs did march through. He thought of himself as a reasonably brave man, but he wanted no part of a Jap occupation and prison camp.

The *Monkfish* was an unfamiliar sub to Griddle. He commanded because her regular captain had been felled by some wretched Asian fever. The second in command, Lieutenant Willis Fargo, was inexperienced, and it was decided that Griddle would take the *Monk,* as she was known, out to sea and retreat to Pearl. Griddle had been on Hart's staff and had previously commanded a sub. It was a logical choice.

This had not made him popular with his crew, who both had liked Jacobs and didn't wish to leave the Philippines without striking back at the Japanese. To date, the *Monk* had accomplished absolutely nothing to that effect, and their failure was grating on the crew.

The *Monkfish* was a reasonably new boat. She had been completed in the latter half of 1939 and was one of the Sargo class of submarines. She displaced 1,425 tons and had a crew of sixty-two. For weapons, she had eight torpedo tubes, four each in the bow and in the stern, and a four-inch deck gun. A pair of 20 mm Oerlikon antiaircraft guns completed her armament.

Griddle squinted through the periscope and didn't care for what he saw. Steaming insolently in front of him was a Kagero-class Japanese destroyer, one of the newest in their navy. She was traveling quickly through the water and in apparent ignorance of the existence of the *Monk,* which was gaining on her.

At first Griddle had been torn with indecision. His orders were to get to Pearl Harbor as quickly as possible, but how did one not attack an enemy warship? Besides, both he and his crew felt a compelling need to do something, anything, to strike back at the Japs. If he were to do nothing, he might also lose what little respect his crew had for him. Other forays had resulted in no attacks by the *Monk*, because no Japs had been sighted or because they'd been in shoal water, where a sub couldn't go, or because the Jap ships had been too well protected. The *Monk* had not yet fired a shot in anger. Thus, they could not pass up an attack on a lone destroyer in deep water, and one where a converging course would put the destroyer in range within moments.

Yet another nagging possibility haunted Griddle and the crew. Was there something wrong with their torpedoes, or was it something else? No one knew, but one thing was certain—far too many torpedo attacks by other subs had been fruitless. Good, solid targets had been inexplicably missed, and often at great danger to the attacking subs.

While a few sinkings had been achieved, it was common knowledge that elite, well-trained crews with first-class subs were accomplishing far less than they should, and that left the torpedo as the reason for failure.

The torpedo in question was the brand-new Mark 14. That it could go more than two miles at forty-six knots was not an issue. What happened when it got to the target was. The Mark 14 was designed to focus on a target ship's magnetic field, streak under the ship, and then explode, which, according to theory, would break the back of the target ship and sink it more efficiently than a normal, old-fashioned impact torpedo.

It was elegant in theory, but it didn't seem to work out in practice, and this concerned Griddle. If they missed the Kagero-class destroyer, they'd have one pissed-off Jap warship to contend with. Not too much was known about the Kagero class, but Griddle's periscope view confirmed that she had what appeared to be five-inch guns, torpedoes of her own, and a clustering of depth charges at her stern. A miss or a malfunction by a torpedo could become extremely uncomfortable.

It was now or never.

"Range?" Griddle asked.

"Two thousand yards" was the reply from Lieutenant Fargo.

Seconds later, four torpedoes were streaking toward the Kagero-class. The target was clear, and they could not miss, not all four of them.

Griddle ordered the *Monk* deeper. They would wait it out under periscope depth. Several stopwatches clicked off the seconds to impact. Now they could clearly hear the screws of the destroyer as she churned the water ever closer to them.

And then the watches were past impact time. Griddle paled. The torpedoes had missed. It was impossible! Not all four of them!

To their horror, they heard the destroyer coming even closer. She had seen the torpedo wakes and was following them to their source. Griddle didn't have to see the destroyer to visualize her slicing through the waves toward them at more than thirty knots per hour.

Then the men of the *Monkfish* heard splashes. "Depth charges," Griddle hollered, and the men prepared to hang on for their lives.

An explosion rocked the *Monk,* sending equipment and men flying in the narrow confines. There were screams of pain as men caromed off the pipes and deck. Another explosion, this time much closer, hurled Griddle against a bulkhead and then onto the floor. The lights flickered, went out, and returned.

Griddle had landed on something soft, and he felt his hand go into the mush of a crewman's skull. The commander couldn't see out of his left eye, and blood was pouring down his face. Waves of pain flowed over him, and he wondered if he could talk.

Another depth charge exploded, this one almost on top of the *Monk.* Griddle felt himself losing consciousness. As he slipped in and out, he wondered if he was going to die. He didn't want to. There was so much to live for. For one thing, he wanted to kill the son of a bitch who'd invented the Mark 14 torpedo.

FRANKLIN DELANO ROOSEVELT LIT the cigarette he'd just placed in the long holder that was as much his trademark as Winston Churchill's cigar was his. The British prime minister was en route, and much had to be decided before the two allies conferred and planned for the continuation of the war that was now raging on two oceans.

But first, there were some unpleasant specifics to clear up. Roosevelt smiled disarmingly at General Marshall and Admiral King. "Gentlemen, just what are the Japanese up to this time?" he asked.

"We're not certain," King admitted. "All indications are that a reconnaissance in force is going to occur, but exactly what the target is, we don't yet know."

Roosevelt inhaled and blew out a perfect smoke ring. He watched it ascend to the ceiling of the Oval Office. "Why don't you know?"

"Sir," King continued, "we can read many of their messages, but not all of them. Part of the problem is manpower, while the other is the fact that their military codes have not been totally broken. A month ago, we had only a couple of score men and women doing this, and they were totally inundated by Japanese communications traffic."

"Which may be why we didn't know about the attack on Pearl Harbor?" Roosevelt mused hopefully. His political enemies were still raking him over the coals for that failure, and he knew it would be a sore point for future generations. He'd been shocked to hear that some Americans were claiming he'd intentionally permitted the slaughter of Americans to get the United States into the war.

"Yes," King answered. "Although there were other factors, not the least of which was that the Jap fleet steamed in total silence, which meant there were no messages to intercept. But, getting back to the people working on the Japanese messages, we now have several hundred and will doubtless have more as soon as we can find them and hire them, but they are still learning their job. We have listening posts on Hawaii and the Philippines as well as here in the States, but the situation is still far from perfect."

"Not in the Philippines?" Roosevelt asked with alarm. MacArthur's command had been reduced to a perimeter that was bound to fall.

King corrected himself. "The Philippine operation has been shut down and the personnel evacuated. Only Hawaii remains operational outside the United States."

"Good. We cannot have anyone with knowledge of Magic falling into Japanese hands. So, where is this Japanese fleet headed?"

"One of three places," King said. "Midway, Samoa, or one of the lesser islands in Hawaii. We think it might be Molokai."

"And what are you going to do about it?"

King's always stern face clouded. "Nothing. Until you release ships from the Atlantic, Nimitz's Pacific Fleet is a shadow. The Japs can come and go as they please, and there's damned little we can do about it."

Roosevelt glared at him. "You know I cannot give you more ships at this time. We are committed to a Europe-first war. You don't have to like it, Admiral, but that's the way it's going to be."

King could only glower. Well before the attack on Pearl Harbor, plans had been drawn up to cover a number of contingencies. Rainbow 5 was the plan that covered a war with Germany and Italy, and a simultaneous war with Japan. It was predicated on fighting an aggressive but defensive war with Japan until the defeat of the other Axis countries was assured. It accepted the painful reality that the United States could not fight a two-front war at that time. This meant that the Philippines were on their own, as was Hawaii, at least until the harbor facilities could be repaired.

Rainbow 5 also realized that ultimate victory was linked to the survival of the Soviet Union and Great Britain as allies. At this time, both were on the verge of collapse. Should either fall, the other would likely follow or sue for a separate peace. Thus, the fall of either Russia or Great Britain would leave Nazi Germany dominant in Europe and invulnerable.

"I know," King muttered.

The truly great fear was the collapse or defeat of Great Britain. If that occurred, Spain would likely join the Axis, who would conquer neutral but pro-American Portugal and then overwhelm Gibraltar, thus isolating the Mediterranean. Should that occur, the Germans would swiftly mop up Egypt, the Suez, and Palestine. They would then link up with Japanese armies attacking Europe. On the way, it was conceivable that they would take the vast oil reserves of the Arabian Peninsula.

The fall of Great Britain might also result in the Nazis' taking possession of the Royal Navy, while a treaty between Germany and England could conceivably result in a pro-German Canada sharing a common border with the United States. It was a nightmare scenario in which the United States would be totally isolated.

Great Britain and the Soviet Union must not be permitted to fall. It was as simple as that, Roosevelt thought. Why didn't King and the others understand? Why didn't the American people understand?

"You know," the president said to the admiral with a forced calmness, "there were those who said I shouldn't appoint you to head the navy. They said that, along with irrationally hating the British, you were an alcoholic and a womanizing lecher. I said I could accept all your faults because you were a tremendous fighter. However, you must work with us to win the war in the way that is most beneficial to the United States in the long run. Admit it, Admiral, even if you wished, you couldn't mount a relief expedition to either the Philippines or the Hawaiian islands at this time. While you may have a number of ships remaining, General Marshall still doesn't have an army. Isn't that true, General?"

"It is," Marshall said.

The American army now consisted of more than two million men, but they were as yet untrained and ill equipped. What newspapers were calling the Arsenal of Democracy existed largely on paper and in people's imaginations. Factories were still being converted to wartime production, and it would be the better part of a year before the newly forming army was ready for offensive operations; what trained units there were had been shipped off to England and Australia.

Australia had been an unexpected problem. With the Australian army off fighting the Nazis in North Africa, the Aussies had quickly realized that they were defenseless against the Japanese. Thus, they had presented England and the United States with a choice: Either American troops would be sent to Australia or the Australian army would be pulled out of North Africa. In response, American troops were landing to defend Australia.

Ironically, the navy was better off than the army despite the disaster at Pearl Harbor. Since it took years to construct a warship, it was almost providential that the buildup of the American navy had commenced nearly two years earlier. Thus, while King fretted over the limited resources presently available, he knew that the fleet under construction was larger than the fleet currently in the water. If only the Japanese would have waited, he thought bitterly, the American navy would have kicked their asses from Hawaii to Tokyo in record time. What really teed him and others off was the nagging feeling that the Japanese were really a second-rate power hiding behind the skirts of a first-rate power, Nazi Germany. The Japs had some good leaders and some good weapons, but nowhere near enough of either.

As if to punctuate that fact, German subs were wreaking havoc along the Atlantic coast in what the Nazis called Operation Drumbeat, while a handful of Japanese subs lurked off Puget Sound, San Francisco, San Diego, and Los Angeles. Flaming war had come to the coasts of America. Burning ships could be seen sinking off both coasts while people stood on the sands and watched.

"The resupply convoy?" Roosevelt asked, interrupting King's thoughts. "When will it depart for Honolulu?"

"As soon as we determine the exact target of the Jap raiding force. It's actually three convoys totaling more than a hundred merchant ships, and they will be escorted by twenty destroyers and light cruisers. Along with military stores, they will carry foodstuffs for the civilian population and as much fuel as we can provide. The fuel situation is causing difficulties, because we had to ensure that the ships in the convoy would be able to go to Hawaii and back without refueling from island stores. There was no point in sending fuel to Hawaii and then having the ships that brought it there guzzle it."

Marshall made a wry comment about a Civil War wagon train that was supposed to bring fodder to Grant's cavalry. By the time the wagons arrived, the horses pulling the wagons had eaten it all. Roosevelt thought it amusing and ironic. King did not.

"Then the fuel situation is truly acute?" the president asked.

"It is," said King. "We lost four and a half million gallons on December 7, when the Japs hit the fuel storage area. A normal shipment from the States gives the islands less than two weeks' supply. At the rate they've been using up what they have left, we don't think there's enough to sustain operations for more than a week or ten days."

"Neither the army nor the navy has sufficient fuel to patrol efficiently and still have enough to fight a battle," Marshall added. "Although, for once, the two services are cooperating in their efforts."

About time, Roosevelt thought. Germany and Japan were the enemy, not the other American services. The president wheeled over to where his cigarettes lay on a table. He made a show of lighting one to hide his concerns. King's comment disturbed him deeply. A week or ten days was all the fuel they had? The convoy had to get through, and the buildup had to begin immediately.

But, of course, nothing could happen until the Japanese raiding force came and went. "What about Hawaii, Admiral?" Roosevelt asked. "Have they been warned?"

"All potential targets have been warned in such a manner as not to betray that the information came from Magic. Fortunately, the Japanese are not all that concerned about radio silence at this time, so we're able to report on their buildup in a general and logical manner. We've said nothing about any infantry being onboard; that would be too much detail and could give away the game. We hope that can be inferred by our people. At any rate, it is far more important that the secret of Magic be kept."

"What arrogance," Roosevelt hissed. "The Japs will pay for this." He then dismissed Marshall. King remained alone with him.

"Tell me, Admiral, are you with us or against us?"

King flushed. "With you. You've given me an opportunity, and I will not fail you."

"Good. While I respect your opinions and wish to hear them, I desire and require your utmost cooperation. You must understand that the decision to implement Rainbow 5 has been made and is no longer an issue."

"Yes, Mr. President. You are aware that everything you said about me, the drinking and the skirt chasing, is all true, aren't you?"

"Yes. Rest assured, Admiral, I do not promote people on their worthiness for sainthood. If I did that"—he chuckled—"we'd never get anything done around here."

As the admiral exited the White House, he saw General Marshall standing by King's staff car.

"Did you notice how he looked?" Marshall asked.

King had. "He looked fatigued, almost exhausted. This whole thing must be a terrible strain on him," he replied.

"Yes, although I fear it may be more than that. He is not a well man. The effects of the polio have weakened his body, and the pressures of running a war are starting to pile up on him. I point this out so you will know how important it is to not aggravate him unduly. If you think he is wrong, speak it, but don't push for a Pacific-first war when he cannot give it to you, even though he wants nothing more than to exact revenge on Japan for Pearl Harbor."

"I know." King sighed. He then told Marshall of his brief conversation alone with the president.

"Good. Think about something else. If something happens to FDR, then who becomes president?"

King paled. "Henry Wallace. Good God, General, the man's almost a Communist."

Marshall smiled. "I wouldn't go quite that far, but he is quite a liberal, and he does seem to think that the sun rises and sets on Joe Stalin and the Soviet Union. Let's face it, under a President Henry A. Wallace, it is unlikely that you would get a rowboat for the Pacific while the Soviets were in any danger whatsoever."

"True enough," King admitted. Roosevelt had earlier agreed to an aggressive defense and had also sent a few additional warships to the Pacific. Not enough to take on the Jap fleet, but at least it was something. This conversation with Marshall was the second lecture he'd received this day on the need to be a team player. He would do it. He would swallow the bile of having to let the Pacific wait and to aid the British and Soviets instead.

God help the Philippines and Hawaii, he thought. On the other hand, God help the United States if Henry Wallace ever became president. Why the hell hadn't Roosevelt taken more care in selecting someone who was only a heartbeat away from the presidency?

CHAPTER 6

As Captain Jake Novacek entered the small, cluttered office at Hickam Field, he started to report formally to his new commanding officer in G-2, the Intelligence Department. Before Jake could utter a word, the colonel behind the paper-strewn desk scowled and abruptly waved him to a chair.

"Novacek, you are the sorriest sack of shit I have ever seen. You are the biggest mistake West Point ever made, and you could spend an eternity with those bars on your shoulder and you still wouldn't be a gentleman. Not only that, your reports are pure, unadulterated bullshit, and they are so barely intelligible that I wonder if you speak English at all."

"I'm glad to see you too, Colonel. I was beginning to think you didn't like me anymore."

With that, both men laughed and shook hands. Colonel Joseph Lawton Collins was forty-six, a man of medium height and a trim, athletic build. He had a square, solid face and clear eyes that hid a wicked sense of humor. Joe Collins had been an infantry tactics instructor at the academy, where the two men had formed a close friendship. Collins had admired the grim determination of the young cadet Novacek, who would not take the easy way out by resigning and returning to his old NCO rank when things got tough.

Collins offered a cigarette, which Jake accepted. "Jake, it's good to see a face I recognize and trust around here. I'm not an intelligence man, I'm a line officer," he told the junior officer.

Jake understood. "I heard a rumor you actually told General Marshall that you didn't want any more Washington desk jobs and he listened." Putting Collins in a desk job was akin to caging a tiger.

"It's close enough." Unsaid was the fact that no one demanded that the army's chief of staff do anything.

"Are you on his list for general?"

Collins smiled. "I'm supposed to get my star in March."

"Congratulations in advance, then. I wish I could get on Marshall's list, although with my luck, it'll be his shit list. In a little while I'll be the oldest captain in the army with an academy ring."

"I know," Collins said. "I got an earful from General Short and Colonel Phillips about your report that the local Japs were harmless. A lot of people aren't all that happy that you were right and that you went on record about it. On the other hand, telling the truth can turn out to be a virtue."

"What do you mean?"

Collins leaned back in his chair and grinned smugly. "Do you know Ike Eisenhower?"

"I met him once, I think. Wasn't he MacArthur's chief of staff?"

"Ike's a temporary brigadier general in War Plans in Washington, and very high on Marshall's list. I wouldn't be surprised if he got a lot more stars before this mess is over. At any rate, just before the attack, someone on Short's staff, maybe Phillips, sent Ike a copy of your report with a notation that this was the kind of asshole Short had to work with and could Ike help them replace you with someone who could actually think."

"Jesus."

"Ike got it just a day or two before the Japs attacked, remembered it, of course, and gave it to Marshall, who wondered why your assessment wasn't believed, especially after it turned out to be correct. According to my sources, Marshall is really pissed off at Short for losing his air force by parking it close together on the ground. If the planes had been dispersed, as you and others had recommended, then the Japs wouldn't have been able to paste them like they did. At any rate, Jake, you are not on anybody's shit list, and both Marshall and Ike are a little intrigued about you."

Jake laughed. "You mean I may make major before the war's over?"

Collins gestured for Jake to close the office door. "Nothing's official, but don't be surprised. It might not come until Short's relieved, but that shouldn't be all that much longer. Short's just being kept on until the situation stabilizes, then he's gone. Keep this under your hat, my friend, but Major General Delos Emmons will replace Short, and I will replace Phillips as chief of staff around here. It's not exactly a combat command, but, with the Japs just over the horizon, it's the next best thing."

Collins ground out his half-unsmoked cigarette. "Now, off the record, what the hell is going on around here? I've only been here a couple of days, and I don't know who I can trust. Hell, I don't even know if the Japs are going to attack or not." He gestured angrily at the stacks of paper on his desk. "And what am I to make of all this crap?"

"First, you can trust Bicknell," Jake said. Bicknell was a lieutenant colonel and the number two man in G-2. "Bicknell's like me. He's a little too rough around the edges for Short's taste. He was a cop in civilian life and doesn't have much military background, but he's good. When you relieve Phillips, he can take over here. For the time being, do what Fielder did and let Bicknell do all the work."

Collins nodded. Short had a reputation for appreciating style over substance, and it was rumored that the deposed G-2, Colonel Fielder, had been given his job because he was sophisticated, suave, and a good dancer, and that he knew little about intelligence work. The point about dancing was significant because Fielder often wound up taking Mrs. Short to social events when the general was too busy.

Collins glared at the papers on his desk as if they were the enemy. "Is any of this important? I've glanced through it, and most of it seems to be from old ladies seeing Japs on their beaches or parachuting onto their roses. There are more alleged sub sightings than the Japs have got subs. What the hell's going on?"

Jake shrugged. "Overreaction and a little panic, causing excessive imagination. When the Japs come, they're not going to skulk around, like these reports indicate. Any Jap saboteur would have to be nuts to land now. Most of the reports you can disregard, especially the parachutes. Some of the sub sightings might be real, but nothing could be done until it's too late, and nobody wants to waste fuel on a wild goose chase."

"You in good enough with the Japanese community here?"

"Enough to know that nothing's gonna happen from them and that no one's hiding any spies. With the major radicals on their way to California, any Japs who would try to sneak in would have no place to hide. A lot of the people in the community really do prefer us over their cousins in Tokyo."

Jake wondered just where that left Toyoza Kaga. To date his information had been perfect. Would it continue if the Japanese did attack? Kaga was a survivor, and that worried Jake. How far would he go to survive? But Toyoza Kaga was one of the real leaders in the community, and Jake would continue to depend on him. What other choice did he have?

"Okay," Collins said. "Now, what's your professional guess? Will the Japs attack again?"

Jake answered without hesitation. "Yes. They'd be crazy not to."

"Can we stop them? What's your assessment of the Hawaiian Division?"

The question surprised Jake. "You'd know that better than I, wouldn't you?"

"First, Jake, remember that I've only been here a few days. Second, while I've read a lot of reports, I really haven't seen the Hawaiian Division in action. I've got my opinions, but now I want yours."

"Okay. The division is too much spit and polish and not well trained or equipped for this war. If this was 1917, they'd be in great shape. Nothing can be done about the equipment, which is as bad as everyone else's, but the training deficiencies could be corrected. If they were going to France to live in trenches, they'd be okay. But that's not going to happen. When the Japs come, the Hawaiian Division's going to fight a superbly trained and highly maneuverable enemy army that'll cut them to shreds, particularly since they won't have any air cover.

"Everybody keeps underestimating the Japanese military, and it's going to cost us dearly if and when they actually do come. Somehow, we've got to stop thinking of the Japs as nearsighted, buck-toothed, and stupid when they've proven they are anything but. As it is currently configured and trained, the Hawaiian Division will fight bravely and hard, but it will be defeated should the Japs come in force."

Collins agreed. It had been his assessment as well. The structure of the Hawaiian Division was a relic of World War I, too unwieldy for the war of maneuver that had just occurred in France and Russia.

To compensate for the lack of mobility, the Hawaiian Division's four infantry regiments had been dispersed across Oahu. Two were in the approximate central part of the island, at Schofield Barracks; one outside Honolulu; and one in the north of the island, near Haleiwa's famous beaches.

"You agree with Short's disposition of the troops?"

"Yes. Under the circumstances, there's not much else he can do. I might be tempted to have a second regiment near Haleiwa, since that's the most logical place for a landing and only twenty miles from Pearl Harbor, but, hell, we've done a bad job of outguessing the Japs lately."

"What's the navy doing?"

"Bailing out as fast as they can. The *Pennsylvania*'s the only big ship still here, and she'll leave in a couple of days at the most. We've got a handful of subs and a few destroyers, but that's it. There are a number of damaged ships, but they aren't going anywhere. A few navy ships are passing through from the Philippines, but all they do is use up what little fuel the navy still has. Most of the navy's shore facilities are shutting down and moving out too. It's a mess, Colonel, and from what I hear, the navy still isn't patrolling more than fifty miles out. The fuel problem again. Of course," he added ruefully, "not many of our planes are in the air, either."

"Then the Japs could be right over the horizon, and, once again, we'd know nothing about it."

"Unless we got lucky, Joe, and we haven't been lucky in a while."

Collins was about to say something when an air-raid siren went off in the distance. "Another false alarm?" he asked. "Somebody spot a seagull?"

False alarms were common, and both men waited for the usual all-clear or for the grim sounds of additional sirens. There was a pause; then the chorus of sirens increased to full volume. Behind the wailing could be heard the *pop-pop-pop* of antiaircraft fire. The Japs had returned.

They were about to run to a shelter when Collins's phone rang. The colonel answered, listened, and slammed the receiver down. "The Japs are landing on Molokai. Damnit, they fucked us again."

Now they could hear bombs exploding. "We needed more time," Collins said angrily.

But we're not going to get it, Jake thought sadly.

ALEXA HADN'T PLANNED to return to teaching so soon, but she had a compelling need to do something. She couldn't dwell on Tim's terrible death, and no amount of moping would bring him back to her. She hoped that working with the lively children would bring a degree of normalcy to her life.

Even though she now had the use of Tim's car, she walked to the school and found that the gentle exercise made her feel good. If she didn't walk the two miles, she rode her bike, which meant that the gas rationing had not yet affected her.

Father Monroe and the students had welcomed her. She cried just a little when the children presented her with small gifts and welcomed her with hugs.

After a couple of days back at work, she knew that her decision had been the right one. It felt good to be active, particularly with the children, who were so innocent and so very much alive.

The one-room school had only forty students, all of whom were at least partially native Hawaiian, in grades one through eight. After eighth grade, the children, most of whom came from very poor families, either dropped out or continued at McKinley High School. McKinley was so racially mixed that it was often disparagingly referred to as Tokyo High. Although most of the students at Father Monroe's school were poor, there were a few whose families did have some money and whose children might go on to the University of Hawaii.

Alexa's favorite student, Kami Ogawa, was one of those who did not seem to have money problems. She was helping Kami with an English essay when the sirens went off, shocking them. For an instant, Alexa froze as the memories of December 7 came flooding back. Then she shook herself free from the past and stood up. "Everybody outside," she commanded, and her young charges obeyed. Father Monroe followed hastily, a stunned look on his face. In single file, everyone trooped out to the freshly dug trenches behind the bare dirt playground. They weren't much in the way of an air-raid shelter, but they would have to do.

Alexa and the children squatted in the dirt and kept their heads down while guns barked in the distance. After a while, she peeked over the lip of the trench. As on December 7, the sky above Pearl Harbor was filled with planes and the dirty black dots of antiaircraft shells exploding. Although farther from the naval base, the school was higher in the hills, which gave her a better view than she'd had at her home.

From behind, she heard the sound of planes and started to cower back in the dirt. "Ours," said Father Monroe. "Go get 'em," he yelled in a most unpriestly manner.

Above them flew several dozen fighters headed out to meet the Japs. "P-47s and P-36s," one of the male students happily informed her. These were followed by six large bombers, which they all knew were B-17s, the superbombers, the Flying Fortresses that were supposed to knock the Japs silly.

"That's the way," Father Monroe exulted. "This'll teach the Japs to take on the U.S. of A."

Alexa felt good about the counterassault. For once America was striking back instead of allowing itself to be punched out. She quickly realized the incongruity of her current emotions and her deep feelings of pacifism. What had Jake Novacek said about being a pacifist himself when the war was over? She was certain Novacek had been joking, but there was more than an element of truth in his statement. Just as her life with Tim had been permanently disrupted, so too were her cherished beliefs about the evils of war. War might be evil, all right, but January 1942 was not the time to be against all wars. In particular not when someone was making a concerted effort to destroy the country she held dear. Pacifism was a luxury she could not afford at this time.

Alexa considered that her school was not likely to be the focal point of the Japanese attack, so she climbed out of the trench to get a better look at the planes. The rest of her flock and Father Monroe followed with varying degrees of difficulty as they ruefully discovered that it was much easier to get into a five-foot-deep trench than it was to get out. Alexa had worn a dress and moved carefully; she was determined not to give the male students a free show.

By now the line of American planes from Oahu's interior had flown past and were rapidly disappearing in the distance. In growing dismay, she recalled the swarms of Japanese who'd attacked the fleet and compared it with the smaller number of American planes that had just flown overhead. The American numbers were so few. Even with the supposedly invincible B-17s, the U.S. force was pitifully small. Perhaps, she thought hopefully, those planes would be joined by others from Hickam and Ewa, and the other fields.

It also occurred to her that she would not be leaving the Hawaiian Islands anytime soon. Perhaps she would never leave, she realized with a shock.

TOYOZA KAGA PUT DOWN THE PHONE and walked to the window of his office. The attack on the harbor and military installations was over. It had begun quickly and ended just as quickly. It was as if the Japanese navy wasn't all that interested in damaging Pearl Harbor again, and he felt that he knew why. They were taunting the Americans and waiting for a reaction.

Only a moment earlier, he'd received a phone call from an associate on Molokai, who'd informed him that the Japanese soldiers were landing at the midpoint of that narrow island. Thanks to his business sources, Kaga knew as much about the situation as anyone in the American military. He also knew that Molokai was undefended. The Japanese would own it in a matter of hours. He hoped that no one in the local police or national guard was foolish enough to resist and precipitate a massacre.

"A tragedy," he muttered. But it was an event he was prepared for. Now it was time to convene a series of meetings with trusted associates who agreed with him that this could be the beginning of a period of agonies for Hawaii's Japanese population.

Unless Kaga's efforts bore fruit, his people could easily find themselves between two fires and with no friends, only enemies. It could easily mean the destruction of everything he had worked for over the past decades. His family, his businesses, everything was now at great risk.

However, he thought as he smiled grimly, it could just as easily mean a time of tremendous opportunity. But first, he had to survive long enough to find out who would ultimately win this conflict.

WITHIN AN HOUR of the attacks on Molokai, Japanese planes began landing on private airstrips near the coast while the marines pushed inland so quickly that astonished and terrified civilians had no chance to flee and were left in bypassed groups.

Mechanics, fuel, ammunition, and other supplies would be ferried out later, and engineers would quickly enlarge the primitive fields, but the effort freed the overcrowded decks of the carriers for normal operations against the American forces.

It had been assumed that the Americans would react quickly to the Japanese presence, and they had. The landing and the swift raid on Pearl Harbor had provoked an immediate reaction. Like angry bees from a threatened hive, the Americans had flown to Molokai with everything that Japanese intelligence said they had.

Commander Mitsuo Fuchida thought it incredible that the American patrols had not found them until Admiral Nagumo's forces were almost under their nose. How could the Americans have been so inept a second time? Had the loss of their fuel hampered them so badly? The Japanese good fortune was incredible.

Fuchida quickly concluded that his presence was not required to assist in the ferrying operations. Instead, he took the opportunity to fly a Zero from the carrier and take part in the battle with the Americans. Actual combat had been denied him for much of the Pearl Harbor battle because of the need for him to observe. Now there was nothing to observe, only the need to destroy the Americans.

The Japanese Zero was simply the best fighter in the Pacific. Fuchida thought it might have an equal in the British Spitfire, but it didn't matter. There were no Spitfires over Hawaii, only American P-36s and P-47s, which paled in comparison with the darting swiftness and maneuverability of the Zero.

The plane was a Mitsubishi A6M2, Zero-sen, navy Type-O carrier fighter Model 21. It could fly at speeds in excess of 330 miles per hour and could stay airborne for eight hours when supplied with external fuel tanks. It had two 20 mm cannons, one on each wing, and could be configured to carry bombs.

Made of an aluminum alloy, the plane was lightweight, remarkably agile, and it could outclimb anything anyone else had. Worse for the Americans, the Zero had come as yet another Japanese surprise, and the Japanese high command was confident that no American had ever seen it before, much less examined it or fought against it.

It did cause Fuchida and his comrades some concern that, in order to cut weight and emphasize speed, there was no armor plating to protect the pilot, and the fuel tanks were not self-sealing. When that potential problem was discussed, some pilots replied with morbid humor that their best protection was not to get shot.

And all the Americans who saw a Zero now, he exulted, were dying. An American P-36 was in his sights, and he squeezed the trigger, sending a stream of 20 mm shells into the plane's body. A plume of smoke appeared by its tail, then a bright flame, and the P-36 rolled into a death spiral. There was no parachute.

It was his second victory that day. Not only were the Americans inferior pilots flying inferior planes but they were vastly outnumbered.

Over his radio, Fuchida heard one of his pilots jokingly complain about the necessity of Japanese planes' queuing up to take a turn at one of the few remaining American targets. This had brought laughter from the other pilots, and Fuchida did not order them to stop chattering. Let them laugh now, he decided; the hard fighting would come later, when the Americans gathered their forces for a real battle.

A B-17 appeared in front of him. Astonishingly large, the bomber was also badly hurt and flying alone. One of its four engines was smoking, and its propellers were stilled. Even so, the three remaining engines kept it on course toward Oahu. The pilot and crew had seen the futility of their efforts and were attempting to flee back to Pearl Harbor.

Fuchida was paired with another Zero, who attacked the tail gun with a quick strafing pass. When this distracted the American gunner, Fuchida swept in and destroyed the gun along with much of the bomber's tail.

The American plowed on through the air, and Fuchida felt a grudging degree of respect. The bomber was a true warrior, and so were the men who flew it.

Warrior or not, the bomber must die. With the bomber's rear vulnerable, Fuchida banked and again attacked from behind. Another stream of shells ripped into the remaining right engine and sent pieces of it into the sky as the machinery disintegrated.

That was enough. The bomber banked to its left and began to glide toward the ocean. Fuchida would get a portion of a kill for this one.

As he watched, the surviving crew members bailed out. Fuchida was sadly confident that the overmatched tail gunner was not among them. The plane was his coffin, and he would ride it to his grave.

A couple of his planes signaled that they were going to strafe the men in the parachutes. "No," Fuchida commanded. "Let them live if they can. They can tell their brothers how good we are."

The commander checked the skies. There were absolutely no American planes in sight. Had the massacre been that complete? Had none of the Americans escaped? He checked with his commanders and was told that ten of his planes had been shot down and another dozen damaged in the brawl. Since Japanese pilots despised parachutes as cowardly, he'd lost at least ten pilots in the overwhelming victory. He wondered where the replacements would come from.

Now the buildup on Molokai could commence without interruption. He was fairly confident the Americans had little left to throw at them. With absolute control of the skies, the Japanese planes could commence taking the American military facilities on Oahu apart piece by piece.

Fuchida radioed that he was returning to the *Akagi*, where there would be a conference with Commander Genda and Admiral Nagumo. Tomorrow he would ferry himself to Molokai and launch and command operations against Oahu. They would continue until the Americans were destroyed and Oahu occupied. He felt a moment of pity for the enemy. They were unquestionably brave, but they were so poorly equipped, and, if the last few weeks were any indication, they were terribly led. He hoped it would stay that way. For Japan's sake, it had to.

"You've got to be kidding" was Lieutenant Jamie Priest's first comment on hearing the orders.

Another of his fellow lieutenants had just informed him that the damaged battleship *Pennsylvania* would slip out that night and, under the cover of darkness, try to make it to the United States.

Jamie had also been informed that he would accompany her on her escape.

Grudgingly, Jamie acknowledged that it made sense. The *Pennsylvania* was useless where she was and, as the day's air raid had proven, would be a prime target for the Japanese planes. She hadn't been hit in this last attack, but further damage was inevitable if she remained. The battlewagon had to get to a California shipyard, where her two forward turrets could be replaced and her ruptured hull plates repaired.

It also made sense to sneak out at night while the Japanese navy was preoccupied with protecting the landing site on Molokai. When Molokai was secured, the Japanese fleet was certain to take up station outside Pearl Harbor's narrow entrance and dare any ships to try to escape.

Yes, there was some danger from submarines and other, smaller, warships, but it was a chance that had to be taken. If they stayed where they were, the Jap planes would surely sink the *Pennsylvania*. If she fled now, there was at least a chance she would make it. It was a lousy choice, but, Jamie thought ruefully, it was the only one they had.

Jamie's position on the *Pennsylvania* was undefined. Normally, he would have been directing fire control for one of the destroyed turrets. Instead, he was given a damage control party even though he had little experience at that grim task. The *Pennsylvania* would depart with only a little more than half of her normal crew and supplies, and her fuel tanks would not be full.

"Perhaps she'll go faster because she's lighter," he heard one of the crew joke.

Not funny, Jamie thought. He also didn't think much of the idea of heading west when they left Pearl and taking the long northern way around the island before turning toward the United States. The idea was to confuse any Japs who might be lurking east of Pearl's entrance and get behind them before making the homeward dash. He hoped the *Pennsylvania*'s commander, Captain C. M. Cooke, knew what the hell he was doing. Jamie didn't know Cooke at all well. Naval captains rarely discussed matters with lieutenants.

"A dash," they were calling it, and he laughed. Now there was a joke. Because of the hull damage, it was unlikely that the *Pennsylvania* would get anywhere near her top speed of twenty-one knots an hour. No, he would have preferred to get as far away from Oahu as fast as they could and the hell with any Japs in the way. If they were caught, they weren't going to get away anyhow.

While they made frantic, last-minute attempts to make the battleship more survivable, the sun slowly went down and darkness covered the harbor. Jamie could see the shapes of the four destroyers that would be their escort to America. They looked terribly small and vulnerable.

The *Pennsylvania* raised her anchor and moved slowly toward the ocean. Their departure wouldn't be at all heroic. They were sneaking out. Jamie looked around at others in the night and saw the same expressions on their faces. They all thought this might be their last night on earth.

CHAPTER 7

■

Oahu is approximately forty miles long and twenty-six miles wide. Honolulu and Pearl Harbor are about a third of the way up the length of the island, which meant that they were about an hour's drive up the one road that led from both sites to Haleiwa, the probable landing place for the Japanese army.

"Take a look at it," Colonel Collins had ordered. "Give me an idea whether we can hold at that point and how long it'll take to reinforce the place if the Japs come."

"When they come," Jake had corrected, and Collins had agreed. How could there be any doubt? he wondered. The Japs had reworked the small airfields on Molokai in record time and now had planes over Oahu almost every minute of the day. Along with attacking fixed positions, the Japanese fighters and bombers struck at targets of opportunity, and that included anything that moved on the road to Haleiwa. The navy was now almost totally gone, and that included the *Pennsylvania*. This meant that the only targets were army ones. A handful of planes remained, but few were fighters. The survivors were scout planes, and PBY flying boats, and were dispersed and hidden.

Jake declined a staff car, choosing a motorcycle instead. He believed that the motorcycle would be less likely to attract attention from the Japanese than a staff car, and it could go cross-country where the road had been bombed.

Even with the advantage of mobility, the drive took four hours instead of one. There were several times when Jake had to hide the motorcycle behind a tree while Japanese planes flew low overhead in a manner reminiscent of their attack on Hickam the preceding December.

Schofield Barracks was the midpoint of his journey, and he arrived during another raid, which delayed him further. This time a Jap fighter got too close, and he cheered lustily when it was blown from the sky by American antiaircraft guns.

When he left, however, several buildings were burning, and one of the guns that had destroyed the Zero had been strafed, its crew shot to a bloody pulp.

Compared with the ride to Schofield, the short haul to Haleiwa was fairly easy, and he made it to the American coastal defenses without further incident.

Jake was not impressed by what he saw. Just under four thousand men had been allocated a front about six miles wide. The defenses were anchored on the northern ends of the Koolau and Waianae mountain ranges. These peaks ran on either side of the island, and in the fertile valley between them was the road from Haleiwa to Schofield to Pearl Harbor. The mountains were more sharp hills and knifelike ridges, and the valley gradually widened until it was twenty miles across at Pearl Harbor.

Trenches had been dug and pillboxes constructed out of sandbags, but where were the mountains of barbed wire that would stop enemy infantry, and where were the big guns that would pound Japanese warships? The largest artillery pieces Jake saw were several batteries of 155 mm howitzers, and they weren't well dug in or protected against counterfire from Japanese warships.

Jake knew several of the officers and asked for their assessment. He was told that, because of the Japanese air attacks interdicting the road from Schofield to Hickam, the brass were now reconsidering their earlier assumptions regarding a landing at Haleiwa. Some were convinced that the Jap presence on Molokai meant a Japanese attack would be against the southern portion of the island, at a place such as Barbers Point or Kaneohe Bay. Thus, that was where most of the construction of defenses was taking place.

Jake had heard this, of course, and asked for their opinions. Almost to a man they felt that the attack would be at Haleiwa, despite what the higher-ups thought. One lanky captain from Arkansas put it succinctly: "This beach is the asshole of the world, and when this is over we'll have been shat on."

Jake rose to the joke. "Shat?"

"Past tense of *shit,* Jake. Look it up."

Collins had told Jake to try to contact him from Haleiwa. Incredibly, the telephone lines were functioning normally, and he got through easily.

The colonel heard a brief commentary that would have meant nothing to someone listening in, but contained words that they'd agreed on to convey Jake's impressions.

Jake heard his superior sigh deeply across the phone. "Get back as soon as you can, buddy. We've got other problems."

"We do?"

"Yeah, people are picking up distress signals in the clear, so this is no secret. Looks like the *Pennsylvania*'s in big trouble."

PROBLEMS HAD COME EARLY for the *Pennsylvania*. She'd managed to exit the harbor and, along with her four escorts, had safely rounded the northern portion of Oahu and headed eastward.

But, by midmorning of the next day, a Japanese plane was seen in the distance. There was no way the plane could have missed them, and this was confirmed when the Jap moved in closer and circled the small force, always staying just out of range.

Jamie and his companions could only hope that they'd put enough distance between themselves and the Japanese fleet covering Molokai to make a long stern chase toward California too difficult to attempt. Just about everyone felt that any threat would come from the air, and not from Japanese surface ships.

Jamie was not totally comfortable with that theory, as the venerable *Pennsylvania*—she'd been launched in 1916—was able to do only sixteen knots and not her normal rated speed of twenty-one. This meant Japanese destroyers could do twice her speed and close rapidly to get into torpedo range. It also meant that Japanese planes could arrive at any time.

Only a few moments later, a dozen Japanese dive-bombers and torpedo planes appeared in the sky to the west. The destroyers maneuvered to form a square with the lumbering *Pennsylvania* in the center. All five ships sent streams of antiaircraft fire into the approaching planes. Several were hit and fell in flames, but the others pressed on, with the blocking force of destroyers bearing the brunt of their wrath. One destroyer was hit by a bomb that blew away its forward turret and left it burning and almost dead in the water. A second was broken in half by a torpedo and sank in only a couple of minutes.

One Val dive-bomber got through and dropped an eight-hundred-pound bomb on the battleship's already damaged bow. The *Pennsylvania* shuddered and plowed on. The Val was not as fortunate. It was blown out of the sky as it attempted to fly away.

Bombs and torpedoes expended, the remaining Japanese planes departed. It had cost them a mere five planes to sink one destroyer, badly cripple another, and they'd done additional damage to the *Pennsylvania*.

The burning destroyer could not keep up with the three other ships and remained back to look for survivors from the sunken one. None of the other ships would be able to stop. To delay was to allow the gap between them and Japanese surface ships that must be on their way to close further.

The rescue effort was doomed. Even though the fires seemed under control, the damaged destroyer would soon be sunk and was just delaying the inevitable.

This was borne out when several Japanese destroyers were sighted in the distance. The two remaining American destroyers promptly steamed after them to do battle. It was a mistake. Almost before they were away, one of the destroyers exploded, lifting out of the water before she settled back and disappeared. She was quickly followed by the second, and word went down that they'd been sunk by torpedoes.

"Can't be," Jamie said in dismay to the men of his ad hoc damage control party as they waited on the deck. The range was just too great, and the explosion was too big for torpedoes. "What the hell do the Japs have?"

Moments later, the *Pennsylvania* shuddered, and a massive plume of dirty water lifted alongside her hull. The impact knocked Jamie to the deck.

"Tell me that wasn't a torpedo, Lieutenant," said Seaman Fiorini, one of the men in the party.

Before Jamie could answer, the big guns on the rear turret began a thunderous long-range duel with the rapidly closing Japanese destroyers. The *Pennsylvania* was alone now, and had to keep the enemy destroyers as far away as possible.

The *Pennsylvania*'s gunners were both lucky and good. One fourteen-inch shell hit a Japanese destroyer, which exploded and disappeared. This caused the remaining three to pull farther out of range, although they continued to shadow the American ship.

Two hours later a floatplane was sighted on the horizon, and everyone on the *Pennsylvania* knew that the Jap battle fleet had sighted her. There would be no escape to California. Jamie was further disconcerted to realize that the Japanese were approaching from the north and not from the west. He realized there had to have been two Japanese task forces, and they had blundered into range of the second one.

Shortly after they were sighted, shells began to rain down on the *Pennsylvania*. At extreme range, none hit, but the splashes were greater than anything they'd seen before.

"Sixteen-inchers," Fiorini said. "Maybe larger. Probably eighteens."

Jamie laughed. "Ain't nothing bigger than sixteen-inchers, and I don't think the Japs have any of those. Besides, who made you an authority on big guns?"

Others in the party laughed nervously. Fiorini had been in the paymaster's office and helped run the battleship's newspaper. Fiorini was not deterred. "Sixteens at least," he said, and the others hooted. It was good to be distracted, if only for a moment.

The *Pennsylvania* was struck by a pair of shells, and she shook like she was in an earthquake. Jamie was again knocked to his knees and, when he got up, saw flames and dark smoke pouring from the gaping ruin that had been her bridge. He wondered if Captain Cooke was still commanding the battleship. Then he wondered if anyone was.

The *Pennsylvania* was well within range of the Japanese guns that were still below the horizon, and she began to absorb additional punishment. At first Jamie and his crew tried to make emergency repairs, but it quickly became apparent that the *Pennsylvania* was doomed and that life above decks was a red-hot hell of raining shell fragments and flying debris.

Bloodily dismembered bodies were piled about, and wounded, many horribly mangled, lay screaming where they fell. Some of the unhurt ran around in confusion and blind terror, interfering with those who were trying to do their duty and fight the ship. Walking was difficult because of the blood that ran down the decks, and several of Jamie's group were hit by debris and body parts. One sailor was swept overboard by a metal fragment, while another was killed when a human arm was driven through his chest like a spear.

Jamie took the survivors belowdecks, where they were shielded from the deadly rain. Anyone not in a turret or protected by the ship's armor was going to die and very quickly. The battleship was fighting back, as the sound of her guns attested, but it seemed that the rate of fire was diminishing as the Japanese shells found their targets.

In the midst of the horror, Fiorini grabbed his arm. "Come with me, Lieutenant. You gotta see this."

Jamie followed Fiorini down another couple of decks. The electricity was flickering, and Jamie was afraid he would be trapped in the dark bowels of a sinking ship, like the men in the *Oklahoma,* and the fear almost paralyzed him.

Fiorini read his thoughts. "Just through here, sir. Remember the hit that didn't explode?"

"Yeah," Jamie said nervously. It had happened a few moments earlier, when a shell slammed into the ship only a few dozen feet from them and they all thought they were dead. While they'd gasped in relief, Fiorini had disappeared for a moment.

Finally, Fiorini paused. "Look at her, but don't touch. She's still hot and may go off."

"Jesus Christ."

Embedded in the decking was a monstrous shell. Its head was buried and out of sight, but the base was fully visible. Jamie was a gunnery officer, and it was larger than anything he had ever seen.

"Hold this," Fiorini said, handing him a tape measure. Jamie complied and measured the shell's diameter. Eighteen inches! It was incredible; no, impossible. The Japs were firing eighteen-inch shells against them. He'd been told that nobody had eighteen-inchers, but he was staring at one.

Fiorini pulled a small camera from his work bag and took several flash pictures while Jamie held the tape. Jamie was about to comment on the camera when he recalled Fiorini's work on the ship's paper.

"These could be important," Fiorini said, and Jamie agreed.

"But first we got to get them out of here."

Somebody hollered that the ship was sinking, and they returned to the fury of the outside world as another Japanese salvo pounded them. By this time, the deck was only a few feet above the water, and the ship was tilted several degrees to starboard. Sailors were leaving the stricken vessel and were able to do so almost by stepping into the water.

"Who gave the order to abandon ship?" Jamie asked.

"No one," came the reply. There was no one left to give the command. The venerable old *Pennsylvania* was defenseless, out of control, and sinking. The remaining turrets had been smashed, and the flame-charred guns were pointed in odd directions. Worse, it appeared that the ship was turning slowly in the direction of the Japanese, the tops of whose ships were now clearly visible as they emerged on the horizon. Jamie counted two battleships and then a third, and the third was a monster. He knew where the eighteen-inch shells had come from.

Jamie, Fiorini, and scores of others stepped from the deck into the water. They swam toward floating debris while the doomed battleship moved slowly past them with stately dignity as shells continued to rain down, killing many of the men in the water. Jamie thanked the facts that he had his life jacket on and that he was an excellent swimmer.

When he reached the debris, he gathered several dozen survivors and lashed debris together to form a raft. While they worked, the *Pennsylvania* continued to absorb punishment as she turned slowly away from the men floating in the water. Either someone was making a heroic charge at the enemy or the ship's rudder was stuck. Jamie thought it was the rudder. He didn't think anyone was in control of the battleship. Looking at the now burning hulk, he doubted that anyone was even alive, much less guiding the vessel.

Jamie watched as the uneven struggle ended. Fiorini continued to take pictures, and Jamie wondered how he'd kept his camera dry.

"Rubber pouch" was the answer. Fiorini then unloaded the film and put it in the pouch. The camera he tossed into the ocean. "No more film."

Moments later the *Pennsylvania* sank by the bow with the giant Japanese battleship virtually alongside her. When it was over, the Japanese ships began to pick up American survivors. Jamie's party was a couple of miles away by this time, but they had no hopes of going undetected.

"We're gonna be prisoners?" Fiorini asked. "I think I'd rather stay in the water and take my chances with the sharks."

Jamie had heard how the Japs treated their prisoners and prayed he'd survive the ordeal.

"They're leaving," someone yelled. It was true. The Jap ships were all turning away at high speed and leaving them in the water. When they were several miles away, the giant battleship must have spotted their group and opened fire with its smaller-caliber secondary batteries. That their target was tiny kept the survivors from being directly hit, but the splashes and concussion knocked them all off their improvised rafts and into the water.

Jamie pulled himself back onto some debris. Fiorini bobbed up beside him and handed him the camera pouch. Jamie took it and was about to pull Fiorini out of the water when another shell landed nearby, covering him with spray and nearly knocking him back into the ocean. Fiorini's face registered surprise and went slack. Then his eyes rolled back in his head and he disappeared into the ocean. The concussion from the shell had created a surge of water pressure that had squashed the life out of him and somehow spared Jamie.

The firing ceased. The Japanese were almost out of sight and over the horizon. Jamie counted about twenty survivors, many of whom were badly hurt. A second tally told him that he was the only officer, and that there was no food or water.

He laughed bitterly. He was the commander of the crew of the *Pennsylvania*. At least the killing had stopped. Now all they had to do was survive.

ADMIRAL CHESTER NIMITZ established his command at San Diego, which disappointed some of his officers, who'd hoped they'd get to stay at the larger and more cosmopolitan city of San Francisco. San Diego had a population of just under 150,000, while San Francisco was more than four times larger.

Almost on the Mexican border, San Diego possessed a fine harbor, and a marine base as well as an existing naval base. Nimitz's move was administrative and had nothing to do with the location of the fleet. Except for a handful of cruisers and destroyers, there were no major warships in the narrow harbor overlooked by the admiral's temporary office.

This day, Nimitz did not see the bay or anything else. His eyes were focused on the report in his hand, and, since he was alone, he made no effort to stop the tears that streamed down his face.

The report confirmed what they had feared—the loss of the *Pennsylvania* and four destroyers with all hands. It was a catastrophe on a par with Pearl Harbor. The American public didn't know about it yet, but desperate calls for help had been sent in the clear and had been picked up by shortwave radios. Amateur radios were supposed to have been shut down, but there were still a number of them listening. There would have to be a reckoning and an explanation, and it would have to come soon. Even with the battleship's crew at less than full strength, the combined crews were in excess of a thousand souls.

Incredibly, because of the chaos at Pearl Harbor, no one was certain who was on the *Pennsylvania* and who wasn't. That infuriated Nimitz. No one should have to die anonymously.

There was a tap on the door, and Admiral Raymond Spruance entered. He had been commanding Halsey's cruisers when Nimitz ordered him back to California. Spruance was a quiet man, but extremely intelligent and decisive. If Halsey was a bull, Spruance was the thinker. In only a short while, Nimitz had come to depend on Spruance's abilities.

Spruance crossed the office and discreetly looked out the window. It gave Nimitz an opportunity to wipe his eyes.

"The Japs have pulled their ships back to the west of Hawaii," Spruance said. "This'll give us a chance to send out floatplanes and look for survivors. I doubt there'll be any, but we'll give it a try."

Nimitz nodded. Could it get any worse? he wondered.

In the Philippines, MacArthur's army was pinned on the Bataan Peninsula and the island of Corregidor. They would surrender in a matter of weeks, a couple of months at the most. MacArthur had been ordered to leave Corregidor so he would not be taken prisoner and paraded through Tokyo as a trophy.

In the southern Pacific, a small American naval force had joined with other small forces from the Dutch and Royal navies. Under a Dutch admiral, they would try to blunt the Japanese offensive in that area. Nimitz thought their task was hopeless.

The British army was retreating down the Malayan peninsula

toward the city of Singapore, and it looked like a disaster there as well. Churchill had proclaimed the place a fortress that would be held at all costs, but everyone knew better.

In both the Philippines and Malaya, the Japanese army had out-fought and outmaneuvered the Americans and the British. This did not bode well for the fate of Hawaii.

At least, Nimitz thought with some satisfaction, he had only the Pacific to worry about. The situation in the Atlantic was no less dire, with German subs ravaging American shipping all along the eastern seaboard and up the larger rivers. In Europe, both England and Russia were reeling under Nazi attacks.

"Opportunity," Nimitz said.

"What?" Spruance asked quizzically.

"Pearl Harbor and all that has followed is not an unmitigated disaster."

"Some'll disagree with that."

"Let them," Nimitz said firmly. "Tell me, Ray. How many battleships have been sunk or damaged by Jap carriers?"

"Nine or ten, depending on how the British count battleships," Spruance answered. "Eight of ours and at least one British."

"And how many carriers have been sunk?"

Spruance grinned. He knew where this was going. "None."

"Right. Now who the devil needs battleships when they keep on sinking?" Nimitz shuffled papers on his desk until he came up with the right one. "Look, we began this war with seventeen battleships to the Japs' ten or eleven. We've lost eight, at least temporarily, but have fifteen under construction. In a year, two at the most, we will have over-whelming superiority in battleships."

"Of course," Spruance said as he took a chair.

"And the same holds true with carriers. We have seven to their dozen or so, but we have another eleven being built, and that doesn't even count the smaller carriers, which we will start producing by the dozens. Can they match that?"

"We know they can't. We know the limitations of their shipyards. Japan doesn't have an industrial base like ours to draw on. While it's a closed society, we're fairly confident they can't add more than a couple of carriers or battleships in the next several years. We already outnumber them in cruisers, destroyers, and subs. If we use our resources properly, we will defeat them. The carrier is the queen of the navy now, not the gunship. Battleships and cruisers will protect the carriers, not the other way around."

Nimitz slapped the desk with uncharacteristic anger. "Yet, we're going to lose Hawaii."

Spruance nodded glumly. Three carriers were operating under Halsey. Their task was to protect Australia. A handful of old, slow battleships under Admiral William Pye was positioned along the California coast. They were there primarily to calm the fears of the populace, not to fight the Japs. If they tried, they'd be murdered.

"If Hawaii goes," Spruance added, "then we'll have to pull out of Midway as well. That big Jap task force we've been listening to seems to have departed. Only Hawaii can be its destination. It'll arrive in a week or so, and, by that time, their planes from Molokai will have softened up Oahu's defenses to the point where a landing will be a cinch."

Nimitz rose and paced the small office. "Our ships are sunk, our carriers are too few, and I'm being told our subs aren't sinking anything because the torpedoes aren't working correctly. Is anything going right for us?"

"Magic is. At least we have some idea what the Japs are up to. Just a shame we can't do anything about it right now. If the Japs ever find out about Magic, we'll really be in a dilemma. We'll be deaf and blind along with crippled."

"Well," Nimitz said, "that's what we need to talk about. I just got word that Magic may be compromised."

Spruance paled. "How?"

"The last of our codebreakers on Hawaii departed a few days before the landing on Molokai. They were on the cruiser *St. Louis*. We believe the *St. Louis* was torpedoed and sunk off the big island, Hawaii."

"Survivors?"

"We don't know. For once I find myself praying there aren't any."

ALEXA RAN OUTSIDE in the night to help Jake with the packages that were stacked in the motorcycle's sidecar. "What have you brought?" she asked with a laugh. "Christmas was a while ago."

It was after midnight, and Jake had awakened her with his knocking on the door. She wore a thin cotton nightgown and had a short robe over it. Neither reached her knees, and she was barefoot.

Melissa Wilson had heard the motorcycle through her open window, and she too came out. If she was surprised to see Jake at two in the morning, she didn't show it. All over Hawaii, people had become nocturnal, as they found it safer to travel slowly at night than to attempt movement during the day, when the Jap planes were out.

Alexa gaped as she handed several packages to Melissa. "What are you wearing?"

"One of my Jerry's shirts and a smile," Melissa said happily. "Don't worry, Lexy, I won't scare Jake away."

Jake pretended he didn't hear the conversation and tried not to stare at Melissa as the three of them moved quickly into Alexa's house. There they pulled the shades and lit some candles. Electricity had been out for a while, as had the telephone lines. There was an air of eager expectation as they opened the bundles. The two women immediately knew what they contained—food.

"Won't this get you in trouble?" Alexa asked as she looked over the array of treasures. There was bread, powdered milk, cans of all kinds, and packages labeled as something called C rations.

"No," he answered, and she saw anger flare in his eyes. "The dumb fuckers were throwing it away. Oops"—he flushed—"I'm sorry."

The women laughed. "We're both familiar with basic military terminology," Missy answered. "I believe that word was little Jerry Junior's first."

Jake laughed, the anger gone. "The bread was decreed stale. It's a little hard, but add water and it'll soften up. You do have water, don't you?"

"A well," Alexa said.

"Good. The canned stuff is dented and therefore not worthy for our boys to eat, and the C rations might have been shipped improperly. It's insane. We may be starving in a few weeks, but some fools still think we're at peace and there'll be an inspection in class A uniforms on Saturday morning. There's a war on, and half the army still hasn't figured it out yet."

"What are C rations?" Alcxa asked. She'd heard the term but had no idea what they were.

"They came out a couple of years ago," Jake said. "Each package contains an unidentifiable meat, lemonade, hard candy, cigarettes, crackers or bread, and toilet paper."

Alexa grinned impishly. "Then the assholes who threw them out should have kept them."

"Absolutely." Jake laughed again. He felt so totally at ease with Alexa and her friend. "I know you don't smoke, but hang on to the cigarettes. They might be valuable soon. Hell, they already are."

That sobered them. "The Japs are on their way, aren't they?" Alexa asked.

Jake shook his head. "I didn't tell you that. But think about something: The Japs haven't hit the civilian water supply, only the military. That tells me they're planning to invade and don't want so much destroyed that they can't sustain themselves after they take over. If all they wanted to do was destroy this place, they'd be flattening everything. No, they're being very selective."

"Do you remember Jamie Priest?" Melissa asked. "He was on the *Pennsylvania.*"

"It's sad, and it's gonna get sadder," Jake said. News of the sinking had just been officially released, and it had cast a further pall on the island. He looked at his watch. "I've got to get back before somebody notices the trash has been stolen."

Melissa got up as well. "I think the baby's crying." The top buttons of her shirt had come undone while she was handling the packages, and Jake tried not to gape at her ripe, full breasts as she whirled and departed.

"I'll escort you to your chariot, Sir Knight," Alexa said. She took his arm, and they walked outside. "I can't thank you enough for what you're doing for us. Melissa's worried sick about little Jerry not getting enough food. She had been nursing, but that's literally drying up and he's eating more and more solid food. I've lost a couple of pounds, but nothing I'll miss."

"I'm glad I can help," Jake said. He thought that Alexa and Melissa had lost more than a couple of pounds each but didn't comment. They were no doubt saving some of their food for Melissa's baby.

Jake was conscious of the feel of her hand on his arm and the occasional brush of her body against him as they walked. This is not happening, he thought.

"Did you really steal trash?" she asked.

Jake chuckled. "It's a skill I picked up as a child when we were really hungry. Amazing what people will throw out, and even more amazing what others will eat if they have to."

Alexa shuddered. "I hope it doesn't come to that."

Jake disengaged himself with reluctance and climbed on the motorcycle. "If it does, it does. Do what you have to to stay safe. Surviving is all that matters, not the price."

"Will you come back again? I'd like to see you, and you don't have to bring presents."

"I'll try," he said as he kicked the motor into life. He would do more than try.

Alexa nodded. "I remember seeing a cowboy movie with John Wayne or somebody like him in it. The heroine told the departing hero to be careful as he went into battle, and we all laughed. It seemed such a silly statement at the time, but I don't think so any longer."

She leaned over and kissed him on the cheek. "Be careful, Jake."

CHAPTER 8

Colonel Joseph Lawton Collins glared at the two men across the table from him. General Short was unaffected by it, but Colonel Walter C. Phillips appeared upset. It struck Collins as mildly amusing that both men would be named Walter C. He hoped they didn't have the same middle name. Or the same father.

As a lieutenant general, Short could afford to disregard Collins's opinions, but news of Collins's pending promotion to brigadier made people like Phillips uncomfortable. Phillips was widely considered to be only barely competent and would likely rise no further. Therefore, the last thing he wanted to do was anger someone who was going to pass him very quickly, and who someday might be his boss.

Worse for Phillips, he had hitched his star to Short's, and the general's star was fading rapidly. It was easy to feel sorry for both officers. They were honest men who were products of a career in a peacetime army, and were not faring well in the shock of combat. Short, for instance, had a lifelong reputation as a highly moral man and a hard worker. Now he would be remembered, if at all, for not being prepared on December 7.

Phillips's presence at the meeting in Short's office was somewhat of a surprise. He was rarely included in anything important, and it occurred to Collins that General Short wanted a witness.

"Colonel Collins," said Phillips. "We all agree that Captain Novacek's assessment of the situation is excellent, but we disagree as to where it points. His feeling that the Japanese will invade at Haleiwa is only that, a feeling. We know that a Japanese force is heading here and we must be prepared for every contingency. We feel that the Japanese may be softening up the southern half of Oahu for an attack at either

Barbers Point, at the west of the harbor entrance, or Bellows Field, which is to the east."

Collins knew precisely where both locations were and took the geography lesson as an insult. "Why not Waikiki? Hell, they could surf in and register at a hotel. No, landings at those sites would put them in the teeth of our field guns and shore batteries. They will land north and get organized. Then they'll ram their army down our throats. At least two of our regiments must be at Haleiwa, not one."

Phillips shrugged. "Look, I know you think a lot of this Novacek. His trip to Haleiwa while under fire was bravely done, and, yes, in hindsight he was right about the local Japanese not being saboteurs, but that doesn't make him right in this instance. We simply have to protect everything."

"And wind up protecting nothing," Collins said, paraphrasing the old military dictum. "What the Japs have proven is that it will be extremely difficult to reinforce any area on the island without air cover. That means we must be dug in close to the point of attack if we are going to stand any chance of stopping them. If they do land at Haleiwa, they will brush our one regiment aside, and reinforcements will be cut to pieces trying to shuttle men north."

"It's seductive," said Phillips, "and we'd stand a good chance of smashing them, but it is too big a chance."

"I agree with Phillips," Short said. He hadn't spoken in a while, and his comment came as a mild surprise. "I don't agree that our northern regiment will be brushed aside so quickly. The Japs may have pulled a fast one on the navy, but they haven't fought our army yet, and I'm confident our boys can handle the little yellow bastards."

Collins shook his head in disbelief. "But look what's happening to the British in Malaya and to MacArthur's boys in the Philippines."

Short smiled grimly. "That's because the Brits have too many Indians and other Asiatics, and Mac has all those Filipinos. No, the Hawaiian Division is made up of real Americans, and they will hold the Japs until reinforcements reach them wherever the Japs try to land."

Short rose and went to a map of the island tacked to the wall. "We have four regiments. The command will be divided into two ad hoc brigades. General Wilson will command the ones at Haleiwa and at

Schofield. General Murray will command the remaining two, and they will be placed to guard Barbers Point and Bellows Field."

Collins admitted to himself that this command breakdown did make some sense. Had the reorganization of the Hawaiian Division gone into effect, Major General Durward Wilson would have commanded the 24th Division, while Major General Maxwell Murray would have taken over the 25th.

Short smiled benignly. "Look, Colonel, I know you mean well, but you've only been here a short time and you'll be leaving us in just a little while."

"I'll be what?" Collins said in surprise.

Short permitted himself a chuckle. "Finally, something I know and you don't. Colonel, I've just gotten orders to send you and a handful of others back to the mainland. I gather that General Marshall doesn't want to take a chance on you becoming prisoners."

"When do I leave?" Collins asked softly. This was not what he'd had in mind. He didn't like to leave jobs unfinished, and that was precisely what was going to happen. He didn't know what plans Marshall had for him and, although intrigued, thought he would rather stay and take part in the fighting.

"We're making arrangements to sneak out a few planes," Phillips said. There was no smugness in his voice. Instead, Collins picked up a hint of regret. He would not be leaving Oahu. "We have a handful of PBYs and a Pan American Clipper that had to make a landing here a couple of days ago. They are hidden and will be used at the proper time."

Both types of planes were flying boats that could land and take off in the water. That trait made them invaluable, as every good-size landing field had been attacked by the Japs.

"Who'll replace me?" Collins asked.

Short appeared to wince. It had been his earlier decision to appoint the incompetent Fielder to the position now held by Collins that had caused so many problems. "Bicknell," the general said. "Novacek will be his second."

"Are you promoting Novacek? He sure as hell deserves it."

Short looked at the ceiling. An explosion rumbled in the distance. If he had listened to Novacek in the first place, he thought, perhaps the situation wouldn't be quite so grave. Perhaps he'd even have a reputation left.

"Yeah," the general said softly. "Promote the SOB."

JAMIE PRIEST HAD NO IDEA which source of his suffering was the worst. Was it the fire from the sun that baked the bare portions of his skin, causing it to blister and resulting in agonies of the damned? Or was it the salt water as it washed over his body and over those blisters and increased his torments?

No, Jamie decided, it was the thirst. In comparison with thirst, anything else was trivial. The thirst was killing him and driving him mad. Had driven him mad? Was he already insane?

He had been at least two days without water, probably longer—he'd lost track of time. Already several of his companions had died or just given up and let themselves slide into the sea to end their pain. All of those who'd been more than slightly wounded in the tragic encounter with the Japanese fleet were dead, and he wasn't certain about the rest. It'd been a long time since he'd spoken to anyone, or heard a voice call out.

At first Jamie and the others had hoped that the ocean currents would push them east toward the mainland, but the winds had been contrary, which meant they'd likely not gone far at all. Floating to California had been a forlorn and ludicrous hope anyhow. Without food or water, they'd have been dead for weeks before they got near the place.

But at least the thought had given them some faint whisper of hope. That hope had vanished when reality set in as time passed. They were adrift in the Pacific without food, water, or shelter, and, while the temperatures weren't at all difficult to endure, the constant exposure to salt water, wind, and sun had scraped them raw.

Maybe the dead were the lucky ones. Jamie knew he would join them very shortly. He had been drifting in and out of consciousness for some time and now was experiencing delirium and hallucinations. There was a whale on the water, and it was staring at him. Impossible, a rational corner of his mind said. Whales go in the water and not on it.

And whales do not have holes in their sides. Okay, he thought, that made it a building and not a whale, but there aren't any buildings in the middle of the Pacific either, so that meant it must be a whale after all.

He heard someone say "easy," and then he felt strong hands lift him out of the water and into the belly of the whale or whatever it was. I'm Jonah, he thought and giggled silently. He tried to say something, but his lips were scabbed over and wouldn't work.

A face looked down on him. There was a light behind the face, and he wondered if it was God talking to him. "Are you from the *Pennsylvania*? If you are, just nod, buddy. Don't try to talk at all."

Jamie nodded, and the face smiled. Damp cloths were placed on him, and he felt their cooling ecstasy. A little water was permitted to seep between his lips, and his greedy body arched to meet it.

"Relax, buddy," said the voice. "There's plenty more where that came from."

The refreshing water partially cleared Jamie's mind, and he felt hands rifling the pockets of his tattered pants and shirt. He was on an airplane, a PBY, and wanted to ask about the others but couldn't frame the words. Then he realized it didn't matter. If he was saved, then so were they.

Jamie felt the surge of power beneath him and the roar of the engines as the plane lifted off from the water. They were airborne, and he was free from the sea and the agonies it had caused him.

The voice returned, and Jamie saw it was a naval ensign. "You ever been to California, Lieutenant?" Jamie shook his head. How did the ensign know his rank? His bars must still have been on his shirt, or there was some information in his pockets. "Well, that's where you're going, sir. You're gonna be safe now. Everything's okay."

The ensign made a move to touch the film pouch that was hung around Jamie's neck. "No," Jamie rasped and jerked it away with a clawlike hand. "Important. Very important."

The ensign nodded and departed. Jamie was satisfied. He had saved the film that Seaman Fiorini had entrusted him with before dying. It was important. Very important. If only he could remember why.

■

THE ISLANDS of Hawaii were over the horizon, only hours away, and Colonel Shigenori Omori stared into the distance as if such actions could will the islands closer and thus end his waiting.

Omori was forty years old, five three, stockily built, and had fairly typical Japanese features and dark hair. The colonel was the commandant of the 450-man field *kempei* detachment, or *kempetei* as it was called outside Japan, that had been detailed to maintain control over the population of Hawaii once it was conquered. As he turned and looked at the mighty transport fleet, there was no doubt in his mind that the conquest would occur.

The *kempetei* were the Japanese secret police, considered by some to be the equivalent of Germany's Gestapo. Omori disagreed. He had contempt for the Nazis and their Gestapo, which seemed to be populated by lunatics rather than patriots. The Nazis killed and tortured for the sake of inflicting pain, rather than for the sake of maintaining control over the population and, thus, the security of the nation. That and their fixation on Jews made them suspect in his eyes.

Omori knew there were sadists in the *kempetei,* any organization with such far-reaching and extralegal powers would attract such people, but using brutality and terror for their own sake was foolish and illogical.

Brutality and terror always had to have a purpose, and ensuring the well-being of Japan and her interests was more than enough purpose, without focusing on ethnic groups simply because they existed. Omori considered Hitler's persecution of the Jews to be a mindless waste of energy that could be better spent hunting down real threats rather than a bunch of shabby misfits. Omori thought it ironic that large enclaves of Jews existed in Shanghai and other areas of China that had been conquered by Japan, and, so long as they obeyed Japan's laws, they were left alone.

When the Hawaiian Islands were conquered, he would have 450 men to help control them. Reality said that they were too few to be everywhere, and that only Oahu would be garrisoned by Imperial marines and the bulk of his *kempetei.* He hoped to place a small contingent in Hilo, on the big island of Hawaii, but decided he might have to satisfy himself with locally recruited informers supported by flying columns of marines to do his work there and on the other islands.

The *kempei* in Japan were somewhat restrained in their actions, while the *kempetei* operating against often hostile foreign populations had few constraints on their actions.

There would, of course, be a substantial garrison of Imperial marines on Oahu, but they were rather ordinary soldiers and not skilled in controlling or intimidating a civilian population. No, the marines would guard the bases, prisons, and airfields, while the real work in securing the islands would be done by Omori's *kempetei* detachment.

As the *kempetei* reported to the army minister, they normally wore army uniforms with special armbands to differentiate themselves from the regular military. In this case, he'd ordered a number of his officers and men to bring civilian clothing along so they could blend in with the many tens of thousands of Japanese who lived in Hawaii.

This fact was disturbing. Many hours of discussion had taken place over how to treat the people of the islands, who constituted three distinct ethnic groups: Japanese, Hawaiian, and American.

Dealing with the white Americans would be simple. They were untrustworthy and would feel his iron fist. He also felt that he understood their fears regarding their women and would exploit them. In particular, respectable American women did not have sex with nonwhites. This meant he could use sexual terror and the threat of it as a means to an end. It also met his personal preferences, and he looked forward to it.

Omori had decided that he would let his personal aide, Lieutenant Goto, pretty much have his way with American subversives. In Omori's opinion, Uji Goto was a true sadist, and he had taken the young man as an aide only because Goto's uncle was a general. The lieutenant, however, could be useful, even expendable if something went wrong.

The native Hawaiians were a different situation. Some anthropologists actually felt they were descended from early Japanese who'd landed on the islands centuries before. Omori thought this was absurd, but his orders were to treat them more gently than the Americans. This would be done until someone stepped out of line, and then they would be dealt with harshly. His research told him that sexual terror among the Hawaiians would be less useful, as they were not as inhibited as the Americans.

The matter of the Japanese on Hawaii was truly unique. Some were totally loyal to Japan, while others were loyal to the United States. Trouble was, no one knew who was who. Word had reached Tokyo that potential leaders of a pro-Japanese government had been interned and shipped to California. Consequently, a puppet government would have to be developed from scratch. This would be accomplished, and very quickly. Four hundred and fifty *kempetei* were inadequate to govern an island like Oahu. They would need a lot of local help.

The Hawaiian-Japanese would be given preferential status and treated with utmost respect. Kid gloves, the Americans called it. They, not the whites, would be in charge. Omori, who'd endured smug patronization from Americans and British in both Washington and London, thought such a reversal of roles would be wonderful to behold. Perhaps he would even take an American mistress.

Along with the *kempetei* detachment, he'd brought a score of Korean women as *ianfu,* or "comfort girls," to satisfy his men and himself. He thought it would be interesting to have American comfort girls in his stable.

Omori sighed. In a few hours the battle would begin. Ahead of the stinking transport on which he and his men were stuffed was an armada of battleships, cruisers, and carriers. The Americans didn't stand a chance.

MISSY WILSON DELVED into the C-ration pack and stuffed something in her mouth. "Kind of bland, but not too bad," she said. "What is it?"

"I think you're eating the toilet paper," Alexa said with a laugh.

"I hope not. There's none left in the stores."

The fragile Hawaiian economy was in danger of shattering. It had been weeks since any ships had come from the mainland, and even the most ordinary items were in short supply. Rationing had helped, but it had reached the point where there was little left to ration. While food was the highest priority, other items, like toilet paper or soap, were running out as well.

At least you could grow food, Alexa thought. How the hell did one grow toilet paper? Or sanitary napkins? All over the islands, fields and lawns had been turned into gardens with edible plants thrusting through the surface. In a while, much of the food problem would have solved itself, but vegetables were so maddeningly slow growing, or at least it seemed like it.

"Thank God for Jake," Alexa muttered.

"You think he'll get in trouble?"

Jake had made several deliveries of "surplus" materials. He'd even helped dig an earth-walled basement under Alexa's house to store the supplies. Jake had insisted that all the items, treasures to the two women, were being discarded by the military for a number of short-sighted reasons. Neither Alexa nor Melissa quite believed him. It was easy to say he was showing them favoritism, but it also seemed that he was stockpiling goods for some unknown need in the future.

"Do you like him?" Missy asked.

"Jake?"

"No, the man in the moon."

"Of course I like him. He's a very good and strong man. Don't you like him as well?"

"Yes." Melissa grinned. "But I think you like him a little differently."

Alexa flushed. "Don't you think it's a little early for such speculations?"

"No. Haven't we all said that times are moving more rapidly than ever and that the old rules don't apply?"

"Are you suggesting that I should marry Jake Novacek? For one thing, he hasn't asked and probably won't."

"All you have to do is encourage him. Besides, Lexy, you don't necessarily have to marry him, just get involved."

"As a protector? Are you suggesting I should be his mistress?"

Melissa shrugged and laughed. "Could be worse. What'd he tell us about surviving? He's a survivor, Lexy. My bet is he'll even prosper in this war. Look, he got himself promoted, didn't he?"

Alexa commented that any thoughts of marriage, or even an affair, were terribly premature with Tim less than two months in his grave. She was going to add that Jake Novacek wasn't her type when she asked herself, Just what was her type?

Jake was strong, intelligent, educated, compassionate, and he respected her. These were all traits that Tim had had in abundance and that she missed terribly.

It was fairly evident that Jake had an almost adolescent crush on her, which was very flattering but was hardly grounds for marriage. Or an affair.

Jake had indeed been promoted and had shown her his new oak leaves with almost childish joy. Funny how a war brought out certain qualities in people while others were left behind. Melissa was right. If Jake survived, he would prosper.

That raised another point. Alexa had just lost one husband to the war, and Jake was a member of the military on an island that was going to be invaded. Did she want to go through all that again? Perhaps events were moving very quickly, but maybe it was time to slow down a little. No, she would keep Jake Novacek as a dear and trusted friend, at least for the time being.

However, the thought of bringing someone like Jake home to her family and friends in Virginia made her smile. He would eat them alive. Not for the first time did she wonder how Jake would be in bed. With guilt she'd found herself thinking more of sleeping with Jake than of being with Tim. She'd justified such behavior by reminding herself that Jake was alive, her husband was not.

"Is he coming by tonight?" Melissa asked.

"Don't know." I hope so, she didn't add. No need to set Melissa off again.

Then the sirens wailed again, and distant explosions made the ground tremble. The two women looked at each other in dismay. In the time since the Japs had taken Molokai, everyone had become expert in the sounds of war. They realized with a sickening clarity that they weren't hearing bombs. It was a naval bombardment.

"No," Alexa said grimly. "I don't think he'll be coming tonight."

JAKE REVIEWED THE REPORTS as they came in. A line of Japanese warships was shelling the defenses on the level ground around Bellows Field while dive-bombers hit anything that moved beyond it.

Colonel Collins burst into Jake's office. "General Short has already decided this is the real thing. One of our subs spotted transports behind the warships. He's ordered the units at Schofield and Barbers Point to move toward part of the Koolau Range that overlooks Bellows."

"It's a feint, and they'll be cut to pieces while on the move," Jake said. "Besides, aren't you leaving? Shouldn't you be packing?"

"Don't be a smart-ass. Everything's up in the air now and you know it. Short thinks Barbers is the target, and Phillips is happier than a clam that his leader's been proven right. Now they're saying the Japs'll shell today and land tomorrow, then attempt a quick thrust up the Koolau to where they can dominate Honolulu and where their long-range field guns can hit Pearl. Both of them are confident the Japs can be stopped."

Jake shook his head. "Whoever holds that part of the Koolau Range dominates the field, and right now that's us. Our guns already overlook the Bellows area and can hit their ships and landing craft, and, no matter how hard they try, they can't knock out all of them. That is why they won't land there. Did you tell him that those Jap transports can slip away under cover of darkness and be off Haleiwa in a couple of hours at most? Did you remind him that those are only light cruisers and destroyers out there off Bellows? Where are the heavies and the battleships? Joe, this is only a feint! The Japs are making us move potential reinforcements away from Haleiwa, which is where they'll be tomorrow morning and we won't be able to do jack-shit about it."

"I told General Short everything, Jake, and he insisted that he'd made a decision and he'd stick with it."

Jake took a deep breath. "Then let me go to Haleiwa and observe."

"Now?"

"Now, Joe. Let me slip away under the cover of night and see what's happening up there."

Collins hesitated. He didn't like the idea of sending one of his most capable officers, and a good friend to boot, off on a possible wild goose chase. But, with Short's mind made up and all decisions made, there wasn't anything more to be done at G-2 for the time being.

"Go ahead, Major Novacek," Collins said. "And I hope you're wrong."

"So do I, Joe. So do I."

THE JAPANESE LANDING and bombardment forces were out of sight as they prepared to launch the assault. Admiral Yamamoto paced the bridge of his mighty flagship and felt that he had again been taught the lesson that nothing goes according to plan.

Yamamoto was particularly distressed by the failures in leadership that had occurred, although he fully understood that he had only himself to blame for much of what had happened.

The admiral now flew his flag on the superbattleship *Yamato,* and, along with the additional battleships and heavy cruisers that constituted the heart of an exceptionally strong strike force, held station about fifty miles west of the bombardment force and the transports. They lay silently and waited for the arrival of an American relief force. Then they would pounce and destroy.

To the best of his knowledge, the existence and strength of the *Yamato* remained a secret. His problem was that he didn't know this for certain. It had been a mistake on his part to send the *Yamato* along with two smaller, older battleships against the *Pennsylvania.* He had thought that the three would dispose of the damaged American battleship in short order and provide the raw crew of the *Yamato* with invaluable combat experience. Instead, the crippled American ship had fought with a ferocity reminiscent of a wounded, cornered animal.

While the *Yamato* had emerged unscathed, the *Fuso* and the *Ise* had been damaged, with the *Ise* forced to depart for Japan for repairs and modifications. There was talk of putting a short flight deck on the *Ise*'s stern and making her a hybrid: half battleship, half carrier. Yamamoto thought it was nonsense and showed what problems lurked beneath the surface of Japan's successes.

When the American warship finally sank and efforts were being made to recover survivors, a periscope had been reported, which caused all the ships to flee the area in haste. American torpedoes might be inconsistent, but no one wanted to test them. When the facts were in, it appeared that the "periscope" had been nothing more than floating debris. The captain of the *Yamato* had reported the possibility of other American survivors in the area but assured Yamamoto that he had shelled them and that they must all be dead.

Admiral Yamamoto was not totally confident. Nor was he thrilled when an officer on the *Yamato* misunderstood his directive that all efforts be taken to ensure that the existence of the great ship remain secret. As a result, he had taken it on himself to execute all seventy-odd survivors from the *Pennsylvania* who had been taken aboard before the periscope fiasco. The young officers who'd carried out the deed were fanatical believers in the code of *bushido* and felt that anyone who surrendered, regardless of the circumstances, was beneath contempt and unworthy of being allowed to live.

In a scathing tongue-lashing, Yamamoto had reminded them that the rest of the world would consider their actions war crimes and be a possible hindrance in negotiating peace with the United States if the story got out. He did not think he'd converted the officers, and, not for the first time, Yamamoto concluded that rigid adherence to *bushido* would spell doom for the Japanese Empire.

The admiral conceded that the giant ship might yet be seen by a sub or a patrol plane, but he was confident that any sightings would be inconclusive, and that the immense strength of the *Yamato* would remain cloaked until her fury could be unleashed against an unsuspecting American relief force.

The Americans had not reacted to the landings on Molokai, which had surprised him, but they had to send a battle force to try to save Oahu. It was inconceivable that the United States would permit 400,000 of her people to be conquered, even if a third of them were Japanese. In order that the invasion portion of his fleet be detected in advance, he had ordered the normal flow of radio transmissions to occur and even concurred in the sending of some messages in the clear that would ordinarily have been encoded.

He checked his watch. Off in the distance, the predawn bombardment would be just beginning. In only a few hours, Japanese soldiers and marines would commence landing on the northern beaches of Oahu. With more than a hundred planes on Molokai and the planes of four supporting carriers, the Japanese air forces would smother the Americans.

"Now," he muttered, "if only their fleet would come."

■

CHAPTER 9

Jamie Priest found it difficult to wear a regulation uniform. The multitude of sores on his body, along with a gash on his back that he'd gotten from a piece of metal, caused him to wince every time something rubbed against his raw flesh. He was also still gaunt and haggard from his time in the water, and his head had been shaved in order to treat other cuts and sores.

"Lieutenant, you look like hell," Admiral Nimitz said in a gentle, joking voice. Beside him, Admiral Spruance smiled.

"Thank you, sir. I have to admit it's pretty much the way I feel."

"You were very fortunate," Spruance said. "The boys in that PBY had just about given up and were going to head for home when they spotted you. No one had any idea you would have drifted that far to the east."

Well, Jamie thought, so much for our sense of navigation. "What about the others, sir? No one seems to know."

"Son," said Nimitz, "you were the only survivor in that cluster of debris."

Jamie's eyes filled with tears and his voice broke. "I'm sorry, sir. I tried so hard to help them."

"We know you did," said Spruance. "Maybe you survived for a reason. Now, show us the pictures and tell us how you got them."

Jamie took a deep breath and got a grip on his emotions. In a plain manila envelope were the developed photos that Seaman Fiorini had taken. The navy had enlarged them to eight by ten, and the developing unit held the negatives. Other copies were en route to Washington. Fiorini would have been pleased.

"Spread them on my desk," Nimitz said eagerly.

Jamie passed one of the glossies to Nimitz. "Admiral, only two are truly significant, and this one may be the most important. It proves that the Japanese ship fired eighteen-inch shells."

The enlarged picture was somewhat grainy, but it clearly showed Jamie holding a measuring tape against the base of a gigantic shell. The unit indicators were clearly visible on the tape.

"Good Lord," Nimitz muttered.

Jamie passed another across. "And this, sir, is the second most important. At the time Seaman Fiorini took this, the Jap was damned near alongside the hulk of the *Pennsylvania*. Even though the Jap is slightly farther away, you can see the enormous size differential."

"Unbelievable," said Spruance. "Like an adult among small children. That Jap battlewagon is twice the size of the *Pennsylvania*."

"At least that much, sir," Jamie added. "The pictures don't give a true indication of perspective. Sir, may I ask who the Jap is?"

Spruance looked at Nimitz, who shrugged for him to go ahead. "Lieutenant, the ship must be their new battlewagon, the *Yamato*. We'd heard rumors that she was nearly finished and that she was big. What we didn't know was how big. We thought she'd be in the same league as our *North Carolina* and *Washington*, at about 37,000 tons, and carry sixteen-inch guns. The *Pennsylvania* displaced 33,000 tons, and this beast must go sixty-five or seventy thousand."

"And carry eighteen-inchers," Nimitz added, still almost disbelievingly. The proportional difference in strength and weight of shell went far beyond the two inches in size.

Spruance shook his head. "Our engineers recently concluded that an eighteen-inch gun was years away in development, and that the Japs would have difficulty doing anything better than fourteens. God, they've euchred us again."

Nimitz stood up and paced his small office. "This also means that we must dismiss any thoughts of using our battleships in duels with theirs. The *North Carolina* and *Washington* are en route to Pacific waters, but they're not going to get even close to that monster unless the odds are overwhelmingly in our advantage." He turned to Spruance. "Ray, all this does is confirm that we're going to have to win this war with carriers and subs, not battleships."

"Even if we had any battleships, we wouldn't use them," Spruance grumbled.

The *South Dakota*, a more modern version of the *Washington* and

North Carolina, was finishing her shakedown training, but that was it. The *Alabama* would be launched shortly, but would not be ready until late in the year. The others in the class, the *Indiana* and *Massachusetts,* would be launched in 1942 but would not be ready until the next year. Not counting the old battlewagons in California waters, the United States would have three battleships in the Pacific.

These ships, however, were all in the 37,000-ton class. The 45,000-ton *Iowa* was scheduled for launch in late summer but would not be available for duty until mid-1943. Even if she were available, the *Iowa* would be seriously outgunned by the *Yamato.*

"No battleships and no carriers," said Nimitz. "All of that means no relief for Hawaii or the Philippines."

"Sir," said Jamie, "are the islands going to be invaded?"

"It could happen at any time," Nimitz answered. Both he and Spruance knew it was about to occur as they spoke, but Lieutenant Priest had not been cleared for Magic information.

"Then I would like to return to sea duty as soon as possible."

"You're entitled to go on leave," Spruance said.

"I'd like to take it some other time." Jamie grinned through cracked lips. "After all, sir, there's a war on."

Nimitz smiled. "So there is, son, but you're not going to be in it for a while. I'm assigning you to staff work here so we can pump your brain about the *Yamato,* as well as the Japanese gunnery and torpedoes. Not too many people have seen the Jap navy in action like you have."

Spruance looked away as Nimitz made his speech. Another Magic intercept had caught an angry Yamamoto castigating someone on the *Yamato* for executing American prisoners. Lieutenant Jamie Priest appeared to be the sole survivor of the last voyage of the *Pennsylvania.* There was no chance he was going back in harm's way at this time.

There was also no chance that either admiral was going to tell the young man of the fate of his comrades.

IN A STRANGE WAY, the scene unfolding below him reminded Jake of his childhood in the hills of Pennsylvania and West Virginia, when he didn't have any money and had to watch the high school football games from up on the higher ground. From such a distance, he had no idea who had the ball or who was winning. All he could see were dots moving slowly and relatively silently across a field. Sometimes he could hear distant cheering or the tinny blare of a band, but the noises seemed disconnected from the events.

Jake had placed himself on a spur of the Waianae Range, which ran down the western side of Oahu. He hoped fervently that he was invisible to the Japanese and that there was nothing on the hill that might attract their fire. The normally peaceful and beautiful white beaches of Haleiwa were about two miles away, but, through his binoculars, he could see events clearly as they unfolded.

The shelling had begun at first light. The American defenses were new and poorly concealed. Raw scars in the earth had shown the Japanese just where to fire, and they had done so to great effect, pulverizing most of their targets. Jake picked out two battleships and four heavy cruisers insolently standing just a couple of miles offshore as they poured thunderous fire into selected areas while transports patiently waited behind them.

The recently dug-in Americans had nothing to respond with and could only absorb the punishment that systematically destroyed all the hard work they'd done. What the ships didn't hit, the planes did. At almost any moment, there were at least a score of Zeros and Zeke bombers overhead. Jake couldn't begin to imagine what it must be like in that thunderous hell on the beaches. Even where he was, he could feel the earth tremble as shells and bombs hit home.

At about ten in the morning, he counted fifty-four landing craft heading toward the beach. If each carried its full complement of twenty-four men, almost thirteen hundred Japanese soldiers were in the first wave. Granted, there were more Americans than that in the area, but the Japanese attack was focused on one point, and the other spread-out American defenders could do nothing to help their beleaguered comrades.

When the landing craft beached on the white sands, ramps on their front ends were dropped, and tiny dots, Japanese soldiers, came pouring out. Jake exulted when some of them fell and actually cheered when one of the landing craft burst into flames from a shell. But it was too little, and the Japanese quickly overran targeted American positions and established a perimeter while the landing craft returned for more soldiers.

Within a few hours, Jake estimated there were between five and six thousand Japanese on the beach, with more arriving almost continuously. Also landed were a handful of vehicles, towed artillery, and small tanks. He saw other dots. These were American defenders fleeing southward down the road to Schofield Barracks and Oahu. Overhead, Japanese planes strafed and bombed anything that moved, and the retreat quickly became a rout.

Japanese gunnery had begun seeking targets farther inland, and Jake decided it was time to leave. He packed his binoculars and mounted his motorcycle. He would go cross-country and not try the road, which was quickly becoming a death trap full of burning and wrecked vehicles. He was not alone in this decision; numerous clusters of men trekked south across the fields.

Smoke could be seen from the small towns in the area. Waialua, with its five thousand people, was in flames, while the coastal village of Haleiwa itself, with only a couple of hundred souls in cottages and shacks, had been flattened by the battle.

Civilians had begun withdrawing when the shelling started, and now they clogged the one narrow road that the army needed for withdrawal of the wounded, evacuation of shattered units, and arrival of reinforcements. There was nothing but chaos on the roads, and Jake could see no sign of American reinforcements heading northward against the flow.

He watched in horror as Japanese planes swept across the narrow road and killed without discrimination. It was like the newsreels he'd seen of the Nazis butchering innocent civilians in France in 1940. It was hard to believe it was happening to Americans on American soil, but the truth lay before him.

Fortunately, darkness would fall in a couple of hours. If the retreating mass of people could stay clear of the fires that would attract planes, they might make it through to Schofield.

So too, Jake thought grimly, might he.

PRESIDENT ROOSEVELT'S FACE was ashen and drawn. His hands shook, and he looked on the verge of collapse. Admiral King resisted the urge to call for medical assistance as he remembered General Marshall's comments about the president's health. What he was seeing was a prime example of the stresses that were destroying the man who appeared in public as strong, unflappable, and buoyantly confident.

Finally, Roosevelt was able to speak. "I know it was expected, but it is still a shock. It's like the death of a loved one who's been dying for months. No matter how much we think we're prepared, it's still a tragedy."

King kept his silence. Roosevelt had just gotten official word of the Japanese landings on Oahu.

"Is there nothing we can do?" the president asked.

King and Secretary of the Navy Frank Knox locked eyes. They had been over this ground many times. Partly as a result of the decision that Germany was the primary enemy, there were few resources available to the navy. Another factor was Japan's unnerving and totally unexpected propensity to be dominant in several crucial areas, and only time, as the American war machine gradually geared up, would shift those dominances.

"The public is going to crucify me if Hawaii falls," Roosevelt said. "Thank God there's time to repair the damage before the next presidential elections, although my party is going to catch hell in fall's congressional races."

"The Japs will take Hawaii," King said tersely. Wait. Had the president just said he was going to run for a fourth term? The third one in 1940 had been unprecedented. Would his health hold up for the current term, much less one more?

Roosevelt tried to rub the pain from behind his eyes with his knuckles. "When that happens, there will be no reason for Bataan and Corregidor to hang on. Do you know the soldiers in the Philippines are fantasizing that we will soon land ten thousand Negro soldiers on white horses to save them? My God, they're going mad over there. How long do you give Oahu, Admiral?"

"Ground warfare isn't my specialty, sir, but my experts say two to three weeks at the most. If the Japs adhere to the pattern established in their earlier attacks, in Malaya and the Philippines, they won't wait too long before advancing. They like to keep their opposition off balance."

"Singapore will soon fall as well," Knox said.

The British and Empire troops had almost entirely withdrawn across the Johore Strait, which meant that only the small island that contained the city of Singapore remained of all Malaya. The British had been outmaneuvered by the Japanese, who'd moved through the jungles instead of using the roads and, when on the roads, had mounted many of their troops on bicycles, enabling them to travel with astonishing swiftness.

"When that occurs," Knox continued, "the Japanese will control all of the western Pacific and be in a position to attack Australia. We will find it very difficult to fend off an invasion down there."

Roosevelt nodded grimly. "Would they do that?"

"It would be a tremendous reach," King answered, "and doubtless not in their original plans. However, neither was Hawaii. Success breeds ambition and this is no exception."

"Perhaps ambition will be their downfall," Roosevelt murmured, and the others nodded. "Tell me, Admiral, when can you mount a counterattack and retake the Hawaiian Islands?"

King was surprised. A counterattack of any force was a contravention of the policy of Germany First. "We need more ships, and we need an army. According to General Marshall, we will have an army well before we have the ships. Let's face it, sir, even though we have a number under construction, ships take years to build, while a soldier can be trained in far less time. If we are going to counterattack by the end of this year, it will be largely with what resources we have now. If you want to wait until the end of 1943, then we will have a fair degree of dominance."

Roosevelt nodded. "What would you need to attack now?"

"Carriers, sir. And a solution to the torpedo problem with our submarines. The days of the battleship are over, except to protect the carriers and for shore bombardment. I wouldn't let any of our battleships go against that Japanese giant unless the odds were heavily stacked in my favor, like the British finally wound up with against the German *Bismarck*."

Roosevelt and Knox agreed. Until the *Yamato* made her entrance, the German *Bismarck* had been the largest warship ever. She'd finally been sunk, but not until she'd been crippled by torpedoes from planes, and only then by the concentrated fire of several Royal Navy battleships and cruisers. The recently arrived information about the *Yamato* had stunned them. Confirming pictures were en route, and it had already been decided that the public would not see them for a long while. Nor would anybody comment on the possibility that there might be a sister or two of the *Yamato* under construction in Japanese shipyards.

"You have three carriers in the Pacific, do you not?" Roosevelt asked of King.

The question was rhetorical. The *Enterprise* and *Lexington* had been in the Pacific at the time of Pearl Harbor, and the *Yorktown* had arrived shortly after. That left the *Ranger, Saratoga, Wasp, Hornet,* and the small *Long Island* operating in the Atlantic.

Roosevelt smiled for the first time during the meeting. "Why do we need carriers in the Atlantic? The German surface naval threat is nonexistent, and the fleet carriers are little use against their subs."

Knox responded. "They will be used to support amphibious operations."

"Which," Roosevelt said, "will not occur for some time. And, when they do occur, can't the carriers be moved from one ocean to another fairly rapidly? After all, isn't that mobility part of their purpose?"

King liked what he was hearing. "At last count, the Japs had nine or ten carriers, but several of them were small, like the *Long Island*. While they doubtless have others under construction, they suffer from the same time constraints we do. Also, light carriers like the *Long Island* are better suited for use against German U-boats, which is why we are converting merchantmen to small carriers. The fleet carriers serve no purpose, other than political, in the Atlantic."

The president winced at the word *political,* and Knox averted his eyes. The very close relationship between Roosevelt and the British prime minister, Winston Churchill, was an ongoing sore point with King and others who felt that the president was far too deferential to British concerns.

"Be that as it may," Roosevelt said, "you shall have your carriers. Not all at once, mind you, as we cannot give even the slightest hint that we are shifting our focus away from helping England and Russia. Perhaps we can do something sooner than late 1943. I leave it to you to come up with a suitable plan."

King was pleased. He had won part of the battle for the Pacific. With carriers, he could strike at the Japanese. It would be too late for Hawaii, of course, but it would occur. Now he could get on with other problems. The torpedoes were a nagging situation. Did they work properly or not? Then, of course, there was the problem with carrier-based planes. Right now, the Japanese Zero ruled the skies, and all the carriers in the world wouldn't change a thing unless there was a good plane on them. Almost all the American carrier planes were F4F Wildcats, which hadn't been tested in battle. King and the other admirals were certain that the Wildcat was superior to the P-36 or the P-40, but just how much better was the question.

All in all, though, King was pleased. He'd gotten the promise of reinforcements and seen the president apparently shake off his unexpected case of nerves. On a really good note, King hadn't been invited to have one of the president's famous martinis. Maybe he'd been too blunt with his commander in chief, but that was okay. In King's opinion, the President of the United States made a lousy martini.

COLONEL SHIGENORI OMORI and his *kempetei* detachment landed on the second day of the invasion. By that time, the Japanese perimeter on Oahu extended several miles inland, and there was no danger from American artillery, which had been either overrun or knocked out by Japanese airplanes and the big guns from the warships.

Omori thought that Hawaii was a beautiful place, and he briefly enjoyed the serenity of walking the beaches and watching the majestic waves as they crested on the clean white sand. He did not, however, permit himself to linger over these thoughts. The time for luxury would come later. Instead, he examined the smashed American defenses, where the dismembered and bloated bodies of the dead still lay where they'd fallen. At least they had died warriors' deaths, he thought. Not like the prisoners who clogged the pens and clustered in numbed groups within their barbed-wire compounds.

Omori walked to one of the pens, where he looked through the fence at the face of the enemy and was unimpressed. "If they were Japanese," he said, "they would be considered as dead. These, however, don't seem to care."

His aide, Lieutenant Goto, laughed. "The Americans aren't warriors. They have no sense of duty or pride. These creatures remind me of Chinese beggars. They are less than human and should be treated as such."

Both by virtue of his position as aide and as a result of his political connections, Goto felt that he could speak more freely than a normal subordinate. Omori tolerated it, sometimes even appreciated it. Even though Goto was occasionally a brute, he was intelligent, a good aide, and not a sycophant, and his connections were a fact of life.

Omori and Goto continued their examination of the area. The civilian population had not escaped completely. Several mangled and bloated bodies were visible in and around the blasted villages, and a number of ragged islanders, mainly native Hawaiian, watched in confusion as the Japanese army moved past them. Any American civilians in the area appeared to have escaped or been killed.

"Schofield will fall shortly," Omori said. "And then we will be on the threshold of taking both Pearl Harbor and Honolulu. At that point, it will become essential that we end the battle quickly. A prolonged struggle for the island is not in our interests. That being the case, what do you think General Tadoyashi will do and how might we help him?"

The first assault waves had been Imperial marines, who had taken surprisingly heavy casualties, but they had been leapfrogged by the reinforced 38th Infantry. The marines had accomplished their purpose by establishing the beachhead; now it was the army's task to complete the conquest. For once, cooperation between the two services had been fairly good. Neither wanted to bear the onus of failure, and both wanted the laurels of victory.

"I don't know," Goto answered after some thought.

Omori smiled. The boy had so much to learn, but at least he was honest. "Terror."

COLONEL COLLINS WAVED Jake Novacek into his office and shut the door. "Jake, in your humble opinion, what're our chances of winning this thing?"

The junior officer laughed harshly. "Slim to none."

After several days of gathering their forces, the Japanese had moved. A double-pronged attack had been launched against the hastily made defensive line that ran across the middle of the island. Both American flanks were anchored on Schofield Barracks. Japanese infantry and armor had probed and, with suffocating air support, breached the line in several parts. As a result, Schofield was surrounded on three sides and was in grave danger of being cut off entirely.

An earlier attempt at a counterattack had been launched over Collins's and Jake's vehement protests. Both men had stressed the fact that any forward movement was hazardous and could be countered by the Japanese. To say the attack had fizzled would have been a compliment. Very few units even reached their jump-off points, and none launched their attacks at the assigned time. Those that finally did make piecemeal attacks were cut to pieces by the Japanese. At least a third of Oahu's garrison was dead, wounded, or missing. If the pocket at Schofield was cut off or wiped out, the casualties would be at 50 percent.

Pearl Harbor and Honolulu were becoming a defensive perimeter with most of the garrison's best soldiers already out of action. As in the Philippines, the Americans were fighting bravely and hard but were being overwhelmed. Within the Honolulu-Pearl perimeter, there was a great deal of confusion, with thousands of soldiers either separated from their units or, worse from Jake's standpoint, noncombat troops who hadn't held a rifle in years. *Useless mouths* was the phrase kicked around at headquarters.

Collins nodded thoughtfully. "You think Short'll surrender?"

"He has to," Jake answered.

"Will you?" Collins asked and saw surprise register on Jake's face. "Look, Jake, I know what you've been up to. After all, I'm intelligence too, aren't I? You're going to bail out of the surrender and go it alone on this island, aren't you?"

"True." In the last couple of weeks, Jake had taken guns, ammunition, and rations from various storehouses and cached them in a number of places on the island. While he had given a good deal to Alexa and Melissa, much more had been buried elsewhere.

"Were you planning to run your own war?" Collins asked with a grin.

Jake took a deep breath. "Sort of. Joe, you ever been in jail?" Collins hadn't. "As a young, dumb kid, I spent a few days in various small-town jails and hated it. A POW camp is nothing more than a jail, only worse. In jail, at least you know how long your sentence is, or that you'll be let out on Monday when you've sobered up. If the Japs put us in one of their camps, you'll have no idea when you'll get out. If ever."

Collins agreed. News of atrocities in Japanese-run prison camps was slowly filtering through to the rest of the world. Both men knew that an extended stay in a Jap camp was equivalent to a death sentence. An ugly, agonizing death sentence.

"And no," Jake said, "I wasn't planning anything as foolish as starting a guerrilla war. The weapons and supplies are reserves in case they're needed, but I was first planning to stay alive, and then I'd organize some kind of resistance, but not a war."

Collins handed Jake an envelope. "I'm leaving tonight on that big Pan Am flying boat. It's been painted black, and it'll be taking off with a full complement of people. You'll be on it."

"What?"

"It's all in the envelope. The navy has a problem. They've lost something important, and they want us to find it, and you in particular have been chosen to do it. The fools sat on the problem until it was almost too late. Apparently some important people were on a ship that got sunk and they wound up on the Big Island. Your job is to find them and make certain they don't fall into Jap hands. That ought to tie in with your plans to skip the surrender ceremonies."

"I'm damned," Jake said.

"Probably. The navy would have the marines do it, but they're all gone, so it's up to us. You'll have a squad of infantry with you. I don't know who these people are on Hawaii, or why they're so damned important, but it was stressed that the Japs cannot get their hands on them under any circumstances, is that understood?"

Jake understood. His orders were to kill them if capture appeared imminent. Good Lord, who were they?

"One other thing," Collins said. "These navy types may have rank on you, and that cannot be permitted to interfere with your duties. You were just promoted to the temporary rank of major, right? Well, that's been changed to a permanent grade, and you now have the temporary rank of lieutenant colonel. Who knows, if this damned war lasts long enough, you might outrank me, although you'll never, ever, be smarter or better looking. Oh yeah, the orders also have you reporting directly to someone in Washington so you won't be court-martialed if you decline to honor Short's order to surrender. It won't mean anything to the Japs, who'll probably chop off your head if they catch you, but it might save your tail in the future."

"Who's the someone in Washington who's now my boss?"

"Marshall," Collins said and chuckled as Jake's jaw dropped.

Jake's emotions were mixed. Rank and recognition were things he'd always dreamed of, but they had come during an enormous and humiliating American defeat, and he was expected to be an assassin if it became necessary.

Collins laughed. "Like I said, we leave tonight. Get your things in order and be back here at ten."

"I'm a bachelor and I'm totally dedicated to the army. There's little to put in order."

"Then go say good-bye to the widder woman you've been seeing and you think I don't know about."

"Bastard," Jake said with a grin as he left Collins.

He didn't want to leave Alexa alone in Honolulu, but at least he'd be free and not in a prison camp. In that case, perhaps he could help her out while attending to the rest of his plans. He would also ask a favor of Toyoza Kaga. Jake had no idea which way Kaga would leap when the Japs took over, but asking him to maintain a discreet observation of Alexa and Melissa was nonpolitical and couldn't hurt.

ALEXA TRIED NOT TO CRY. With Tim gone, Jake had become her friend and her anchor. That and the fact that she was genuinely fond of him made the thought of his leaving all the more upsetting.

Damn the military and its secrets, she raged inwardly. All Jake had been able to tell her was that he was departing for someplace that night. But if he had been going stateside, she realized, there would have been no need for secrecy. He hadn't said he was going to the mainland, which meant he would still be someplace on or near the islands. Interesting.

On the plus side, Jake had brought some more supplies and a bottle of white wine, which she, Melissa, and Jake had finished. They'd had to drink it warm, but it still tasted good.

Melissa said she heard the baby crying and left the two of them sitting on the couch. Jake's large hand was enfolded by Alexa's two.

"The last time you left me," she said, "I told you to be careful. I should have waited until this."

"It worked once, say it again."

She smiled and kneaded his hand. "Be careful. Now, what words of wisdom do you have for me?"

Jake took a deep breath. Life was already awful on Oahu, and it was going to get much worse. He had arrived during the day and been faintly surprised at the lack of Japanese air activity. The ruined buildings, charred vehicles, and cratered fields he took as a matter of course. The Japanese were all focused on the area around Schofield and the dissolving defense line north of the Honolulu perimeter. The result was that Honolulu enjoyed a temporary reprieve, although the rumblings of bombs and shells echoed in the distance while clearly visible fingers of smoke reached skyward.

"Last time I told you to survive. Just do that, Alexa—survive. Do whatever you have to do, pay any price, just survive. Cheat, lie, steal, anything; it doesn't matter what you have to do as long as you survive. Stay alive and I can look for you. If you don't, I can't."

She squeezed his hand harder. "When will the army surrender?"

"A few days, maybe a week. In the meantime, you and Melissa get into the city and stay in the crowds. You don't want to be two women alone out here when the Jap army comes through."

"But will it be that much safer in Honolulu?"

"Who knows? But it can't be worse than here. Maybe after the surrender you can come back, but not until then. Stay with crowds. There's always safety in numbers. Dress ugly and don't wear makeup or wash your hair. Tell Melissa to dye her hair back to its normal color, whatever that was. Don't do anything to draw attention to yourself or make yourself attractive. If that fails, then there's nothing left but to endure what you must and do what you can to survive."

Survive, Alexa thought. *Survive* was today's vocabulary word. Jake had said he'd look for her, and that gave her some hope. "When should we leave?"

"The sooner the better. Pack now and be ready to move at a moment's notice." He checked his watch. "I've gotta go."

Light was fading as they walked to the motorcycle. I'm going to be more alone than I have ever been in my life, Alexa thought. Melissa was a good friend, but she had her own priorities, a son and a departed husband.

Alexa put her hand on Jake's arm and felt the strength of his muscles. "Jake, I will do everything I must to get through this, and I want you to survive as well." She then put both her arms around his neck and kissed him on the lips. "And then I want you to find me, understand? Please find me."

Jake was shocked speechless. She was just about as tall as he, and he was almost as frightened by the intensity in her eyes as he was delighted by the feel of her body against his.

"I understand," he finally managed to gasp. Now all he had to do was figure out a way to get back from the big island of Hawaii to Oahu with only the Jap army and navy in the way.

ADMIRAL YAMAMOTO POUNDED his desk in frustration. His plans were falling apart. Where were the Americans? Why hadn't they sent a fleet to relieve Oahu? How could the Japanese navy fight the climactic and decisive battle that would knock the Americans out of the war if the Americans didn't cooperate?

Since when, he reminded himself wryly, did the enemy cooperate during a war? It was a lesson that was continually learned and relearned by admirals and generals everywhere.

Commander Yasuji Watanabe nodded tolerantly. He was as close to a friend as Yamamoto permitted himself while on duty, and only he was privileged to see such rare displays of uncontrolled temper. Technically, Watanabe was Yamamoto's aide, responsible for coordinating logistics, but Yamamoto used him as a sounding board when circumstances directed.

The admiral rose and paced his office. The battleship *Yamato* was in calm waters, and there was very little motion as she knifed through the sea. That and the sheer size of the ship made for a stable platform.

"We cannot win a war of attrition," Yamamoto continued, "and we cannot permit the Americans time to rearm. Have you seen the reports from Fuchida on Molokai? He's already lost half his planes. The Americans may not have any fighters, but they do have antiaircraft guns and they use them quite well. Add those to the pilots we are now losing from the carriers and we may have a serious problem to resolve. Damn their foolishness anyhow!"

Watanabe concurred. The foolishness referred to was the Japanese pilots' continuing resistance to wearing parachutes. Flouting direct orders, the carrier pilots either didn't take them, or didn't hook them up when in their planes. Their excuse was that sitting on a parachute made flying awkward. Everyone knew better. A parachute was a violation of *bushido*. A warrior dies in battle; he does not parachute away from the foe. That this attitude took the lives of highly skilled and virtually irreplaceable carrier pilots didn't faze them one bit.

It did, however, faze Yamamoto, Nagumo, and Fuchida. Carrier pilots were excessively trained in Yamamoto's opinion, and there were too few of them to use as reinforcements after lives were thrown away. Planes could be built by the thousands, but where would the pilots come from? He had tried to get modifications to the rigorous training program but had so far been unsuccessful. Even Commanders Fuchida and Genda, both products of the system, concurred that changes had to be made or Japan would run out of carrier pilots long before the Americans did.

As a result of casualties already taken, Yamamoto had made the decision not to send Nagumo's carriers on a raid through the Indian Ocean to Ceylon after Oahu fell. No, they would need time to regroup before striking toward Australia. The Royal Navy bases at Trincomalee and elsewhere would keep for another day. Fortunately, the Royal Navy contingent in the Indian Ocean was not a great threat. At least not yet.

"Watanabe?"

"Sir?"

"If the Americans are not going to rise to the bait, then we must end this as soon as possible. Please inform General Tadoyashi that there is no need for him to hold anything back. The Americans simply are not coming. Please tell him that I would appreciate it greatly if he would use whatever force is necessary to bring this campaign to a quick and decisive halt."

Part of the plan was that Tadoyashi's army would strengthen itself and mark time for a few days as a lure for the American fleet. It was now obvious that the gambit had failed and was to be discarded.

After Watanabe left, Yamamoto regretted the part of the bargain with Tojo that had compelled him to use carrier pilots on Molokai, instead of asking for more expendable army pilots. Army pilots would have been at least as effective, but no, he'd had to promise that naval personnel would fly from Molokai. As a result, Fuchida had lost more than fifty planes and pilots, an entire carrier's worth of irreplaceable pilots. Anyone, Yamamoto angrily reminded himself, even a half-trained army pilot, can land on a field. It takes great skill and training first to find and then to land on a moving carrier in an angry and tossing sea.

At least General Tadoyashi could now proceed without any constraints. This meant that terrible things would occur on Oahu if the Americans didn't surrender. Yamamoto wondered if this was another decision he'd regret.

·

CHAPTER 10

"Ladies and gentlemen, this is your captain speaking." The voice sounded tinny over the intercom, but it got everyone's attention. "Weather and the Japanese permitting, we will be departing momentarily. The smoking lamp is off and will not be lit. We will be flying at two hundred miles an hour, at a height of six inches, and this is the first time I've ever flown anything this large."

Joe Collins shifted uncomfortably. "Another unemployed comedian. I'll have him shot when we get to California."

The voice on the intercom was unperturbed. "Seriously, folks, my name is Lieutenant Commander Meagher, and I've flown this plane for years for Pan Am as well as being part of the Navy Reserve. You're on a Boeing Model 314 flying boat, and we have a range of just under four thousand miles, which should get us to California with no fuel problems. Under civilian conditions, we could carry a crew of eight and seventy-four passengers, and even sleep forty of them in bunks. As we are no longer civilians and have been designated the *C-98*, we now have a crew of only four, which means you can get your own damned coffee. We have fifty-one passengers plus all their equipment. Our cruising speed is 184 miles an hour, and we are 2,300 miles from San Francisco, so you can do your own math and determine the length of the flight. Oh yeah, the heads don't work."

"I really am going to kill him," said Collins.

"We will be flying extremely low in order to avoid detection, so keep your windows closed and you won't get wet. And, for those of you who were expecting a nonstop flight, sorry, but we will be landing on the Big Island to let off some passengers."

"That's us," Jake muttered from his seat beside Collins. Behind him, Sergeant Will Hawkins and eleven other men acknowledged the obvious in silence.

Jake had just met Hawkins, a rangy young man in his mid-twenties who exuded quiet confidence and competence. Hawkins assured Jake that all the men on the plane were volunteers, and not deadbeats people were trying to dump.

There was grumbling from some of the others. Collins checked his shoulder to see if the shiny star that designated his early promotion to brigadier general was still there. One of the reasons he'd been promoted ahead of schedule was to be the ranking officer on the plane in case anyone had problems with the change in schedule. One blimpish-looking colonel muttered a few comments about correcting things, but a steely glance from Collins settled the matter.

"I can't believe this thing is going to get off the ground," Jake muttered.

The plane had been taxiing on the waters off Ford Island along Battleship Row. The cadavers of the sunken ships were dimly visible through the windows as reminders of the disaster.

With a roar, the giant flying boat surged forward, and, after a gut-tightening eternity, it lifted off the water and banked southward.

There were no more flippant comments from the pilot as the plane flew over the shattered fuel storage depot and out across the enemy-controlled Pacific. As explained to Jake and Collins, the flight plan was a replay of the attempt to free the *Pennsylvania*. It was presumed that the Japs could not be everywhere and would have most of their ships and planes watching anything trying to escape east. The flying boat would head south, drop off Jake, and then head well south again before finally turning east toward California.

As promised, the plane flew almost shockingly low over the water, and it seemed to Jake that the whitecaps were lapping its belly. The pilot made one more terse comment about absolutely no smoking. It was a reminder that the plane was built for civilian purposes and not armored; therefore, any hit from a Jap gun could ignite the full load of fuel.

Once Jake saw the silhouette of a destroyer a few miles away and thought they'd had it, but luck was with them and the plane droned on undetected toward Hawaii. The trip from Oahu was not a long one, but it seemed to take forever for the dark shape of the Big Island to come into view.

There were no lakes or rivers on Hawaii where the big plane could land, so the pilot set her down in the gently rolling swells off Manuka Bay, near the southwest tip of the island.

Rafts were launched, and Jake and his little army paddled off toward the beach. Even before they were ashore, the plane taxied away and lifted off into the darkness. The people Jake was to rescue were miles away, and it would be too dangerous for the flying boat to wait. Jake's orders said some other form of pickup would be arranged once he found the lost naval personnel, who were waiting patiently but well inland. He hoped they were well hidden. In case there was more than one group of navy people wandering around, Jake had been given a sign and a countersign, which he'd shared with Hawkins in case something happened to him.

After they waded the last few feet to the dry ground, they hid the rafts and Jake reviewed his resources. Counting himself, he had twelve men, along with food, ammunition, medical supplies, and radio equipment. He was effectively stranded in what was very likely going to become enemy-occupied territory, and considered himself a well-armed and modern Robinson Crusoe.

As they picked up their gear and headed inland, Jake could only wonder what on earth made this mission so important.

IT AMUSED COLONEL OMORI that the Americans would take such care to blindfold him. Under other circumstances, it would have been insulting and demeaning, but not now. Instead he thought it was a pathetic gesture. General Tadoyashi had sent a messenger under flag of truce to ask for a conference with General Short. Short had accepted, and Omori was the messenger.

To make the effort more meaningful and show the importance of his mission, Omori wore the insignia of a major general, one rank above his real rank of colonel, as the Japanese army did not have brigadier generals.

The blindfold was but a formality. With planes flying overhead with impunity, there was little the Japanese military didn't know about the American situation. It was, however, interesting to hear the comments from the American military as he was passed through their lines. They foolishly and arrogantly presumed that he didn't speak English. The insults he understood and expected. He would have been surprised if they hadn't been said, and there was nothing he hadn't heard before.

The overheard comments about food and ammunition intrigued him, as they confirmed that the Americans were having an awful time getting either commodity to the front lines. It appeared that, while there was enough ammo, there wasn't much food. This was disturbing to him, because the Japanese army hadn't brought all that much either. It was, however, a matter that could only be dealt with later.

Finally, he was shown to an underground bunker and his blindfold removed. He did not blink at the change in light as that would have shown weakness.

General Short and Colonel Phillips entered the room with a third man they identified as an interpreter. "We will not need one," Omori said in English. "There will be no misunderstandings between us. What I have to say will be perfectly clear."

The interpreter left. He would doubtless spread the word that the fucking little Jap spoke English and people should watch what they said. Omori knew he had thrown away a small advantage but felt it would help in speaking with Short, who looked nervous and had a tic in one eye, and Phillips, who simply looked exhausted. Both men appeared gaunt, and their uniforms fit them poorly.

"General Short," Omori said firmly, "the purpose of this cease-fire is to permit you to save lives by surrendering. Your forces at Schofield have been destroyed, and we now hold the high ground overlooking Ewa and Barbers Point. Without sounding overly dramatic, your cause is doomed and further struggle will only result in needless deaths."

Just the day before, Japanese infantry had streaked down the western side of Oahu on bicycles and achieved a foothold on the Waianae Range overlooking American positions. Under the protection of naval guns, the Japanese army had dragged howitzers up the heights and begun shelling down into Pearl Harbor's defenses with devastating effect. Preoccupied as they were with the bulk of the Japanese army before them in the valley between the two ranges, the American army had been powerless to dislodge the Japanese.

Short lowered his eyes. "I am not authorized to surrender."

"I understand," Omori said gently. "You must notify your superiors in Washington. Do that. We will grant you a forty-eight-hour cease-fire. However, that cease-fire is conditional."

"And what are the conditions?" Phillips asked.

Omori kept his eyes fixed on Short. Phillips was inferior in rank and powerless; he would be ignored. "You will make no effort to move forces or strengthen your defenses. Of course your men will make repairs, but that is all. Further, you will cease work on any demolitions to take place before Oahu falls. In your position, I would be planning to dynamite anything that we might find usable. To do so would be regrettable, and we would treat such actions as banditry. Do I have to remind you that, in my nation, bandits are executed?"

Short nodded. "I will relay your message."

"And add this to it, please. I know you are concerned that we are Asian barbarians, and there is some truth to that. Our way of waging war is far different from yours. The longer the fighting goes on, the less it is likely that I will be able to hold a conquering army in check. Bloodlust, once aroused, is a terrible thing to see and is almost impossible to stop. If you surrender immediately, I will guarantee the safety of the civilian population and assure you that military prisoners will also be unharmed."

"Will you abide by the Geneva Convention?" Short asked, almost plaintively.

"General," Omori said, "neither your nation nor mine ever signed that convention. We will treat your prisoners in accordance with Japanese law and custom."

Omori watched as both men paled. "Gentlemen, you are presuming that life for your prisoners will be harsh, and that is correct. It will, however, be life, which is more than they will have if the fighting continues." He rose. It was time to end it. "You are not in a position to either quibble or negotiate terms. You will inform us of your intent to surrender, or your soldiers will be massacred and your civilians left to the mercies of our troops. You have forty-eight hours. In twenty-four hours we will give you an example of the totality of our determination to destroy you."

"THE SILENCE IS DEAFENING," Alexa said as she pulled some weeds from among her growing vegetables. "And frightening. I never thought I'd find the sounds of war reassuring."

Melissa wiped the sweat from her forehead. "It's strange, but I don't trust it either. Silence means the fighting's stopped, and that's good, but it's a sure bet that Jap general didn't show up to surrender to us."

News of the meeting between Short and the Japanese general had sped across the island with incredible swiftness. Exactly what had been said remained secret, but it could have been only one topic: surrender.

Alexa stood and wiped the dirt off her knees. "I like your hair. Is that the original color?"

Melissa grinned and stuck out her tongue. She had taken Jake's relayed instructions to heart, and her once-radiant blond hair was now a very mousy light brown and cut short. Alexa had hacked at her hair as well but felt that her natural color was bland enough. That and baggy, dirty clothing made them appear sexless. She hoped.

"Honey," Melissa said with an affected drawl, "it's been so long I don't recall. Even my roots have been known to lie."

Alexa looked down the road and saw people moving along it. They had packs on their backs. Groups of refugees were taking advantage of the cease-fire to move to places of greater safety. "I think it's time to go, don't you?"

Melissa nodded. They'd packed suitcases and were ready to leave on short notice. "Think our gardens'll be here when we get back?"

"I hope so." The cease-fire had lasted for almost an entire day. Rumor was that it'd last for another, but who knew what the Japs might do instead of honoring their word?

"I think," Alexa said, "we have enough time to clean up and double-check what we've packed. Jake said we should dress ugly. He didn't say we had to be filthy." At least not yet, she thought. Why did she have the nagging feeling that this shower might be her last for a long time?

A PORTION of the front lines was about two miles north of the small city of Waipahu, population six thousand, which lay directly between

Schofield and the base at Pearl Harbor. The city itself had been destroyed by Japanese artillery on the heights above the plain and by batteries now south of both Schofield and Wheeler Field.

The American defenders took the unexpected cease-fire as an opportunity to dig out collapsed trenches and strengthen bunkers. They took turns at eating and resting, all the while keeping an eye on the Japanese positions only a mile away.

"White flag," a sentry yelled. Sure enough, a white flag was visible above a known Japanese position. Word was passed down, and the battalion commander, a harassed-looking major, joined them. After a few minutes, a couple of figures appeared pulling a cart. The white flag was on a pole attached to the cart.

The major looked through a high-powered field telescope as the small party advanced. It was apparent that it was difficult for them to pull the cart over the rough terrain, and they fell a couple of times. For some reason, the sight reminded the major of a Passion play he'd seen once where Christ stumbled under the weight of his cross. The thought chilled him.

Something was wrong with the two men. They were naked, and then he realized they weren't men. The two naked people pulling on the cart were women, white women.

"I want two unarmed men to go out there with blankets to cover them and then help them with the cart," he said. A dozen volunteers raised their hands. There was anger, not prurience, on their faces. They knew what the Japs had done to the women.

Under a white towel attached to a branch, two soldiers advanced through no-man's-land and up to the slowly advancing cart. They covered the women with blankets, which were totally inadequate for the job, and assumed their burden.

After agonizing moments, they made it to the American trenches, where the major had a good look at the women. They appeared beaten and tormented. Their bodies were bloody and covered with cuts and bruises, some of which still oozed blood, and there was the hint of madness in their eyes. The sight was so disturbing that most of the soldiers averted their eyes.

"Who are you?" the major asked gently. The women were white, and he thought he knew the answer.

"Nurses," one managed to answer through swollen lips while the other one began to tremble uncontrollably. "From Schofield," she added.

The major examined the cart. It had high sides and a canvas top, and looked like it had come from a farm. "What's in the cart?" he asked and wondered if he really wanted to know.

"Heads," the first nurse answered and began to cry. "Our boys' heads. The Japs are killing their prisoners."

FRANKLIN DELANO ROOSEVELT LOOKED dejectedly out the window. Winter in Washington is a damp and usually unlovely time of year, and this day was no exception. It was raining fitfully over the nation's capital and in the president's heart.

"Do we have a choice?" he asked.

General Marshall, Admiral King, Secretary Knox, and Stimson all either shook their heads or looked away. General Short had earlier relayed the Japanese ultimatum and the forty-eight-hour deadline. Now they had knowledge of Japan's barbarity.

The two nurses were survivors of a group of at least a dozen captured when Schofield had been overrun. All had been gang-raped, but the two had been chosen to survive while the others had their throats cut.

The two survivors had then watched while fifty American POWs were selected at random from a holding pen and decapitated. The message the two brutalized nurses delivered was very simple. If General Short did not surrender, ten Americans would be executed every hour that went past the deadline. Also, there would be no protection for the civilian population. General Tadoyashi was explicit on this point. If there was no surrender, he would turn the 38th Division loose on Honolulu as he had on Hong Kong in an orgy of raping and looting.

"I'm still waiting for my answer," Roosevelt said. "Do we have a choice? For God's sake, if there is, tell me!"

"There is none," King answered. "I recommend surrender."

"As do I," Marshall said, and the two secretaries nodded agreement.

"General Short is required to surrender the entire Hawaiian archipelago," Marshall added, "and that includes Midway."

Roosevelt shrugged. Midway was an island base over a thousand

miles north and west of Hawaii proper. Its presence on the archipelago was a geographic quirk.

"What do we have there?" the president asked.

"Nothing anymore," King said. "We'd hoped to use it as a forward
and unsinkable aircraft carrier, but the invasion of Oahu outflanked it
and made it irrelevant. We evacuated the last of the personnel a day or
two ago. The Japs'll get a couple of empty islands and a fairly usable
airfield if they want it, but Midway is no longer of any importance."

"Then let them have it too," Roosevelt snapped. "At least tell me
that Magic is safe."

"We've taken steps to ensure that it is," Marshall said.

"That's not quite a yes," Roosevelt muttered. "But I guess it'll do
for the time being."

King was anxious to get back to his office. "Will that be all, sir?"

The president smiled, but it was an expression devoid of all happiness. "No. I have one more task for both you and General Marshall. I
told you I want the islands back. When can you do it?"

King hid his surprise. "As I said before, by the end of 1943 we'll be
strong enough to take on the Jap navy."

"As will the army," Marshall said. "But it may mean deferring some
actions in Europe."

"This year," Roosevelt said. "By the end of summer."

"Impossible," King said, and Marshall concurred.

"That is your assignment, gentlemen," the president said. "If you
can't do it, I'll find someone who can. I will not abide having nearly
four hundred thousand Americans under the Japanese heel. I want you
to be creative and clever. I want you to do whatever terrible things you
must to mount a successful operation, but you must succeed. I want
those islands back."

"Yes, sir," they chorused.

King stole a glance at Marshall, who looked away. There was only
the faintest chance that they could muster enough strength to take
back Hawaii. However, they might be able to hurt the Japs, or at least
let them know that America wasn't dead and buried. Yes, thought
King. They could do at least that much.

"One other thing," said Roosevelt. "Just don't give away the secret
to Magic."

■

THIS TIME the terrible silence was broken by the sounds of marching feet and the music of an approaching military band. Incredibly, it sounded like something by Sousa.

The military portion of the surrender was complete. The Japanese occupied Pearl Harbor and other facilities, and the American prisoners of war had been marched off in long, grim lines to camps that were being built near Wheeler and Schofield, in the center of the island.

Now it remained for the Japanese to take possession of the civilian portions of the city.

By the time the parade reached Honolulu's McKinley High School, the crowd of spectators had grown to several thousand people of all ethnic backgrounds. Alexa estimated the Japanese military contingent at several hundred small and grim-faced men with bayoneted rifles on their shoulders. The rifles were long and looked like oversize toys being held by children. But the soldiers weren't children. They were the conquerors. Despite everyone's fears, the Japanese had lived up to at least one part of their bargain: They had not turned their army loose. Discipline had been good, and fears of atrocities were diminishing. So far.

"They don't look so great, do they?" Melissa said softly. "Kind of like houseboys in uniforms."

Alexa agreed that they did not look frightening at all. How had they defeated the American army on Hawaii so completely and with such apparent ease?

An English-speaking officer came forward and announced that this was one of several flag-raising ceremonies that were taking place and would signify the Japanese occupation of the islands. The flagpole in front of the school was empty. The American flag had long since disappeared. The Japanese would not be able to stomp on it and desecrate it.

The Japanese officer stated that newspapers would soon publish a complete list of rules and regulations, but he would summarize some of the more important ones.

First, all adult males over the age of sixteen were to report to special locations for the purpose of forming work gangs to repair the damage caused by the fighting. Failure to show, he added, was punishable by death. Alexa thought this order would help the Japanese round up strays from the military who were trying to hide in the civilian population. She wondered if that included Jake.

Second, all women and children were to be occupied in the growing of food. With that, Alexa agreed heartily. Food shortages were getting worse.

Third, hoarding was punishable by death. Alexa gasped. Did that include the cache of rations under her house?

Fourth, all civilians would bow to Japanese soldiers regardless of rank. There would be instructions on how to bow correctly, but it would be at a fifteen-degree angle and would be held to a count of five. When a man in the front of the crowd laughed, the officer made a quick signal and soldiers dragged him away and, while a woman screamed, ran a bayonet through the meat of each of his thighs.

"Next person who laughs, dies!" the Japanese officer yelled while the man writhed in bloody agony on the ground. With a nod he allowed the man to be taken away by his friends, leaving behind a bright red pool of blood and a throng of people shocked to silence.

At another signal, the band began playing a slow, stately melody. To Alexa's surprise, the Japanese soldiers joined in and sang with enthusiasm and reverence. When it was over the officer told them that this was the Japanese anthem, the *Kimigayo*.

"In the future," the officer concluded, "you will stand and show reverence when you hear this melody as you did for 'The Star-Spangled Banner.' This is your new anthem. You will respect it."

THE CLIMB through the thickly shrubbed and heavily wooded hills of the island of Hawaii was more tedious than arduous, and it took Jake and his men a couple of days to reach their objective.

When they did, a handful of tattered sailors greeted them with enthusiasm and relief. It was obvious they'd never expected to be found by anyone. After checking on those who were lightly wounded, Jake got on with his task.

"Now, where's your boss?" he asked, and several sailors directed him to a path that led up a hill.

"But no one's allowed up there, sir," one young ensign said and stood before him, blocking the path.

Jake grunted something vulgar and pushed past the man. He had gone only a couple of hundred yards when he came to a decrepit shack. Thinking that the situation was totally incongruous, he knocked on the door. After a moment, it opened and a disheveled and exhausted looking man Jake guessed to be in his mid-forties stood before him.

"I told you people to stay away," the man said and stopped as he realized this was somebody new. "Who are you?"

"Raven," Jake said.

"Nevermore," the man said after a moment's hesitation. "Next time we get more original call signs." He smiled and held out his hand. "I'm Commander Joe Rochefort, and you must be the cavalry."

Jake introduced himself and was pleasantly surprised that Rochefort's grip was firm and strong. Maybe he always looked like a frazzled college professor? At least his target now had a name. His orders had denied him even that basic piece of information, and he wondered why.

"We're the infantry, Commander, not the cavalry. We had to walk here, and you'll have to walk out."

"Name's Joe, Jake. I'm not big on rank. Besides, I think we're equal."

Jake grinned. "And we're on land and not a ship. Since I'm in charge of getting you out of here, I'm supposed to command this part of the enterprise."

Rochefort shrugged. "Makes sense. Do me a favor, though, don't come up here unless it's a real emergency."

"Fine."

There was no opportunity for further talk as Jake found that Rochefort's sailors hadn't eaten much in several days. Hawaii may have been paradise in some people's eyes, but food did not grow on trees. It had to be searched for and found.

The hungry sailors ate army rations with a gusto that amused some of the soldiers, who didn't think that anyone, even a sailor, would be dumb enough to like them. Jake made a mental note that their rations were limited and the addition of eight healthy appetites would reduce their limited inventory in a big hurry.

Also, the eight men had only two pistols among them. Jake's twelve had ten brand-new M1 Garands with a number of clips of ammunition each, along with two Thompson submachine guns. Jake had a .45 automatic pistol. When he'd mentioned to Hawkins that it would be good for close-in combat, the sergeant had spat on the ground and said he had no intentions of fighting anyone close in.

"I'm glad you came," Rochefort said after the men were fed. "After the surrender, I was afraid we'd been forgotten."

Jake blinked. He'd stayed off his radio since landing for security purposes. "Then it's official."

"Over and done. Short surrendered everyone on every island, and that includes us. I can't, of course, but what about you?"

Jake wondered about the "of course," but didn't ask. "I never planned on it, so this is a godsend in a way." Then he told Rochefort of his orders that the commander was never to fall into Japanese hands.

"No surprise," Rochefort said solemnly. "Do you wonder why?"

"Of course, but I'm under orders not to ask."

"Then let me clarify something for you. Back on Oahu, I ran a radio listening post. We would sit back and wait for the Japs to talk. With a big enough antenna, we could listen to what they were talking about in Tokyo. Most of the time, they didn't bother to use code for the mundane and routine reports and such, and this gave us excellent insights into the Jap mind.

"When they did use code, we were stumped, but we could still extrapolate much of their intentions from the number and frequency of their messages. We could also determine that, when senders and receivers moved, the Jap fleet was at sea and where it was headed. I've established a crude listening post at the top of that hill, which is why I keep it secured. The receiver's in that abominable shack, and the antenna is strung up to a tree. Other than letting the navy know we're here, we've only listened and not sent. The Japs, by the way, have announced that anyone with shortwave radio equipment will be shot."

Jake nodded politely. The story was interesting but intriguingly incomplete. What Rochefort did for the navy was great, but hardly worth killing him for. Listening to unencoded messages was something that anyone could do, and guessing movements from unreadable coded data was also not that special. Commander Joe Rochefort wasn't telling the truth, the whole truth, and nothing but the truth.

CHAPTER 11

Admiral Raymond Spruance glanced up at the interruption and smiled tolerantly. "Gentlemen, now that we are all here, we can begin."

Lieutenant Jamie Priest winced and took a seat at the end of the long table. Even though Spruance seemed to be a pretty easygoing and regular guy, it did not behoove junior officers to piss off admirals by being late for meetings, no matter what the reason.

Nor was Spruance the only admiral at this meeting. Rear Admiral Charles A. Lockwood was present. Lockwood commanded the American submarine forces in the Pacific, and his presence at the meeting was a surprise to Jamie as he was supposed to be in Australia. Lockwood, a belligerent man on the best of days, looked angry and glared at Jamie, probably because Jamie didn't wear the insignia of a submarine officer.

Next in rank was a Captain Winters, and Jamie knew nothing about him. Nor did he know about a Lieutenant Fargo, who wore the badge of a submariner and who looked at Jamie with an expression that asked: Why the hell are we all here? A young but thin and plain-looking civilian woman with glasses was present to take notes.

"Gentlemen," Spruance began, "this is an informal meeting to discuss the situation with our submarines and our torpedoes. Our discussions will be preliminary, anecdotal, and nonscientific. All of you are here because you have had unique experiences that may help shed some light on the problem. For that reason, I want this discussion to be free from any concerns about rank."

Jamie wondered just how freely junior officers could actually speak in front of seniors. Unfortunately, he felt he was going to find out fairly shortly.

Spruance continued. "Admiral Lockwood is here because he commands our subs. Captain Winters is here because, as an engineer with the Bureau of Ordnance, he helped design and build the Mark 14 torpedo. Lieutenant Fargo is here because his sub, the *Monkfish,* unsuccessfully used Mark 14s to attack a Jap destroyer with results that were almost tragic. Lieutenant Priest is here because, as an officer on the *Pennsylvania,* he saw the other side of the coin. That is, he saw Japanese torpedoes at work, and there are few around who can lay claim to that dubious honor."

Jamie flushed as the others looked at him with expressions ranging from surprise to respect. Even Lockwood stopped glaring at him.

"Lieutenant Priest is now a member of our staff," Spruance added, and Jamie noticed that the young woman had looked up from her reading glasses and smiled tentatively at him. The smile made her look far more attractive than he'd first thought.

The mention of Japanese torpedoes brought forth several frank comments. Spruance, Lockwood, and Winters all admitted that at first they had doubted the range and speed of the Jap torpedoes and felt that the *Pennsylvania* and her escorts had been hit by an enemy sub that had actually been much closer than the Japanese surface ships. Jamie admitted he'd had his doubts as well.

"But now we know better," Spruance said. "The Japs have a torpedo they fire from surface vessels. It's called the 'Long Lance' and with good reason. It has a range of more than ten miles compared with the Mark 14's two and a quarter, and leaves no wake, which means it's oxygen-powered. I might add that it has a helluva lot greater hitting power than ours as well."

"It also works," Lockwood snapped, which earned him a glare from Winters. "There's a smaller version for their subs that is also better than the Mark 14."

Spruance gestured for peace. "We know we have a problem. What Admiral King, Admiral Nimitz, and I want is a solution, or at least the beginning of a solution. Gentlemen, there are very few submarine targets in the Atlantic; therefore the bulk of our torpedo targets will be here in the Pacific. This is our problem, and we must move to solve it."

Spruance reprised the situation as he understood it. Torpedoes were being fired at Japanese shipping, but many of them were either malfunctioning or missing. No one was entirely certain which. He then invited Captain Winters to describe the torpedo.

Winters had the no-nonsense look of an engineer, and he also seemed put out that the worth of the Mark 14 torpedo was being questioned. "We built the best torpedo in the world," he said firmly.

"At least until the Japs showed up with theirs," Lockwood interjected.

Less subjectively, Winters went on to describe the Mark 14. It had a magnetic trigger that was designed to explode when it was affected by the earth's magnetic field as a ship passed overhead. The torpedoes were to be set at depths that would ensure this would occur. When it worked, the explosion would break a ship's keel and sink her more efficiently than a contact torpedo.

The Mark 14 could also be used as an impact torpedo. It had a sophisticated detonator that was supposed to explode the torpedo when it hit an enemy's hull.

Problem was, as Admiral Lockwood growled, it didn't work out that way. He turned the floor over to Lieutenant Fargo, who described the *Monkfish*'s attack on the Japanese destroyer.

"Our new commanding officer, Commander Griddle, was an experienced submariner. The targeting was good, but not one of our four torpedoes hit. As directed, they were all set to run under a target, and we believe they did. But not one exploded."

Winters shook his head in disbelief. "First of all, four is far too many for one target. You just cannot fire torpedoes so wastefully. Second, you must have done something wrong. I would like to talk to Mr. Griddle."

"He's in a San Francisco hospital," Fargo said stiffly. "He lost one eye during the depth charge attack that took place right after we missed, and may lose the other. As to what we did, I double-checked everything that Commander Griddle ordered, and while he was doing it. I even saw the destroyer through the periscope and confirmed range, course, and targeting plot. There were no mistakes. The torpedoes were set to detonate at the proper depth and they didn't do it."

"And this is just one incident out of many," Lockwood said. "There are reports like this coming from all over the place."

"I can only add," Winters said, "that the torpedoes should be exploding. We've checked the ones remaining on the *Monkfish,* and there's nothing wrong with them. Is it possible, Admiral Lockwood, either that your officers are not following regulations in the heat of battle or they don't know enough about engineering?"

Fargo bristled. "Sir, we followed all directions. I would also add that, as a Naval Academy graduate, I have a damned solid knowledge of engineering."

Lockwood leaned forward and glowered at Winters. "Look, I know everyone at BuOrd thinks my boys are a bunch of undisciplined, raggedy-assed pirates, but that's not so! They're brave, yes, even reckless, but they're not stupid. Every one of them wants to make a kill and get his ass home in one piece."

Jamie turned to see how the woman was taking the dialogue. She looked up at him, and he saw sadness in her eyes.

"We're getting nowhere," Spruance said with a touch of exasperation.

Now, Jamie thought. "Sir, may I ask a question of Captain Winters?"

"Of course."

"Captain Winters, I was late for this meeting because of a phone call I got from a friend. He too worked on the Mark 14 and said something that disturbed me. Sir, was the Mark 14 ever live-fired with a warhead at a target?"

Winters nodded. "I know where you're coming from, son. The Mark 14 was thoroughly tested."

Jamie persisted. "With respect, sir, that isn't what I asked. Was a live torpedo ever fired at a target ship, and, if so, what were the results?"

"I don't want to bore you with the scientific details, but rest assured that the Mark 14 was thoroughly tested."

Spruance stepped in, his curiosity piqued by Winters's evasion. "Captain, answer the young man's question. Yes or no?"

"To the best of my knowledge, perhaps once. Perhaps not at all."

There were gasps of surprise, and Jamie thought that Lockwood's jaw was going to hit the table as it dropped.

"Why not?" Spruance asked.

"Admiral, the Mark 14 is a very sophisticated and complex weapon. That translates into expensive. Each one of them costs ten thousand dollars, which is why I'm upset that four were fired at one small target. It's unnecessary. To further answer your question, test firing was done with dummy warheads at targets in large pools. That way the torpedo could be recovered and used again. The torpedoes passed under dummy hulls and would have exploded had they contained warheads."

"Sweet Jesus," Lockwood said in disbelief. "You mean that no one ever saw one of these bastards explode on a target?"

"If you put it that way, that's true. However, it was the opinion of BuOrd that test firing would be both expensive and redundant. The torpedo works."

"Except when it doesn't," Lieutenant Fargo said with ill-concealed disbelief.

Spruance called for silence. "All right, here's what we're going to do. We'll hold live-fire testing here and now."

"I protest," said Winters.

"Noted. Now, we have the *Monkfish* in port and she has a dozen Mark 14s left. Captain Winters, you will again confirm that the torpedoes are in working order and you will oversee their being fired at targets."

Winters nodded sullenly.

"Lieutenant Priest, your job is to organize the shoot. Find a couple of relics we can tow out to sea and fire at, along with ships and planes for observation. I don't think it'll be necessary to fire all twelve of Lieutenant Fargo's expensive torpedoes. Four strikes me as sufficient."

"I'd like to fire a couple more to test the impact trigger," Lockwood requested. "Remember, it doesn't work too well either. Personally, I think it's just too damned fragile."

It looked like Winters was about to object, but then he thought better of it. His expression said he would get his day in court and was confident he'd be vindicated.

Spruance adjourned the meeting. As the group left the room, Jamie mentally began to organize his task. He was pondering when he felt a light tug on his sleeve. It was the stenographer. She was shorter than Jamie, thin, maybe an inch over five feet, and in her early twenties. "Hi. Sir, I'm Sue Dunnigan, and Admiral Spruance thought I might be able to help you with the clerical work on your project."

"Great," Jamie said with a grin that surprised him.

■

THE PROCESS of informing California that he'd found Nevermore, also known as Commander Joe Rochefort, was elegant and simple. As directed, at eight in the evening Hawaii time, Jake radioed a single letter of the alphabet. It was *A,* which meant that Rochefort had been found and was well. Other letters meant different things. *B* would have meant that Jake and his soldiers were still looking, and *C* that they hadn't a clue as to where Nevermore was. Still other letters would have indicated that Rochefort was injured and whether he could travel, while the letter *X* said he was dead.

P was the most dreaded signal. It meant that Joe Rochefort was in Japanese hands.

The one-letter signal was sent three times, at one-minute intervals. Jake wondered what would happen if the soldier entrusted to listening had gone to the can at that exact moment. He would know in just under two days, when he would receive an alphanumeric response that would give him further directions.

As a precaution, Jake had moved the radio several miles from what they now referred to as their base camp when he transmitted. It was considered extremely unlikely that the Japanese would be able to pick up such a quick message, and even less likely that they would be able to act on it, but no one wanted to take chances. They would, however, wait at the base camp for the return transmission as receiving the message was a passive action. The station in California could be broadcasting to the moon for all the Japanese would know.

Rochefort and his assistant, Holmes, spent most of their time up at his shack, listening, or doing whatever they did, and this left Jake time to work with his little army. He also interrogated the other sailors as to whether or not they were the only survivors of the sinking of the *St. Louis.* The cruiser could have had a complement of over a thousand men, and it seemed highly unlikely that only these eight had been spared.

Jake was able to confirm that the sinking had taken place out of sight of land, and that many hundreds had taken to lifeboats. It could be presumed that others had made land safely, but the sailors told Jake that Rochefort had forbidden them to try to search their fellow crewmen out or make contact with them.

They also mentioned that they didn't know Rochefort was even on the *St. Louis* until he came ashore with them, and that they still didn't know who the hell he was.

Good, Jake thought. The fewer who knew, the better.

Forty-seven hours after sending the message that all was well, they received the response. The first two digits were numeric and represented the number of days in the future when the pickup would be made. The next four digits were the time, and the final two were the location. The value of three was subtracted from each number or letter to give the true message.

"Jesus, Colonel"—Hawkins laughed—"they sure do make something complicated when given half a chance, don't they?"

"I don't know about you, Sergeant, but I kind of like it that way. The more careful they are, the more likely we are to pull this off."

"Ah, sir. When the naval people leave, will you be going with them?"

Jake had been cleaning his rifle and squinted down the barrel. The question made him think of Alexa and so many others he knew. At least Alexa was likely safe, but the army people were in prison camps. It would be an easy call to say, yeah, he was going with Rochefort, and back to a land of hot coffee, doughnuts, warm beds, and clean uniforms, but somehow it wasn't all that easy.

"No, I think I'll stay here. The navy'll be back sooner or later, and they'll need some army help to get untracked."

Hawkins grinned. "Thought you were going to do that. We've been talking it over, and we'd like to stay with you. Maybe we can really start our own little army, sir."

Jake suddenly found it difficult to talk and nodded his thanks. Hawkins and his men were willing to follow him and put their lives in his hands. It was overwhelming and reminded him just what he found good about being in the military. Now all he had to do was make sure their efforts and risks weren't wasted.

TOYOZA KAGA WASN'T SURPRISED when he was summoned to meet with the already infamous Colonel Omori. As one of the remaining important Japanese whose loyalty might lie with Tokyo, he considered the meeting almost inevitable.

They met in Omori's headquarters at Schofield, and the colonel came right to the point. "We are forming a provisional government, and you will be an informal part of it."

Kaga bowed. "I'm honored." He did not miss the fact that he had been ordered to serve and not asked to volunteer.

Omori waved at a stack of papers. "One of my tasks here is to go over the records held by the American military and the FBI. They make for interesting reading. In some quarters you would be considered undesirable and disreputable, but you are successful and discreet as well as pragmatic. It is also true that you have a son in the service of Japan. You must be very proud of him."

"Very much so," Kaga replied.

"I believe I can use you as a liaison between myself and the remainder of the Japanese community, who, I am sad to say, have not entirely welcomed us. This, while not completely surprising, is perplexing and disappointing."

"Give them time, Colonel. They are terribly confused. Many of them have family on the American mainland, as well as back on the Home Islands, and some even have sons in the American military. Others are waiting and wondering when there will be an official annexation of Hawaii as a province of Japan."

Omori looked surprised. "That will happen soon. Haven't we made it perfectly clear?"

"Forgive me, Colonel, but most people, myself included, recognize your sincerity but do not believe you are in a position to speak for Tokyo. In short, we are afraid of supporting Japan and then being bargained back to the United States, where we will be subject to American justice that will be extremely harsh."

Omori glared at him as he recognized both the truth of what Kaga was saying and the fact that he had said it. Such an argumentative response in Japan would have merited at least a sharp slap across the face. Here it simply pointed out the differences between the Japanese of the Home Islands and the Japanese of Hawaii.

"Then we will be patient," Omori finally said and dismissed Kaga.

As Kaga left, he had his driver pass the crude prison camps where thousands of American soldiers lived almost without shelter. Already they looked gaunt from lack of food and sunburned from exposure. Then, as he drove back to Honolulu, he passed long columns of men, American civilians, who were going to work assignments. Most would work as laborers in grueling circumstances.

Kaga leaned back in his seat and pondered. The distribution of wealth was in its early stages, but what was going to occur was obvious. All those with white skin were being deprived of their jobs and livelihoods, and put to work as a heavy labor force. The hard work, coupled with short rations, was already taking its toll, and many of the workers in the columns looked like they were scarcely able to shuffle along. Omori didn't seem to care if civilians under his jurisdiction died, and Kaga wondered if that was part of a plan. He would have to discuss this with some of his closest and most trustworthy friends.

Closer to the city, life was far less brutal. There, almost every field and vacant spot of land had been turned into a garden, and the crops were starting to come in. Perhaps that, he thought, would alleviate most of the now pervasive hunger problem. Kaga had to admit that the Japanese idea of turning those parts of Oahu that had been sugar or pineapple plantations into rice paddies was potentially a good one. The work was backbreaking, but the Japanese government insisted that younger, stronger American women work at least two days each week in the paddies.

He passed one such project and ordered his driver to slow down. Close to a hundred American women were knee-deep in brown water. They wore either shorts or skirts with the hems tucked up into their waists, and were hunched over as they did something to the little plants that peeked out of the muddy water. That had been the first problem to be solved—the retention of water. Without any lakes or rivers of consequence, Hawaiian agriculture was dependent on the abundant rainfall and the water that percolated just below the volcanic surface of the land.

Kaga told the driver to stop. One of the workers looked familiar. It was the woman that Jake Novacek had asked him to look out for, Alexa Sanderson. At least, Kaga thought grimly, she was alive and healthy.

ALEXA STRAIGHTENED UP and bent backward to ease the pain in her lower back. A Japanese soldier who was overseeing the group yelled at her, and she went back to work without any comment or change of expression.

Beside her, Melissa groaned. "God, I hate this," she whispered.

The soldiers frowned on too much conversation, although this day's guard seemed not to care very much. His yelling at Alexa appeared to be more to keep his sergeant happy than out of any degree of nastiness. Alexa thought the Jap soldier looked more like a lost kid than a terrible enemy.

"I only hope we get to eat some of this," Melissa added. "I'm really getting worried about Junior."

Melissa had left her son with an older woman in the neighborhood while she went out to work. As a woman with a small child, she might have been exempt from the work gangs, but the field workers were also given additional food because of their strenuous tasks. This meant she had more for Jerry Junior.

Alexa agreed silently. At least the women were being given enough food to get by, while the men were fed less than minimal rations. She'd heard someplace that one of the Japanese strategies was to keep the men so weak that they wouldn't be able to think of rebelling or sabotage. From the looks on the men's faces, it was working and after only an extremely brief time.

"Of course," Melissa whispered and giggled, "I could always put out for that guard. He seems to be enjoying our legs and what he can see of our boobs when we bend over. I really think he likes his women all sweaty and covered with mud."

"I heard he has the clap," Alexa said sweetly. "But go ahead if you must."

She then wondered how many women already were trading sex for favors from the Japs. It was almost inevitable. For a woman, sex might be the only weapon or item of value she had left. Alexa wondered if Melissa would trade sexual favors for food for her son and decided that, under the circumstances, she probably would. Then she wondered whether she would do the same to prevent starvation or physical harm. The thought repelled her, but she could not deny the likelihood. Jake had said survive, and survive at all costs.

The Japanese strategy seemed to be to strip all semblance of dignity and respect from their civilian prisoners. And that, Alexa realized, was exactly what they were. The Japanese were not an occupying force that permitted the civilian world to function as before. No, they were restructuring the entire economy and social fabric of the islands.

The thought occurred to her that aching muscles from planting rice might someday be the least of her worries.

•

THE GENTLEMAN from the Portuguese embassy, Rodrigo Salazar, was a little nervous. He was a low-ranking functionary and had never been in the White House, much less met President Roosevelt.

"Please understand," Salazar said in correct but halting English, "my country and I are merely the messengers in this unfortunate situation."

By early 1942, Portugal was one of a diminishing number of neutral nations left among the major powers. In Europe, the others were Switzerland, Spain, Ireland, and Sweden. To a large extent, their neutrality was a fiction. Portugal was unofficially with the Allies, while the other nations were more or less in the Axis camp. Some of this was geographic pragmatism. Switzerland and Sweden bordered Axis powers, while the Spanish government had been supported by Hitler in their civil war and had a long land border with Nazi-dominated France.

Ireland, of course, hated anything British and was only now coming to grips with the fact that the United States, the land where so many of her sons and daughters had emigrated, was allied with Great Britain, whom she despised.

Portugal, facing westward on the Atlantic, and thoroughly distrusting neighboring Spain, leaned toward the United States. Portugal also had diplomatic ties with Tokyo, which made her useful for the unofficial exchange of messages.

In the New World, most of the nations of Latin America were in the Allied camp, while the larger nations of South America—Brazil, Argentina, Chile, and Peru—still straddled the fence.

"This is amazing," Roosevelt said as he handed the message to his secretary of state, Cordell Hull. "First they conquer Hawaii and now the Japs expect us to provide food for the Hawaiians."

"It confronts a hard reality," Hull said. "The islands do not grow enough food to support their population, and the only way to prevent starvation is to permit ships to bring food. Japan does not have surplus food, so that leaves us. We may have instituted rationing and be feeding other nations, but we will always have food for our own people."

"The Japanese say it will only be for a short while," Salazar said. "They are converting the islands into a self-sustaining agricultural economy, and this process should be completed within a few months.

In the meantime, they require a convoy of food each month to feed Americans in Hawaii."

"And none of this good food will reach their army, will it?" Hull asked sarcastically and then apologized when he saw the discomfort on Salazar's face. "Of course it will, and please forgive me. I did forget that you are the messenger and not the message."

Salazar grinned. "At least you will not have me beheaded."

"Not immediately," Roosevelt said. "How many ships do we need each month?"

Salazar checked his notes. "It depends on the size of the vessel. Between twenty-five and fifty. You do understand that the Japanese will not permit American flagged ships to enter Hawaiian waters, do you not? They understand that declarations of war on them by some of the South and Latin American countries are without substance and will accept ships flying those flags."

"Ducky," Hull said with uncharacteristic candor.

"We accept," Roosevelt said. "I will not permit Americans to starve if there is any way I can prevent it."

After a moment's polite conversation, Salazar departed.

"I wish to see King and Marshall," Roosevelt said. "Perhaps there's something useful they can make of this."

Hull demurred. "The Japs'll be watching the convoy like hawks. I'm sure they are familiar with the legend of the Trojan horse."

Roosevelt started to make a pair of martinis. "What we do and how we do it are the military's problem. I do think, however, that they could be looking so hard for a Trojan horse that they might miss something more obvious, such as submarines landing men and supplies."

The thought pleased him, and he began to chuckle.

·

CHAPTER 12

Staff Sergeant Charley Finch was just about the only American who was delighted by the Japanese attack on December 7. Charley was a supply sergeant who had access to the vast warehouses that housed the army's store of supplies.

At thirty-eight, short and overweight, Charley had been preparing for his retirement from the army by padding his nest. He had sold substantial amounts of material and army equipment to international dealers at a tenth of its worth. Even with this fragment of value, he saw thousands of dollars coming in, which he cabled to an account at the Bank of America in San Francisco. It was, he thought, foolproof.

At least it was until he got greedy and sold stuff to some local people who got stupid and then got caught, at which point he began to sweat bullets. The local crooks' possession of military goods had brought in the FBI and, if it hadn't been for the Japanese attack, would have seen him arrested when they traced it back. As it was, he'd been tipped off, and, while the bombs were fortuitously falling, he'd set fire to a couple of warehouses, figuring that "bomb damage" would account for any shortages.

He'd been right, and the FBI forgot about trivial matters like missing equipment and went chasing more important targets.

What he hadn't counted on was being thrown into a POW camp. The conditions were brutal, the food was totally inadequate, and the guards were sadists who took great delight in beating prisoners to bloody pulps for the most trivial of reasons. They thought it was fun for one guard to direct a prisoner to perform one task while another would come along a few seconds later and change the order. Then the first guard would brutally beat the hapless prisoner for not carrying out the original assignment. If the prisoner tried to protest or did anything other than stand and take it, the beating got even more severe. Already, several prisoners had been beaten to death. Everyone knew it was a sadistic game the guards played, but there was nothing anyone could do about it.

So far, Charley had not been caught in it, but he figured his luck had run out when a pair of guards called him by name and dragged him out of the camp, so terrified that he could barely stand up. It'd happened to a lot of soldiers; not all of them had returned, and many of those who did come back had been beaten pretty badly.

Charley was dumped in the back of a truck and forced to lie on his face while he was driven a short ways. He knew where he was going— the *kempetei* headquarters.

He sat for several hours on a hard stool while he sweated and worried. Finally, two new guards grabbed him and dragged him into an office where he confronted a Japanese officer. His knees weakened and he almost fell as he recognized the officer. It was Colonel Omori, the head of the *kempetei* and a man whom others described as Satan himself. Beside him stood Satan's helper, Lieutenant Goto.

"Sergeant Finch," Omori said, "you are a crook, a liar, a thief, and a coward. Do you know what we do in Japan with people like you? We execute them, that's what."

Finch moaned in terror, and Omori continued. "The FBI destroyed most of its more important files before we took over. Yours they didn't consider important. It's ironic, isn't it? Had we not attacked, you would have been in an American prison. Now you're in a Japanese one."

Finch did not respond. He was too frightened.

"Do you like prison, Sergeant Finch? Are the guards treating you kindly enough? Perhaps a couple will come and visit you tonight."

"I'm fine, sir," he stammered.

"Would you like to leave the camp and live in comfort?"

Charley turned wary. What was the Jap offering?

Omori continued. "Comfort means good food, clean quarters, liquor, and even sex. Wouldn't you like to spend the rest of the war regaining your weight and fucking women?"

Now Finch was intrigued. "Yes, sir."

"Good. I want information from your camp. We know there's a radio in there, perhaps more than one, and we know there's a camp hierarchy that is a potential source of resistance. Also, the FBI agents in Honolulu have disappeared. We think they are disguising themselves as prisoners, and we would like very much to talk to them."

Charley nodded. He knew this was something he could not refuse to do. The comment about the guards' conduct meant that his denial would be his death warrant. The guards would stomp him into the ground of the camp.

"We will devise a way for you not to get caught. For instance, we will take you out each day and return you each night to the camp, at least for the short term. Your story will be that you are inventorying the contents of several warehouses for us, and that we've given you the choice of doing it or being killed. Your friends will understand.

"Once you've given us the information, you will be taken from the camp and housed separately for the duration of the war."

Charley liked the idea. There were risks, like how would he explain it away later, but later might just be a long ways in the future. He would cross that bridge when later actually arrived.

Omori opened a drawer and pulled out a pair of pliers. "These belong to Lieutenant Goto. Do you know what he does with them?"

"No, sir." All of a sudden Charley felt that events had taken a wrong turn.

"The lieutenant likes to use the pliers to make people cooperate. First, he uses them to pull out fingernails and toenails, and then to crush fingers and toes, knuckle by knuckle and joint by joint. When that is done, he'll either pull out a person's teeth or use the pieces as a hammer to break the teeth off just below the gum. I understand the pain is excruciating."

Charley was sweating again, and he had the sudden urge to urinate.

Omori looked fondly at the pliers and smiled at Goto, who just stared at Charley as if he were a lower form of life. "Then the lieutenant likes to use them to crush a person's testicles and nose. Maybe he'll just put loose folds of skin in them and squeeze with all his strength until the ends meet. It all proves that interrogation can be done quite effectively and with inexpensive and unexpected tools." Omori smiled. "Do you know why I'm telling you this?"

Charley understood. "So I'll know what'll happen to me if I double-cross you."

Omori beamed. "Excellent."

Lieutenant Goto signaled, and two guards suddenly pinned Charley's left hand to Omori's desk. Goto took the pliers and smoothly yanked out the nail from the little finger. He waved the little piece of Charley as a trophy. Then, as Charley was gasping with pain and shock, Goto crushed the first knuckle of the same finger with the pliers.

The guards released Charley, who howled and writhed on the floor. "Why?" he groaned as he clasped his damaged hand. "I said I'd cooperate."

"I know," Omori said, looking down on him. "This was to guarantee it. The pain you've just felt will be a thousand times greater if you fail me. Also, you have now been tortured by the Japanese for insolence and failure to cooperate fully. This means you can return to the camp as a hero. The medics there will be able to treat your wounds, and you will now be trusted by those in charge."

Charley let the guards help him up. The pain was almost controllable, although his finger throbbed like it was on fire. Omori was right on both counts. The pain was an investment. Hell, if he survived, and he had every intention of doing so, he'd get a Purple Heart for this, maybe even some other medal. And he knew damned well that he wasn't going to cross Omori for anything.

"AMAZING," Jake said as he looked at the slender silhouette of the sub offshore. "You navy guys can get a sub across the Pacific and right up to the coast of Hawaii with more precision than a bus arriving at a destination in a city."

"No traffic," Rochefort said.

The transfer had so far gone off without a hitch. Jake had figured it would take three days to reach the rendezvous point, so he allowed four. That gave them more than enough time to travel and to reconnoiter on arrival to ensure there were no Japs in the area. Japanese presence would have been very unlikely, as the only Japanese military on Hawaii was a very small contingent in Hilo.

The sub surfaced at three in the morning, a time chosen because it was dark and just about everyone who might see it would be asleep. Again, this was a small chance, as the area was desolate and almost uninhabited.

The rafts arrived with additional supplies for Jake and his band, and were filled with the men who were leaving Hawaii. There was a slight change in the passenger list; two of Jake's men had decided they really didn't want to spend the war as guerrillas on Hawaii, and Jake had permitted them to leave. Volunteers were all he wanted. The departing two were offset by the two marines from the *St. Louis* who did want to stay. Rochefort didn't have a problem with that, and Jake figured that he was a little ahead with the trade-off.

Finally, Rochefort waded out to the last raft, which bobbed in knee-deep water. "Jake, I truly appreciate everything you've done, and, good God, I wish you the best of luck," he said.

Jake and the commander shook hands warmly. "I'll see you someday in California," Jake said.

"God willing."

"Joe, I want you to do me a favor. Here's a letter I've written, with some thoughts I've put down. After the sub's been under way for a couple of hours, please open it and read it, but not before. Will you do that?"

Rochefort was a little puzzled but agreed to Jake's request. He settled into the raft and was taken out to the looming bulk of the submarine. She was the *Cachalot* and had been present at Pearl Harbor during the attack.

Like all subs, the *Cachalot* was small and cramped, and stank of oil, sweat, urine, and stale air. Rochefort soon found that his quarters was a folding bunk that he was expected to share with at least one other officer. It was going to be a miserable voyage, but at least he was headed to safety.

Even if he had wanted to read Jake's letter right away, he wouldn't have been able to as he spent nearly half a day helping the sub's skipper get everyone and everything squared away.

When he finally got a moment's rest, he recalled the letter and unsealed it. As he began to read, his expression changed from anticipation to astonishment.

When he was through, he folded it carefully and put it in his pocket. "Jake, you are a son of a bitch," he muttered with a mixture of anger and admiration. Then finally he laughed. "Yeah, a real, no-good, rotten son of a bitch."

ADMIRAL SPRUANCE LOOKED through the window of the PBY at the panorama below. A sizable fleet was stationed around the target area. "Congratulations, Lieutenant Priest. I gave you virtually unlimited authority, and I see you exceeded it. Are there any ships in the navy not involved in this experiment?"

Jamie grinned. "I presumed you wanted this done right, sir."

In the couple of days since the meeting, Jamie had been almost frantically busy, and, if it hadn't been for Sue Dunnigan's help and connections, he might not have completed the assignment in the time allotted.

First, he had to acquire target ships. By going through local registries, Sue was able to find a couple of ancient freighters that hadn't gone anywhere in a couple of years because their engines were completely shot. These had been towed to the target area and anchored.

Then it was necessary to have a number of destroyers stationed in the area to keep the curious away and to make sure that errant torpedoes didn't sink a friendly ship. A more distant screen of destroyers and light cruisers was employed to keep out any possible Japanese submarines. None had ventured as far south as San Diego, but there was always the first time.

After that, the rules of the test were developed. It was decided that the *Monkfish* would fire two torpedoes at the first ship while submerged and fire the second pair at the remaining ship while on the surface. The *Monkfish* had fired at the Japanese destroyer while submerged, but other attacks and misfires by other boats had occurred both on the surface and while submerged. From anecdotal evidence, it seemed to make no difference whether the sub was submerged or not—the torpedoes just weren't exploding.

All four torpedoes would be fired at a range of a thousand yards. If either target ship remained, Lieutenant Fargo of the *Monkfish* had permission to try impact shooting with an additional two torpedoes.

Captain Winters was confident that both ships would be sunk forthwith. "Hell," he'd said with a laugh. "Those tubs are so rusty a near miss'd make them fall apart."

With that Jamie agreed. Winters was so certain of his torpedoes that he bet a dinner in town with Fargo and Jamie. Jamie didn't begrudge him his happiness. He was a scientist and engineer, and looked forward to the results of an experiment that, while expensive, would get people off his back. In the couple of days since the meeting, Jamie had found Winters to be sincere and hardworking, although more than a little stubborn about his beloved torpedoes.

As an added bonus, an experimental sonar system had been mounted on one of the destroyers. It was hoped that it had been fine-tuned enough to hear the torpedoes in the water and ascertain what occurred when they were fired. Sonar could determine the direction and distance of an object but not its depth. Even so, it would be invaluable if the targets were missed. At a thousand yards on a sunny day and with a calm sea, Captain Winters was confident his torpedoes would hit.

"Where's Winters?" Spruance asked. Admiral Lockwood was on one of the destroyers, while Sue Dunnigan was onshore.

"He's on the sub, sir, managing things. Uh, and that's why we're making the first shots submerged. He's claustrophobic, and we want to get the boat up as quickly as possible."

Spruance stifled a smile. "Then let's get on with it."

Jamie confirmed that all was in readiness, then spoke into the radio. "Captain Winters, the admiral wishes you to commence when you are ready."

Almost immediately, the *Monkfish* reported a torpedo fired. Seconds later, the sonar operators said they heard it running in the water.

Anxiously, Spruance and Jamie counted down until time of impact. Nothing.

"Sonar," Jamie called. "What do you hear?"

"Torpedo is still running and the sound is fading. It's like she's getting farther away."

Okay, Jamie thought. One malfunction. An angry Winters said he was firing the second, and sonar again picked it up. A little later, the results were the same. No hit and the torpedo continued on.

"Surfacing," radioed an obviously shaken Winters, and, seconds later, the sub emerged from the sea and took up station to fire at the second hulk.

From the PBY, they could see the torpedoes leave the tubes and head directly for the target before they submerged to run under it. Sonar reported them running loud and true and, again, nothing. No hits and the torpedoes continued on, out into the ocean. Jamie turned toward Spruance, who looked perturbed.

"Sir," came Fargo's voice on the radio, "we wish to fire two impact-trigger torpedoes with the normal mechanism and two with triggers we've made ourselves."

"Go ahead," Spruance said and then muttered under his breath, "Can't hurt."

The first impact torpedo hit the target ship and exploded. This brought relieved cheers from everyone on the plane. The target immediately began to settle in the water. The second torpedo arrived a moment later and, to the astonishment of everyone, clearly bounced off the crippled target without exploding.

"Unbelievable," said Spruance.

The *Monkfish* then shifted and quickly fired two more torpedoes at the remaining target ship. These, Fargo reminded them, had had their triggers altered by one of the sub's mechanics. Both hit and exploded, sending the rusty hulk to the bottom in a minute.

There was nothing more to be seen, and the PBY headed back to shore.

"Well," said Spruance. "We've raised questions and possibly resolved some of them. We'll tell Admiral Lockwood that his subs are to override the hull-detecting trigger mechanism and go impact only." Then he recalled that only one of the first two impact triggers had worked. "I will strongly suggest that our people see just what the *Monk*'s people did to make their triggers work better than the original ones and copy it."

Unsaid was the fact that it would take time, maybe months, for all the changes to be made. Many American subs were at sea and wouldn't even know about the changes until they returned to port. All present hoped they *would* return to port and wouldn't be sunk by angry Japanese warships after failed attacks with the flawed Mark 14s.

Unsaid too was the fact that this was a patch, not a solution. At least, Spruance thought ruefully, they could now begin to fight back more effectively.

The admiral reached over and clasped Jamie on the shoulder. "Good job, Lieutenant. That was a well-designed test."

Jamie flushed. "Thank you, sir. Miss Dunnigan did a lot of the work for me."

Spruance laughed. "I'm not surprised. When the Congress gets

around to permitting women to enlist, she'll be one of the first officers. She's a navy brat. Her father served with me back on the *Mississippi*. He was a chief petty officer and a fountain of knowledge. He
was killed on the *Arizona*, you know."

Jamie hadn't known that. There hadn't been enough time to find
out much at all about her, except that she was pleasant, intelligent, and
sometimes very intense. Now he knew why. Jamie quietly resolved to
find out more about her. While far from a raving beauty, she was
growing on him.

SERGEANT HAWKINS SIGHTED his rifle and pretended to squeeze
the trigger at the distant but clearly visible target. "Bang," he said.

"One dead Jap," Jake said. "Good shooting."

"Sir, I could nail him if you'd let me."

"Sure, and you'd get us all killed."

The Japanese officer was about three hundred yards away. Hawkins
was a crack shot and could have dropped him easily.

However, the Japanese officer was the leader of a column of infantry that looked about platoon strength. That meant the Americans
hidden on the hill overlooking the Japanese were outnumbered three
or four to one. However tempting it might be, they were not going to
give away their position, even their existence, to a Japanese patrol who
had no idea they were being watched.

"You'll get your turn," Jake said.

These were the first Japanese the small group of Americans had
seen outside Hilo, and it looked like they were nothing more than a
probe to see what lay in the interior of the island. Half an hour earlier,
four trucks, a staff car, and the platoon had driven up and parked at the
intersection of two dirt roads. From the casual way they moved about,
it appeared that they didn't expect to find anything exciting. Just a
drive in the country.

Jake was grateful the hills in the area were so thickly covered by
shrubs and low, twisting trees. His small army could hide within feet
of the Japanese and wouldn't be seen unless a Jap was lucky enough to
stumble over them. Since the Japs were road bound, this was highly
unlikely.

It was tempting to kill one or two Japs and then retire into the boondocks, but Jake nixed the thought. It was not yet time to let anyone know they existed.

"More Japs," Private Dunbar whispered. Another column of trucks began to emerge from a valley about a half-mile away. All the more reason not to draw attention. The new column, also four trucks and a car, drew up to the first group and stopped. Now their numerical disadvantage had doubled.

"Gang's all here," one of Jake's men commented.

"Oh, shit," Hawkins snarled. "They've got prisoners."

A half dozen men in blue denim had been thrown from the back of one of the trucks. They clustered together on the ground while the Japs circled them. The Americans on the hill could hear distant laughter.

"Sailors," said one of the marines. "Probably some of our guys from the *St. Louis*. And there's not a damned thing we can do to help them, is there, Colonel?"

"That's right, not a damned thing," Jake said grimly.

"Now what the hell?" Hawkins muttered.

The American prisoners had been pushed behind one of the trucks. Their hands had been tied in front of them and then to the truck. They stood there, a pathetic little group, while the rest of the Japs loaded up in their vehicles.

"Bastards are gonna make them walk to Hilo," said Dunbar.

"I don't like this," Jake whispered. His stomach tightened. Something terrible was about to happen.

The vehicles started up and began to move slowly down the road. It was straight for about a mile, and Jake could see everything as it unfolded. At first, the prisoners were able to keep pace with the slowly moving truck, but then the truck speeded up and they had to try to run. The sailors were doubtless weak from wounds and hunger, and they hadn't gone more than a few yards at a trotting speed before one of them stumbled and fell. It was like a bowling ball hitting pins. First one man fell, then the others dropped until they were all being dragged by their bound hands along the dirt road.

"Stop, you motherfuckers!" screamed Hawkins.

Instead, the Japanese vehicle continued to accelerate. The six men bounced along the road like children's toys in a sickening dance of bloody death. Whatever screams they made were drowned out by the sound of the trucks and the distance involved. Jake wondered if the sailors were all dying in stunned silence.

A few moments later, the Jap column and its hideous cargo were out of sight. Jake and his men stood in silence. Several were crying in anger and frustration, and Jake felt tears on his own cheeks. The Japs would pay for this.

"You gonna radio this in, sir?" Hawkins asked.

Jake thought for a moment. It would be risky, but the truth of the Japanese atrocity had to be told. He had a code and a list of frequencies to use. He would take the chance. "Yeah. Tonight when it's real late and all the little yellow bastards are sound asleep."

Jake wondered how the sailors had been caught since the Japs had been so casual in their patrolling. Was it bad luck? Hey, even a half-hearted attempt at hiding should have worked. Or had they surrendered in the desperate hope they'd be treated fairly? Then it struck him that maybe they'd been turned in by a local. He might never know, but the possibility would make him redouble his caution.

Hawkins nodded. "I learned something today, sir."

"What's that, Hawk?"

"No fucking way I'm gonna be taken prisoner."

ADMIRAL YAMAMOTO FELT that Prime Minister Tojo was not quite the man for the job of leading the nation. Perhaps Tojo was a good army minister, but it looked like the combined duties of army minister and prime minister were overwhelming. Yamamoto thought Tojo was not enough of an internationalist to cope with being prime minister. The result was a man who was nervous and looked like he hadn't slept in weeks.

"More military successes, Admiral?" Tojo asked with a brittle smile.

"Some, but nothing grand. We have defeated a joint Anglo, Dutch, and American squadron in the Java Sea and are consolidating our landings in that area. The naval portion of the noose is tightening around the Americans in the Philippines. With MacArthur having abandoned them, it is only a matter of time before they too surrender."

"It's taken the army enough time already." Tojo sniffed. "The Americans are outnumbered and starving."

The comment surprised Yamamoto. In effect, the prime minister had just criticized the army minister, himself. "Very shortly," the admiral said, "our fleet will sail into the Coral Sea and strike at Port Moresby as a precursor to invading Australia."

"And the operation against the British in the Indian Ocean remains canceled?"

"Regrettably, yes. We are stretched too thin, and our men and equipment are too fatigued to undertake it at this time."

Tojo agreed that it was regrettable but made no further objection. Yamamoto knew the capabilities and limitations of his fleet. If he said the raid was a bad idea at this time, then so be it.

"And Hawaii?"

"Organized resistance is over. The army is withdrawing, and our marines are garrisoning Oahu and the Hilo region of Hawaii. Some of the fuel depot is already repaired, and tankers are en route to begin stockpiling oil. When that occurs, Oahu will be a truly viable fortress."

Tojo nodded. "You are aware that the first American food convoy is on its way. The *kempetei* will be on the alert to ensure that the Americans don't try to sneak in spies or saboteurs."

"I'm certain Colonel Omori will do an excellent job, Prime Minister. However, that does bring me to a point. It might appear that he is being overenthusiastic in his application of authority. A case in point might be that massacre of prisoners the Americans are screaming about."

While the army had led the patrol, it had been the handful of *kempetei* operatives escorting them who had ordered that the Americans be dragged to death behind the truck.

"The Americans were outlaws," Tojo said. "According to international law, they were subject to execution. However, I agree that a little more prudence was called for. I am also surprised that the Americans found out about it and so quickly. Any thoughts, Admiral?"

"Prime Minister, I said that organized resistance had ceased, but there still remain some incidences of disorganized resistance. The death of the prisoners might have been observed, and the information either radioed or telephoned to someone able to get it out of the islands. We have evidence that there are other stray American military personnel in the area, and the information may have come from them. If nothing else, this will definitely discourage any remaining Americans from surrendering, which could be unfortunate."

Tojo concurred. He would discuss it with his army subordinates. "There are those who feel that such harsh actions may hasten the Americans to the conference table."

"Have you seen any indication of that, Prime Minister?"

Tojo was surprised at the sarcasm in Yamamoto's voice. "None yet, but it will come."

The prime minister rose. The audience was over, but the admiral wanted the parting shot. "I hope it comes soon, Prime Minister. In a short while, the American fleet will be strong enough to confront us on even terms. In a while longer, we will be dreadfully outnumbered and facing the possibility of defeat."

When Yamamoto left, Tojo sat alone in the room. He was close to despair. Why hadn't the Americans asked for a truce, an end to the conflict? He felt totally inadequate. Events were running out of his control. He was like an engineer on an accelerating train whose brakes wouldn't work. He had to prevent a crash.

However, he did not agree with Yamamoto about the *kempetei's* actions being counterproductive. No, he felt that the screws could be tightened even more on the Americans in Hawaii.

ALEXA KNEW that the Japanese colonel was mentally undressing her and ignored it. At least he was a little more subtle than his assistant, Lieutenant Goto, who had practically fucked her with his eyes as he admitted her to Omori's office.

Goto's hand had brushed her hip as she passed him in the doorway, and it was not an accident. She was glad that she had worn an older dress, one that came well below her knees and was baggy as a result of weight loss. Jake would have been proud of her. In her mind's eye, she looked absolutely sexless.

"Be seated," Omori said in only slightly accented English. "I am pleased that you could meet with me, Mrs. Sanderson. First, let me extend my condolences on the tragic loss of your husband."

"You're very kind."

"You must be wondering why I requested the opportunity to talk with you, Mrs. Sanderson."

Indeed she was. It had come as a request, but few were foolish enough to decline such a summons from the head of the *kempetei*.

Alexa thought it amusing that Omori made any implication that the meeting was voluntary. The "invitation" had come the day before and said that a car would pick her up.

The office was fairly small and sparsely furnished; a slightly ajar door led to what appeared to be sleeping quarters. She wondered if that was where Omori lived. She caught a glimpse of an Asian woman in the room and concluded she must be one of the prostitutes the Japanese were rumored to have brought with them.

Alexa smiled. "Before we get to that, may I ask you a question, Colonel?"

Omori was mildly surprised. "Certainly."

"When will the schools reopen? I have almost forty students who haven't been inside a classroom in several months, and this is not good for them. They should not be idle."

Omori nodded in apparent sympathy. "I understand your concern. However, it will not happen for a while. Perhaps not until fall. All schools will remain closed until we can reorganize the curriculum. As Hawaii is now part of the Japanese Empire and the Greater Southeast Asia Co-Prosperity Sphere, we must change the local schools' academic focus toward Japan. Instead of American history and values, schools will teach everything that is Japanese, including the language to those who don't know it."

"I see," said Alexa. His answer confirmed a rumor she'd heard earlier. To the conqueror went the spoils, and the schools.

"Now, Mrs. Sanderson, may I come to the reason you're here? Are you aware that there was a dossier on you in the FBI offices?"

"No," she said in genuine astonishment. It must have had to do with her pacifist activities and openly stated opinions. She was shocked to realize that the FBI was even remotely interested in what she did and said.

"The FBI destroyed many of their files, but they did not get to all of them, and yours was one of a number that remained. Tell me, Mrs. Sanderson, are you still a pacifist?"

"I consider war to be awful, and now I have personal proof of that awfulness," she answered carefully.

"Then you would be willing to do what you can to bring a peaceful end to this terrible conflict, would you not?"

Alexa felt a trap opening. "Within reason."

"I am aware that you have influence in Washington, and, therefore, your comments on war might be listened to. We have prepared a series of statements that we would like to publish under your signature."

He handed her a sheaf of papers, each of which contained several paragraphs of virulently anti-American propaganda. After she read them a second time, Alexa returned them to Omori. "These go too far," she said. "They would proclaim me as a traitor to the United States. I'm sorry, but I cannot sign them."

Omori shrugged. "And afterward, we would like you to broadcast a number of prerecorded radio statements supporting the written statements. We will, of course, prepare the scripts for you."

Alexa was puzzled. Hadn't he heard her decline? "I'm sorry, I can't do that."

"Are you aware that your friend Father Monroe was arrested yesterday?"

"For what?"

"Insulting a Japanese officer. The punishment can be as extreme as death by beheading."

Alexa's mind whirled. Father Monroe was a good man. A bit naïve, perhaps, but not one to go about insulting their conquerors. "There must be a mistake," she said.

"Would you like to see him?"

Without waiting for an answer, Omori took her arm and led her outside and across a road to a building that looked like a warehouse. Inside, the walls were bare with a number of cruel-looking hooks hanging from rafters. From one of them dangled Father Monroe. He was naked and blindfolded, and his hands were tied behind his back. A rope from his wrists was connected to one of the hooks, and his feet were tantalizingly but barely in touch with the ground. Alexa watched in horror as he groped for the ability to stand and ease the pain in his extended shoulders.

"The effect of suspending him from his hands as we have," Omori said, "is to slowly dislocate his shoulders. As you can see, he is suffering terribly."

Alexa was appalled. "That's barbaric."

"Not to us. We believe in quick, severe justice in these circumstances. A trial would simply be a costly and unnecessary delay. Punishment must occur immediately and must deter others from doing the same thing. However, we do not consider the incident with Father Monroe serious enough to require his death."

"How long will he be like this?" Alexa wanted to vomit. Under the blindfold, Father Monroe's face was a mask of pain. Bruises and welts showed where he'd been beaten, and there was a puddle of urine and feces on the floor. She felt ashamed to be looking at his old, frail body in his humiliation and pain. She could not, however, stop staring. It was so horrible as to be unreal. It must be a nightmare from which she would soon wake up.

"He will remain where he is for twenty-four hours. Of course, he might be dead well before that, which would be a shame. However, he could be released if you agree to work with us. If you decline, he could easily die. Perhaps I will just leave him up there until that happens. If he's stronger than he looks, he could be in agony for days."

Alexa took a deep breath. The trap had been sprung and she was helpless. "All right," she said sadly. "I'll sign the statements."

Omori led her back to his office, where she quickly signed all the papers he put in front of her. She didn't reread them. There was no point. "We could have forged your signature," he said, "but this is so much better. We will get back to you when we're ready to record your speeches. As an added benefit for your cooperating with us, you will immediately start getting better rations, and you will no longer be required to work in the rice fields."

Alexa mumbled her thanks. She would share her additional food with Melissa and the child. Perhaps some good would come of her humiliation.

When Alexa left to be driven back home, Omori turned to Goto, who had been watching the proceedings with interest. "Did you see how easy that was? Had I tortured her, she might have resisted out of a sense of outrage and courage, and made herself a useless martyr. But, by my threatening someone else and making her responsible for that other person's fate, she folded immediately. Americans are very predictable like that. This is an extremely effective technique you can use in your own future interrogations."

Goto nodded politely. He understood that Omori had gotten his desired result, but to Goto it had been an empty result because Mrs. Sanderson did not yet truly fear Omori and the *kempetei*. He preferred the more direct and painful approach. Not only was it equally effective, but it was so much more satisfying.

Omori laughed. "Besides, I have further plans for Mrs. Sanderson. I had no idea she was so attractive. American women are so tall and arrogant, and it is so marvelous to reduce them to a more primitive level. The next time she's here, it'll be far more interesting for both of us."

Goto smiled. He did not think Mrs. Sanderson was attractive at all. Not only was she so much taller than both he and Omori but she was older than he was. Goto preferred his women to be both smaller and younger. Much younger.

CHAPTER 13

Dear Joe,

By the time you read this, you should be well on your way to safety. I wish you the best and hope that your efforts against the Japs will be successful and end this war so we can all go home. I also want you to know that your friendship and companionship were appreciated, and I look forward to renewing them at a more congenial time and place.

Now for the hard part. I concluded fairly early on that there was more to what you were doing on Oahu than simply monitoring radio messages you couldn't understand. Like a good soldier, I didn't go searching for answers, but you and Lt. Holmes accidentally provided them. You navy guys seem to forget that other people have brains, and you totally ignored the possibility that I spoke Japanese. I do, although not that fluently, and it was impossible not to listen in when you and Holmes discussed your problems in what you thought was secrecy.

That means I know you've broken at least some of the Jap codes and are reading their mail. I believe you called the program Wizard, or Magic, or something along that line. Great work. Keep it up and we'll nail the little yellow bastards.

You're a good man, Joe, and I know you'll show this letter to the right people even though it means you've got some egg on your face. Let the military know that Jake Novacek and his little army are alive and well on Hawaii and that I know a real important secret.

I don't want to blackmail anybody, but these are desperate times and I don't wish to be left out to dry. I believe that I can do important things here on the Big Island, and I believe it is equally important that I'm not captured. (Note: Joe, I have no intention of being taken alive, but things can go wrong, can't they?)

I don't want to leave here for the comforts of California while so many of

my friends are suffering in prisons and from hunger and other privations. Pass
this note on and get me some help for them.

Thanks,

Jake Novacek, Lieutenant Col., U.S. Army

General George C. Marshall placed the letter on his desk. Then he
rubbed the bridge of his nose. He had a terrible headache, and this
piece of news wasn't helping at all.

Across the room, Admiral King grinned sardonically. "Helluva
note, isn't it?"

"Rochefort's a man of honor," Marshall said. "A lesser man might
have just destroyed the letter. After all, it makes him look just a little
foolish, doesn't it?"

"True, but you're right. Rochefort is honorable. A little embarrassed perhaps, but honorable. Fortunately, he's damned brilliant, so
he's forgiven his sin. Holmes's punishment for having a big mouth is
that he has to continue working with Rochefort. Now, what do we do
about it? We jumped through hoops to get Rochefort out because of
his knowledge of Magic, and now we have your man Novacek wandering around Hawaii with it. Should I send another sub to pick him
up?"

The general thought about it. It had taken several weeks for the sub
carrying Rochefort to make harbor and for the offending letter to get
by courier to Washington. During that time, there had been intermit-
tent contacts with Novacek on Hawaii as he and others, like Fertig on
Mindanao in the Philippines, began resistance movements. Novacek
had already formed cells of sympathetic civilians and located a handful of other stray military personnel on the islands. Right now, all they
were doing was observing and reporting, but who knew what their potential might be.

"No," said Marshall. "Novacek is in too deep. If we ordered him to
leave, he'd think of some reason to evade the order and stay. What Novacek appears to want is involvement in the war. What we have to do
is figure out how to give him that without causing the whole Jap army
to try to catch him."

King nodded. "I was hoping you'd say that. The president wants the
islands retaken, and it struck me that we may have a forward base already in place."

"What do you want him to do?"

King stood and stretched. "I haven't the foggiest idea yet. All it is right now is an intriguing possibility. Hell, our torpedoes are beginning to work, which means the Jap navy is looking over its shoulder at us, and now we've got a bunch of GIs an hour's flying time from Pearl. I don't know what we're going to do, but Nimitz is working on the problem, and he's got some bright boys on his staff. I want to know if I can work with Novacek. After all, he's army, and that means he's yours."

Marshall laughed softly. "Maybe we can work with him and Doolittle. That man still wants to launch army bombers from your carriers and bomb Tokyo."

"That," King said thoughtfully, "is just not going to happen. There will be no carriers cruising west of Hawaii until Hawaii is retaken. However, maybe we can find a new target for the ambitious and imaginative Colonel Doolittle."

ALEXA'S SECOND SUMMONS to Colonel Omori's office came only a week after the first. As before, she dressed very conservatively, even shabbily, and wondered why she'd been called. After all, she had more than lived up to her part of the bargain. She had signed all the news releases they'd asked her to, and even seen drafts of what she was to record. To protect Father Monroe, she would make them and hope for the best later on.

On the positive side, the increased rations enabled her to feed herself better and get some more food to Melissa and her son. Alexa thought of asking for favored treatment for Melissa but decided against it. Why draw unneeded attention to her friend, who continued to work the fields while Alexa watched the child? Father Monroe had left Honolulu and was reportedly recuperating north of the city from his injuries, both physical and psychological. In short, the man had been broken.

When Alexa was seated in Omori's office, she saw that the door to his room was fully open and the cover on the large American-style bed was pulled down. She knew through the grapevine that he also had a residence in a Honolulu hotel suite. The *kempetei* colonel did not want for creature comforts.

Omori entered, gestured for her to remain seated, sat down himself, and smiled. "As before, I'm glad you're here."

Alexa nodded and muttered something polite.

"Your work on amending the script drafts is very thoughtful. The changes will be accepted, of course."

Alexa smiled inwardly. She had made a couple of apparently cosmetic changes that would make the English more halting and less correct. She hoped they would signal any listeners who knew her that she was doing the broadcasts under duress.

"At this point," Omori continued, "I have additional uses for you. I wish you to be involved in the new social life of Hawaii to show just how well the island's white population is being treated. I wish you to be my escort at a number of functions that are upcoming."

"I don't know what to say," Alexa said with total truthfulness. The proposal stunned her.

"You will, of course, become my mistress."

"Absolutely not," she snapped.

"Starting tonight. You see"—he smiled—"I understand exactly how to manipulate you."

Omori pushed a button on his desk, and the door behind Alexa opened. Lieutenant Goto stood there with a naked young girl in his grasp. Alexa gasped as she recognized Kami Ogawa, her student. Kami looked like she was in shock. When she recognized Alexa, she moaned and cried out for help.

"Other than embarrassment," Omori said, "the girl hasn't been harmed. Yet. Whether she is or not is totally up to you."

As if scripted, Goto shifted Kami so that one of his hands was free. He ran it over Kami's young breasts and down to her almost hairless crotch. Kami tried to evade his probing finger, but Goto was too strong and she cried out in pain as he penetrated her. Goto laughed, and Alexa saw his erection straining against his uniform trousers.

"Will you release her unharmed?" Alexa asked through clenched jaws.

"Of course. You have my word of honor."

Alexa wondered just how much honor Omori had, but, as before, she had no choice. If she did not agree, Kami would be assaulted by the pig of a lieutenant, and God only knew who else.

"All right," she said softly.

Omori smiled and signaled Goto and Kami to leave. "You will go to my room and wait. I'll be about an hour attending to other business. My servant's name is Han. She will assist you, and you will do precisely what she tells you. Her English, by the way, is fairly good. She is quite intelligent and educated for a Korean."

Han was a round-faced and plump young Korean in her mid-twenties. She was pleasant and seemed slightly sympathetic as she took Alexa to Omori's room. There she handed her a large drink of fruit juice.

"Take this," Han commanded in accented English. "It contains a medicine that will relax you."

Alexa refused at first, but Han was insistent and she drank. After a few minutes, a feeling of languid euphoria began to envelop her and she realized that the "medicine" had been a narcotic, probably opium or morphine.

"He will undress you himself," Han said. "Just do what he says and you will be fine. Do not even think of arguing or complaining, and please do not struggle. He will hurt you if you do, and he will continue to hurt you until you give in. And believe me," she said grimly, "you will give in. I saw him gouge out the eyes of a woman who resisted him and then, when he was done, turn her over to his troops. Once upon a time I did not wish to give in. He made me regret that, and I no longer argue. I would die a long and terrible death if I did, and so will you."

A while later, Omori arrived. Without preamble or comment he stood Alexa by the side of the bed, where she swayed gently. She was still fully clothed except for her shoes and socks, which Han had removed for her. Even without them she was several inches taller than Omori.

Omori unbuttoned her dress and slid it down to her ankles. Her slip followed, and then her bra and panties. Then he examined her slowly and carefully. He ran his hands over her, caressing her breasts and buttocks, and squeezing her nipples until she whimpered.

Omori was particularly fascinated by the patch of light-colored hair at the base of her stomach, which he stroked several times. She was so much more robust than a Japanese woman. They tended to be small and dainty, not strong like this one. The Koreans also tended to be larger than Japanese women, but Omori thought the Koreans were cows. There was a statuesque sensuality to this American, and she aroused him.

"You are too thin," he said huskily, "you must eat more."

Alexa said nothing. He laid her on her back on the bed with her head on the pillow and her legs apart. He undressed himself and, after a few additional and perfunctory caresses, mounted her and entered her. He thrust hard for a few moments, groaned, and it was over. Alexa wondered through her mental fog, Now can I go home?

No. It was just beginning. He had claimed his ownership and now intended to enjoy it.

Han had never left the room, and she brought towels, which she used to wipe them both, along with more to drink. Omori also drank and talked about things that went over Alexa's head. The drinks contained more of the drug, and she felt herself spinning out of control but not caring. If the drug shielded her from the degradation she was enduring, then she would be thankful for it.

In an astonishingly short while, Omori was hard again and took her a second time. This time he was far more gentle and persuasive, and Alexa felt ashamed as her body betrayed her by responding to him. When he was done, Han appeared again. Now she too was naked, and she began to caress and kiss the most intimate parts of Alexa's body until Alexa moaned in unwanted pleasure and cried out.

Then Han showed her how to return the favor. Alexa started to protest until Han hissed a sharp reminder about Omori hurting her that reached what level of consciousness still remained. She gave in, and the two women grappled on the bed in a drug-induced passion while Omori watched and laughed, his eyes glassy from the drug. Alexa wondered if she looked like that.

Finally, the two women fell back on the bed, sweat-soaked and exhausted. Through her stupor, Alexa glanced at a clock. The night was almost over. Soon, perhaps, she could go home. Omori looked at his watch. "Once more," he commanded and sat on the edge of the bed. He forced Alexa to kneel before him and guided her face to his crotch. "But this time in a new way."

Alexa accepted him into her mouth and began to rock back and forth as he gurgled happily. She no longer cared. There was not even the slightest thought of resistance, only acquiescence. She no longer had any worth or dignity, only shame and humiliation. She was a piece of property owned by Omori.

In a corner of her mind, she recalled Jake saying that she should do anything to survive. Omori groaned, and she tasted him. She wondered if there was anything worse that could happen to her if she was to survive.

JAKE EXULTED SILENTLY when he received the radio signal that told him his letter to Joe Rochefort had made its way to Washington and been accepted.

He had maintained the original camp in the hills as a base from which his patrols crept out to keep an eye on the Japanese and recruit selectively from the local population. He had followed the primary rule of not letting each small group of volunteers know of the existence of the others. They suspected, of course, but knew nothing for certain. Only Jake knew them all. As his second in command, Hawkins knew more than the others, but not everything.

The Japanese in Hilo remained quiet. The island was just over four thousand square miles, and much of the terrain was extremely rugged. Mountains on the triangular-shaped island lifted several thousand feet into the air, and there were at least two active volcanoes, Mauna Loa and Mauna Kea, along with the craters of many dormant or dead ones. The eastern side of the island was more lushly overgrown than the west, which was windswept and comparatively barren. Because it was easier to hide there, they stayed in the eastern half even though that put them dangerously close to the Japanese garrison at Hilo.

There had been no repeats of the large patrols that had captured and massacred the American prisoners. Jake estimated there wasn't more than a battalion in Hilo along with a small detachment of *kempetei*. Hilo had a population of nineteen thousand, second only to Honolulu. Most of the other places on the island were hamlets of several dozen to several hundred people. Thus, it was fairly easy for Jake's command to remain undetected.

The island of Hawaii was fertile, and there was a good deal of farming and ranching in the valleys and along the coastline. This meant they had access to food growing both wild and on farms, which had alleviated the problem of hunger for the time being. Several sympathetic landowners had begun to help Jake's small army, and he was encouraged to note that some of these good people were of Japanese descent. Obviously, the invasion was not a unanimously popular undertaking.

The Japanese army in Hilo was more interested in overseeing the distribution of food shipped in from the States via Honolulu than in exploring the countryside. Spending time in Hilo was much more pleasant to the occupying Japanese than patrolling through jungles and up volcanoes in search of rumored and elusive bands of Americans. As a result of this neglect, Jake's patrols had found another dozen American sailors and a pair of stray marines in the near jungles of Hawaii.

Counting the civilian volunteers who did not travel with him, his army had grown to almost a hundred men. Unfortunately, more than half had no weapons, and many of the weapons they did have were civilian shotguns and rifles. They would not be taking on Imperial Japan's finest anytime soon.

"Good message from home, Colonel Jake?" Sergeant Hawkins asked as he plopped on the ground by Jake.

"Y'know, when we get back to the States, Sergeant Hawk, you're going to have to quit calling me Colonel Jake."

Hawkins grinned. An easy form of camaraderie had grown among the handful of men who formed the nucleus of Jake's force, and he and Hawkins were now close friends. "You get us back to the States, and I'll call you anything you want. So what's the message, sir?"

"It's interesting. They're going to send us some more men, but they specified that some would not be combat types. We now report directly to Nimitz in San Diego, and he's very interested in our keeping our cover and not being found by the Japs."

"I like the man already," said Hawkins. "I just can't believe we're working for the navy."

"Don't worry, Hawk; we're still in the army. Let's just say we're coordinating real closely with the sailors. One of the things they told us to watch out for was stretches of level and solid ground. What does that mean to you?"

Hawkins thought for a second and laughed. "Planes. The sons of bitches want us to look for places to land planes. Damn, this could begin to get real interesting."

"Is this going to be the end of our litany of defeats?" asked Roosevelt.

"There are no guarantees, sir," said General Marshall. "But it is the right thing to do. The longer our forces in the Philippines hang on, the weaker they get and the more casualties they take."

"Japanese prison camps are brutal, aren't they? Our boys will be terribly mistreated if they surrender."

"Yes, they will, Mr. President," Marshall said glumly. Beside him, Admiral King kept silent. The bulk of the men on Bataan and Corregidor were army, not navy, and it was the navy that was unable to relieve them.

Roosevelt was visibly upset by the news that General Jonathan Wainwright, now commanding the Philippines, wished to offer to surrender his command to the Japanese. Wainwright saw the obvious— that there would be no reinforcements or relief, only prolonged agony. He had said that he felt he could hold out for several weeks more, even a couple of months, but for what purpose? The longer the siege went on, the more weakened the men would become. Thus, when the inevitable occurred and the Americans in the Philippines did surrender, they would have even less ability to withstand the privations of Japanese camps.

The time to surrender and save lives was now. The president knew he would be castigated for it, and accepted that as a fact of political life. "Is there no good news anywhere?" he asked.

King answered. "Intelligence says the Japs are gathering for a thrust into the Coral Sea as a prelude to taking Port Moresby. Warned as we are, we hope to ambush them."

Roosevelt nodded. Again he felt exhausted. His strength seemed to ebb so much earlier each day. "See that you do."

The sun-drenched beach south of San Diego was far from a solitary place. Even so, both Jamie Priest and Sue Dunnigan were in their own private worlds and able to ignore the several dozen people who were in view. Even the sounds of a foursome of drunken sailors and their dates failed to penetrate their shells. If it had been the weekend, the place would have been packed with humanity. But this was a work evening; the many thousands of military personnel were at their bases, and the tens of thousands of civilians in the area were working overtime producing bombers and the other materials of war that were just beginning to pour out of American factories.

Sue pried the top from a bottle of beer with an opener and handed the bottle to Jamie. "Was it that bad?"

He had been quiet since he'd picked her up and driven the short distance to the beach. The area was so lovely, so calm, that it was almost possible to forget there was a war on.

"I had to dredge up some memories I'd been trying to forget," he replied.

She tucked her legs under her knees and took a bottle for herself from the cooler. Going to the beach had been her idea; the inquest had been the navy's. Jamie looked so drawn and forlorn that she wanted to hold him to her and rock him like a baby. He was so thin and frail in his swimming trunks, she found it difficult to think of him as an officer, and a hero who'd survived both the Japanese and the ocean. At least the burns from the sun had gone and the cut on his back was a barely noticeable scar. He was pale, and the early evening in the sun would do them both some good.

When it came to thinness, she wryly thought that she matched him, bony limb for bony limb. Sue considered herself slender to the point of skinny and bemoaned what to her was an almost total lack of a bosom. At least she didn't look foolish in her two-piece bathing suit like so many plump women did. She saw that the waist of her suit had ridden low and her navel was almost exposed. She pulled it up while thinking that, if she had better hips, it wouldn't slide down so much.

This was the first time she and Jamie had done anything social. Their relationship had been very cordial but based entirely on work. Even the times they'd had lunch together had been because of the pressures of work, not because they wished to enjoy each other's company. She hadn't planned on suggesting anything like this evening at the beach, but he had looked so distraught after the inquest that she thought it was a good idea.

The Navy Department had finally commenced an investigation

into the loss of the *Pennsylvania*. The sinking of a single ship, even a battleship, had largely been lost in the immensity of the disasters that had befallen the U.S. Navy since December 7. It seemed unlikely anyone even cared anymore.

Finally, however, four elderly and unimportant admirals had made the journey from Washington to interview Jamie Priest, the only known survivor of the sinking. In Jamie's words, the admirals had been more than a little pissed that they had to travel to California instead of Jamie coming to them, but Admiral Nimitz had made it clear that he wanted Jamie to remain in San Diego. Thus, the four admirals trekked across the nation on a series of trains and buses, suffering through the inconsistencies and delays of a transportation system still paralyzed by the impact of war. They took the opportunity to loose their anger when they interrogated Jamie.

Now he shook his head in frustration. "I didn't have the answers they wanted. They couldn't get it through their heads that I was just a lonely and lowly officer who wasn't assigned to anything in particular, who didn't know squat about the battle, and who spent the entire time scared to death. They wanted to know what was happening on the bridge and got angry when I told them I never got on the bridge. I thought one of them would have a fit when I said I wasn't certain where the bridge was. They didn't even care how those guys died in the water, although I got the hint they thought I could have done something better to save them. The bastards."

He finished his beer and took another one from Sue, who let him know she liked being called Suzy by her friends and he now qualified. "I guess they felt they wasted a trip, and they're right. I don't know what they wanted, but they should have known they wouldn't get it from me. They'll just have to wait until the war's over and they talk to the other survivors."

If there are any, Suzy thought. She'd caught snatches of conversation between senior officers that told her otherwise.

She decided to redirect his thoughts and pointed out the glories of the sun reflecting off the waves. It didn't work.

"Japan's out there," Jamie said.

"So's Hawaii," she answered softly.

Jamie bit his lip. "God, I'm sorry. I haven't given a thought about you losing your father. I must sound like a spoiled child."

"Just a little," she teased. She was gratified that he did seem genuinely contrite. A lot of guys wouldn't have cared.

"Tell me about your dad," Jamie said.

She leaned back on her elbows and drank in the sun. She took off her glasses, and the world beyond a dozen feet away became a pleasant blur. She wished she was naked and could let the sun play over her entire body as she liked to do on some of the more private beaches in the area. She wondered what Jamie's reaction would be. Shock? Dismay? Delight? Maybe someday she'd find out.

"Not much to say. He was a good man, a good father, and a good sailor, and I loved him very much. He encouraged me to get an education, which I did. He served with Spruance, which is how I got this job as his clerk at the tender age of twenty-four. Being a sailor, Dad was gone for long stretches of time, so I got used to him not being there. My mother lives in Oakland. They got divorced a few years ago, and she remarried some guy who works in a factory. The guy's a jerk, and I'm really disappointed in Mom, but I guess she needed the security."

Suzy took another beer for herself and snapped off the top with more force than was necessary. She's hiding her anger too, Jamie thought, but not very well.

"Dad died on his battleship," she went on. "Now they're saying the *Arizona* will be a permanent tomb or memorial when we retake Hawaii. I'd like that, and I know he'd like that. I could visit there and know where he is and that he's finally safe."

"In the meantime, we do what we can," Jamie said.

He was proud of his work. Already a partial solution had been found for the problem of the torpedoes running deeper than set. The weight difference between the test warheads and a real warhead was significant enough to cause a torpedo to run ten feet deeper than expected. Adjusting the settings was all that was needed, although there was concern that the earth's magnetic field was producing variances that also affected the settings.

The situation with the impact detonators was still not totally resolved. It was now a given that they were too sensitive, and there was talk of copying a more reliable British design. In the meantime, mechanics onboard submarines tinkered with each torpedo to make them all more effective.

"When you write your book, put me in it," Suzy said with a grin.

"My what?"

"You heard me. After the war, you will write a book about your experiences, and I want to be in it. As the heroine, of course."

Write a book? Funny, but the thought intrigued him. "Okay, I'll write a book. And I'll put those four admirals in it in all their glory."

Perhaps a book would be a way of telling the world about the quiet courage of people like Seaman Fiorini, and about his photos, which might have influenced the course of the war.

They finished their beers, and Suzy broke out sandwiches. As they ate, she couldn't help but think that her father would have liked Lieutenant Jamie Priest.

CHARLEY FINCH HAD NEVER INTENDED to be a traitor. All he ever wanted was a little peace and comfort for himself and a way out of the prison camp. If it meant ratting on a couple of his buddies, well, so what? He'd done it before, and he'd do it again if the situation was right.

All he thought the Japs would do about the POWs' command situation in the camp was to smack the guys involved around a few times, maybe put them in solitary for a while, and everything would get back to business as usual. Hell, everything had been fine so far. His "duty" outside the compound was now considered normal by his fellow prisoners, who actually awaited his returns with eagerness. Along with the others who worked outside the barbed wire, he had become a font of information regarding the outside world and even "smuggled" in excess food. His buddies in no way begrudged him the fact that he ate his fill from Jap leftovers and brought only what he could hide and carry. What the hell was he to do—they'd all laughed—push a handcart or wheelbarrow full of Jap goodies in each day? Only Jake knew that Colonel Omori made Charley take the food. It made him more valuable and trusted by his fellow prisoners.

All this was now threatened, even destroyed, by the punishment Omori was inflicting on the four American prisoners, which Finch was forced to watch. He was behind a screen and the POWs were blindfolded, but he had the nagging, crawling feeling they knew he was there.

Goto was clad in only a loincloth, and his short, muscular body glistened with sweat and the prisoners' blood. He had worked the men over with his pliers as they hung from the rafters by ropes tied under their armpits. All their fingers and toes had been smashed, as had their noses and teeth. Now Goto was finishing the job by battering each man's chest and back with a baseball bat. As another blow landed, a soldier groaned and Charley heard the nauseating sound of a rib snapping.

Goto laughed and pounded the kidney area of another man. Blood had begun to ooze from their bowels. At least they were through screaming. The first few hours had been terrible with their howls of agony.

Goto shifted and began a series of savage uppercuts with the bat on the prisoners' testicles. He had done this earlier, and their balls were swollen like purple grapefruits that looked like they would burst.

"Enough," Omori said, and his lieutenant looked disappointed. "Cut them down and have the other prisoners retrieve them."

Charley was surprised. Earlier, Omori had said he would have them executed. The colonel looked fatigued. Charley had picked up enough Japanese to overhear that the colonel had spent the night drinking and fucking some white woman. Lucky bastard. It also looked like the colonel had been using drugs, and Charley found that intriguing.

The soldiers whispered that Goto had been dipping his wick in some local pussy all night as well.

"Don't worry, Sergeant Finch," Omori said, "they will die. Only it will be in full view of their comrades and over a great period of agonizing time as the prisoner medics try to save them. Since they don't have the resources to do any such thing, their efforts will simply prolong the men's death agonies."

Charley shuddered. Jesus, what a sadistic bastard.

"You have kept your bargain," Omori said. "And I will keep mine. We have captured two FBI agents and now have the two men who commanded the prisoners. You will not return to the camp. You will be reported as killed for insolence. Instead, you will be installed in a cottage just off the base and out of sight of the other prisoners. You will be fed and have liquor and the services of one of the Korean whores."

Charley thought he'd been promised a white woman like the one Omori was screwing, but he didn't press it. "Thank you, sir."

"When the time comes, I will have other duties for you."

Charley was again surprised. He had thought this was a one-shot deal. Of course, he realized ruefully, he'd also thought the four men would be relatively unharmed.

"There are Americans loose on several islands," Omori continued, "and I believe you would be perfect in flushing them out."

"What will you do with them, sir?"

Omori glared at him angrily. The question was impertinent. "They are outlaws, Sergeant; what do you think we do with outlaws?"

Charley Finch bowed deeply in apology. "I understand fully, Colonel Omori." And he did understand. If a few more died so he could stay alive and well, that was just tough shit. It would be years at the earliest before the United States returned, and Charley Finch had best look out for Charley Finch. He knew it would be difficult to explain his prosperous survival when so many others were dead and dying, but that was something he would resolve when the time came. Maybe he would move to Japan? Hell, after he'd helped them, the Japs would welcome him with open arms, wouldn't they?

■

CHAPTER 14

It was time to do something constructive, Jake thought, long past time. He and his men had spent more than enough days hiding and organizing, and now they had to show the people of the big island of Hawaii that there was an American presence nearby, and that it was capable of hurting the Japanese.

This wasn't something he'd decided on lightly. His mission was to stay hidden and await orders. However, he had to live in the area, and that required the assistance of the handful of people on the farms and in the villages outside Hilo. Many of them were wavering in their support of America, and others felt that the Japanese were invincible and would stay forever, making it necessary to reach an accommodation with their new masters.

Jake believed it was time to change a few minds. Fortunately, the Japanese proved very cooperative in the matter.

Those farmers and villagers in the area who were not of Japanese or Hawaiian extraction were often subject to brutal treatment by wandering patrols of occupying soldiers, who, without anyone to stop them, had become more and more adventuresome. In particular, the Chinese were often treated terribly. It was Jake's opinion that the soldiers were out plundering on their own while their commander in Hilo drank himself into a daily stupor.

As the Americans were on the move from one campsite to another, a terrified child told them that the Japs were at a farm owned by a Chinese family just a couple of miles down the road. Jake took with him only his regular soldiers and two of his marines. The remaining handful of add-ons and sailors were ordered to stay in place. Most didn't have the experience needed for this. Jake wondered if he had it either, but he kept that disquieting thought to himself.

The Japs were still at the farm when they arrived and appeared totally unaware of impending danger. Hawkins counted eight of them, and several were lurching around drunk. All had rifles, although several rifles were leaning against the neat white frame house. An army truck was parked by the farmhouse, but it didn't look like anyone was in it. A barn, again white and neat, was behind and to the left of the farmhouse. The buildings were surrounded by acres of fields, in which wheat and vegetables grew several feet tall. Part of the area had been turned into a rice paddy. The whole place exuded prosperity and the results of hard work.

"If we do this right, sir, this could be a turkey shoot," Sergeant Hawkins said.

Jake nodded. "Then let's make sure we do it right. Jesus, what's that?"

Jake focused his binoculars on the slightly open door to the barn, past which it was difficult to see. A naked woman stood against it. Her arms were spread wide, and her hands had been nailed to the door. Her head was slumped on her chest, and she had been disemboweled. A sausagelike strand of entrails hung down her belly. Other cuts and slashes were visible on her body, and another body lay in the barn. It appeared to be an adult man.

Jake had sent two men to reconnoiter the other side of the farm. They reported that there were no other Japs in the area and no sign of any other civilians either.

"They killed them all," Hawkins said and spat on the ground.

Jake took one group of men and Hawkins the other. The idea was to get at the Japs with converging fire from two angles to hit them before they had a chance to react. No one would fire until Jake did and until they reached their assigned positions, about a hundred yards from the farmhouse.

They crawled through the fields and reached their places without being seen, even though their movements must have disturbed the vegetation. The Japs were too drunk to care. They would be leaving soon for the comforts of Hilo, Jake thought, and then they'd get them. He didn't want to attack when they were in the house, which they could use as a fort.

The Americans didn't have long to wait. A group of Japanese lurched and staggered out of the house laughing and carrying bags of loot. It was too much to ask that all would line up neatly for him, but six of them were outside at the same time and were easy targets. When they started to pick up their rifles, he knew there was no time to wait.

"Fire," he yelled, and his five men let loose and were immediately followed by Hawkins's group.

Four of the six Japanese were hit immediately. Their bodies jumped and fell, then lay still. The remaining two tried to aim their rifles but were riddled by additional bullets. A seventh Jap came running from the house and right into a hail of bullets, which hurled him backward. The eighth jumped out a window and ran into the barn. He had a pistol in his hand and looked terrified.

"Mine," Hawkins said and darted to the barn before Jake could speak. He lunged through the door and rolled into the darkness inside. A moment later there was the sound of a pistol shot, followed by a full clip emptying from an M1. A moment after that, Hawkins emerged and waved at Jake. A Japanese pistol stuck out from his belt.

Jake's soldiers checked the rest of the farm. The man in the barn was dead, and it looked like he too had been used for bayonet practice. A girl, about ten, was found dead in the bed in the farmhouse. She had been raped repeatedly and then had her throat cut. Like the others, she had been dead for a couple of hours.

"I don't know what the Chinese do about their dead, but let's bury them quickly."

"What about the Japs?" Hawkins asked.

Jake thought for moment. "Put the bodies in the truck and we'll drive it into the woods. Maybe it'll take them a long time to find it. And don't forget to take their weapons."

Later, as they hiked back to their camp, Jake sensed the uplift to his men's spirits. They had finally struck back, and it felt good. They might have to play hide-and-seek with the Japs for a while, but Hawaii was a big island, and they could take advantage of every rugged inch of it.

Better, the people of Hawaii would soon know that the Americans were still around.

"Hawk," Jake said, "why did you go into that barn alone?"

"Lotsa reasons, sir. If I hadn't, you might've, and you're more important than I am. Also, the fucking Japs pissed me off. I like Chinese food."

■

THE TWO JAPANESE SOLDIERS detailed to take Alexa home had been ordered not to attack her. They obeyed but decided the orders allowed them to paw and fondle her. When they arrived at her home, they pushed her out of the car and onto the lawn.

Her return attracted Melissa, who helped the stunned and half-naked woman up from her hands and knees and into the house. It was barely dawn, and none of their few neighbors appeared to notice the event. In a handful of terse sentences, Alexa told her friend what had happened and said that she wanted a bath.

Melissa drew the bath and helped Alexa into the comforting hot water. She watched sadly as her friend attempted to wash away all vestiges of the terrible night. It wouldn't work, of course, but Alexa had to try, and she scrubbed her body with an almost manic fury, even putting the soapy washcloth into her mouth, which made her gag. Her stomach was empty, so she could only retch.

When Alexa finally tired, she left the tub and lay down on her bed. Melissa then called for a doctor she knew who was very discreet. He was of Hawaiian extraction and was still permitted to practice. He examined Alexa, gave her a pelvic exam, suggested she douche, and left them.

Somewhat revived, Alexa filled Melissa in on the details.

"Do you have a diaphragm?" Melissa asked.

"Of course. I was so stupid. I didn't think I'd need it."

"Just make sure you take it the next time. It won't save you from some of the sick games he likes to play, but it should keep you from getting pregnant by the bastard."

Next time? Pregnant? Alexa hadn't given that a thought. Dear God, would it happen again? Yes, she realized, it would happen again. And again, and again, and again. The colonel had made it clear that she was his possession, his mistress. There would be more times with him mounting her, more sessions with Han, and more times with her sucking Omori's penis and tasting his semen. She wanted to be sick.

Melissa stayed with her as long as possible through the day, even offered to stay the night with her child, but Alexa said no. She would deal with her problem herself.

Thus, she was alone and the house was dark when the rear door burst open. Three men dressed in dark clothes and hoods grabbed her, and one covered her mouth with his hand before she could scream. She had been ready for bed, and there were no lights on.

One man was the leader. "Please be quiet, Mrs. Sanderson, we are not your enemy. We wish to talk with you. Will you promise not to scream?"

Alexa agreed. Once again she saw no choice.

"What do you want?" she asked when they released her. They didn't behave like burglars. "And why those hoods?"

The leader handed her a robe, which she put on eagerly. She'd been wearing only a short cotton nightgown. The act of tying the robe around her waist comforted her.

The leader gestured for her to sit down, and he did as well. The other two took up stations as guards, looking out the windows. "I am sorry that I was too late to help you in your dealings with Omori. I can only hope that I can now be of assistance. As for these ridiculous hoods, it is better for everyone if you do not know our faces at this moment."

"Then you know what happened?"

"Yes. He raped you. He forced you to serve him in order to save someone else. The Japanese will do this wherever and whenever they can. The threat of sexual assault is a weapon of terror for them."

Alexa started to cry softly. This stranger had called it rape, and, while she thought it was rape, Alexa wondered if others would think the same way. After all, Omori hadn't beaten her, hadn't held a knife to her throat, hadn't even actually threatened to hurt her, although Han had said he would. Alexa knew that, in some people's eyes, this lack of violence would make her seem a willing partner in what had occurred. She knew better, but others would judge from the smug safety of distance. But she had saved Kami, which she told the intruder.

"No," said the leader sadly, "you didn't."

Alexa was stunned. "Omori swore he wouldn't touch her!"

"He didn't. His pig of a lieutenant, Goto, did. He raped her all night and then turned her over to a couple of his men, who passed her around like a child's toy."

Alexa sagged. It had all been for nothing.

"It gets worse," he said. "Kami managed to free herself and ran away. Some of my, ah, friends found her and drove her to a place near the ocean for safety. That was a mistake. In her shame and despair, she walked into the sea and never came back."

As Alexa reeled from this new blow, she caught a catch in the man's voice. "What was she to you?" she asked.

"My grandniece," he gasped. "A lovely flower that had only half bloomed. She was my wife's brother's son's child and the joy of my years. She was only half Japanese, and that made her inferior in some eyes but not mine. She was deeply loved and will be missed forever."

They were silent for a moment. "What do you want from me?" Alexa asked.

The man sighed. "Nothing can bring Kami back, and nothing can eliminate your night with Omori. What I can do is ensure that nothing further happens to you. I wish to move you from here to one of the other islands. There you will be with friends of mine and out of Omori's reach. There are comparatively few Japanese military in the islands, and Omori doesn't have the resources to search for you."

"How much time do I have to think it over?"

"None. I want you to leave now. You are not the only woman in Omori's stable. There are two other Americans who've already been turned into opium addicts and whores by him. He will use you for a couple of weeks, and then you will be passed around to a succession of other Japanese officers. What happened to you last night was bad enough. How would you like to service half a dozen men each time? In six months, I predict you will be dead of drug usage, or dying of it, or of syphilis."

The hooded leader knew this wasn't the truth. So far, Alexa Sanderson was the first woman Omori had attacked, but it was felt that she needed to be frightened into moving.

Alexa was convinced. She would go, and right now. "Let me pack a few things. What about my friend? Will you take her?"

The leader shrugged. "If she wishes it. However, if it is the friend we saw you with, she has a small child. I doubt that she would wish to live the life of a refugee with him."

And that, Alexa thought, tells me that there will be danger where he is sending me. However, she decided it would be far better than the lingering agony Omori had in store for her. He was right. Melissa was better off where she was. Alexa wanted to say good-bye to her friend but decided against it. Melissa was safer in a state of honest and plausible ignorance.

"Now, please take off the mask," she asked.

He did as requested, revealing the face of a Japanese man well past middle age. She looked into his eyes and saw deep sadness that was possibly as great as her own, along with strength and more than a hint of cruelty. This man would be a terrifying enemy.

"Who are you?"

"I am Toyoza Kaga, and I am a merchant in the area. I am Japanese born, but I have no wish to see the Japanese military succeed. Is that acceptable, or does the fact of my race offend you?"

"Do I have a choice?" Alexa asked grimly. "How will you get me off the island without the Japs"—she caught herself and flushed while Kaga smiled slightly—"I mean, without Omori's men finding me?"

"That will not be difficult. Each night scores of fishing boats leave and return without the Japanese caring. Our occupiers have done nothing to hinder commerce between the islands. Quite the contrary; it is in their best interests to encourage fishing to help feed the people. You will be on one of the boats."

Alexa rose. She felt strength and hope returning to her. "All right, let's get going."

COLONEL JIMMY DOOLITTLE THOUGHT he had seen everything in his years in the army and the air corps. Now, he knew he was wrong.

Doolittle was forty-five and had taken a slightly unusual route toward higher rank. Instead of attending West Point, he had graduated from the University of California and later earned a doctorate at MIT. He had joined the army in 1917, resigned in 1930 to work in private aviation, then reenlisted as a major in the summer of 1940.

As the short, trim colonel walked along the beachfront with Admiral Nimitz, he could only gawk at the array of planes floating before him. None of his experience had prepared him for what he was seeing and what he thought the admiral was going to tell him.

Finally, he found his voice. "Admiral, what the hell am I supposed to do with these big, ugly monsters?"

Nimitz grinned. "Bomb the Japs."

Lined up before them and in the waters of the bay were eight flying boats. They looked like so many gargantuan geese on parade and, from the upward cut of their bows, seemed to be mocking him. But Doolittle knew one thing: He was a bomber pilot, and flying boats were not bombers. The fact that they rested in the water precluded them from having bomb bays. They were slow, fat passenger planes, not warplanes.

He sighed. "What do you want bombed, and why me, sir?"

Nimitz explained in reverse. He said that Doolittle had a reputation as an intelligent, creative, and flexible commander. Doolittle's original plan had been to bomb Tokyo using sixteen B-25 bombers that would fly from a carrier, bomb Tokyo, and land in China. Doolittle's abilities while training for this army-navy foray had impressed the navy, which had asked for him to be seconded to their command.

"And let's face it, Colonel, not too many navy pilots know anything about large bombers, and these planes are going to be just about the largest bombers the world has ever seen."

Doolittle thought he knew the answer but had to ask. "And my target? It's no longer Tokyo, is it?"

"No, it's not. Your target is the fuel depot at Pearl Harbor. According to our intelligence sources, it is nearly rebuilt now, and, when it is finished and filled, Pearl Harbor will be a viable forward base for the Japanese. As it stands, the Japs have only a scratch force in and on Oahu, and the longer we can keep things that way, the easier it will be to retake the islands once we have achieved naval superiority. Therefore, your job will be to destroy that depot just like the Japs did to us."

Doolittle saw the irony in the situation. "And why not launch my B-25s from a carrier?"

Nimitz smiled. "Let's just say we have other plans for our carriers. Besides, once launched, where would you go? Hawaii is in the middle of nowhere. Flying to China would not be an option, as it would be if you bombed Tokyo. You'd be forced to land in the sea if you used B-25s. However, with modifications and drop tanks, these flying boats can take you from California to Hawaii and back."

Doolittle whistled. "The Japs'll never expect a plane that can do that trick."

"You will have the fullest cooperation from both army and naval engineers in reconfiguring those passenger craft into weapons. May I presume you already have some thoughts?"

Doolittle smiled. It would be a helluva challenge, but the admiral was right. And yes, there were a few thoughts percolating in his skull.

"Two questions, Admiral."

"Shoot."

"First, let's say I arrive over Pearl and I see targets that may be more inviting than a fuel depot, for instance, a row of sleeping carriers. How much discretion will I have?"

"All you wish. That's one of the reasons we chose you."

Doolittle felt like jumping in the air. "Fantastic! Now, sir, when do you want me to be ready?"

Nimitz smiled benignly. "Yesterday."

COMMANDER MITSUO FUCHIDA GREETED his old friend Minoru Genda with heartfelt warmth as they met in what had been the officers' club of Wheeler Field, out by Schofield Barracks. After they'd exchanged pleasantries and treated each other to a drink, Genda brought up the reason for the meeting.

"Fuchida, you have done a marvelous job of, first, reducing the American forces on Oahu and, second, rebuilding this devastated base. May I assume that all your planes and pilots have been transferred from Molokai?"

"You may, indeed. The fields at Molokai have been dynamited, which makes them useless for anyone else, although they could be rebuilt fairly quickly. I must admit, I am not comfortable with so many potential airstrips so close to Oahu and no one watching over them."

Genda agreed. "Unfortunately, our resources are stretched thin. However, you are flying patrols over all the islands, aren't you?"

"Of course. But with only sixty planes at my disposal, I have only a handful on overland patrols at any given time. I am afraid that most of what goes on in the islands is unseen by my men."

Fuchida was forced to divide his air resources among ocean patrols, which were deemed more critical because they looked for carriers; antisub duty off the entrance to Pearl Harbor; overland patrols; and the maintenance required to keep the planes in the air. At least a third of his planes were being serviced at all times. In the event of an attack, he was confident almost all of them would rise to fight, but the situation stretched his current overland patrols thin, too thin, in his estimation. "You know, Genda, I lost nearly a hundred pilots taking Oahu," he said.

"A high price," Genda said solemnly. The hundred pilots were equivalent to the flying crews of two carriers. Replacements were arriving, but they did not appear to be of the same quality as those killed, and this fact made both men uncomfortable.

Genda brightened. "At any rate, I have good news for you. Your work here is done. You are needed with the fleet."

"Marvelous." Fuchida could barely contain his enthusiasm.

"Nagumo is taking the carriers south through the Coral Sea to Port Moresby. He hopes to lure the Americans to battle and inflict a crushing defeat. He has been told that you are the best man to command all the fighters."

Fuchida inhaled deeply. It was an enormous honor. "I will do my best."

Genda clapped his friend on the shoulder, a most un-Japanese gesture of camaraderie. "Your best will be more than sufficient, my friend. We hope, a thrust toward Australia will knock both them and New Zealand out of the war and secure our southern flank. After that, we can destroy the British in the Indian Ocean if the remainder of the Americans won't fight. Perhaps," he said solemnly, "it will end the war."

Fuchida shook his head. *Perhaps* had been said too many times. "I am not that confident. I saw how desperately the Americans fought to keep this place, and I do not think they will let the loss of Australia, or even several of their carriers, deter them. Do you know there are still Americans active and fighting on the other islands?"

Genda was surprised. "I had no idea."

Fuchida laughed harshly. "It's not something that either Admiral Iwabachi or Colonel Omori wants publicized. Just the other day a patrol was ambushed and wiped out on Hawaii, only a few hours away from Hilo, and we can do nothing about it. We know that there is a great deal of clandestine radio activity, which we cannot pin down, and every third sailor on the food ships must be a spy, regardless of nationality. Frankly, my friend, I would not doubt that our conversation will be reported to Washington tomorrow."

Genda laughed nervously. Was the man serious? They were virtually alone in a large room. Native Hawaiians made up the serving staff, and there was a sprinkling of American Negroes working in the kitchens along with other Hawaiians. These were civilians who had worked at the base before the war and professed no love for the United States, which had treated them harshly. No, Fuchida had to be kidding. "It can't be that bad," Genda said.

"It isn't," Fuchida responded, "but it's bad enough. You do know that we are not getting the full support of the Japanese community here, don't you, and the Hawaiians are almost totally unresponsive? We've been here for almost five months, and there's been no official clarification of our long-term policy regarding the islands, and the Japanese and Hawaiian people who would be our allies are beginning to worry and wonder."

The two men rose and stepped outside. The Hawaiian sun had bathed the lush green land in brightness. Even the scars of the recent battles looked cleansed and unthreatening. With the low mountains as a backdrop, it should have been a vision evocative of the grace and elegance of Japan itself. Instead, it had taken on a sinister, hostile appearance, with the mountains looking like so many rows of sharks' teeth.

"You ask about our policies? I sometimes wonder if we have one," Genda said.

"We are a long way from making this place our own," Fuchida responded. "I sometimes wonder if we will have the time."

LIEUTENANT GOTO STOOD at attention before Colonel Omori and Admiral Iwabachi, and looked at his two superiors with studied insolence. He knew he was the son of an important man and had far more political pull than either of the senior officers who glowered at him. He had nothing to fear.

Omori shook his head in disbelief. "I cannot believe you would be so stupid, Goto, as to perpetuate what is a near uprising among the Japanese community. I gave my word that the girl would not be harmed and you went and fucked her and, worse, turned her over to your men. Now she is dead, the woman I wanted to serve as my mistress has disappeared, and the Japanese community is outraged. Is it possible that you are incapable of thinking beyond your prick?"

"I only did what a soldier should do with a captive woman,

Colonel," Goto said unrepentantly. "The people who are claiming she was pure-bred Japanese are lying. The girl was certainly part Japanese, but she was a mongrel with Hawaiian and American blood, which makes her less than nothing. There is no reason for anyone to get excited."

"I am concerned that you disobeyed an order," Iwabachi snarled. "I have only a few thousand men to govern these entire islands, and I depend on the goodwill of the Asian people to do that. Whether she was a mongrel or not, many people believe that she was Japanese and that you caused her death."

Goto's response was almost a sneer. "I did not force her to walk into the ocean, sir. That was her own stupid idea. So she got fucked, so what? Every woman will get it sooner or later."

Iwabachi was a terrier of a man, considered a fanatic by many. His faith in all that was Japanese was absolute, and he prayed for the honor of dying for his emperor. At a different time and place, the admiral would have been sympathetic to Goto's position. Today, however, he had an unruly set of islands to govern. He decided to play his trump card.

"Lieutenant, the girl's last name was Ozawa. It is being said that she was distantly related to our Admiral Ozawa, even though she was a mongrel."

For the first time, Goto looked uncertain. Admiral Ozawa commanded the naval detachments in action against Indonesia and Malaya, and was considered the logical successor to the revered Yamamoto, should anything happen to him.

"It can't be," Goto said without conviction. "I don't even think that's her last name. It was Ogawa, not Ozawa. We must refute the lie."

Omori did not quite agree. "That is too simple. Refuting a rumor often does nothing but give it credence. Like many rumors, it will have a life of its own. We can only wait for time to cause it to die down. In the meantime, you must go. I am assigning you to command the *kempetei* detachment on the island of Hawaii, at Hilo. There are guerrillas loose on the island, and your task is to find them and destroy them."

Goto bowed and sighed in some relief. His punishment would be a minor one, and the banishment to Hilo would only be temporary. Besides, while there he would have the opportunity for glory and independent command, and there had to be very young women in Hilo. It could have been a lot worse. It was good to have clout.

"AND WHO BESIDES the southern congressmen support this incredible idea?" President Roosevelt asked as he shook his head in disbelief.

"General DeWitt," said General Marshall.

Roosevelt sighed. DeWitt was the commander of the Western Defense Command, which included California. Shortly after the attack on Pearl Harbor, he had convinced the president and others that the resident Japanese were a threat to the safety of the country and quickly had them removed to concentration camps. Liberals, even those in Roosevelt's own party, were calling it a travesty of justice in that many of those removed were American citizens, both native-born and naturalized, and others were too old and feeble to be considered threats. It didn't matter. General DeWitt felt that the only good Jap was either a dead one or one who was locked up.

Roosevelt had reluctantly acquiesced. The mood of the country had demanded it, and he had rationalized that the Japanese-Americans would actually be safer in concentration camps than out on the streets and subject to mob justice.

But this request from a small group of senators and representatives astonished him. They proposed a trade of the Japanese civilians held in California camps for those white American civilians in Hawaii.

Senator Theodore Bilbo, a Democrat from Mississippi, was the spearhead for the plan. His rationale was simple: First, white people were being abused and going hungry in Hawaii; and, second, white people should never be held prisoner by nonwhites. Thus, with so many Japanese in our prisons and so many white Americans in theirs, a trade seemed like a logical step.

Roosevelt handed the paper containing the proposal to Marshall, who passed it to Admiral King. "Tell me, does the esteemed Senator Bilbo know he is under investigation for illegal activities involving war contractors?"

Marshall smiled tightly. "He must. Everyone else is aware of it."

Roosevelt jammed his cigarette into an ashtray. "And what would he have us do with the nonwhite population of Hawaii? Just write them off and leave them under their oppressors? Doesn't he realize that what he proposes would be a virtual signal of abandonment of the islands? It would tell the world that we have withdrawn from Hawaii forever."

"I don't think Bilbo has thought that far." King snorted. "Personally, I don't think the dumb son of a bitch can think to the end of his nose."

"I'm being crucified by the press," Roosevelt said. "Walter Winchell is saying the most terrible things about Hawaii to his radio audience, and the *Chicago Tribune* is printing news of appalling atrocities, most of which is false. Even Father Coughlin has decided to reignite his career by blaming me for everything. Tell me, gentlemen, are there any real plans afoot to liberate Hawaii and relieve me of this god-awful burden?"

The two senior military men stole quick glances at each other. Under FDR, security in the White House was not the best in the world. At one time they had even restricted the president's access to Magic information because of his maddening tendency to leave papers lying around, or to share the information with advisers who had no clearance to receive it. In particular, this applied to his friend and military adviser Major General Edwin "Pa" Watson, who was garrulous and sloppy with the documents he received.

"There are plans in the development state," Marshall answered cautiously. "But there is nothing we can or should discuss at this time."

"So I should say nothing in response to these attacks?" Roosevelt asked, and both men nodded. "This is so much more difficult than I ever thought it would be," the president said sadly. "Thank you for your time, gentlemen. If you don't mind, I'm not feeling well and am going to take a nap."

Marshall and King watched as the president wheeled himself out of the office. He was gaunt and gray, and had difficulty maneuvering the chair.

"If he feels as bad as he looks," King said as they were leaving, "then he is in really bad shape."

Marshall did not comment. He was deeply disturbed by the state of the president's health and what that portended. His worst nightmare was that Vice President Henry A. Wallace would accede to the presidency.

.

CHAPTER 15

Sergant Hawkins chuckled in the darkness. Like all of them, he was camouflaged and his face smeared with dirt, which made him almost impossible to see. "Colonel, this is getting to be like Grand Central Station. How much longer do you think we can continue landings at this place?"

"This may be the last," Jake said as he stole a glance at the almost sheer cliffs to their rear. "Of course, the last one was supposed to be the end of it. This one is a surprise."

The overusage of the bay where they had originally landed by flying boat was a concern to them all. So far they had been both lucky and good in that there were few people in the vicinity and even fewer Japanese patrols. It was a situation that could not last forever, and the delivery they were waiting for was unplanned.

In the preceding several weeks, the submarines had lined up almost like buses or, as Hawk preferred to think, trains. The military had not abandoned Hawaii; instead, it was apparent that the tiny force on the island was to be built up. Toward that end, subs had disgorged a platoon of well-trained and highly skilled Marine Raiders. They were commanded by First Lieutenant Sammy Brooks, a small, dark-complexioned young man with an Annapolis education and a ferocious desire to kill Japs. His brother was a prisoner in the Philippines.

The original handful of soldiers and marines had grown thanks to the infusion of navy refugees and a few selected civilian volunteers, including a handful of women. As a result, Jake gave Hawkins an unauthorized battlefield promotion to second lieutenant. Brooks had no problem with that, and, to Jake's surprise, his superiors in California agreed and confirmed it.

Along with much-needed supplies and equipment, other subs had landed a score of army engineers under a burly, middle-aged Swede, Captain Karl Gustafson, and his job was to find a place where planes could be landed and hidden until they were needed. "Not for too many planes," Gustafson had stressed. "Maybe a dozen or so."

Jake had thought it would be easier to hide a herd of elephants in a small church and not be noticed by the congregation, but he was pleasantly surprised at the skill shown by Gus and his men in identifying suitable locations. It was stressed that any landing strip should not look like one until it was time to use it. They were fortunate in that the ground was rock solid and flat enough in many areas, which meant it was necessary only to keep their basic efforts hidden. This could be done by moving foliage to key spots, and Gustafson was very good at hiding things.

Additional equipment and personnel also meant an improvement in their communications with California and other places. They maintained infrequent but steady contact with other guerrilla forces, primarily those under Fertig in the Philippines.

It was good to know they were not alone. Jake was secure enough to refuse additional help. A hundred or so men and women could be dispersed and hidden, while a larger group would be that much more difficult to both hide and feed.

The marine platoon still used the 1903 Springfield, and not the M1 Garand as their rifle. However, they did use the same .30 caliber bullet, which meant the supply situation was difficult but not impossible.

So, Jake wondered as he jerked his attention back to the present, what are we doing on this beach tonight? Instead of California calling, this time the message had been from Oahu and said to expect a "package."

At only a few minutes past the target time, he heard the quiet rumblings of a well-tuned diesel engine. After a while they saw a small fishing boat coming close to the shore. With its shallow draft, the darkened craft eased up to within a few feet of the sandy beach.

They watched as the three-man crew guided someone out of the cabin and awkwardly down into the shallow water. The fishing boat's crew was calm even though they had to know that a score of weapons were aimed at them.

"Your package can walk," Hawkins muttered.

"I don't know why, but I'm surprised," Jake said.

The "package" stood in the waist-deep water while the boat backed away. It was then that they realized the person was blindfolded and wearing an awkward and too-large cap.

Finally, hat and blindfold were removed. Jake gasped when he saw the hair and realized it was a woman, and, as she waded slowly and awkwardly toward land, he knew exactly who she was.

"Alexa," he said, and the sound of his voice startled her. "Over here."

"Jake? Oh, God. Is it you, Jake?"

They met where the water was knee-deep. She almost fell into his arms, and he held her tightly. Some package, he thought. He squeezed her, and she returned the embrace with that fierce strength that once had astonished him.

Finally, she broke free and looked at him. In the night he could see sadness on her face and tears streaming down her cheeks.

"I survived, Jake," she said, and her voice cracked with sobs. "I did what you said. I survived. I did whatever I had to, and now I'm here. I had no idea it would be so awful just to go on living." With that, she sagged on his shoulder and allowed him to lead her inland as the rest of the column formed up around them.

THE AMERICAN SEAMEN on the craggy and inhospitable island of Lanai had been fools, Charley Finch concluded. The idiots could have remained in hiding for all eternity. Living would have been uncomfortable and harsh, but it would have been better than what had happened to them and how it was likely to conclude.

The seven men had been marooned when their transport had been sunk off the coast in an attempt to flee to California. The fools had then started robbing the local people for food, and the civilians had reported them to the police. It had been only a matter of time before the *kempetei* picked up on the fact that Americans were running loose on Lanai and behaving like ordinary bandits.

Charley Finch's job had been to make contact with them and pretend that he was an escapee from the camps on Oahu. He located them after only a couple of days, and they welcomed him with open arms, even allowing themselves to think that he was some kind of savior. Other than knives, they had no weapons, and, had he been part of a Jap patrol instead of a lone, unarmed American, they would have fled safely into the interior. As it was, they stayed put because he told them the area was clear. It had been a fairly simple matter to leave a trail that the *kempetei* could follow. Charley's only real concern was that the Japanese might kill him by mistake.

That, it turned out, was not a problem. Colonel Omori had accompanied the combined *kempetei* and Japanese marine patrol, and the seven Americans had been taken into custody with barely a whimper. Now they stared at him in disbelief and horror. All had been beaten bloody in a brutal interrogation coordinated by Omori.

"I am satisfied," the colonel concluded. "These poor creatures know absolutely nothing."

No surprise, Charley thought. "What will you do with them, sir?"

Omori shrugged. "As I've told you, according to international law, they became outlaws by not surrendering." He nodded to a *kempetei* sergeant, who drew a pistol, held it against the skull of one of the sailors, and casually blew his brains out. The others began to moan and cry out, but the sergeant moved quickly down the line, and all were dead within a few seconds.

"I believe that was fairly merciful, don't you, Sergeant Finch?"

"Yes indeed, sir."

"They are not worthy of our time and resources. I must admit, however, that you did an excellent job of finding them. We will return to Oahu and plan your next assignment."

"May I ask what it might be?"

Omori smiled. "Lieutenant Goto has been on Hawaii for only a short while, but he has confirmed that there is a sizable American group operating in the interior. It will be a much more difficult assignment than this, but I am confident you can locate them and lead us to them."

Charley did not share Omori's enthusiasm. However, he was not in a position to argue. On a previous occasion, the colonel had reinforced the fact that, if Charley either balked or failed, he would be returned to the prison compound and the prisoners informed that he had been a Judas to them. Charley shuddered. The POWs would tear him to little bloody pieces. So, he thought grimly, he would do what he had to. But there was nothing wrong with making his situation more pleasant while he waited.

"May I ask a favor, Colonel?"

Omori froze him with a glare. Dogs did not ask for favors, and it was apparent from his look that Omori thought more of dogs than he did of Charley Finch. "What?"

Charley bowed. "Sir, it involves my living conditions. The food and the refreshments are excellent, sir, but I would like something other than the Korean woman you gave me."

Omori laughed. The sergeant had been assigned one of the homeliest of the comfort women he'd brought with him. She'd spied on Charley for Omori and reported him to be harmless and not even a good lay. "Do you want a Japanese woman?"

Charley professed shock. "No, sir. I am not worthy."

"That is right, Sergeant Finch. You are not worthy and you never will be. Only a Japanese man is worthy to screw a Japanese woman. Yet you have performed faithfully. I will get you an American, a young white woman. Would that satisfy you?"

Charley said that it would, and Omori walked away from him. It occurred to the colonel just who would be assigned to fuck Charley Finch. He had met her while questioning people regarding the disappearance of Alexa Sanderson. She was otherwise useless and would be perfect.

THE ENGINEER from Boeing was short and skinny, and had thick glasses. His 4-F draft status, which precluded him from entering the military because of physical problems, was virtually painted on his forehead. If, however, he could turn the giant flying boats into bombers, neither Colonel Doolittle nor Admiral Spruance would care about his physical appearance.

The engineer's name was Bart Howell, and he was as pompous as he was frail. They were gathered outside an immense hangar, and Howell began to speak. "As I saw it, the problem was the hull of the flying boat. In a conventional bomber, the bombs are stored in racks in the belly of the plane and released more or less simultaneously through a large bomb bay. This is impossible since the watertight integrity of the flying boat must be maintained. A bomb bay would be an invitation to a sinking."

"We understand that," Spruance said with mild impatience. "Have you come up with a solution?"

Doolittle stifled a grin. If the little prick hadn't, then they'd wasted a trip out to the desert and someone would get his butt ripped. Spruance was mild-mannered and polite to a fault, but he didn't suffer fools.

Howell took out a handkerchief and wiped his glasses. "Yes, sir, we have."

The blunt statement startled both men, even though it wasn't totally unexpected. Howell led them into the cavernous hangar, where a series of wooden struts resembling the skeleton of a giant whale had been constructed. "Gentlemen," Howell said, "this is a mock-up of the hull of a Boeing 314 flying boat."

Doolittle pointed to a series of short metal chutes in the interior of the plane that canted toward the back and ended in the hull.

Howell smiled. "That, Colonel, is the solution. A large bomb-bay door would collapse from the pressure of the water both on landing and on takeoff. However, we concluded that a dozen or so small holes wouldn't result in enough seepage to cause a problem. The metal chutes are bomb racks designed to hold one 250-pound bomb each, or a large number of four-pound incendiaries. With the holes in the hull angled toward the tail, the pressure on the hull is minimized and, prior to landing and takeoff, a series of dead bolts will be used to secure the hatches. There will no doubt be leakage, but nothing you can't control with some pumping while on the water, and it will simply drain out when airborne."

Doolittle walked around the skeleton craft. The solution was so simple and so elegant.

Howell continued, "Someone must remove all the dead bolts so that a trigger mechanism in the cockpit can actually open the hatches and release the bombs."

"How accurate will the bombing spread be?" Spruance asked.

"Not very," Howell admitted. "In a way it would be like firing buckshot from a shotgun. The higher up the plane is, the wider the spread. I strongly recommend low-level bombing to ensure any semblance of accuracy."

Doolittle couldn't imagine the tiny engineer ever firing a shotgun, but he agreed with Howell's estimate. High-level bombing was extremely inaccurate with conventional bombers, and this would be far worse. Nevertheless, it was now evident that the giant flying boat could be transformed into a weapon that could fly to Hawaii and back.

"Mr. Howell, when can you have these racks made and ready for installation?" Spruance asked.

Howell smiled proudly. "I presumed you'd like them, so I've had the machine shops working on them day and night. We now have enough for three planes and will have the rest in a week. Then we can begin installation and practice."

"Excellent, Mr. Howell," Spruance said and then added somberly, "I know I don't have to tell you how important it is that no one finds out about your work."

Howell wiped his glasses again and shook his head tolerantly. "I assure you of my discretion, Admiral. However, even a nearsighted idiot like me understands that you are not configuring a long-range plane like this as a bomber so you can attack Seattle. I hope you destroy all the Japs on Hawaii."

Doolittle smiled. He was beginning to like the little man. Perhaps the guy would like a drink? "So do we, Mr. Howell," he said. "So do we."

LIEUTENANT JAMIE PRIEST looked across to where Suzy Dunnigan sat taking notes. He tried to catch her eye, but she didn't look up and he dared not move. He was by far the most junior officer in the room, and his job was to make like wallpaper until and unless someone asked him to do something.

Admiral King and General Marshall had arrived in San Diego the day before via a grueling ride in a bomber. Now, after a night's rest, they and their small staffs were more than eager for the briefing Admiral Nimitz had prepared. As usual, Admiral Spruance was with Nimitz. Admiral Halsey was out with his carriers off Australia.

This was the first time Jamie had seen either King or Marshall in person, and he was a little awed. He'd been introduced and gotten a perfunctory handshake from King, who seemed more interested in Suzy's legs—her skirt was very short as a result of cloth shortages—and a kind comment from Marshall about the *Pennsylvania*. It made him wonder if everyone knew about his ordeal.

Nimitz stood. "Gentlemen, what we have prepared for the Japs is what my staff has started calling Operation Cork. In the absence of something more stirring, I suggest we keep the name. It was selected because the idea is to cork up the Japanese fleet in a spot where we can get at them, and that spot is Pearl Harbor."

Nimitz stepped to a wall chart of the Hawaiian Islands. "Admittedly, Cork violates virtually every military principle, particularly since it is predicated on the enemy doing precisely what we wish them to do, rather than what they have the ability to do. However, I believe it is inevitable that the Japs will take their main fleet to Hawaii, and do so shortly after the base becomes viable to them as a result of the completion of repairs to the fuel storage depot. When that occurs, they can use Pearl as a base for striking at the West Coast or, more likely, Alaska.

"We do not believe they will attempt a landing in California, Washington, or Oregon, but we do consider it strongly possible that they will send a bombardment force to California, or land troops at points in Alaska. If they do, the terrain and distance will make them very difficult to dislodge."

There was a shuffling as that statement was digested. Shelling of American cities had not yet occurred and would cause panic when it did. Even worse was the thought of the Japanese in Alaska, parts of which were closer to Japan than they were to the forty-eight American states.

King swore under his breath, while Marshall was silent. Japanese assaults on the West Coast might spell an end to the Germany First strategy. The shelling of San Francisco or Los Angeles would result in political pressure to concentrate efforts on Japan that could not be ignored. The results would be tragic. King might like the idea of Japan first, but Marshall knew that strategy could cost the United States the war.

Nimitz was satisfied that he had their undivided attention. "As you've informed me," he continued, "neutral diplomats in Tokyo are picking up hints that Hawaii will be formally annexed by Japan in either July or early August. We feel that a ceremonial showing of their fleet will occur to reinforce Japan's intentions."

"The fucking bastards," King said. Jamie looked at Suzy and saw her quick grin. The daughter of a sailor had heard far worse. "Their annexing Hawaii would be a taunt for us to come and get it. So what're we gonna do to stop it?"

"At the very least," Nimitz responded, "we have to destroy Pearl as a base. Toward that end, you know of our plans to send Colonel Doolittle on a raid to destroy the fuel depot."

"A waste of his efforts," King grumped. "Almost as nonsensical as his original idea to bomb Tokyo from a carrier."

Nimitz smiled. He had been chosen by King to command in the Pacific and wasn't affected by his boss's surly attitude. "Agreed. Even Doolittle would rather attack juicier targets than fuel tanks. If the Jap fleet presents itself, he will attack it. If the Japs don't come, of course, he will still hit the fuel. At the very worst, it would delay their ceremony."

Marshall was incredulous. "But he'd attack with only a handful of converted flying boats? It would be suicide."

"It is not intended to be suicidal. Risky, yes, but not suicidal," Nimitz said. "There are other plans afoot to hit the Japs and to keep their planes on the ground, or"—he smiled almost impishly—"safe on their carriers. Also, now that the torpedo problem has been largely solved, we will swarm the islands with our subs once the Japs arrive."

"And our carriers?" Marshall asked.

"One of my staff," Nimitz said and nodded toward Jamie, who flushed as he realized why he was there, "pointed out that a light carrier escorted by destroyers looks from a distance just like a fleet carrier escorted by cruisers. We are preparing a decoy force of escort carriers and destroyers to cruise at a distance off Spain and Portugal and then turn north. Along with a few discreet leaks at cocktail parties in Madrid, we hope the information will be passed on to the Japs that we have conceded the Pacific to them while we take on the Germans. In the meantime, our fleet carriers and their escorts will rendezvous around Samoa. They will wait for the signal that the Japs are corked and then attack. If a landing is feasible, we have a division of infantry, the newly constituted 24th, ready to depart at almost a moment's notice."

"Jesus." King sighed. "It would be great to pay the bastards back for what they did to us at Pearl Harbor by killing them right there at Pearl Harbor."

Nimitz agreed. "They tricked us because we were overconfident.

We hope they are just as overconfident and can be tricked just like we were."

Little more of substance was said before the meeting adjourned. There would be further discussions after lunch. Neither Jamie nor any of the other junior officers would attend. The afternoon would be free. He finally caught Suzy's eye, and she nodded.

King turned toward Nimitz as they left the room. "God damn, I hope it works. Operation Cork? Not exactly heroic, but I hope history records that we shoved a cork right up their asses."

SHORTLY AFTER ARRIVING at Jake's base camp, Alexa informed him that she needed time alone. He didn't ask for a reason and permitted her to go into the interior with a couple of local women as companions and protectors. While it tore at him to see her so tormented, he accepted that there were times when people had to be alone with their thoughts before they could share them.

When she returned after several days, Alexa smiled tentatively at him and suggested they go for a walk after dinner. It was still light when they got to a spot that Jake thought she would like. There was a small pond, and they could sit on a flat rock that looked down on the clear water, where fish about the size of minnows flitted in apparent joy in their search for food. The place was almost totally hidden by sheer cliffs, and, without being ordered, Sergeant Hawkins had discreetly placed guards around the tops. Jake knew this and was glad that they were out of sight.

Carefully and completely, Alexa told him everything that had happened to her and to Melissa. She spoke of the backbreaking work in the fields, of watching Father Monroe being tortured, and of her finally agreeing to speak treason for the Japanese. She told him in detail of her night of sex and drugs with Omori and Han, and then of Kami's rape and suicide. "Somehow I will get over it. I'm not certain how, just yet, but I will," she concluded.

When she was finished, he held her hand tightly. "You didn't have to tell me this. Omori used you and raped you, and then you got away from him. You did what you had to, and I'm glad, really glad, because that means you're here. You're with me and you're safe. And I'm glad you tried to save Kami. You're not responsible for her death, Goto and Omori are."

She smiled tentatively. "I did have to tell you. If I didn't, you'd always wonder just what happened, and I think it would eat at you. Now you know, and you can judge for yourself whether I did the right things or not."

"There was nothing else you could have done, Alexa. Everything was out of your control. You were his pawn. If you hadn't done what he wanted, you'd be dead or wishing you were. Life is too precious; I'm glad you didn't give it up."

"I know. Did you know the women you sent with me while I was out thinking were also assaulted by the Japs?"

"No," he said. "Frankly, I never gave it a thought."

"We talked about it. One of them was raped only once, the other by a dozen soldiers. We told each other everything, and then we cried. It helped to realize I haven't been alone. In fact, I may have been fortunate. I wonder if there will be any women in Hawaii who weren't attacked by the time this all ends. If it ever ends," she added. "The Japs use sex as a weapon, a tool, to achieve their ends. And we're supposed to respect them?"

Alexa took a deep breath and looked up at the darkening sky. Some of the larger stars were already visible. "Just think. In six months, I've gone from a docile, wealthy, college graduate navy wife to a widow who's been assaulted by a Jap officer, who's betrayed her country, and who's now a refugee in a guerrilla camp. What's the saying? That which doesn't kill me, strengthens me? I guess I must be getting terribly strong."

She allowed him to put his arm around her shoulders, although he made no effort to draw her closer. He understood and sympathized far better than she realized. Someday, he thought, he'd tell her of the terrible and sometimes drunken assaults some men had made on him when he was a boy, in particular those weekends he'd spent in county jails for minor offenses. Growing strong enough to resist them had been a marvelous revelation.

She shuddered. "I'll never be as strong as you are. My life was always so sheltered. Damn the Japs. Damn Omori and Goto."

"Goto's here on the island, Alexa. We'd heard about Kami's death, although I didn't connect it to you. Goto's been banished until it blows over and is stationed in Hilo."

"Are you going to kill him?"

The ease with which she asked the question surprised him. If her ordeal hadn't strengthened her, it had apparently hardened her. "If the opportunity presents itself. I'm not going to risk what we have here for personal revenge."

"And what do you have here, Jake?"

He explained about the secret base the engineers were building. "Our first priority is to stay alive and undiscovered by the Japs in Hilo, or by their planes. I'm glad they don't seem to have too many planes to look for us. Whether we can build an airstrip and keep it quiet or not is another point, but we're doing our best."

"I've enlisted in your army, haven't I?"

"Yep."

"Good. I want to do what I can to help. Will you get me a gun and teach me to shoot?"

He decided not to tell her that the military used rifles and not guns. "I will. Gladly."

"Good," she said and tucked her head under his chin. "Now just hold me very strongly. I need strength, Jake. I don't have all that much myself, although I'm working on it."

Jake did as he was told and reveled in the feel of her body next to his and the fact that she had so much implicit faith in him. She smelled clean and good, and her breath was hot on his chest.

Jake counted his blessings. Alexa was here and safe, and considered him a part of her future. Despite the pain she'd endured, he liked that. Whatever wounds she still felt, he would help her heal them.

Then a pragmatic thought intruded. By helping Alexa escape, Toyoza Kaga had totally and completely decided whether he was Japanese or American.

After a while, Jake grinned into the night. Alexa was sound asleep and snoring slightly. Maybe the healing had begun.

COLONEL OMORI NODDED as Toyoza Kaga entered his office and took a seat. "The people still hate us, don't they, Kaga?"

"It will take time, Colonel. Wounds do not heal overnight. It would have been far better for Goto to have been tried, either here or in Japan. Then people would know that justice was being done and not deferred."

Omori shook his head angrily. "Impossible."

Kaga knew it would have been difficult to prove a crime, even under normal circumstances. Kami had committed suicide, and could not testify against Goto for the rape. And it was highly unlikely that the enlisted men who had also raped the child would ever come forward. In Kaga's opinion, they were headed toward Japan if they were not there already.

"Then you will just have to live with the circumstances until the emotions fade."

Omori accepted that. He had expected as much. "And your son, is he doing well?"

Kaga's only son, Akira, had been brought by ship to Oahu. Kaga had been told that Akira's return was a gift from the Japanese government for his presumed loyalty. His son had lost a leg in the fighting in China and was no longer of any use to the Japanese army. Kaga's heart ached at the pain his son was feeling, but, as usual, he masked his emotions. "He is improving, thank you," he replied.

Akira had volunteered for the Japanese army while he was a student in Tokyo, a fact that made his father loyal in the eyes of Omori. He had become an officer and been assigned to duty in China. What Omori didn't know was that Akira had quickly become disillusioned, even horrified, by what was occurring there. On returning home, Akira had filled his father's ears with tales of the Japanese army's butchery. In particular, he told of the incident called the Rape of Nanking, in which tens of thousands of civilians had been raped, tortured, and murdered.

Now Kaga knew there was no honor in Japan's enterprise or in its intentions for the people of Asia. Both Toyoza and his son had begun to meet with a small circle of friends who shared this view. A number of them were young and of military age, and several had even served in the Hawaiian National Guard. This fact had begun to give both men interesting thoughts.

Kaga feigned a proud smile. "My son has served his emperor well. Even so, I am glad he is home."

"As am I. Perhaps your son will speak to the people of Oahu of his experiences. It might help our cause."

My, my, Kaga thought. The man will actually help us recruit followers. Akira could meet openly with the people of Oahu and selectively with others without attracting attention.

"We will need gasoline to travel," he said, as a merchant would. "And a vehicle. I can supply a driver."

"No problem at all," Omori responded loftily.

"Then I am sure we would both wish to help."

As Kaga departed for his home and his son, he wondered how he could have been so infatuated by Japanese successes. He had served in the Japanese army against the Russians at Port Arthur in 1905. There he had seen the ruling military caste's excesses, brutality, and contempt for life. He had been an enlisted man and treated with scorn at best by his superiors, and seen the lives of his comrades wasted in desperate assaults on Russian barbed wire. The Japanese army had succeeded, but only after crawling over the piled corpses of its soldiers.

Following the war, Kaga had deserted and, with assistance from relatives, found passage to Hawaii. How could he have been so stupid as to think only a few decades could change the minds of the masters in Tokyo? Worse, if Omori probed deep enough, he would find that Toyoza Kaga was a felon because of his desertion.

Kaga had thought that his past was well behind him. Now he knew better.

•

CHAPTER 16

*T*he congressman from Ohio was short and overweight, which partially contributed to his sweating profusely, even though it wasn't all that warm. A Democratic representative from an ethnically Italian district in Cleveland, Dominic Cordelli had been an FDR backer since Roosevelt won his party's candidacy for the vice presidency in 1920.

As luck would have it, FDR's loss had also been FDR's future gain. He was governor of New York when Herbert Hoover became reviled as the cause of the Great Depression. That the charge was unfair, and that Hoover was a decent and hardworking president, was irrelevant. Someone had to take the blame for the economic catastrophe, and it had occurred on the Republican Party's watch, which resulted in Roosevelt's victory in 1932.

In 1932, Dominic Cordelli had been swept to office on his president's coattails and, like Roosevelt, never left. He had supported FDR on every issue, including Roosevelt's ill-advised attempt to stack an uncooperative Supreme Court with more malleable members.

Cordelli did not have difficulty getting brief meetings with Roosevelt, and the representative, both wise and cunning, did not abuse the privilege. He had to wait only a couple of days before seeing the president, while other petitioners waited a lifetime.

Admiral William Leahy, the president's chief of staff and soon to be chairman of the Joint Chiefs, had arranged the meeting and was with FDR, who quickly noticed Cordelli's agitation. "Dominic, my friend, be seated and tell me what's on your mind," Roosevelt said.

Cordelli wiped his sweaty brow with a handkerchief that had been clean earlier in the day. "Mr. President, I need a favor. No, not a favor. Perhaps information and assurances would be more like it."

Roosevelt shrugged and smiled disarmingly. "Ask."

"I have a niece, a Mrs. Alexa Sanderson. Her husband was killed in the attack on Pearl Harbor."

"Dreadful," Roosevelt said with genuine sympathy. Then he turned impish. "Sanderson doesn't sound terribly Italian, though."

"She's not. She's a WASP from Virginia and related on my wife's side. The problem is that the niece is still in Hawaii. The FBI has been out to see us because she's making radio broadcasts and signing documents that could be considered treasonous. I want you to know that my niece would never do such a thing except under extreme duress. The FBI may be thinking of prosecuting her for something she was forced to do or say with a gun pointed at her head."

Roosevelt stole a glance at Leahy, who had been briefed when Cordelli had asked for the meeting. This had enabled Leahy to do a little research.

"Have you heard the speeches?" the admiral asked.

"Yes. The FBI was kind enough to play a couple for me. The language is convoluted and awkward. It isn't hers. She's highly educated and simply doesn't speak that way." Cordelli managed a wan grin. "Hell, it sounded worse than some of my constituents. No, sir, she's reading from a prepared script, and I'm convinced she's being forced to do it."

Roosevelt smiled. "If that is the case, she cannot be charged with any crime." He looked at a note that Leahy had handed him just before the congressman's arrival. The president leaned forward and looked intently at Cordelli. "Can you keep a secret?"

"Of course," Cordelli said.

Roosevelt spoke in a conspiratorial whisper. "It does not surprise you that we are in contact with certain elements in occupied lands, does it?"

"Not at all."

"Good. Well, what I am going to say must not leave this room, is that understood?"

"Of course," Cordelli responded eagerly. Both men knew he would tell his wife.

"Your niece is among several who have been forced by the Japs to send messages like that. We know they have been forced to do it."

"Poor Alexa." Cordelli sighed. "My wife is upset enough as it is without her thinking of Lexy being mistreated."

"Without going into detail," Leahy continued for Roosevelt, "I can assure you that your niece is no longer under Japanese control. She has been moved by our people to a different location in the islands, and there will be no further broadcasts of that sort by her, although, of course, some old ones might be replayed. She is not out of danger, but she is much freer than she had been."

Cordelli exhaled in a whoosh of relief. "Thank you."

They shook hands, and the congressman departed.

"You know what I wish?" Roosevelt mused.

Leahy smiled. "I have no idea, sir."

"Just once, I wish that the FBI would learn a little about tact and discretion. Why should the President of the United States be so involved in so minor a problem?"

Leahy smiled. He knew better. Roosevelt was exuberant at being able to give his friend Cordelli some good news. That simple act had lifted some of the stress from FDR's shoulders. That he had been able to be angry at the FBI was an added bonus. Admiral King and General Marshall had been right. The way to keep FDR alive and well was to keep him happy. Helping Congressman Cordelli was the perfect tonic. As to Roosevelt's lament about the problem being too small for him, Leahy knew that was so much hogwash. The president had enjoyed the whole thing immensely.

Franklin Delano Roosevelt had had a good day, and that was all that counted.

LIEUTENANT UJI GOTO KNEW he wasn't much of a warrior, but his new commander at Hilo, Major Osami Shimura, was even less of one. Shimura was short, fat, flabby, lazy, and dissolute. He was generally drunk by noon, and Goto thought he might be using opium as well.

Shimura also was a coward. He had close to five hundred men at his disposal and had done nothing to rid the island of Hawaii of the American guerrillas who, in the opinion of Goto and other more determined officers, operated with impunity outside Hilo.

"Too many," Shimura had said on several occasions. "There are hundreds of them out there just waiting to ambush us. Our job is to hold Hilo, not run all over this wretched island chasing shadows."

Goto wondered how a group of well-armed Americans could become shadows, but he said nothing. He had read the raw intelligence data and knew there was only a very small American force in the field, somewhere between fifty and a hundred, and they would not be able to stand up to a battalion of Imperial marines if they were cornered.

Of course, Goto acknowledged that cornering them was the problem. Hawaii was four thousand square miles of jungle, mountain, and volcanoes, some active, in which the Americans could hide. As a boy visiting relatives, he had hiked some of the trails and knew that a full division of Imperial marines might not be able to root them out unless they had to stand and fight for something they deemed important.

With an active campaign out of the question for the immediate future, he settled into a fairly comfortable existence. Like the other officers, he got drunk almost every evening and spent many of the nights in the local brothel. The madam, a fat Hawaiian with many gaps in her smile where the teeth had rotted out, quickly understood his unique pleasures. She made certain he had access to several girls in their early teens, although she had been disturbed by his requests for girls who were even younger. So far, she had not been able to get any prepubescent children for him, and that disturbed Goto as well.

Of course, if he could get back to Honolulu, with its larger population, his needs could be more readily fulfilled. In order to get back, he had two choices: First, he could wait out the necessary time, as Omori had suggested, or, second, he could do something outstanding that would require him to be sent back to Honolulu regardless of what the civilians thought. Who gives a shit, he snarled to himself, what the civilians think?

Thus, it was with some eagerness that he greeted the foul creature who stood before him. "Sergeant Finch, you are to be congratulated on all you have done for Japan. I can only hope you will be as successful here."

Finch was uncomfortable but tried to hide it. He should not have been sent to Goto's quarters, where his presence might be noted. Even though it was night and he was wearing civilian clothing and a hat, someone might have recognized or remembered him.

"As always, Lieutenant, I will do my best."

"It was easy for you on Lanai. The Americans there were total idiots and there was really no place for them to hide. Here on Hawaii, it will be different."

Indeed it would, Charley thought. Finding the guerrillas would be the first part of the problem.

"How will you explain yourself?" Goto asked. "You will appear to them as a reasonably healthy POW. How will you explain yourself?"

Finch bowed. He had not been invited to sit. "I'm fortunate in that most of the POWs on Oahu have been sent to Japan. I will say that I escaped during transit, made it to Molokai by boat, was hidden on a farm, and then fled to Hawaii with the purpose of meeting up with the Americans. It is a simple story, and one they won't be able to check out."

Goto grunted. Finch couldn't tell whether he agreed or not. "When you find the Americans, how will you contact us?"

"Sir, on Lanai I was able to drop notes in a stump by the road. This island is too big for that sort of thing. I'm afraid I will have to desert the Americans when the time comes."

That answer did not totally please Goto. It meant that Finch could be used only one time and that his fat commander would have to be induced to move rapidly, something that just wasn't likely.

However, like Finch, Goto had no choice. He would use the tools at hand, not the ones he wished he had.

ON THE OTHER SIDE of Hilo, Lieutenant Sammy Brooks, USMC, crouched in the hole he'd dug in the side of the hill overlooking Major Shimura's quarters. Shimura had commandeered a large and stately house on the outskirts of Hilo that must have belonged to someone with money.

It was daylight, and he had several hours more to wait. Beside him was his rifle, the '03 Springfield he thought of as his best friend. Brooks was an outstanding shot, and, in his opinion, the Springfield was a more accurate sniper rifle than the new Garand being issued to the army. Screw the army, he thought, he'd keep his Springfield.

As a marine, he had been well taught in the craft of stalking a prey. He would not be found except in the unlikely circumstance that someone literally stumbled onto where he was hidden. He knew that what he was doing was against Jake Novacek's orders, but he just didn't care. It was impossible for him to be on the same island with a pack of Japs and not strike out at them. He'd heard of Novacek's ambush of the Jap patrol and knew that the Japs hadn't launched any offensive against them. He was confident the same would be the case this time.

Brooks hadn't intended an ambush. His original plans were for several days of in-depth reconnaissance of the Hilo garrison, but, when he realized how small and ineffective the Jap force was, he knew he could strike and flee into the interior with little concern.

He had lied to both his commander in California and Novacek. His brother wasn't in a Jap prison camp. His brother was dead. Word had come from the Philippines, through a civilian who both knew his brother and had seen him die, that Captain John W. Brooks had been bayoneted for insolence en route to a prison camp after the surrender at Bataan. His insolence was begging for water. He was then buried alive in a sandpit by fellow prisoners, who would have been killed themselves had they not cooperated. When the grievously wounded man had clawed his way out of his grave, he had been reburied. John W. Brooks did not escape death a second time.

Although he detested it, Sammy Brooks understood the need for patience. Already he had spent almost a day in his hole. He ate sparingly of his rations, drank sips from his canteen, and relieved himself into a hole dug in the bottom of his hideout. The waiting was agony, but he would be well paid for it.

Finally, shadows faded into a gray night. There were plenty of stars, which was both a blessing and a curse. His target would be easy to see, but so would he as he fled. He would count on confusion and a defensive reaction to his attack to enable him to get into the safety of the hills.

A car pulled up in front of Shimura's quarters. A guard got out of the front seat and ran to his station at the rear of the house. The driver exited and opened the rear door for the fat major to get out. He then ran to the porch to open the door for Shimura, after which he would take up duty as a front sentry. Brooks knew that they changed every four hours from a guardhouse that was a couple of miles away.

In short, Shimura's security was incredibly lax.

The major walked to the house and waited for the guard to open the door. The range was three hundred yards. Brooks squeezed the trigger, and there was a startling blast of sound and light. Shimura's head exploded in a froth of gray and red while the sentry gaped in astonishment.

"Damn," muttered Brooks. He'd been nervous, and his shot had ridden high. He had aimed for the Jap's torso, not his head. It was too easy to miss the smaller skull. He had been lucky.

He worked the bolt and fired a second time, dropping the shocked guard beside his master. The second guard raced from the back, and another bullet toppled him. This was excellent. Anyone who had heard the gunfire was unlikely to investigate, and there was no one to notify the other soldiers at the guard shack. Someone in the area might phone, but it was unlikely. No one would want to get involved. The Japanese reaction would take time.

"Three for three," Brooks exulted and laughed, and then he turned somber. "That's for you, Johnnie," he sobbed.

He gathered his rifle and his gear and began the lonely trot into the hills.

It never rains in sunny Southern California, at least that was what Jamie Priest had always thought. This day, however, had brought a torrential rain and a cold wind off the ocean, and neither showed any sign of letting up.

He and Suzy Dunnigan had moved their picnic from the beach to the small, two-bedroom bungalow that had belonged to her father. It was a mile away from the ocean, and, by the time they got there, parked the car, and got their things from it, both were soaking wet and cold.

No matter. While there was no furnace in her house, there was a Franklin stove, which, after only a few minutes and a handful of wood, gave off enough heat to dry their swimsuits while they dined off a blanket that was spread on the floor by the stove.

Suzy had chosen a white wine from a California vineyard he'd never heard of. Jamie's perception of California wines was that they were cheap and bitter, and he found himself pleasantly surprised by the richness of the taste. The wine, coupled with the radiant heat, made them feel warm and mellow.

Jamie spent a couple of minutes examining the house. There were a number of pictures of Suzy's father, along with a couple of her as a thin and serious-looking child, and the house exuded a fairly masculine air.

"Dad bought this place after the divorce. I only moved back a few months ago. I graduated from Stanford last June and always thought my dad would move back here and take possession. Then, after he was killed, I didn't have the heart or courage to change anything." She laughed softly. "However, I had already moved into the larger bedroom and taken over the big bed. My stuff is in his closet. Even before Pearl Harbor, I didn't think he'd mind if I took it over."

"I like it. What will you do with it when you leave to serve your country?"

Congress was on the verge of approving women in both the navy and the army. With Nimitz's endorsement, Suzy was a virtual shoo-in for officers' school or even a direct commission in what would be called the WAVES, the Women Accepted for Voluntary Emergency Service. She thought someone had strained hard to make the acronym work for the navy.

But it was a sore point insofar as Jamie's request for a transfer to a combat command had again been denied.

"I'll probably rent it out. Do you think you'd be interested?"

Jamie thought that he might. It would beat the hell out of the bachelors' quarters he shared with several dozen close friends.

"Yeah, since I'm not going anyplace, I might just take you up on it."

She reached over and took his hand. "Jamie, you know they can't send you out. You may be the last of the *Pennsylvania*'s crew, and they can't risk you. You'll be promoted, and you still have a great career if you want to stay in the navy when the war's over, but you know you won't see any more combat in this war."

Jamie knew it, but he didn't have to like it. Everything she said was correct. He'd been informed that his promotion to lieutenant commander would come down any day. They both thought it was overdue and probably delayed because of uncertainty regarding his role with the doomed battleship. Privately, Jamie thought the four pissed-off admirals who'd traveled to see him had stonewalled it for as long as they could.

"Don't feel bad," she said and squeezed his hand. "Whatever happens, I won't be getting shot at either. With a little luck, I'll be back in San Diego doing what I've been doing, only wearing a uniform."

"That's important to you, isn't it? The uniform."

"Because of my father, yes."

"And that's why you like me, right? Because I look so good in a sailor suit?"

Suzy laughed and squeezed his hand harder. "Who says I like you?"

"Don't you?"

"Of course," she said with a smile. "And it doesn't bother me at all that you won't be in combat. You've seen more than enough of it. I don't want you hurt."

Jamie was delighted. Even though he knew she was fond of him, it was the first time she'd said it. He wondered if the fact that they were just about finished with the second bottle of wine had anything to do with it.

He reached for her, and she came toward him on the floor. He kissed her very gently, and she didn't respond. God, he thought, have I misjudged? "I guess I shouldn't have done that."

She shook her head and smiled. "I don't know why, but you surprised me. Try again."

He did as directed. This time her lips parted and she melded into him. She slid across his lap and kissed him back. To his delight, her tongue was exploring his as eagerly as he was hers.

This time Suzy was wearing a one-piece bathing suit. They parted, and Jamie slid the straps off her shoulders and pulled it down to her waist. Her breasts were small, but he thought them indescribably lovely. He caressed them, then kissed her nipples until they hardened while she ran her hands over his buttocks and held the erection that strained against his swimsuit. She wriggled to help him as he slid her suit over her hips and down her legs. Then she undressed him and they caressed each other as they lay on the carpet.

She was lithe and small, and he thought he had seen no one more beautiful as he ran his hands, lips, and tongue over her body. He wanted to take her right there, but Suzy got to her feet.

"Not on the floor," she said and giggled. She pulled him into the bedroom, and they fell onto the bed. She wrapped her slender legs around him and drew him onto her and into her. They both groaned and climaxed quickly. It was too soon, but they knew they had all night to get it perfect.

The next morning, they made love for the third time. Then they took a bath and did it again. They would be late for work but didn't much care.

"Remember what I said about you renting this place?" she asked. They were still naked and back in bed.

"Of course."

"Well, why don't you move in now? You can sort of get used to it while I'm still here. You can even save on your laundry bill, since we won't be wearing much in the way of clothes."

Jamie thought that was a marvelous idea with one concern. "But what about your neighbors? What'll they think?"

"Screw the neighbors," she said firmly. She sat up so that her breasts hung almost into his face. "Let 'em think what they want. Besides, don't they know there's a war on?"

AKIRA KAGA'S RIGHT LEG had been amputated just above the knee. It was a challenge to walk with crutches, but he was the kind to rise to challenges, and he had become surprisingly mobile in only a short time.

With his father driving, and accompanied by two *kempetei*, he began speaking to groups of civilians throughout Oahu. The majority of the people he addressed were Japanese, although a few Hawaiians did attend. He never saw a white face in the crowds.

Akira and his father worked hard on what he would say and precisely how he would say it. He wanted the underlying meaning thoroughly comprehended by the Japanese of Hawaii. The two *kempetei* men weren't particularly subtle, and, besides, they were kept drunk by friends of Toyoza Kaga.

Akira told his listeners that the Japanese soldier was brave and resilient, traits that were essential when fighting in China, where there were no supplies and less in the way of medical care, facts that required them to loot the enemy and local civilians.

He saw surprise on their faces. No supplies? No medicine? Why couldn't Japan take care of her fighting men? Many of his audiences had donated money to help Japan defeat China, their long-standing enemy. Where had it gone?

Akira then told them of the tens of thousands who'd died fighting the Chinese and how the Chinese kept on coming. Japan would persevere, he said, no matter how many Japanese had to die to accomplish it, and no matter how many more years it would take. Japan, he said, would ultimately conquer vast China, a land that was as large as a mighty ocean and in which the Chinese were forever retreating. It might take a hundred years of agony, but Japan would prevail.

He saw a stirring in the crowd. In effect, he had told them that the war between Japan and China would never end. They had not been informed of the scope of the casualties, and this too shocked them. Heavy casualties, no supplies, no medicine, and no end in sight to the killing? Japanese soldiers reduced to looters and beggars? This was not the stuff of glory.

Akira responded to the accusations of atrocities committed by the Japanese in China. They were not true, he said, although it was sometimes necessary to take food from the peasants since the Japanese army didn't have enough for itself. He said it was sometimes necessary to punish uncooperative Chinese by destroying their property or even executing them. He added that a Chinese woman should feel honored to be taken by a Japanese soldier, even if she initially resisted. As his eyes traveled the crowd, Akira noticed a number of people preparing to leave, their heads down in shame.

Then he told them that his travel back to Hawaii by ship had been fraught with danger because of the ever-present menace of American submarines. "But we did not fear them, even though they did sink several in our convoy," he said boldly as it sank in on his audience that Japan did not rule the oceans. He had further told them that the supply line from Japan to Hawaii was as tenuous as the line from Japan to the troops in China. Hawaii was out on an indefensible limb, and many looked nervously at one another.

"I believe that soon Hawaii will be annexed to the empire of Japan," Akira said. "When that happens, I will rejoice. That means that the Americans will be forced to fight a decisive battle against us, and, despite their material assets and the overwhelming size of their country, we will prevail. No matter how devastated Hawaii is as a result of the coming battle, we will win. It won't matter how many thousands of tanks or planes they have, or how many hundreds of warships they hurl at us, it won't matter. Hawaii's cities and farms may be destroyed, but we will rebuild. Tens of thousands of Hawaiians may die, but Japan will be victorious.

"Some of you have seen the factories and shipyards of America, and, while Japan has nothing like them, Japan does have the courage of her people, who are willing to die in their millions to secure their country's future. America's vast material superiority will amount to nothing. Even if Germany is defeated by the Allies and we have to face the combined might of the United States, Great Britain, and China, we will be victorious. It doesn't matter that America's army now numbers in the millions and its soldiers are not like the drunken louts who were stationed here and were defeated, they are not Japanese."

As he finished to tepid applause, he saw that most had understood clearly and were looking at him with new respect. He had told them that the Japanese army was inept and guilty of the worst imaginable atrocities. Japan was doomed, and a mighty battle could easily be fought on and for the islands. Simple numbers told them that the United States had a population a third larger than Japan's. Combine that with Great Britain's, and add the vast but incompetent legions of China, and an ugly picture of a war of attrition was drawn. Japan might be able to distance herself from China's hordes but never from an angry and vengeful United States and Great Britain.

Later that evening, Akira and his father met with a select handful of young men in the back of a dry-cleaning business owned by Toyoza Kaga. Guards watched for unwelcome guests while the two *kempetei* slept away in their beds. The alcohol had been augmented by a mild narcotic, and they would not awaken for anything less than a volcano.

For this group, Akira was even more specific. "Japan has been accused of terrible atrocities in the war with China. Let me tell you that they are all true. I volunteered for Japan's army because I thought her cause was just and the empire was good. I no longer think that. I saw what happened in Nanking with my own eyes. I saw women and children raped and murdered by the thousands. I saw Chinese men bayoneted to death for no reason other than that they were Chinese. To my shame, I took part in those evil actions. I killed helpless people and raped innocent women."

He tried to block out his memory of a terrified woman who had submitted to him while her baby whimpered.

"Perhaps," he said bitterly, "the loss of my leg was in payment for my sins."

Kentaro Hara was an old friend and peer of Akira's. "Would it have been saved if Japan's army had provided decent medical support?"

"Probably," Akira admitted. "Infection set in after a while. We had to use bandages salvaged from the dead and then washed as best as we could."

His friends were appalled. "And our troops are really that bad?" Hara asked. "Japan's army is noted for its discipline. What is happening?"

"Madness," Akira said, "and incompetence. I did what I did in a moment of rage and fury. We had been fired on from a village, and a friend of mine was killed. In other instances, the replacements from Japan aren't up to the level of the men they are replacing. The second- and rear-echelon soldiers are little more than half-trained criminals who have been conscripted and abused, and who have no wish to be in China. There have been incidents of soldiers murdering their own officers."

That brought gasps, and even Toyoza Kaga was surprised.

"What can we do?" Hara asked sadly. "Japan will be defeated and the Americans will be on us in a rage for revenge."

Akira smiled. "That is why we are here. We must organize and be ready to support the Americans when they invade. They must be made aware that not all Japanese support Tokyo. Not all are old fools or young radicals, like I was. We must be willing to pay for their understanding with our blood."

"Excellent," Hara said with an enthusiasm that surprised both Akira and Toyoza, "but how will we let them know we are here, and what should we do? It is rumored that Americans are active on Hawaii. Do we have a means of contacting them?"

Toyoza Kaga spoke for the first time. "I will work on that," he said innocently and saw the look of comprehension on the others' faces. When they laughed, he knew that Akira had chosen well, and he was proud of his son.

LIEUTENANT GOTO FULLY AGREED that punishment had to be given out for the deaths of Major Shimura and his guard. The second guard might yet die from his wounds, and his fate, whether he died or not, was part of the planned retribution.

What did surprise Goto was that Admiral Iwabachi had overruled

Colonel Omori regarding its severity. Iwabachi wanted blood for the harming of his men and he wanted it in copious amounts, while Omori urged relative restraint. Deaths had to occur, but Omori wanted far fewer than Iwabachi did, and he wanted the native Hawaiian population insulated from the reprisal. It struck Goto as ironic that the admiral was endorsing acts not dissimilar to those that had seen him banished to Hilo.

The new commander of the Hilo garrison was Captain Isamu Kashii, and he held the post by virtue of being more senior in rank than the other captains. In his mid-thirties, Kashii was a firebrand and a fanatic, totally the opposite of the late, unlamented, and cowardly Major Shimura. Kashii wanted to kill Americans, and Goto wanted to help him.

A hundred men and women were chosen from the population. People of Japanese extraction were excluded from the reprisal, but, regardless of his orders, Hawaiians were not. When Goto had commented that the Hawaiians were likely to be sympathetic to Japan, Kashii had told him it didn't matter. They were all suspect in his eyes. Kashii could not even begin to comprehend the thought of the assassin being a lone warrior. He was vehement that the murderer had to have had help.

This was more like it, Goto had exulted. Shimura had been a pussy, afraid of his own shadow and more interested in entertaining himself with booze and drugs than in searching out the Americans. Let the blood flow.

As a result, the hundred doomed men and women had been chosen, some at random and some because they hadn't shown enthusiasm for the Japanese cause, then interrogated with utmost brutality by Goto and some of Kashii's men. Many couldn't walk and had to be helped into the sunlight by those who could, while several were blind. Their eyes had been gouged out. The remainder of the Hilo population had been ordered to witness the punishment, and there was an audible moan by the assembled thousands as the tormented victims were led to the place of death.

Ten thick wooden stakes had been driven into the ground. They rose more than six feet tall and stood in front of a higher wall of sandbags. A Model 92 heavy machine gun mounted on a tripod stood about fifty yards away, while the two-man crew looked grimly at the empty stakes.

Moaning and numb with terror, the first ten were tied to the stakes. Captain Kashii signaled, and the machine gun commenced an insanely loud chattering that drowned out all other sounds. The victims jumped and writhed as the bullets tore into them, sending a spray of blood and flesh into the air. Then everything was still, and the bodies lay limp in their ropes. After a few seconds, some people in the crowd started screaming, but they were ignored. Soldiers untied the victims and dragged their bodies to the wall behind. A couple of them twitched and may still have been alive.

A second ten were brought forward, tied, and machine-gunned. The process was continued until only the last ten remained, and they too were tied to the now badly splintered stakes. The ground before them was so soaked with the blood of the preceding victims that red puddles had formed, and the crowd had ceased screaming or crying out. The mound of dead and dying behind the stakes had become a stack of bloody, raw meat as bullets that missed their targets had smacked into the bodies.

With the last ten in place, Kashii gave another signal, and ten soldiers with bayonets on their rifles took their places, one in front of each victim. Kashii bellowed an order, and the soldiers began their practice. First, they lunged their blades into the meat of their victims' inner thighs, then the muscle of the upper arms. The last ten shrieked for mercy, but there was none. More thrusts slashed at their buttocks, the backs of their calves, the cheeks of their faces, their eyes, and, finally, slashing, disemboweling thrusts to the victims' stomachs finished it.

Even so, it would take a while for some of them to die. The crowd was dismissed, but soldiers stood guard over the bloody place. Kashii ordered that no bodies be removed for at least twenty-four hours as an example.

The captain strode over to Goto and smiled. There was blood spattered on Kashii's uniform. "Well, that ought to keep them in line. If it doesn't, we'll do it again and again until it does."

The man loves to kill, Goto thought, and then laughed harshly to himself. And Omori thought *I* was a problem. At last, he congratulated himself, I am serving under a real leader.

"Some of the people in Hilo will move out, Captain." Goto's intelligence operatives told him that several hundred had already departed and more would follow. In a little while, Hilo could be a ghost town.

"Let them," Kashii said. "There will be no food for them. They'll come back."

"Captain, any more clues as to the murderer or his helpers?"

"The killer was an American. One had been seen skulking around the day before, but it was unreported and apparently had happened earlier under the lax administration of my predecessor. But no, I did not get any information regarding specific assistance given to the assassin. Now I don't need it. A message has been sent. I am confident it will not happen again."

Goto agreed with Kashii. The Americans would be cowed by what had happened and would not attempt such a murder again. Unless, of course, someone struck at Kashii in revenge for this day. Goto saw how the captain's actions might have launched a spiral of violence.

Good, he thought. Finally, he felt he was serving under a Japanese warrior.

•

CHAPTER 17

Lieutenant Brooks was appalled at the Japanese reaction to his killing of Major Shimura. Still, Jake felt compelled to read the young lieutenant the riot act, which he did with a vengeance.

It had taken Brooks several days to return from Hilo through Japanese patrols that were suddenly out in force. Prudently, he had taken a circuitous route back to the main American camp, and it was only then that he found out about what was being called the Massacre of the Innocents.

"I never thought the Japs would do anything like that," Brooks had said with sincere contrition. He had never dreamed that he would cause anything so awful to occur, and the news had made him physically ill. He had killed an enemy soldier, which was what he had been trained to do.

"You never thought is right," Jake had snapped. "Look, I'm sorry your brother was killed in the Philippines, damned sorry, but that doesn't give you the right to go off and start your own private war. If I'd known you were going to shoot that Jap, I'd have stopped you from leaving camp. That Jap you killed was so stupid he was one of our best allies. Now they've replaced him with someone who can actually think, and that's likely to cause still more people to die."

"It won't happen again, sir."

Jake pushed his face right up to Brooks's. He was taller than the small, wiry Raider. "Damn right it won't. You take any actions without my orders and I'll bust your ass right down to buck private. Is that understood?"

"Yessir."

"And another thing. I have just promoted Hawkins to the temporary rank of captain. Whether or not I have that authority, I don't care.

I just want it clearly understood that he's in command and not you if something should happen to me. Understood?" Brooks's head bobbed up and down. "Good. You're dismissed."

Hawkins came over as Brooks departed, his shoulders slumped in dejection. "Everybody makes mistakes, Colonel, but he made a doozy. A hundred dead people because of his actions is a little hard to take. We gotta help him live with that so it doesn't destroy him."

Jake agreed. "I'll ease up on him tomorrow. You're right, I don't want to destroy him as an officer or as a person. Let him spend a night thinking about it, though. Now, let's talk about our new member. Who the hell is Charley Finch, and why does he make me uncomfortable?"

Hawkins chuckled. "For one thing, if he's been on the lam for a couple of months, like he says, he looks too well fed and plump to me."

"Right. Did you know him before the war?"

"I knew of him, but I never really met him. I saw him a few times at the NCO club and knew he was in supply, but we never hung around."

"What was his reputation?"

"A low-level crook and overall shady character, which may explain why he is so plump and juicy. He's one of those guys who could hustle his way out of anything, so he may have been doing exactly what he said he was, being fed and cared for by locals and by stealing anything that wasn't nailed down."

Finch had arrived the day before. He claimed that he'd escaped from a Japanese work gang a couple of months earlier, and that his fellow prisoners had all been shipped to Japan. He said he'd been hidden by sympathetic Hawaiians on Oahu who'd helped him make his way to Maui, where he'd stayed with an old Hawaiian woman who'd cared for him and kept him hidden. Then, as Finch explained it, she died and he made his way to Hawaii all by himself in a small boat he'd swiped.

"It's a great story," Jake said, "and there's nothing that can be verified. His fellow prisoners are gone, the old lady's dead, the boat's stolen, and he's already said he can't quite recall the people on Oahu who helped him because he was so sick at the time. He may not be a yachtsman, but he just could be good enough to take a small boat from Maui to Hawaii. It's less than thirty miles from one island to the other, and I don't think he'd ever even be out of sight of land on a sunny day."

Hawkins grinned. "I take it you don't trust him."

"Hawk, the old army was a small club, and the garrison on Oahu was an even smaller chapter of that club. Everyone knew everybody else, and, yeah, I knew about good ol' Sergeant Charley Finch. Hell, everybody did. You're right, he was a minor crook and a total shit. Keep this under your rusty helmet, Hawk, but he was under investigation by the FBI."

Hawkins whistled. "Why?"

"Stealing army stores and selling them. I got involved in my intelligence capacity because the FBI thought he was selling weapons to gangsters and other people who didn't like the United States."

"Jesus, now what?"

"Well, we gotta remember that he was never arrested, never indicted, never tried, and never found guilty. Who knows, he may be innocent of anything major."

Jake thought of the supplies he'd "liberated" before the surrender. Did they make him different from Finch? "At any rate, he's the type of person who actually could show up fat and healthy when everyone else is starving, and that doesn't necessarily make him a crook. In fact, it might make him the kind of cunning son of a bitch who could help us."

"Okay, Colonel Jake, then what does it really make him?"

"Someone we watch very carefully, Hawk. Either he's telling the truth, or he's doing things I don't even want to think about."

Hawkins took a deep breath as he realized what Jake was implying. "The killing on Lanai? Those seven guys who got caught by the Japs? You think he had something to do with that?"

"It's almost too awful to contemplate, isn't it? I can't believe a fellow American would have anything to do with it, but I can't get the possibility out of my mind. Nobody has any proof, and you can't send somebody to jail on my hunches. On the other hand, if Sergeant Finch is such a damned great hustler, he may be an invaluable asset to us. We're gonna use him, Hawk, but"—Jake grinned tightly—"we're going to watch him like a hawk."

▪

THE GIANT FLYING BOAT wasn't particularly difficult to get or keep airborne, although keeping it on the straight and narrow in a stiff desert wind was a challenge, even for a skilled pilot like Colonel Jimmy Doolittle.

Below him were a series of rectangles painted in white on the flat and barren ground east of San Diego. They were approximately one thousand feet by one hundred feet and were intended to simulate a very large ship, and a ship that was anchored. Doolittle and Nimitz had concluded that anyone could hit a tank farm full of large and combustible oil storage tanks. It would take real skill to hit a carrier if, by chance, one was in Pearl Harbor at the time of the strike.

The priorities were ironically like those given the Japanese on December 7. First were the carriers. In their absence, the oil storage tanks. Nowhere on the list were battleships. Even if there were battlewagons in Pearl, they were to be ignored in favor of the carriers and the oil storage facilities. My, Doolittle thought, how the mighty have fallen. His personal opinion was that battleships were particularly dramatic dinosaurs that could do damage only if they were permitted to get within range. The purpose of a plane was to keep them out of range and to sink them.

After numerous attempts, Doolittle and the other pilots had come to the conclusion that the Boeing Model 314 flying boat was a lousy bomber, and that hitting any target was extremely difficult.

Of course, if they'd been able to use one of the new, secret Norden bombsights, it might have been different. High command, however, had nixed that idea. Too much chance of the bombsights falling into enemy hands, they'd said, which pretty much told him what they thought of his chances for survival.

This conclusion was further reinforced when Doolittle was informed that he would be promoted to brigadier general on his return, and not before. He understood fully. Enough generals had been killed or captured in this war. They did not need another one for the Japanese press to trumpet as a triumph. Colonels, even bird colonels, were a dime a dozen.

The massive plane came in over the target at five hundred feet. Five other planes flew at the same height over other, similar rectangles.

The original eight planes had been reduced to six because of maintenance problems and had been cannibalized for parts.

The bombardier signaled and released the bags of flour that served as dummy bombs. The plane shuddered slightly as the bombs were dropped, and Doolittle pulled hard to lift her out of harm's way. In his mind he could visualize scores of antiaircraft guns shooting at him, while a dozen Zeros streaked downward to blow him out of the sky. He decided that he must have been nuts to have volunteered for this.

"Got some hits," exulted Bart Howell from the tail of the plane. The skinny little engineer was usually airsick, but this time he actually looked happy. Then Doolittle saw the caked puke on the front of his coveralls. Doolittle laughed. Howell was giving his all for his country, even his lunch.

Howell had worked day and night to install and then modify the bomb chutes, and those efforts had caused Doolittle's and the other pilots' impression of him to increase immeasurably. So what if he sometimes was a pompous jerk; the pompous jerk knew what he was doing.

"This is the right altitude, isn't it?" Howell asked.

"Yeah," muttered Doolittle, "five hundred feet." There had been a number of attempts at altitudes that were higher and safer, but the only consistent hits came from flying low. It was almost treetop level, only there wouldn't be any trees on the ocean. Five hundred feet was almost tantamount to suicide unless something happened to distract the fighters. With surprise on their side, they might just be able to make it through the antiaircraft storm, but the Zeros would follow them and swat them into the sea. "God help us all," said Doolittle.

SERGEANT CHARLEY FINCH THOUGHT that he might just have outsmarted himself. Local Hawaiians had been very helpful in getting him in touch with someone who got him in contact with others who finally took him to the American camp. No one was suspicious of him until he actually made it to the American base and realized that the commanders were people he knew personally or had heard of.

Somehow, Captain Jake Novacek had gotten promoted to light colonel, and Sergeant Will Hawkins was, even more incredibly, a captain in this ragtag army. Neither event boded well in Finch's opinion. Novacek had been in intelligence, G-2, which probably accounted for his suspicious nature, and Hawkins had been one of the straight shooters who'd always looked down on Finch's schemes. It was unfortunate, but there was little he could do about it right now.

What Novacek had done was very impressive. The camp was well organized and the people well armed and disciplined. Finch was afraid it would be a little tougher nut to crack than had been anticipated. The presence of marines and army personnel meant that he could be in grave danger should the Japanese find the place and attack. These weren't the confused and lost souls he'd led to destruction on Lanai.

Finch was pleased that Novacek had assigned him to work with the storage of supplies. Other than being a natural fit because of his background, the task enabled him to figure out how the American force was organized. It also surprised him just a little to realize that he now thought of the Americans as "them" and not "we."

Finch hoped his position would give him a chance to feed himself a little better than the rations that were provided. Despite the fact that Hawaii was fertile and grew just about anything, food was a chronic problem. The guerrillas did grow crops in a manner intended to make the fields look wild, and they did get other supplies from sympathetic and supportive locals, but they seemed to be always on the edge of scarcity.

In one regard, Finch gave Novacek grudging respect. The group he was with was the central command, but there were satellite enterprises that were very important, and about which he could find out very little. The problem was that only a handful of people knew what they did and where they were, and he wasn't yet one of them.

He'd figured out that there was a radio station somewhere nearby. Hell, that had been common knowledge way back with Omori. But something else was going on that required a lot of material, and he didn't know what it was. There were some disturbing references to airplanes that couldn't possibly be true. Novacek did not have an air force, so what were they talking about?

Or could they? He had to find out. If Novacek's force was planning something big, Finch had to find out so he could tell Goto and Omori. If he could do that, then he could count on an even bigger reward.

It occurred to him that the fact that the Americans were dispersed would likely mean there would be survivors when the Japanese finally acted on his information and attacked. That would be yet another good reason for his not ever returning to the United States. He laughed. As if he needed another one.

The only other disturbing thing about the camp was the virtual lack of women. What few there were were either native Hawaiian or Chinese, and he'd had his fill of those. The only white woman was the widow of some navy guy, and she spent as much time as possible around Novacek, who was very possessive about her. That meant she was very much off-limits. Novacek was a burly guy who'd rip the arms off anyone who touched her.

Besides, Finch knew who she was. Alexa Sanderson was the bitch Omori had been fucking back on Oahu. She was okay as far as looks went but definitely not his type. She was too tall and too elegant, as well as too strong willed for him. He grinned. Omori had done all right by Charley Finch after the Lanai job—he'd seen to it that he'd had the services of one very classy American blonde.

EVEN THOUGH Admiral King had flown in a private plane from Washington, and thus managed to avoid the abominable hassles of travel, he was tired and more irritable than usual.

He finished reading the report and almost threw it across the table, where Admirals Nimitz and Spruance watched tolerantly.

"This is bullshit," King finally said. "This isn't an offensive or a counterattack. Hell, it doesn't even qualify as a raid. It's a fucking pin-prick if it works and not even that if it doesn't. I expected a plan, not a stunt like this."

Nimitz was unfazed. "It's the best we can do without a real fleet."

King's eyes flashed angrily. "That is not my fault. If I had my way, every ship in our navy would be over here fighting the Japs instead of helping the goddamned British. And it's damned sure not my fault that you lost two carriers in the Coral Sea."

The battle of early May had been the first in which the combatant ships had not seen each other. It had been entirely fought by carrier planes. The *Lexington* had been sunk in the fighting, while the badly damaged *Yorktown* had foundered and sunk while limping back to San Francisco. Had she been able to go only the shorter distance to Pearl Harbor, she might have made it. Most of her crew and almost all of her pilots had been rescued, but the task force commander, Admiral

Frank Fletcher, was among the missing. The *Yorktown* was yet another casualty from the attack on Pearl Harbor and the subsequent loss of Hawaii.

The Americans were certain they'd sunk one Japanese carrier and damaged two others. More important, they'd stopped Japan's thrust toward Australia. Nimitz and Spruance were satisfied with the outcome, although it meant that the United States in the Pacific was almost as totally out of carriers as it was of battleships.

"All right." King sighed, his anger spent. "What do you need?"

Nimitz answered. "*Hornet* and *Enterprise* are all we'll have available for the next round. I want more carriers. All of them."

King snorted. "You don't want much, do you? Roosevelt wants them in the Atlantic when we invade German-controlled North Africa in November, and I don't have to tell you how important it is that we succeed. As much as I opposed it, North Africa's a go, and a defeat there would knock us back a long ways."

Nimitz and Spruance had long heard the rumors that an attack was pending, and now it was confirmed. It meant that they had only a small window of opportunity for action in 1942, but, if that was what FDR wanted, that was what the president would get.

Nimitz pressed that point, and King took a deep breath. "All right. You get *Saratoga*, *Wasp*, and *Ranger*, but on one condition. They must not be unduly risked, and they must be returned to the Atlantic theater by mid-September."

"They won't be risked," Spruance said. "No carrier will move against the Japanese unless the pinpricks we're devising actually work."

King was far from convinced. "You think they can?"

Nimitz answered. "I'm reminded of a story I read about a wasp or hornet, or maybe even a bee, getting inside a moving car with four people in it. When everyone tried to swat the pesky little insect, the car lost control and crashed. All four were killed and the wasp flew away. In fact," he said with a slight smile, "I've just decided to rename this pinprick Operation Wasp. It fits marvelously and sounds better than Operation Cork."

"I just hope you're right," King said. "At least it does look like the Japs will be coming to Hawaii."

Listening stations in the United States had decoded diplomatic messages to the effect that the annexation of Hawaii was going to occur in midsummer. It stood to reason that the Japanese would make it an impressive show, and that meant the presence of a sizable portion of their fleet.

"At the very least," Nimitz continued, "we should be able to embarrass them with a raid on the fuel tanks. At the best, we might actually do great damage. But rest assured, our carriers will not move unless there is an excellent opportunity for success. If there is little or no chance, our fleet will not move from Samoan waters. At the worst, we will have sacrificed nothing more than a few dozen brave men, but it will not be a catastrophe. With a little bit of luck, we could hide the fact of the loss for years."

Nimitz didn't like having to make that last statement, but he understood the realities. Failure was an orphan, and the United States couldn't afford to have another debacle like Pearl Harbor.

"Do I know everything I should about this venture?" King asked.

Spruance chuckled. "Hell, we're still making it up as we go along."

Nimitz's eyes twinkled. "Thanks for the carriers, Ernie; now, what about escorts? Same terms as with the carriers. We'll get them back to you in September and we won't risk them."

"What do you want?"

"Battleships, Ernie. I want the *North Carolina, Washington, South Dakota,* and *Indiana.* You know that the Japs will show up with at least the *Yamato* to go along with their carriers. They didn't build that monster to put her in storage. If she's there, I want revenge for the *Pennsylvania.* No, we're not going to set up a duel. I just want surface protection for the carriers that'll pack a wallop if we need it."

A task force built around five carriers and four battleships would be a powerful one, but still much weaker than what the Japanese could put against them. It would also be much smaller than the fleet the United States had under construction and would have afloat in a year or two if they wished to wait that long. They didn't.

"The *Indiana* won't be ready by then," King said and ventured a small smile. "Maybe I can do something else for you."

COLONEL OMORI SAT in the back of his car as it rolled slowly down the almost deserted streets of Hilo. The few people who remained were that handful of Hawaiians and Japanese who were sympathetic to the Japanese cause, or who pretended to be that way. Omori trusted none of them. The rest, the majority, had gone inland to the other villages and hamlets to escape the possibility of yet another massacre. Omori gestured, and the driver stopped quickly. The colonel got out, and Lieutenant Goto, who'd been in the front seat, quickly stepped alongside him.

Omori looked toward the mountains that glared down on Hilo. The colonel could almost feel enemy eyes on them. If the Americans ever got artillery on the hills, they could pound the small Japanese garrison into little pieces. The two Japanese destroyers at anchor in Hilo Bay gave him some comfort. Their four-inch guns would return fire at anyone who chose to insult Japan.

At least for now they would, which made it all the more imperative that the Americans be rooted out. The size of the island and the difficult terrain—forested and nearly jungle on the Hilo side, barren and craggy on the other side—meant it would be impossible to find the Americans without help.

Omori scuffed idly at a pebble with his boot. He fully understood the difficulty Goto was having in finding the Americans. "And your Mr. Finch, has he produced?"

Goto shrugged. "He's disappeared into the interior, and we believe he's in contact with the Americans. What he's found out, we won't know until he gets back to us."

"The American presence is as big an insult as is this abandoned town," Omori said with a touch of petulance. "Tell me, are the Americans here capable of doing anything to disrupt the coming arrival of the fleet?"

"Then it's true?"

"Indeed. Yamamoto will personally command a major force that will arrive in late July. They will bring with them an official proclamation declaring the Hawaiian Islands to be part of Japan. Now, what can the Americans do about it?"

Goto pondered a moment. "When will the navy's arrival be announced?"

"When the fleet arrives, and not sooner." Omori did not need to add that, after that, the entire world would know.

"Then the Americans will be helpless. They might try something childish to embarrass us here, but they have no military capability that would hurt us."

This was Omori's assessment as well. Yet he was not totally comfortable with the almost cavalier dismissal of the American guerrillas. The fact that they survived, perhaps even thrived, pointed to a sophisticated organizational and support structure. They should not be taken lightly.

A part of him recalled that, somehow, Alexa Sanderson had been spirited away. Omori was confident that she was with the Americans in the hills of the Big Island. When he found her, she would be turned over to Goto, and, when that sadist was through, the rest of the army could have her. She had caused him embarrassment and aggravation beyond her usefulness. More important, her presence on the island meant that she'd had help on Oahu. The Americans had to be destroyed.

Goto read his mind. "Do you want Captain Kashii to send patrols out farther into the hills? The captain would very much like to go chasing the Americans."

Omori nodded. "Yes. Keep the Americans worried that a Japanese patrol could be right behind them."

Even as he said it, the colonel knew it was wishful thinking. An entire army could hide in the hills and crags that glowered down on him. It was an amazing island. There were even active volcanoes and flowing lava out there. How the devil did an army deal with a lava flow? The Americans would be found either through Finch's treachery or blind, dumb luck. He'd put his money on Finch.

KENTARO HARA LAUGHED and bowed. "How do I look? Am I not a worthy soldier of the empire of Japan?"

Akira Kaga laughed at his friend's antics. "No, you do not look like a Japanese officer. For one thing, you are too neat."

Hara pretended to be hurt. "I have my pride."

"And so do the Japanese soldiers," Akira answered seriously, "but they show it in different ways, and looking slovenly is one of them. The true warriors in the Japanese army are contemptuous of spit and polish. They prefer to affect the look of a rugged warrior, a seasoned campaigner; thus, their uniforms always look like they've been stolen from someone larger and slept in for a great while."

Hara sighed as he took off the Japanese army tunic that had been made for him by one of several seamstresses employed to copy Japanese uniforms. It had been determined that it would be easier and safer to have them made by trusted people. Thefts would alert the Japanese to the fact that not everyone wearing a uniform was on their side. The conspirators' infiltration was something they wanted kept hidden for as long as possible.

Akira was pleased with the progress they'd made. Already there were enough uniforms to outfit thirty volunteers, and he had more than that ready to fight.

"All right," Hara said. "I'll get something that doesn't fit, but I won't be happy. It won't be up to my standards."

"Screw your standards." Akira laughed. Behind him, his father entered the room.

"A marvelous display," the older man said.

"Too bad they don't allow one-legged officers in the Japanese army," Akira said with regret. Although several of his volunteer force had experience in the national guard, none had served in the Japanese army and none had seen combat. His men would have the benefit of his experience, but he could not lead them.

"Is there still no word as to what will be expected of us?" Hara asked.

"None," Toyoza answered honestly. The Americans on the Big Island had been silent about what a rebel force of Japanese might be used for. The message sent to Colonel Novacek had been received with surprise and apparent delight. The colonel had responded that he would be happy to coordinate with a force of Japanese-Americans at a time in the not too distant future.

But as to what, when, and where, Novacek had not said. Either he was being prudently tight-lipped regarding his plans or he hadn't figured out what to do. Toyoza Kaga suspected the latter. A force that could pass as Japanese was not to be squandered.

"Weapons," Akira said. "What good are all the uniforms in the world if we don't have weapons?"

"The Americans said they would take care of that," his father said tolerantly. Again, just how they would accomplish this had not been mentioned.

"And I want to lead, Father," Akira said angrily. "No, I have to lead."

Toyoza Kaga nodded his head sadly. He had regained his son and did not want to risk losing him again. "I know. It will be done. I've contacted a doctor who will direct the making of an artificial leg for you. You won't be able to run or march very well, but, yes, you will be able to lead."

CHAPTER 18

Jake rubbed his eyes and squinted out into the near dark that signaled the end of one of the longest nights of his life. He had been up all night, and only anticipation was keeping him going. He longed for a cup of coffee, but that was a commodity that had been unavailable for a very long time, along with cigarettes and beer. He rarely smoked, but he craved a cigarette now.

Standing beside him, Captain Karl Gustafson fretted and worried. Gustafson was a large and rawboned man with an out-thrust jaw. An engineer for more than twenty years in civilian life, he wore what remained of his uniform in uncaring disarray. Unlike most Swedes, who were impassive and calm, he paced nervously, waiting like an expectant father to see if his idea was a good one or if it would die at birth.

Small fires staked out an area more than a hundred yards wide and half a mile deep. It was a rectangle that ran from the top of an ocean cliff and ended well inland. Both Gustafson's and Jake's greatest fears were that the lights would be seen by the wrong people and missed by the right ones. Farther inland, but on a line from the cliff, their radio sent out a beeping signal every minute. The radio beeps were long-range homing devices, while the rectangle outlined by the small fires was the ultimate destination.

There was a risk of detection, but, despite their apprehensions, it was deemed a small one. The Japanese knew the Americans sent messages from the interior of the island and had made little attempt to stop them. It was also routine for the Japanese not to send out patrol aircraft at night. They'd gotten used to seeing nothing and had stopped looking. What few planes they did use to patrol over Hawaii came during the light of day.

There was even less of a chance of detection from the ground.

First, no one lived in the vicinity, and, second, the Japanese didn't send ground patrols this far west of Hilo. While they had stepped up their efforts near Hilo since the massacre, this part of the Big Island might as well not have existed.

Jake noted that the daylight was not that far off. There was a definite glow to his rear, indicating that the sun was about to rise over Hilo. He hoped the Japs had slept soundly.

"Yes!" said Gustafson exultantly. He pointed out over the darker western sky.

"Can't see a thing, Gus," Jake said as he stared into the gloom.

"Then clean your eyeballs and look where I'm pointing."

A few seconds later, Jake did see the dark silhouette against the sky. Almost immediately, the plane dipped gently and landed between the rows of fires. One down. Jake felt like applauding, and a couple of the score of men with them did clap their hands.

In intervals of two to five minutes, the rest of the flight touched down. Immediately, the wings of the F4F Wildcats were folded and Gustafson's people covered the planes with camouflage netting that resembled the barren landscape of western Hawaii.

As this was happening, other men ran with straw brooms to wipe away the tire tracks.

"Plane! Freeze!"

The yell had come from a lookout and was their worst fear. If they were detected, their efforts were doomed. They all dropped to their knees and curled up. One of the pilots was slow to respond and had to be manhandled to the ground.

"Clear," yelled the lookout. He looked a little shamefaced. The "plane" he'd seen over the hills leading toward Hilo had been a large bird. Jake slapped him on the shoulder and told him he'd done the right thing by being cautious. Privately, Jake thought he'd aged a decade in the few minutes since the warning cry.

Eleven planes had landed. There were supposed to be twelve. The flight leader was Lieutenant Ernie Magruder, USN, who looked too young for his rank. He had a pencil-thin mustache that didn't make him look mature. Jake guessed his age at twenty-one.

They waited awhile and then, sadly and reluctantly, gave up on the stray plane. The sky was bright and the fires were put out. "Nielson didn't make it," Magruder said softly. "Helluva way to go."

"Could he have found his way back to the carrier?" Jake asked.

Magruder shook his head. "Not a chance. No way on earth he could have found an unlit carrier in the middle of the ocean, particularly since the carrier would have moved out in another direction. Nielson was a volunteer, Colonel. He knew his orders and he took his chances." Magruder added the last statement with more bravado than Jake thought he felt. The idea of flying off to death in an endless ocean sent a chill down his spine. God bless Nielson, he thought.

The pilots' orders had been to make no effort to survive in the event of engine failure, getting lost, or some other problem. They all knew the success of their mission would be compromised if they were taken alive, or even if their remains or the wreckage of their planes were found. If they were unable to complete their mission, they were to dive straight into the sea. Death would be quick, and the plane would sink to the bottom of the ocean, where both plane and pilot would be lost forever.

Magruder took a deep breath. "Eleven out of twelve ain't too bad, now, is it?"

"It's outstanding," Jake said fervently.

He turned and found he already had a hard time seeing the planes through the netting and the dirt that had been piled against them. They would be invisible from the sky, and no one ever came along this stretch of harsh ground. When night fell again, they would be moved a little farther inland, to where they would be half buried. There, the pilots would double as mechanics to prepare their planes for their mission.

"This is Hawaii, isn't it?" Magruder asked, surprising Jake.

"You didn't know?"

Magruder grinned. "Hell no, sir. We volunteered for a mission to kick some Jap ass. Then we were shipped out to Africa and flown to a British carrier off India. We've been virtual prisoners for a couple of weeks and never let out on deck or had any casual contact with the Brits. When we launched, we were told what direction to go and how long to fly. Other than that, this could be Ohio for all I know." He laughed. "After we arrived, they said we'd be filled in on the details, although, if this is Hawaii, I'll bet you two bits we're gonna hit Pearl Harbor."

Jake hid his surprise. American planes launched off a British carrier and without any real idea where they were going? Incredible. But now he had an air force.

"Yeah," Jake said, "this is Hawaii, and you're the Hawaiian Air Force. And yeah, you're gonna get a chance to kick some Jap ass."

Magruder nodded. "Great. Only let's call this Nielson Force, after the poor guy who didn't make it."

JAMIE PRIEST HELD TIGHTLY to the slender body of Suzy Dunnigan. "This is wrong, you know," he managed to say. They were both choked up with emotion brought on by the reality of her imminent departure. It was harder than either realized to let go of what had been a marvelous time together.

"I know," Suzy said, wiping a tear off her cheek. "Here I'm going off to war while you wait at home. It's supposed to be the other way around, isn't it? I have to go, but don't be too sad. After all, it's not like I'm going very far or for very long."

Congress had finally authorized women in the military, and Suzy's nomination had been endorsed by both Nimitz and Spruance, which made for immediate acceptance. She would spend a month or two in training, which would begin sometime in August, and then be commissioned an ensign in the WAVES. She hoped she would be stationed back in San Diego, but they acknowledged that anything was possible when it came to the navy.

"I'm glad you're taking care of the house," she said. "That's a big worry off my mind. I never really cared for the place until my dad was killed. Now, it's all I have left of him." Jamie felt honored by her trust and hugged her again.

Jamie had begun by regularly spending the nights with her and then, after a few weeks, had officially changed his residence to hers. Some on Nimitz's staff were shocked, but the two lovers didn't care. Jamie and Suzy had ignored the world and spent every waking moment reveling in the pleasure of each other. A previous remark about clothes referred to the fact that, on weekends, they spent all possible time as naked as the day they were born. The weather was balmy, and nudity simplified and expedited their lovemaking. Suzy had even managed to initiate the fairly conservative Jamie into the delights of swimming naked in the ocean at night and making love in the sand.

He would miss all that. More important, he would miss Suzy Dunnigan. He had told her, even brought up the subject of marriage, but she had demurred. She had to wait until her tour of duty was completed. She owed that to her father, and Jamie could not argue the point. Both hoped they would not have to wait until the war was over and life was more settled. Forecasts put the end of the conflict as far out as 1950, which depressed them both. She loved him, but she had a duty to perform that was as strong as his.

Outside, a cab pulled up and honked. They embraced once more, and she departed, walking briskly and not looking back.

As the cab pulled away, Jamie felt a desperate loneliness. So this is what it's like, he thought, for wives and mothers to send their men off to war. At least Suzy would be spared the likelihood of combat, although many places that would have been considered "safe" in previous conflicts were well within the range of bombers, and transit across the ocean was subject to attack by submarines. He hoped that she would be assigned stateside.

He still chafed at the restrictions on his going back to combat but had come to terms with them. Nimitz had been explicit—no combat. With so much time now on his hands, Jamie would work harder and longer on his duties on Nimitz's staff, and on Operation Wasp in particular.

ADMIRAL ISOROKU YAMAMOTO PACED the stern of the giant battleship *Yamato*. He was alone except for Commander Watanabe, his confidant and sounding board. All others knew enough not to interrupt him while he walked and thought.

Around him in Hiroshima harbor lay the bulk of the fleet preparing for its foray to Hawaii. He would command a mighty armada of carriers, battleships, and cruisers that would overwhelm the American navy; that is, if only the Americans would cooperate.

Yamamoto was confounded by the inconsistencies in intelligence-gathering capabilities. Intelligence gathering had never been a Japanese strong point, and its weaknesses were now glaringly apparent and irreparable. It was far too late to develop a force of operatives and observers who could operate behind enemy lines.

The first problem was the recently concluded battle of the Coral Sea. Just what had happened, and who had won? The Japanese navy had proclaimed a victory, which, in tactical terms, was correct. But the Japanese fleet had been forced to withdraw without accomplishing its objective, a landing at Port Moresby on New Guinea. Didn't that failure constitute a defeat of sorts? It was very likely that sober analysis in future years would declare the battle a draw, and that disturbed the admiral. The modern Japanese navy had a string of victories that stretched back almost a hundred years. Had it ended with a draw in the Coral Sea?

A draw? Japan could not be victorious if they only fought draws. The preponderance of arms, real and potential, lay with the United States and her primary ally, Great Britain. If Japan continually fought draws, she would run out of ships and men well before the Allies did. There could be no more draws. There could only be victories.

Tactically, though, the battle had been a Japanese victory. The United States admitted to the loss of the carrier *Lexington,* and there had been no information regarding the *Yorktown* since then. Pilots had reported the *Yorktown* to be severely damaged; thus, she'd had to go someplace for major repairs.

Even though there were only a handful of intelligence sources on the American West Coast, it was difficult to hide a carrier in the few port facilities where the *Yorktown* could be repaired. She had not been seen in any of them, nor had other observers seen her go through the Panama Canal to a place on the East Coast. It was conceivable that she had taken the long way around South America, but it made no sense to risk a damaged ship in such an arduous journey.

No, he concluded, the *Yorktown* had sunk and the Americans had not yet admitted it. Even if she were suddenly and magically to appear in an Allied port, she was likely too badly damaged to fight again for a long while.

Japanese losses in the Coral Sea had been minimal in comparison. The light carrier *Shoho* had been sunk, along with a destroyer, and two fleet carriers, the *Shokaku* and the *Zuikaku,* had been damaged and had returned to Japan for repairs. They would not take part in the coming campaign, so each side had lost the use of two fleet carriers for the immediate duration. Japan, however, would get her fleet carriers back in a matter of months, while the *Yorktown* and *Lexington* were lost forever to the Americans. Yamamoto had to ensure Japanese victory before they were replaced by the massive American building effort.

Of most serious concern was the loss of nearly eighty experienced pilots. The deaths of so many at one stroke meant that the reserve pool of qualified carrier pilots was severely depleted. If the Coral Sea had been a victory, it occurred to the admiral that it had been a Pyrrhic one and, to paraphrase the ancient general, how many more could Japan sustain?

There were other concerns gnawing at the admiral.

"Watanabe, where are the remaining American carriers?"

"According to intelligence sources, sir, they are in the Atlantic."

Observers along the Panama Canal had spotted the *Enterprise* and the *Saratoga* moving through the canal and into the Atlantic. The report meant that there were no American carriers in the Pacific Ocean. Why? Again, intelligence had speculated that the Americans were gathering their forces for a strike against the Germans, and that it would involve a landing either in Africa or in France.

But could it also presage a sneak attack against the Japanese? After all, it would be a fairly simple matter for the two carriers to disappear into the ocean, head south, and return to the Pacific by way of South America. A damaged carrier might not be able to make the harsh transit, but undamaged ones could do so with relative ease. The American carriers could also transit into the Indian Ocean by way of South Africa and then into the Pacific. Either way, it was unlikely they would be seen until they wanted to be. The South American route was almost totally uninhabited, while the British controlled the horn of South Africa. It occurred to him that two or more American carriers could be sneaking up on him in much the same manner as the *Kido Butai* had snuck up on Pearl Harbor. On the other hand, if the American carriers had truly departed for the Atlantic, the Pacific was a Japanese ocean.

"We need confirmation," Yamamoto said to Watanabe. "If the Americans have abandoned the Pacific, then we have an opportunity to do great damage to them, and possibly bring an end to this war. We can land troops in Alaska unopposed, as well as bomb and shell the cities of California. After annexing Hawaii, we can humiliate the United States and bring her to the negotiating table. It doesn't matter if they won't come out and fight. We will have our victory."

Following the attacks along the American West Coast, Yamamoto hoped that the postponed operation to put a landing strip on Guadalcanal would be reconstituted. A Japanese air base on Guadalcanal would threaten New Zealand and Australia and, coupled with additional victories against the American West Coast, might just knock those two semi-independent nations out of the war. He acknowledged that it was far more important to defeat the United States and sign a treaty with her. If America left the war, Great Britain and her minions would collapse. Guadalcanal would have to wait.

Watanabe had said nothing. He was there to listen, not to speak unless specifically asked.

"Confirmation," Yamamoto repeated and pounded his mangled hand against the railing. "We must confirm that the Americans are in the Atlantic."

ALEXA SANDERSON SMILED DOWN at Sergeant Charley Finch, who returned the smile uncertainly. The woman who generally stayed so close to Colonel Novacek had scarcely acknowledged his existence until this moment.

"Sergeant Finch, I haven't had a chance to welcome you. I've been preoccupied with other things, and that's rude of me."

Charley smiled tentatively. "That's quite all right, ma'am. I guess there are a lot of things going on that're more important than me."

She sat on the ground beside him. "Jake—I mean Colonel Novacek—is away for a few days, so that gives me a chance to check up on things. I'd like to ask you a few questions, if I may?"

"Go right ahead," he answered with a certainty that he didn't feel. What the hell did she want? Maybe she was attracted to him. He changed his mind about her attractiveness. Even though she was dressed in men's clothing, there was no doubt she was damned good-looking. He felt a stirring in his groin. It had been a helluva long time. He wondered if Novacek was screwing her.

"I want to know what's happening in Honolulu," she said. "I know it's been a while since you were there, but your information is probably better than anybody else's."

Charley was both relieved and disappointed. "I spent most of my time in hiding, ma'am. From what I could tell, and from what people told me, it's a pretty miserable place. The Japanese military is everywhere, and their secret police are the nastiest people on the face of the earth."

He watched as her eyes clouded. The comment about Omori's secret police had struck home. Alexa waited a moment, then continued. "How are the people getting on? What are they eating?"

Charley shrugged. "I can only tell you what I heard, and that's that anyone who's white is having a rough time, while anyone who isn't is doing okay. There's enough food to go around now, but nobody's gonna get too fat from it."

She laughed softly and glanced at his still prominent paunch. Thanks to their Spartan rations, it was disappearing, but far from gone. "I got this"—he grinned—"while hiding out with that old lady. She must've thought she was going to feed an army for a hundred years. It might've been illegal to hoard, but I'm kinda glad she did."

"You know I lost my husband, don't you?"

"Yes, ma'am. A lot of good people died that day."

"Did you have family in Hawaii? Friends?"

What should he tell her? he wondered. "No, ma'am, although I do have a girlfriend in San Francisco. Want to see her picture?" It was a spur-of-the-moment comment but seemed logical.

Alexa nodded and Finch pulled a snapshot out of his wallet. Alexa's eyes widened as she saw it. "She's very pretty," she finally said. "What's her name?"

"Nancy Winfield," he said, improvising quickly. Nancy Winfield was somebody he'd known back in the States. He wasn't certain what the name of the person in the picture was. "And she is prettier than I deserve. I sure know that, and I remind myself about it a hundred times a day. At least," he said sadly, "I used to. God only knows what's happening to her now. She probably thinks I'm dead."

Alexa put her hand on his arm. "Perhaps we can send a message that you're all right."

"That would be great," Charley said sincerely. Even if they did send a message, it would be to an address where no one named Nancy Winfield lived. They would assume she'd moved and forget about it. "Thank you, ma'am."

Alexa stood and brushed the dirt off her khaki slacks. She smiled at the sergeant and walked off. When she was far enough away, she allowed her eyes to well up with tears.

"You're going to die," she whispered angrily. "You're going to fucking die, Charley Finch."

THEIR MAIN RADIO WAS in a hut near the top of a hill. It was large, and Jake's soldiers had quipped that the radio was about as portable as a dead elephant. The antenna was on a tall tree a little ways away. Unless you were close and knew what to look for, it was invisible.

The Japs were looking for it, so Jake hadn't had the set and antenna placed on the highest hill in the area. That would have been too obvious. Instead, the tree-covered hill was one of scores like it that jutted up in the rugged terrain and were otherwise not significant.

Someone always stayed by the radio in case a message came in. There was a planned schedule, but you could never tell when something important might arrive, especially now that it looked like big things were about to happen. So far, only a handful in the main area knew of the planes' arrival, but it was only a matter of time before the secret became common knowledge. They had to be used fairly soon or any element of surprise might be lost.

Jake didn't have to take a turn in the radio hut, but he rather liked doing so. It felt good to have a roof over his head, and the privacy he insisted on while up there was a splendid relief. His Morse code skills had improved to where he could receive a message without screwing up.

He might be alone, but he was safe. The shack was protected by Hawk's soldiers, who kept out of sight and gave him the illusion of privacy.

The isolation gave him a chance to think without the distractions of routine command. He stripped off his uniform and relaxed in his army shorts and sleeveless undershirt. He was filthy, but so was everyone else. Back home, people might have bathed once a week or more, but not here. There was sufficient water, but it was primarily for drinking and cooking, not bathing and showering. Crude containers had been devised to hold rainwater and springwater so that some washing and showering did occur, but it wasn't on a frequent basis. Jake sniffed. He hadn't had a chance to clean up in more than a week. Hawk had made the comment that it was part of their camouflage. "If you smell like a jungle, you'll be mistaken for one," he'd said.

Small quantities of soap were made from ashes and sand, and were strictly rationed. As a result, everyone, even the women, kept their hair very short. Jake thought Alexa looked very attractive in a haircut that would have seemed short on a man only a few months ago.

Maybe it would rain and he could let Mother Nature hose him down. But even rain wouldn't help the tattered condition of his clothing. Like everyone else's, it had been reduced to little more than rags. His underwear was so bad it reminded him of the type old ladies said you should never wear in case you got in an accident.

He stepped outside and looked up at the star-filled sky. No rain in sight, but there was a breeze that was comfortable on his bare skin. Although he was not a stickler for discipline, he insisted that his men— and women—be suitably dressed, rags or not. States of undress were tolerated only in situations such as this, where there was a degree of privacy.

Jake sighed and went back inside the shack. When would the radio open up and tell him when and how he was to use the pilots and planes? The obvious target was Pearl and its rebuilt fuel depots. If that was the case, what were they waiting for? The British carrier and the American pilots had run tremendous risks to get to him, and those efforts should not be wasted.

He shuddered when he thought of the danger. Not only had the pilots run the risk of getting lost or being discovered but they had made the trip with extra fuel and bombs strapped to the lower sides of the wings of their F4Fs. Like most people who don't fly warplanes, he hadn't given a thought to how the bombs would arrive. He hadn't known that no pilot in his right mind—which was damned few of them—would try to land a plane with the bombs hanging below the wings. The smallest bump as they landed and they would have blown up, taking plane and pilot with them. No, bombs were always ditched in the ocean before landing.

Instead, Ernie Magruder and his cohorts had flown their lethally dangerous devices across the ocean in the night and had landed safely—bombs, fuel, and all. Now the pilots were hiding near their planes, doubtless playing cards and drinking the homemade booze that Jake tolerated for those off duty.

Another plus was the fact that they'd not yet been detected. Despite an apparent change in attitude, Japanese foot patrols still hadn't come close to them. It was as if the Japanese garrison in Hilo was holding back and waiting for something to happen. Jake wondered if this Japanese reluctance to act had anything to do with the arrival of the planes. He had no idea what it might be, but he did feel there was a pattern of activity developing.

This stalemate could go on forever unless the Japs at Hilo were heavily reinforced, which Jake concluded was inevitable. The American presence would have to be eradicated sometime.

If the Japanese did begin sizable sweeps of the island, it would be a disaster for Jake's men and women. They would be on the move in a harsh land and separated from their food sources. Death or capture would be only a matter of time. They could run and hide, but they had to eat. They would have to abandon the radio, which would leave them alone as well. It was a miserable thought.

He lay back on the twin bed that someone had found and put in the shack. The bed, mattress, and pillow were other reasons to take a turn waiting for the radio to hum. It was a strong and honored tradition that whoever slept in it was responsible for cleaning the sheets and pillowcase. Jake thought that was getting off cheaply.

So what would happen if their efforts failed and they were discovered? He would have to kill himself to keep the secret of Magic from falling into Japanese hands. He also felt that a number of others, Alexa included, would take their own lives as an alternative to what would happen if they were captured. After all, hadn't the men on Lanai been prisoners who'd been executed because they were considered outlaws? As more and more was found out about conditions in Japanese prison camps, there were those who thought the victims of the Lanai massacre had been the lucky ones.

On the positive side, Brooks and Hawkins ran their respective units well enough, while the new guy, Charley Finch, seemed competent enough to help out coordinating supplies. Hawkins was a jewel, and Brooks had shaken off his depression caused by the massacre in Hilo.

Jake didn't quite trust Finch yet, and Alexa seemed to dislike him, but there was nothing they could hang the guy for. Maybe he was one of those unlovable people who just did their jobs. After all, since when had this become a popularity contest?

Alexa had volunteered to observe Finch, and Jake had accepted her offer. This was something she could do without being obvious because she was a civilian, and because she was in charge of those supplies unique to women problems. Jake chuckled when he thought that his command had to be concerned with sanitary napkins. There were only a dozen women in his group, but they had to be cared for, Alexa was perfect for the job, and it got her close to Finch. Sergeant Finch got his ass all puckered up when either Jake or Brooks came by, and he almost ignored Hawkins. Alexa watching Finch removed one problem from Jake's plateful.

Jake was satisfied that the Charley Finch problem would resolve itself, presuming that there even was a Charley Finch problem.

I'm getting paranoid, he thought with a yawn. He pulled the top sheet over his body and closed his eyes. If anything came in over the radio, a bell had been rigged to ring and wake him. The mattress felt like the lap of luxury and reminded him of a world long gone. It was so comfortable he wondered if he would be able to sleep.

He grinned in the night. If he did fall asleep, maybe he would dream of Alexa. She and he had grown remarkably close since her arrival, and he wondered what direction the relationship would ultimately take. He hoped to find out before too long. Or too late, he thought grimly. Damnit, let something happen.

CHAPTER 19

■

Commander Joe Rochefort strode into the conference room and plopped a stack of papers on the table. As usual, he was the antithesis of a smart-looking officer. He looked like he'd slept in his uniform, which had often happened. At his own office, he frequently wore a robe and slippers.

"Morning, Jamie," he said genially. "Catch up to me yet?"

Lieutenant Commander Jamie Priest grinned back. "Not yet, sir, but I'm working on it."

Despite many more years of devoted service to his country, Rochefort was only one grade higher than Jamie, and very likely to stay there. If it galled him, however, he didn't show it. Joe Rochefort had more important things to do.

"You'll be at the meeting?" Rochefort asked.

"Yes, sir."

Jamie had only recently been cleared to get Magic information. His new rank had nothing to do with it; a number of people with far lower rank, even enlisted men, had Magic clearance because, as Rochefort said with a sarcastic laugh, "If they didn't, then a lot of damned admirals would actually have to do some work."

He was right, of course, and there were many admirals and generals who hadn't a single clue that Magic existed, while sergeants and petty officers, possessors of knowledge that could change history, passed them in the hallways.

Having the information provided by Magic had been both a blessing and a curse. It had been a blessing because Jamie now knew so much more about what was going on with the Japanese. It was fascinating to read not only their minds but their mail.

The curse part was twofold. First, it further hammered home the fact that he would never get into a position where he might be taken prisoner and the information extracted from him. Only a handful of key people with Magic clearance had been permitted to leave the States, and none into positions of danger.

The second part of the curse brought him back to the nightmare of the *Pennsylvania*. He'd found and read the intercepts in which Yamamoto had tried to stop the execution of the American survivors. The Japanese admiral had apparently failed, and that meant Jamie truly was the only survivor of that disaster. The knowledge brought a numbing feeling, and he wished Suzy was there for him to talk to.

But she wasn't, and it was something he had to resolve by himself. Jamie'd received a handful of letters in the short while she'd been gone and sent some himself. They loved each other and missed each other.

He also found that Suzy had received Magic clearance. She'd never even hinted at it. It did mean that they could talk about the *Pennsylvania* and other things when she finally returned to him. Magic clearance also meant she wouldn't be supervising a mess hall after she finished training.

Admiral Nimitz arrived and took a seat at the head of the table. Admiral Spruance wasn't there, which puzzled Jamie.

Nimitz went straight to the point. "What do you have for us, Joe?"

Rochefort grinned. "In summary, the date of the Japanese arrival at Pearl and the makeup of the Japanese force."

Rochefort went on to say that the Japanese fleet under Yamamoto was scheduled to arrive at Pearl Harbor on July 20. It would stay for two weeks while the islands were formally declared to be Japanese territory.

"There are six carriers in the First Air Fleet under Nagumo," Rochefort said. "The *Akagi, Soryu, Hiryu, Kaga, Ryujo,* and one other. We don't have the name just yet. There are two battleship divisions. The first consists of the *Yamato* and the *Musashi,* both of their giants. The *Musashi* is a surprise. I didn't think she was ready, and she might not totally be. This could easily be her shakedown cruise."

Standing in the corner of the room behind Nimitz, Jamie shuddered. Two like the *Yamato*? How would the navy handle them?

Rochefort continued. "The second division consists of the old battleships *Kongo, Haruna,* and *Kirishima.*"

"I thought we sank the *Haruna* in the Philippines," Nimitz said with some surprise.

"Apparently not," Rochefort responded. "I guess we gave the Medal of Honor to a pilot for sinking the wrong ship."

An American airman named Colin Kelly had been awarded the medal for having sunk a Japanese battleship by ramming her with his crippled plane. Either he hadn't sunk the *Haruna* or he'd hit a different ship. An air force pilot could easily have mistaken a Japanese cruiser for a battleship.

Or, Jamie thought with dismay, the whole incident had been fabricated to make something heroic out of the catastrophe that had befallen the American army in the Philippines. He decided he didn't want to know.

"There will be a number of cruisers and destroyers as escorts, and a brigade of infantry on transports who will depart after the ceremonies," Rochefort said. "Right now it looks like the Japs will land them in the Aleutians, and then the fleet will foray down the coasts of Oregon, Washington, and California. The only thing possibly holding them back is their fear that our navy really hasn't vacated the Pacific."

Which they hadn't. Jamie now knew that the American carriers had returned to the Pacific, along with other carriers and battleships. They were waiting in silence off Samoa, twenty-six hundred miles south of Hawaii.

Rochefort put down his papers and smiled like a cat. "Yamamoto is bitching that he can't get confirmation our carriers are actually in the Atlantic and not looking over his shoulder."

Nimitz nodded. "He will get that confirmation fairly soon." He paused and added, "We hope."

Jamie felt like purring. It was his idea about deception that was going to be implemented. If it worked, he would have done his best to strike back at the sons of bitches who had sunk the *Pennsylvania* and massacred her crew. Even if it didn't work, he'd given it a helluva shot.

Nimitz stood. "We'll get this to Spruance as quickly as possible."

"What about Halsey?" Rochefort asked in surprise.

Nimitz smiled gently. "For a man who deals in secrets, you don't know everything, do you?" he teased. "Halsey is sick and Spruance is going out to replace him."

Jamie had heard the rumor and was not as surprised as Rochefort. He was, however, not entirely comfortable with the decision, though it wasn't his to question. Halsey was sick, and Fletcher was missing and presumed dead. That left Spruance to command the Samoan force.

But Jamie wondered if Spruance was the right man. He'd worked for him and knew him to be extremely intelligent, and considerate of his subordinates. But were these the attributes of a battle leader? Was he aggressive enough to lead an American attack force against superior odds? Halsey wouldn't have flinched. But Spruance?

ALEXA WALKED THE DIRT PATH to the radio hut. It was early night, and there was no trouble seeing by the light of the myriad of stars above her. She didn't notice the glorious display, though; she was there for a purpose.

She reached the flimsy door and knocked. "Who's there?" came Jake's muffled reply. She smiled. He must have been sleeping already.

"I am," she answered and stepped in. Jake sat up in the bed and scrambled to cover himself with a sheet. He was wearing an undershirt and shorts. Poor puppy, she thought. He looks so confused.

Jake smiled and yawned. "What's up?"

Alexa pulled the stool from beside the radio and sat down by the bed. "I want to talk. All you have to do is stay there and listen."

"Okay."

"Jake, do you know how evil so much of the world is, and how much of it I've seen?"

He reached out and took her hand. "I know what you've told me. I can't begin to imagine what your ordeal was like, though. As to the rest of the world, there's a lot of good out there too, not just evil."

Good answer, she thought. "You remind me of Tim. He was a good man and, despite being a professional naval officer, an innocent and naïve man. He saw good in the world and thought there was more of it than there was bad. He thought his job was to protect the good. I see a lot of him in you. You're a good man, Jake, a very good man."

Jake flushed. "Hey, Alexa, I'm far from perfect. Don't canonize me just yet, okay?"

She laughed. "I said good, not a saint. Also, you have a sense of honor, don't you?"

"What do you mean?"

"You could have left the islands and returned to California a long time ago, couldn't you?"

"Sure, but I thought I could do some good here, maybe even do something to defeat the Japs."

"Honor," Alexa repeated. "There are those who say that innocence and naïveté are essential for there to be honor. I don't know if they're right, but I'm glad your sense of honor required you to stay instead of taking the easy way out. If you hadn't done that, I wouldn't be sitting here alive today. If you hadn't stayed, you wouldn't be planning something big against the Japs, would you?"

"No secrets in this small town," Jake said with a laugh.

"Honor," she said again. "Will you do something for me, with me, but following my instructions to the absolute letter? It's very important to me. Will you honor my request? Will you honor me?"

He squeezed her hand. "Of course."

"Jake, do you love me?"

He took a deep breath. "Yes," he said with a whisper. It was all he could manage.

She smiled gently, confidently. "Then help me. But don't move unless I tell you to; don't say a word unless I ask you to. I will do everything, understand? Everything."

Jake nodded, and she pulled him to where he stood silently on the dirt floor. She looked at him for a moment, then pulled the undershirt over his head, paused, and slid his shorts off. She stared at his powerful body while his erection grew. He looked at her questioningly but made no move, no sound. Jake was a statue.

"You are going to purge me," she finally said and touched him softly on his chest. Her fingers felt like fire to him. "You are going to remind me of how much I loved Tim, and you are going to help remove the stench of Omori from both my body and my mind. You are going to be my knight and rescue me from the dragon that eats at me. Help me, Jake."

She undressed and stood naked in the starlight that came through the open window by the bed. Jake had never seen anyone or anything so beautiful. Her breasts were firm and full, and her belly flat. The legs that he'd admired the first time he'd seen her were as magnificent as he'd dreamed.

Jake longed to tell her, but she touched his lips with her finger and reminded him to be still and unmoving. She told him to lie down on his back in the bed. He grabbed the sides of the bed to stay in control. He understood that she needed it to happen this way, and he would not betray her.

She straddled his thighs and caressed his chest, letting her hands wander down to his belly and his erect penis. When she stroked that, he groaned and thought he would explode.

"Not yet," she said in a husky whisper and let go of him.

She slid forward so that her breasts hung down into his face. "Take them, Jake."

She guided her aroused and full nipples to his lips, and he devoured them with hunger and tenderness. Then she slid backward over his thighs, and he entered her easily. She rocked back and forth with her eyes closed, while he gripped the sides of the bed so tightly he thought it would break.

Finally, she threw her head back and groaned; then, seconds later, Jake exploded inside her.

He caught his breath. Her eyes were open, and she was looking at him with a strange half smile. "May I hold you now?" he asked softly.

"I used you."

Jake held out his arms. She came down to him, and he held her tightly to his chest. "It's okay," he said and laughed. After a second, she laughed with him.

"I thought it would be, soldier boy," she said as she kissed his chest and shoulder.

"I love you, Alexa. Always will."

She lifted up and kissed him on the cheek. "Then I guess I'll have to learn to love you, won't I? It won't take long at all. You're a good teacher, and I'm an easy learner."

Alexa pulled him out of the bed, and they sat on a mat on the dirt floor. She slid the bucket over, and they took turns sponging each other with the tepid water, joyously lingering over each other's bodies. They let the night air dry them and returned to bed, where they made love again, this time without restraints or inhibitions. They guided each other's hands and lips over their bodies with an eagerness that surprised and delighted both of them.

Then they fell into a deep sleep. Alexa would later recall it as the best night's sleep she'd had in months.

"OPERATION WASP?" Roosevelt said with a derisive laugh. "Why not call it Operation Cheap or Operation Shoestring? This is warfare on a totally inadequate budget, and the slightest misstep will bring disaster."

"Then we will not make any missteps," Admiral King said firmly. "Only a few handfuls of personnel and planes will be risked. It's sad, but they will scarcely be missed if we are defeated. The few major units we have will not move until and unless we are certain they can do so with relative safety. There is nothing in these plans that is contrary to what we agreed upon. If everything falls into place, we will defeat the Japs and even stand a chance of liberating the islands. With the resources available to me at this time, that is all that can be expected."

"If it fails," Roosevelt said grimly, "I want those people in the Hawaiian hills off that island."

King thought this would be virtually impossible in the event of defeat, but he kept silent. Congressman Cordelli must have been talking to him again about the plight of his niece. King felt sorry for the man, and for FDR too, but he was not going to jeopardize a number of warships and planes to rescue some debutante who'd managed to find herself in a war zone. Hell, he thought, there were thousands more in even worse shape in the Philippines, China, and Hawaii. At least Cordelli's niece had a sort of freedom in the hills, which was vastly preferable to a prison camp. As to Novacek and the rest of them, well, they were soldiers or marines and they were all volunteers who understood the risks. No, rescue in case of failure was not likely at all.

Roosevelt's hand twitched nervously. "And I don't want any prisoners paraded through the streets of Honolulu and then executed. What have you done to ensure the safety of any of the men shot down?"

"We've taken steps," King assured him. "I cannot guarantee perfection, but the navy'll do its best to rescue our boys should it prove necessary."

"Do what you can," the president said wearily. "And do what you have to. We need a victory, Admiral, and we need a big one."

■

THE RETURN of the *Monkfish* to hostile waters had been something that freshly promoted Lieutenant Commander Willis Fargo had been wishing for. This, however, was not quite what he had reckoned on. He'd hoped for a patrol in the vastness of the open sea, and the chance to catch unsuspecting Japanese ships. Instead, he felt he and his crew were almost literally in the mouth of a very angry dragon.

Shit.

The *Monkfish* had been sent on a solitary and extremely dangerous mission to Hawaii. If there were any other American subs in the area, Fargo hadn't been told of them and they hadn't made themselves known to him. He was alone in a little boat in the middle of a gigantic ocean.

Actually, he wasn't in the middle of the ocean anymore. Land was very close and clearly visible through the periscope, which was raised scant inches above the water. He squinted and swiveled the scope until he was confident that no enemy ships or planes were in sight. It was early evening, and he could see lights on in some of the buildings and even see people moving around.

The absence of major shipping was puzzling. After all, he was only feet off the coast of Oahu and staring at the entrance to Pearl Harbor. En route, he had taken a look at the port of Honolulu as it nestled under the promontory called Diamond Head. Both the city and the island looked deceptively normal. He could almost imagine that the war hadn't occurred and that he could spend the night getting his ashes hauled in one of the more elegant sin spots of Honolulu. It was a façade, of course. Horrors were taking place in a gentle land that once had been thought of as the nearest thing to paradise in this life.

If the lack of Japanese shipping was a puzzle, so too were his orders. He had been specifically forbidden to attack anything en route to the Hawaiian Islands from San Diego, no matter how tempting it might be. Rounding the southern tip of the Big Island and heading north to Oahu, he had seen a couple of Japanese merchant ships but had withstood the urge to sink them. Now, off Pearl, the anchorage was noteworthy for its emptiness. He couldn't see far into it, of course, but no major ships had come and gone in the time the *Monkfish* had carefully approached and then lay in wait.

And then there was the second portion of his orders. He had been told to penetrate as far as possible into the mouth of the anchorage and stay there, hidden, until an entire Japanese fleet steamed in. Again, he was not to attack. He wondered if the top brass had any idea just how well he'd done in penetrating the Japanese defenses of Pearl. He'd have a helluva tale to tell when he got back. *If* he got back, he corrected himself somberly.

He could, however, attack when the Japanese fleet attempted to exit. However—God, how he hated that damned weasel-word—he must make certain that it was the fleet trying to leave and not just a ship or two heading out on routine patrol. When he'd asked Admiral Lockwood for a clarification, the admiral hadn't bitten off his head, as was his normal practice with junior officers who asked questions. Instead he'd been quietly sympathetic with Fargo's predicament.

"You'll know, son, you'll know. If the Jap fleet starts to come out in a big-ass rush, then it'll be your time to act."

So what the hell was going on, Fargo wondered. He wouldn't run out of fuel or food; extra quantities of both had been stuffed into his already cramped vessel, but how long was he supposed to sit there like a bump on an extremely dangerous log?

At least he'd found what he hoped was a fairly safe place to hide the *Monkfish*. He was off to the side of the entrance of the harbor and opposite Hickam Field and Fort Kamehameha, about where the antisubmarine boom had been. The boom had been destroyed and not yet repaired, which surprised Fargo. So much for the myth of Japanese industriousness, he thought.

The ruined hulk of an American destroyer jutted out of the water by the shore. In the channel, the water was more than forty feet deep, but, alongside the entrance, it sloped upward to well under that. Thus, it was fairly simple to lie alongside the wreck and stay submerged during the day, only rarely raising the periscope for a look-see. At night, he cautiously raised the *Monkfish* to where he could open the conning tower hatches, let in some fresh air, and recharge the batteries. His only fear was that a Jap officer would come and inspect the hulk, or some kid would use it as a fishing pier. Otherwise, he was confident that his boat merged with the background.

The wait was unnerving to both him and his crew in the crowded and stifling submarine, but they gradually got used to it. What the hell, Fargo thought, what choice did they have? He allowed normal conversation but forbade any loud or sudden noises. His crew called this "Fargo's Don't Fart Rule."

Fargo'd gotten command of the *Monkfish* because he was familiar with her and her crew, and had taken her safely from Hawaii to California. Commander Griddle had never fully recovered from his wounds and had been given a medical discharge. This was Fargo's opportunity, and he wasn't going to screw it up. If Admiral King wanted him to penetrate the harbor and lie in wait, then he would do it. Hell, he'd taken the *Monkfish* right up the Japs' asses.

He chuckled as he decided he didn't really like that analogy.

JAKE NOVACEK MET his unexpected allies in a small dilapidated house outside the village of Kahuku, just off the northernmost point of Oahu. It was, he thought, about as far from Honolulu as you could get and still be on Oahu.

He had arrived in one of Toyoza Kaga's fishing boats, hidden in a false compartment in the hull. It stank of old fish, and now so did he. Jake was sure Alexa would love this.

He'd landed at night and been hustled off to the house where Kaga and his son, Akira, were waiting.

"You give off a delicious scent," Toyoza said, grinning. "Try not to get near any cats."

"After the war, I'll never eat fish again," Jake said, then got to the point. Every minute on Oahu was fraught with potential danger, and he wanted to get back to Hawaii and Alexa as quickly as possible. "I understand your dilemma, Toyoza. You have men but no weapons."

"Correct."

"And we have Japanese uniforms," his son added. Akira paced the small room with a pronounced limp. He was still trying to adjust to an artificial leg.

"What will you do with weapons if I get them for you?" Jake asked both men.

"Kill our common enemy," Akira responded.

"They will be Japanese," Jake persisted.

"I know," Akira said sadly. "But that is how it must be. We will kill Japanese soldiers just as many white people must kill their German and Italian cousins. Japan is now our enemy. It may have taken some of us a while to realize it," he said with irony, "but we understand it now."

"How many are you?"

"Just under fifty," Akira answered, and Jake noted that the older man was deferring to the younger.

"If I were to question their loyalty," Jake said, "you would tell me that they are all totally committed to your cause. However, I have to tell you that a solid cadre that was smaller in numbers would be better than a more dubious larger group."

"I understand," said Akira, "but I am certain of them. They have all been initiated, shall we say."

Akira explained that the group had kidnapped two Japanese soldiers when they were drunk and off duty. Each conspirator had plunged his knife into the body of one of the soldiers and, therefore, had shared in the murder. The corpses were then dumped into the ocean and, according to Toyoza Kaga, were considered to have deserted. Foul play was not suspected by the military police or *kempetei*.

Jake was both shocked and impressed by the cold-blooded callousness of the act. He decided he wanted neither Toyoza nor Akira as his enemy. "If I get you weapons, you must swear to follow my orders. I don't know exactly what is going to happen or when, but it will be soon, and whatever you do must not be premature and jeopardize it."

"We understand," Akira said. "Now, what and where are the weapons?"

Jake grinned. During the Japanese siege and invasion, he'd cached away quantities of army supplies in the wild hope that they'd someday be useful. Now his foresight was going to be rewarded.

"I can get you several dozen Springfield rifles and several hundred rounds of ammunition. There are a couple of crates of grenades and a dozen .45 automatics and ammunition. You'll have to clean the weapons because they're in the ground, and I'm sure they're rusted pretty badly. If that's not enough, you'll have to get other guns from what you referred to as our common enemy."

"Magnificent," Akira said. "How far away are they?"

"They're in several places," Jake said, "one of which is only a mile from here. Now"—he paused—"I would like a favor from you, Toyoza."

"What is it?"

"When you sent the woman, Alexa Sanderson, to me, she left a close friend behind. The friend's name is Melissa Wilson, and Alexa is concerned about her and her small son. Can you check on her?"

Jake thought he caught a wariness in Toyoza's eyes. It passed in an instant, if it had existed at all.

"I will do that," Toyoza said and stood up. "Now let us get to the rifles."

COLONEL SHIGENORI OMORI WAS REPELLED by the utter lack of secrecy in Admiral Iwabachi's headquarters. Everyone and his proverbial brother appeared to know the timetable for the arrival of the great fleet and Admiral Yamamoto. How could they keep the Americans from finding out?

Iwabachi was unimpressed by his concern. "Let them find out, Colonel. Let the Americans come and we will defeat them. Let their sympathizers here rise up, and we will squash them like the insects they are. I am confident that our navy can handle theirs, and I am doubly confident that you know everything that is going on in the islands. Surely you can't be afraid the little band of Americans on Hawaii will try something."

Omori had to concede the point. He knew of absolutely nothing amiss on Oahu, and the situation on Hawaii, while an aggravation, was contained. So why did he feel uneasy?

Iwabachi laughed. "Yamamoto will see what we have accomplished in so short a time and be pleased. Perhaps it will even mean a promotion for us."

Omori smiled and nodded. He was not as impressed with Iwabachi's efforts as the admiral was. While the fuel tanks had been reconstructed, only half of them were full. Nothing had been done regarding clearing the wrecked American ships from where they'd been sunk, and the antisubmarine boom had not been repaired. Shore batteries that had been smashed by the bombardment remained that way, and the antiaircraft batteries were less than half effective. Pearl Harbor had a long way to go before it could be considered a fortress.

Of course, there were reasons for this situation. Iwabachi's orders had been to concentrate on the fuel storage tanks and, when that task was complete, to develop the defenses. It had been stressed that Oahu without fuel was useless. Iwabachi had not been given adequate resources to do much more than the first job, and the remaining tasks had been pushed further and further back. Omori did not think Yamamoto would be pleased, regardless of what Iwabachi thought.

He and the admiral ate in what had been the American officers' club, and it still disturbed Omori to see American Negroes moving about in the kitchen and cleaning the tables. This was another area in which he and the admiral disagreed. Despite the fact that the Americans were technically civilians and certainly not white, Omori considered them a possible threat. Iwabachi had laughed at him and asked him how a handful of shambling, ignorant people with black faces could ever threaten Japan.

After the meal was over, Omori returned by car to his office. With the removal of the remaining American prisoners to Japan, he had moved his operations to Honolulu. Only the Japanese naval air section remained at Wheeler Field. That consisted of two score Zeros and a handful of reconnaissance craft, along with their pilots, mechanics, and a small number of guards. This was something else that Omori felt was inadequately done. The islands needed more planes and more soldiers. Perhaps that lack would be corrected after Yamamoto arrived.

He sighed as his car neared the hotel where he kept a suite. There would be liquor and the pleasure of watching the Korean woman, Han, perform with another American woman. The hell with it. If Iwabachi wasn't concerned, why was he?

.

CHAPTER 20

Reinhard Hardegen had commanded the sequentially numbered *U-123* before the start of hostilities between Germany and the United States. His and a handful of other boats had been sent to American East Coast waters in what was called Operation *Paukenschlag,* or Drumbeat. They'd launched themselves furiously against unprotected and unsuspecting American shipping. The drum they had beaten was the American merchant fleet.

It had been what Hardegen and his comrades referred to as yet another "happy time," as ship after ship was sunk off the American coast. U-boats boldly went up the Mississippi, the St. Lawrence, and into the port of New York. Hardegen himself had seen the city's skyline and marveled at it. The Americans had been totally inept in their antisubmarine defenses. It was as if they never thought war would come to them. The Germans exulted as the idiots had even kept their city lights on, which enabled tankers to be silhouetted against them in the night.

Hardegen had been ruthlessly efficient, although not unnecessarily cruel. He had not shelled lifeboats; slaughtering the innocent was not in him. Once, he had positioned the *U-123* between the shore and a burning tanker that he was shelling with his deck gun. He did not want to accidentally send shells from the gun over the tanker and into the crowds of Americans gathered on the nearby beach to watch the show. He wondered what they'd thought when the *U-123* had emerged before them, almost literally a stone's throw away.

The American defenses still weren't particularly good, although they were improving. There was just too much shoreline for the Yanks to patrol, and they had too many bad habits to break. The Americans were likable, but so undisciplined, Hardegen thought.

And discipline was what made Hardegen a good member of the Kriegsmarine, the German navy. He had spent the last few months as a training commander, but the navy had been asked to find out what the American fleet was up to. In short, where were the carriers? Despite lingering injuries, he would do his duty to the best of his now limited abilities.

Hardegen had been at the U-boat base at Lorient, on the western coast of France, when the call came in. The *U-123* with its new skipper had been the only sub in port, and her captain had just suffered an attack of appendicitis. With mixed emotions, Hardegen had essentially commandeered his old boat and taken her north.

Her crew had been looking forward to more leave time in France, where they had been celebrating cheating death one more time in the riotous manner that was traditional with submariners. There'd been tons of food, copious amounts of liquor, and eager French whores. Still, the command from Admiral Doenitz would be obeyed.

Hardegen's orders had been to cruise north and try to find a suspected American task force off Iceland. He was to locate and observe and not commit any rash acts. Confirmation of the presence of the American fleet was deemed more important than another kill.

This suited Hardegen for two reasons: his sub had left suddenly and without torpedoes, and he had no death wish.

Thus, Hardegen squinted through the periscope and tried to make sense of what he saw anchored in the mist. American destroyers formed a protective outer screen, and it was difficult to see clearly because of the weather. He would make no attempt to penetrate further.

He made a notation and turned the periscope over to his executive officer. "You make a tally, and we'll compare," he said.

The other officer nodded and began his observations. Finally, he stepped back. "I make it five large carriers with a possible sixth in the distance. There are three battleships and a number of heavy cruisers. From their silhouettes, I believe they are all Americans."

Hardegen nodded. "I counted only five carriers and no sixth one in the distance. However, I defer to your younger eyes. Please signal that we have located the American fleet and give its probable disposition."

"Five carriers or six?"

Hardegen thought for a moment. How marvelous that Berlin had even thought to look in Iceland for the Americans. And what were they doing there? Obviously there were big plans afoot, and his discovery would be a major part of upsetting them.

"Let discretion be our guide. Tell them six."

At the secret codebreaking complex at Bletchley Park, England, the codebreakers exulted. Hardegen didn't know it, but he was as safe as a baby in its crib. They had recorded both his orders sending him to Iceland and his brief report. He'd been allowed to exit Lorient without interference, and his return trip would likewise be uninterrupted; thus allowing him to amplify on the American armada he thought he'd seen off Iceland.

LIEUTENANT COMMANDER FARGO KNEW the totality of overwhelming, shuddering fear. The ocean outside the thin hull of the *Monkfish* throbbed as immense, angry, and fearsome life vibrated through the water and resonated within the submarine.

Like his German counterpart half a world away, he was close to a massive fleet. In this case, the term *close to* meant feet and not miles.

"Jesus Christ," Fargo muttered. "How many of the fuckers are there?"

He had spotted the approaching Japanese armada on a routine periscope sweep. Along with two of the largest battleships he'd ever imagined possible, he had noted a number of carriers before prudence told him to down periscope and lie on the floor of the harbor entrance and act like a piece of mud. Even though one of his men had tied debris to the periscope to make it less visible, he wasn't going to chance it with the entire Japanese navy cruising past him.

Instead, he and his men tried to identify the type of ship by the sound of its screws as it rumbled by. Assuming that the first two were the battleships and the carriers had followed, they were comfortable in estimating that at least a dozen major warships, heavy cruisers or larger, had entered the confines of Pearl Harbor, with still more coming. The enemy fleet was at least as large as the entire U.S. naval force that had been assigned to Pearl Harbor on December 7.

But they'd had to enter through the channel single file, and they'd have to leave the same way. The channel was just too narrow to permit more than one of those leviathans to pass at a time. Fargo recalled that there had been real fear during the Pearl Harbor attack that one of the American ships would be sunk in the channel and plug it up. At one point, the entrance was only about a quarter mile wide, and the navigable portion much less than that.

Fargo smiled as the noise level finally abated. Smaller ships, destroyers or light cruisers, made a different, lighter sound as they too entered the anchorage in a stately parade.

"Where the hell they gonna park them all?" he heard one of his men whisper. The sailor didn't know just how many ships there had been when the entire American fleet was in the harbor. He also had no idea how big the harbor was. It would require planning, but Pearl could handle a very large number of ships.

But there was still only one narrow entrance.

If, as Admiral Lockwood had explained, the Jap fleet might come out in a helluva rush, then they might not be looking for one small submarine right at the entrance to the harbor.

Maybe, Fargo thought and smiled, he would get a chance to do some real damage and still get away.

The sound of the ships finally ceased. He waited until he knew the wreck was in shadows and carefully raised the periscope. With it only a few inches above the water, he looked around. The entrance to the harbor was empty. The Japs had disappeared inside. He swung the scope and looked out onto the ocean. A picket line of destroyers was in view but several miles away. It was highly unlikely they were looking in his direction. They would be watching for an enemy that would come from the sea if it came at all. He was as safe again as he had been before the Japs had arrived. The *Monkfish* was inside the Japanese defense perimeter.

Hell, Fargo thought. He had indeed sailed right up their asses.

AKIRA KAGA WAS GREETED as a long-lost brother by the pilots stationed at Wheeler Field. He wore his real Japanese uniform for the occasion, and the young men were suitably impressed by the decorations and the wound he had suffered for Nippon.

He had invited himself for a tour and an opportunity to talk to the men stationed in what had become an isolated outpost that still bore the scars of the battles earlier in the year.

Only a handful of buildings at the airfield had been repaired sufficiently to use, and a surprisingly small number of planes was lined up along one runway.

Schofield Barracks was in even worse shape, which was one reason why there were no Japanese soldiers in the area. There were only the pilots, their mechanics, and a handful of Japanese marines as guards. The prisoner of war pens were vacant and stood as haunting reminders of the American defeat. Akira wondered how many of those thousands who'd been imprisoned there were still alive. Judging by the emaciated condition of those he'd seen before they'd been shipped off, few would have survived the long voyage to Japan. It was something else that Japan would have to answer for.

As he looked around, it occurred to Akira that the place was even more poorly defended than it had been on December 7.

A Captain Masaka had greeted him warmly and introduced him to the other men who appeared glad to have him there as an interruption to a boring existence.

After his talk to the troops, which was different from the one he gave to the civilians, Akira asked for a further tour of the facility, and Masaka was happy to oblige. Akira limped badly, but he was able to keep up with the captain. His determination in using the artificial leg was beginning to show dividends.

"Tell me," Akira asked, "why are you stationed here and not at Hickam, Ford Island, or the other strips closer to Honolulu and Pearl?"

Masaka grinned. "I wish we were. But Admiral Iwabachi fears sabotage, so he had us put as far away from Hawaiian people as possible. That and the fact that the other fields are still unusable made this the logical choice."

Masaka's statement confirmed what Akira had heard and observed. As everywhere else, the damage done in the fighting here had not been repaired. Of course, the Japanese in Oahu didn't need a lot of airfields with only a couple dozen planes at their disposal. But it did explain Novacek's interest in Wheeler's vulnerability.

"Are the planes always parked this close together?" Akira asked. The Zeros and scout planes were almost wingtip to wingtip.

Masaka shrugged. "Admiral's orders, and admirals always know best, don't they? We have only a squad of guards, and they can't watch the planes if they're scattered all over the place. I know it's like how the Americans had theirs when we attacked them, but there are no American ships, and, besides, we're in the middle of the island, where we'd get plenty of warning."

"Of course, when Yamamoto's fleet comes, any concerns will all become immaterial, won't they?"

"Precisely." Masaka beamed. "And perhaps I can get a billet in Honolulu, where I can have a little fun with the local women. We get some prostitutes bussed here every weekend for those who can't get off duty, but they are usually quite ugly. It is a miserable existence here in the middle of paradise."

Akira laughed sympathetically with the young man. He wondered how many combat missions Masaka had flown. Probably only a few, maybe none.

Akira walked around the area a little longer, taking note of the locations of the sandbagged guard bunkers. Mentally, he answered the question Jake hadn't asked: He could take Wheeler and destroy the planes. But then what? A simple raid would result in some killings and destruction, but if it were an isolated instance, the attackers would be hunted down and killed. Admiral Iwabachi would be particularly furious when he learned that Japanese had done this, and his vengeance would be terrible.

No, this had to be part of something much bigger than simply embarrassing the Japanese, and he was pleased to be participating in it.

CHARLEY FINCH SMILED CONTENTEDLY as he sorted supplies. After what had seemed an eternity of furtive looking, he now had knowledge that was useful. A few casual comments and a couple of glances at documents he wasn't supposed to see had told him that the Americans were up to something. Security in the camp was lax, and everyone seemed to think that everyone else was totally trustworthy. This had given him a golden opportunity, and he had made the most of it.

Incredibly, Novacek had gotten his hands on an airplane.

But what the hell was he going to do with it? Finch now had a solid idea where it was located, but he had no idea what kind of plane it was, or what it was going to be used for.

He could rule out a bomber, although stripped-down B-17s had flown from California to Hawaii last December. A bomber needed bombs and more fuel, and Charley was confident that Novacek had neither in any serious quantity.

So that left somebody's personal, civilian plane, a leftover from before the war. Perhaps there was even more than one, but how did that change matters? Those were dinky-ass things with no range and minimal bomb-carrying capability.

Still, they could carry small bombs and could be fitted with machine guns.

That must be it, Charley decided. Fucking Novacek must be planning an attack on a Japanese outpost, and Hilo was the logical answer. All the Jap garrison at Hilo had was a couple of small seaplanes that they used to pretend they were scouting. Now all he had to do was get the information to Lieutenant Goto and collect his reward. He wouldn't be able to guarantee the total destruction of Novacek's group, but he could sure cut their balls off.

"Oh, there you are."

Charley looked up quickly. It was Alexa Sanderson, and she was smiling at him. She sure was looking better since she and Novacek had started screwing each other's brains out. The relationship was an open secret in the community, with no one disapproving. Charley didn't care who she fucked.

"Jake wanted me to give you a message."

"Sure," he said.

"He wants you to go to a couple of the farms by Hilo that've been supplying us with food. Tell them we'll need additional supplies and we'll need them fast."

"Uh, how fast, ma'am? They can't grow what they don't have."

Alexa laughed easily. "Of course not. Tell them to gather what they can and have it ready at the prearranged sites within two weeks. For some reason, Jake thinks we may have to move from here fairly quickly, and he'll want supplies positioned where we can get at them."

Two weeks? Now he had a time frame for whatever they were up to. "I'll leave tonight. Who will I take with me?"

"Do you need anyone?"

He shrugged. "Not really."

"Good," she said, her smile even wider. "Jake thinks we'll be short of men, so if you can go alone, that'd be swell."

When she left, Charley hummed happily. He had just been handed a gift from above. He could leave and give the information to Goto and, if necessary, come back to this stinking little camp. The fact that they'd have to move quickly meant that it wasn't going to be only an air raid. He could tell the obnoxious lieutenant that there was going to be an infantry attack on Hilo in conjunction with the air attack.

AS COLONEL OMORI HAD PREDICTED, Admiral Yamamoto had not been pleased with their efforts. He and Admiral Iwabachi had been summoned to the admiral's flagship, the *Yamato*, and were seated with Yamamoto in a conference room. Outside, the might of Imperial Japan lay at anchor in a stunning array of battleships, carriers, cruisers, and destroyers. The population of Honolulu had stood by the tens of thousands and gaped at the awesome might of Japan. Now maybe some of the nervous fools, those who were upset by the death of that girl, and all the others would realize just who was going to win this war.

Yamamoto glared at both men. "I had expected to see a fully functioning port and naval facility," he said through tight lips, "not this collection of ruins and rusting hulks."

Iwabachi also contained his anger. "With profoundest respects, Admiral, then you should have seen to it that I received the resources to accomplish the task. Not even the best of carpenters can drive nails without a hammer. Tokyo gave me seven thousand men to control all these islands and to contain many thousands of prisoners. They gave me few mechanics and skilled workers, no equipment, and no food."

"What about the American men and equipment?"

Iwabachi laughed harshly. "Despite orders to the contrary, much of the port facilities and material that had not been damaged in the fighting were destroyed by the Americans. We executed some of those responsible, of course, but it was too late. The damage had been done.

"We used the prisoners and civilian workers, but they were indifferent workers at best, and some even committed further acts of sabotage. Then, as a result of the food shortages, they weakened, which slowed progress even further. After a while they became useless, which is why I had the prisoners shipped to Japan. I was told that my priority was the repair of the fuel storage facilities, and that task has been fulfilled. Even now, fuel is being added to them from your tankers. Any other work done by us was to provide suitable living quarters and to repair the roads. And, of course, I had to resolve the food situation."

Yamamoto tapped the fingers of his mangled hand on the table between them. What the arrogant junior admiral had said was correct. Tokyo had not been fully confident that Hawaii could be held, so it had not provided the wherewithal to do a proper job. The government emissaries who expected to see the annexation of a radiant jewel in the middle of the Pacific would be disappointed, but they would have to deal with that fact.

But his presence now meant that this situation would change. Only moments before, he had received confirmation that the American carriers were in the Atlantic, off Iceland, and preparing for an undetermined action against Germany. Exactly what they were up to didn't concern him. He didn't care if the Americans tried to cruise up the Rhine. His only concern was that they were far away from Hawaii.

The sole remaining Allied force of significance in the Pacific was a British squadron that had taken up a position in Australian waters in anticipation of a move in that direction by Japan. Yamamoto had sent a pair of old battleships, a small carrier, and a dozen heavy and light cruisers toward Australia to threaten it and further mask his move to Hawaii. Now it seemed that the effort had not been necessary. The Americans were gone. The Pacific was Japan's. The world would soon know that the fleet was in Hawaiian waters, and Tokyo would shortly announce that the annexation would occur. Representatives from Nazi Germany, along with emissaries from several puppet and neutral nations, had accompanied the fleet.

"On Saturday, August first," Yamamoto said, "the Hawaiian Islands will be proclaimed a province of Japan. That is only a week from now, which is not enough time to change matters. When the fleet departs, which will be within a couple of days after that, I will leave you sufficient resources to carry out the following tasks.

"First, the airfields at Hickam, Ewa, and Barbers must be repaired. Second, the shore batteries and antiaircraft installations must be reconstructed."

"Will I receive additional forces to man them?" Iwabachi asked.

"Of course," Yamamoto snapped. "Then I want the wrecks removed from the harbor."

Iwabachi nodded. "It will take a tremendous effort to remove the carcasses of the sunken battleships. It was not something I attempted to do because, even with the best of resources, it would take an enormous amount of time and effort."

This time Yamamoto agreed. "Which is why it is your last priority." He turned to Omori. "The existence of the American guerrillas on Hawaii is repugnant. What will you do about it?"

"To be candid, Admiral, there is very little we can do. We know they have a radio and communicate regularly with California, but we have been unable to locate it. We cannot triangulate in such rugged terrain. Right now, we place it in an area of over a hundred square miles, which, given the harshness of the land, means we could march ten feet away from it and not see it. The same holds true with the guerrillas themselves. They can stay out there forever until I get sufficient troops to mount a series of massive sweeps that would wear them down and cut them off from their supply bases."

Yamamoto had seen the Philippines and other areas of the Hawaiian Islands. He knew precisely what Omori's problem was. American guerrillas were still active in the Philippines and even on the relatively small island of Guam. Only time would wear them down.

"You would need a division," Yamamoto said. "It must wait. Are they capable of disrupting the annexation proceedings?"

"They might try something," Omori said. "But they are only a handful and could do little more than cause an embarrassment. They would also have to transport themselves from Hawaii to Oahu, which I do not consider likely as it would be suicidal."

There was no more to be said, and Yamamoto dismissed them. On the deck of the battleship, Omori spent a moment gazing at the splendor of the Japanese navy. He swelled with pride at the force that had humbled the Americans and taken this jewel from them.

Now all he had to do was ensure that what he'd told the revered admiral was correct. He would contact Goto and make certain that he was doing all that could be done to keep pressure on the American guerrillas. If anything happened, Omori was confident it would be near Hilo, where the Japanese garrison was relatively small, which made it a potentially tempting target. Only a raving idiot would think of attempting anything disruptive with the fleet in the harbor along with a brigade of infantry on troop transports. No, any move by the Americans would be at Hilo.

So why did he have the nagging feeling of doubt that something was going to go wrong? He would double and redouble his efforts to ensure that the ceremony went off without a hitch. After that, did he really care?

ALEXA WATCHED from behind a tree as Charley Finch headed off in the direction of Hilo. He was alone and carried some rations in a field pack, along with a rifle across his shoulder. He lumbered more than walked, and it was obvious that the sergeant was not in good shape. Too bad, she thought.

It would take Finch a couple of days to get to either Hilo or the farms he was supposed to visit, and a couple more to come back. If he came back. She wondered if he would actually visit the farms. Perhaps she had misjudged him. After all, there was nothing definitive to hang on him, just the very strong suspicion that there was more to Sergeant Charley Finch than there should be. If he came back and if he had completed his assignment, she would have a lot of her suspicions allayed. But not all of them. She could not get the photograph out of her mind. How had he gotten it?

Jake walked up behind her and put his hand on her shoulder, massaging it gently. "Are you solving the problem?"

She felt his strength and drew from it. She pressed backward so that she was leaning against him. It was a very comforting feeling. What she was doing was so far removed from her previous life as a docile navy wife that it was terrifying. "Sure am, Jake."

"We just got the word, Alexa. It's going to be the early morning of August second."

Alexa thought quickly. What the devil day was today? It was so easy to lose track out in the wild. Ah yes, August second was a week away. Perfect.

"Are you worried?" she asked.

"Damn right I am. I still don't know everything that's going on, and that's the best way. But I do know that if our part of this fails, we could be running for our lives from thousands of angry Japs. We'll have proven that we're a lot more dangerous than they thought, and they won't stand still for that. We'll have a devil of a time hiding or getting away from here."

She shrugged. It was easy to be fatalistic. "If that's the case, Jake, then we run. And if we can't run, then we die. Like I said before, I'm not going to go back as a prisoner."

"Me neither," he said gently as he hugged her and nuzzled the back of her neck. Soft hairs grew there, and he thought they were fascinating.

"We all have to die sometime, don't we?"

"Yeah," he answered with a harsh laugh. "I just don't want it to be right away. I'd kind of hoped to spend more time with you. Like maybe thirty years or so."

Alexa took his hand and led him away. Several other people were about and trying not to look at them. When they were alone in the shadows, she turned and kissed him. "Then let's spend what time we have together. I know a marvelous place in the bushes where we can make love. I find you very attractive now that you no longer smell like fish."

Jake hesitated. "There's a helluva lot to do between now and next Sunday."

"An hour?" she teased. "You can't spend an hour making love to the woman you love?"

Jake laughed and felt himself growing warm. "An hour I can spend."

ADMIRAL NIMITZ HAD HIMSELF driven out to the isolated ocean cove where the five giant seaplanes bobbed at anchor. First there had been eight, and then six, and now another had fallen to mechanical problems.

Nimitz thought it was incredible that such massive and ungainly things could ever get airborne. However, once they did reach the skies, they became long-winged and as graceful as one of the great birds that flew the oceans.

"Colonel, you are either the bravest man I've ever known or the craziest."

"Probably a little of both, sir."

"You realize what we're doing, don't you?"

Doolittle's orders were to be over Pearl Harbor at just before dawn on the morning of Sunday, August 2, 1942. Exactly how he would do that without proper navigating equipment and in the face of possibly contrary winds was his problem. He had five massive flying boats all reconfigured to carry bombs. They could make it to Hawaii and, just maybe, all the way back. There was no other plane on the face of the earth that could do that.

It was presumed that some planes would be lost in the raid, and that the remaining planes would be damaged, perhaps severely. The cripples were to fly as far as possible toward the United States and then land in the ocean. Ships would try to find them and pluck them to safety. It wasn't much of a chance, but it was something.

Doolittle's men were willing to put themselves at risk, but not to commit suicide. There had to be at least the ghost of a chance of survival. Of course, no one wanted to be captured by the Japanese. A fast death would be the best that could happen in that case.

"Yes, sir, I understand fully, and so will my men," Doolittle said. "We're going to do unto the Japs as they did unto us. We're going to hit them just before first light, when their slanty little eyes are fast asleep. I do have a question, though."

"Go ahead."

"My five planes aren't all that's involved in this, are we?"

Nimitz smiled. "If I recall, you were more than willing to take a flight of B-25s over Tokyo without any assistance, weren't you?"

Doolittle winced and grinned. "Sorry, Admiral. I shouldn't have brought it up."

"Colonel, let's just say that you shouldn't be surprised at anything that happens. Like I told you so long ago, people say you're the right man for this mission because you are so flexible in your thinking. That's why you've been given carte blanche regarding the choice of targets."

There was, however, a priority to the targets. First, he was to attack any carriers in the harbor. Second, he was to hit the fuel storage depots. Battleships were a very low priority. Not only were his bombs too small to do much damage to them but the huge battlewagons just weren't all that important anymore.

The great unspoken fear was that Doolittle's planes would make it through Japanese defenses only to find that the carriers were no longer in the harbor. It wouldn't take them long at all to sortie into the open ocean once the alarm was sounded.

The second fear was that his planes would waste their bombs on empty storage tanks. Intelligence sources said that only half the depot's tanks were full, but they didn't say which half.

There were twelve men on each of the five planes: a pilot, copilot, navigator, radioman, bombardier, and gunners to fire the machine guns that had been installed as defenses against the Zeros that were sure to swarm them. It had been hoped that the guns would provide a disconcerting sting and help the seaplanes get through.

Doolittle thought they were a waste of time and men. He had sixty men with which to take on the Jap navy and the defenses of Pearl Harbor.

Why the hell, he thought wryly, hadn't he stuck with something simple? Like bombing Tokyo.

CHAPTER 21

*L*ieutenant Ernie Magruder paced the distance from the cliff to where the planes would commence their runoffs. In a few days he would launch eleven Grumman Wildcats against the might of Japan. The Wildcat was a good, solid plane, although obsolescent and due to be replaced by a newer Grumman model. The newer plane was not going to be risked in an operation as chancy as this. There was too much possibility of it falling into Japanese hands.

The Wildcat carried six machine guns but only two one-hundred-pound bombs. It had a range of just over seven hundred miles, which meant they would not have all that much time over Pearl during the raid. In and out, drop and run, shoot and scoot were his instructions. Even so, there probably wouldn't be enough fuel to take them back to the Big Island if they had to do much fighting or high-speed maneuvering, so they were to land on abandoned strips on Molokai. From there, they were to run like hell and hide. Ironically, these now-abandoned fields were the ones that had first been used by the Japanese earlier in the year. Locals had helped repair them after the Japanese left.

The Wildcat was considered overmatched by the Zero, which was faster and more maneuverable. But Magruder knew that his plane could still cause a great deal of damage to the Zero, which had a wonderful propensity to blow up when hit, while his tough little plane could absorb punishment and get away.

His job wasn't to take on the Zeros. His task was the carriers, if any, and the fuel. He had been told that his appearance over Pearl would be a complete surprise to the Japanese. Magruder sincerely hoped so. It was the Japs who had a death wish, not Ernie Magruder of Montgomery, Alabama.

Of course, that presumed he and his trusty planes got airborne in the first place.

"What's the problem?" asked Captain Gustafson. "You take off from a little ship in the middle of an ocean, don't you? So what's wrong with jumping off a cliff?"

Magruder laughed nervously and conceded that the jut-jawed captain had a point. Launching from Hawaii was planned to be simplicity itself. Three abreast, planes were to taxi as fast as they could downhill toward the cliff, then launch themselves into space. According to Gustafson's calculations, the planes would drop but a few feet before becoming stable flying machines. Magruder had his doubts and could visualize himself plummeting a thousand feet into the ocean. "Captain, I just want you to know that, if this doesn't work, my last words will be 'You fucked up, sir!' "

Gustafson laughed hugely. "What's the saying? If you can't take a joke, you shouldn't have enlisted? Well, son, you've enlisted and here you are. Now, if you know a better way of getting your planes in the air without building an airfield that the Japs would spot, you tell me."

Magruder didn't. "Now that I think of it, getting in the air might just be the least of my problems," he said. "I have to find Pearl Harbor at dawn and without attracting attention, blow up the place, and then get safely out of there. Jumping off a cliff is a piece of cake in comparison."

Gustafson nodded sympathetically. Magruder was only half his age and had his whole life before him. In the short while they'd been together, he'd begun to think of Magruder as the son he and his wife never had.

Gustafson was an immigrant from Sweden who'd arrived as a teenager. Before coming, he'd been told that the United States was a land of soft and spineless people who would never fight and couldn't bear to be uncomfortable. Novacek, Magruder, and so many others had shown that assessment to be a lie. He put his hand on the younger man's shoulder. "You can do it, Ernest."

Magruder laughed. Nobody called him Ernest. "Thanks, Pop."

"Now," Gustafson said, "let's see if that still we rigged up is working all right. We have a couple of days to prepare for your mission, and I think we could all use a drink."

∎

AFTER WHAT SEEMED AN ETERNITY, Jamie Priest had finally gotten a letter from WAVE-in-training Suzy Dunnigan. She said that she was doing well in the classroom portion of her training, and that the physical part was a breeze. Recalling her taut and lean body as they swam, ran, and made love, he had no doubt that she could march or hike circles around her peers.

Her only negative was that she had just come down with the flu and was puking her guts out. She said it was the navy's fault for sending her from sunny California to Chicago. Jamie laughed at the joke. It was July, and the Great Lakes Naval Training Center was probably hotter than San Diego, so maybe it wasn't the flu. Maybe it was something she'd eaten, like navy food, for instance.

Every day he had his security clearance brought him new discoveries and revelations. He now understood that Great Britain had been fully informed of the navy's masquerade off Iceland. Thanks to some clever carpentry, the smaller vessels had been made over to look like their bigger brethren. Viewing from a distance, the German sub had been fooled and Berlin had passed the erroneous information on to the Japanese.

The British had intercepted both the message from *U-123* and the subsequent signal from Berlin to Tokyo. They had forwarded the information to Admiral King in Washington, where it had been relayed to both Nimitz in San Diego and Spruance in the Pacific. Jamie wondered if King's noted antipathy toward Britain had moderated. He doubted it.

You see what you expect to see, had been the plan. It had grown from that long-ago offhand comment by Jamie. The *U-123*'s was not the only sighting of the phantom fleet. A Spanish warship had been permitted to get close enough to see and then been abruptly ordered out of the area. The Spanish were ostensibly neutral but leaned heavily toward the Axis. The second confirmation must have really dazzled the Japs, he thought.

Another consequence of Jamie's new status was the realization that Jake Novacek led the guerrillas on Hawaii and that Alexa Sanderson was there as well. Every time he thought of it he had to stifle a grin. He could see Novacek as a guerrilla, but Alexa? What the hell had happened to the quiet girl who had been the wife of his friend? Alexa Sanderson was almost a socialite, not a soldier. But then, he thought solemnly, circumstances force changes. Sometimes you have to adapt or die.

When Nimitz found out that he knew Novacek, Jamie was called into the admiral's office. "Commander, do you realize that you are among a handful of people who have any idea who this fellow is?"

Jamie didn't. "Sir, I'm very surprised."

Nimitz gestured him to a chair. "Novacek is responsible for at least two aspects of Operation Wasp. Joe Rochefort worked with him for a short while and thinks highly of him, and the only other recommendation I've gotten is from a General Joe Collins, who sent a favorable report on Novacek to General Marshall. Some think Rochefort's a little crazy, and I have no idea who this Collins person is, although I accept Marshall's opinion of both him and his reference. Novacek might not be one of Marshall's Boys, but Collins certainly is, and, if Novacek pulls this off, he might well be one too."

Jamie stifled a grin. Even on a good day, Rochefort was at least unique, and crazy might not be that far off the mark. However, Rochefort was crazy like a fox. As to Jake becoming one of General Marshall's favorites, Jamie found himself strangely pleased for someone he hadn't known at all before December 7.

"Sir, I was very impressed with what little I saw of him," he said and then explained that he really knew Alexa Sanderson far better. "All I can say is I think that we're in good hands with Jake Novacek, and I'm very glad that Mrs. Sanderson is as well."

Nimitz had only a dim recollection of once meeting Tim Sanderson, and none of his widow, although he recalled the name as a result of queries from some congressman. Admirals often had a hard time recalling junior officers with whom they had no contact, and Nimitz was no exception, even though he epitomized courtesy and consideration.

"It's a strange world, Commander," he said, "and it's about to get even stranger in a couple of days, isn't it?"

"Yes, sir."

"I don't want this to fail," Nimitz said gently. "There may be only a handful of people involved, but they are all human beings and I don't want anyone to die needlessly. Novacek has control of at least a couple of parts of Operation Wasp, and I like to think he's up to it."

"I think he is, sir," Jamie responded. He thought it both astonishing and in character that Nimitz would be so concerned about people. Once again, he felt honored and proud to serve with the man.

"Well, you get back to your work, and if you can think of anything else about Novacek, you tell me," the admiral said.

"Sir, may I ask you a question? It may sound impertinent, but it isn't."

"Go ahead."

"The way I see it, sir, there are at least five parts to Wasp, and most of them are supposed to occur around dawn of the second, and with forces approaching from all over the place. Do you really think that can be coordinated?"

Nimitz smiled tightly. "Nope. What we all hope for is that at least a couple of the disparate parts actually do work. You're right that it's impossible to time things so well when forces are converging from thousands of miles away from each other and different directions. I can only hope that, as events do unfold, the Japs are kept off balance and confused. That may just give us a level of success.

"As to the five separate events, if one succeeds, then it's a pinprick to the Japs and we'll have lost. If two or three are successful, then we've won a small victory. Four or five, son, and we may have won the war."

ADMIRAL RAYMOND SPRUANCE was fifty-six years old and, not counting time at the Naval Academy, had spent more than thirty of those years as an officer in the navy. During that time, he was acutely aware that he'd never seen combat. Spruance had risen to command as a result of his skills, even though he lacked the flamboyance and apparent belligerence of some of his peers.

Spruance was quiet and unassuming, efficient and unperturbable, and those traits worked for him particularly well in times of stress. He was considered cautious, but that was only because he wished to accomplish his goals with a minimum of human cost. However, Spruance clearly understood that there had to be at least some human cost when engaged in war. Even the most lopsided victory would result in some casualties for the victor. He also understood that too much caution brought other dangers, caused by missed opportunities and letting an enemy take the initiative. Caution, therefore, could be as much a vice as it was a virtue.

"I will call the dance," he muttered. "I will not become a punching bag."

"What?"

Spruance grinned at his companion, Captain Marc Mitscher. "Pete" to his friends, Mitscher was a year younger than Spruance but, with his weathered and craggy face, looked decades older.

"I was thinking out loud," Spruance said, "and mixing metaphors at the same time." They were in Spruance's quarters on the carrier *Hornet,* the flagship of the American task force that was anchored off Samoa. Spruance commanded the fleet, while Mitscher commanded the air arm.

Mitscher grinned. "Don't let too many people hear you doing that. The men are worried enough as it is without an admiral who talks to himself. Don't worry about mixing metaphors, though. Most of our pilots think a mixed metaphor is a Mexican drink."

"What do you think of our orders, Pete?"

He shrugged. "Ours not to reason why?"

They had discussed them numerous times. Spruance was to do battle, but only if the circumstances were right, and he was not to take any undue risks. The navy would make their move only if Operation Wasp was successful.

But how would they know it was successful? What if the Japs located the radio transmitter on Hawaii and knocked it out? What if Wasp was successful and no one could relay the information in a coherent manner?

Wasp was warfare on a shoestring, and every one of the few people involved in it could be killed and the operation still be successful. It would be tragic if his fleet was in the middle ocean awaiting word that would not come in time to use it. An opportunity bought with American blood would be lost because he would not permit "undue risk."

"What would happen if we lost this battle?" Spruance asked.

"I don't think about defeat."

"I forgot," Spruance said drily. "But indulge me. What would happen if this fleet were destroyed?"

"We'd replace it and the navy would replace us. Hell, we've got more than a dozen fleet carriers under construction right now, and it hurts my head to think of how many battleships, cruisers, and destroyers we'll have in another year or so. It'd be tough, but we've the resources to make good any losses."

"So I'm not Jellicoe, am I?"

Admiral John Rushworth Jellicoe had commanded the Royal Navy at Jutland in the previous war and was the subject of many naval studies. Jutland was the largest naval battle in world history to date, but Jellicoe had been acutely aware that Britain had no backup fleet and defeat by the Germans would turn the oceans over to their mortal enemy. Britain would then be blockaded and starved. Britain would have to sue for peace.

Jellicoe knew that he alone could lose the war in a single afternoon. Britain could not make good on her losses; thus, Jellicoe had been quite content to let the Germans return to their bases after an inconclusive battle.

"You're right, Admiral," Mitscher said softly, "you're not Jellicoe. If anybody's in that position, it'd be Yamamoto. He's got just about all the navy Japan has and just about all she'll ever have. Japan cannot replace her losses in any significant manner."

"So why are we being so cautious, and how would you now define *undue risk*?"

Mitscher grinned. "I'd define it a lot more loosely than some people."

Without putting it in so many words, their orders strongly implied that the American task force should not even begin to move northward unless Operation Wasp was successful. Even under the best of circumstances, that meant the Americans could not arrive within range of Oahu for two to three days after the critical morning of August 2.

"I think we should give ourselves a head start," Spruance said. "I think we should be ready to pounce on them as soon as we can. If Wasp works, I don't want the Japs to have a couple of days to solve their problems. I want to hit them hard and fast, and before they know what's happening to them."

Mitscher almost felt like purring. "Excellent."

Spruance and Mitscher walked to the bridge and looked out on the ships that surrounded the *Hornet*. "We'll divide the force into two groups. The carriers, the fast battleships, and other ships that can maintain speed will be in the van. The old battleships, slower cruisers, and supply ships will bring up the rear. That way, if we're wrong and all the Japs in Hawaii start chasing us, the old and slow ships will have a head start. Maybe some of them can get away."

Mitscher visualized Jap ships erupting from Pearl Harbor like angry bees or wasps from a hive. The Japanese had enough power to over-whelm the entire task force, not to mention a divided one. Spruance was going to divide an inferior force in the face of a superior enemy. Who the hell said he was too cautious? If events didn't work out, Spruance would have put the entire fleet at risk of being sunk.

But what if the Japs couldn't get out of their hive? Mitscher thought that would be the irony of Operation Wasp. Spruance was right. Brave men were going to put their lives on the line in an outrageous attempt to stop the Japs. Being prepared for the results of their efforts was the least they could do.

The captain's wrinkled face split wide with a grin. "Then let's us get this fleet moving."

Lieutenant Goto felt like spitting in the face of Sergeant Charley Finch. Goto believed that using turncoats and traitors like Finch brought dishonor to Japan's warrior race. He sometimes thought that defeat with honor would be preferable to victory aided by scum like Finch.

However, Finch had brought important news. Goto and Captain Kashii had been surprised and impressed by the audacious American plan to attack Hilo. Now they would be prepared and would inflict a stinging defeat on the Americans. Along with being prepared to re-pulse the minor aerial attack, Kashii would send two companies of in-fantry on trucks to where the plane or planes were based.

For his part, Finch considered his work done. He had no desire to return to the American base camp. He wished to get laid and get rich, in that order. He made it clear that both Omori and Goto owed him a lot.

"That disgusting snail," Kashii snarled after Finch had left them. "He expects to be treated like a lord when he should have his head cut off and shoved up his ass."

Goto laughed. "I wonder how he'd like the view."

Both men had been drinking homemade liquor to pass an other-wise dull afternoon and had added a couple more drinks to celebrate their new find. They weren't drunk, but the raw booze had loosened many of their inhibitions. Finch was out getting screwed by one of the local whores. He'd wanted a white woman but decided to settle for what was available, which wasn't much.

"I am quite certain that Colonel Omori has an interesting end in store for Sergeant Finch," Goto said. "Perhaps even something like what you have in mind. Personally, I would like to see him cut to little pieces and forced to watch while pigs eat his living flesh."

"I like that idea," Kashii said and lumbered to his feet.

Outside, Sergeant Charley Finch stood frozen in horror. His hand was scant inches from the knob. He'd gotten his ashes hauled real fast by an ugly whore and wanted to talk some more with Goto. He still wasn't fluent in Japanese, but he understood what Goto and Kashii were saying well enough to get that he was going to be betrayed by the Japs. Any thoughts of a reward were now gone. He had to be concerned with his survival.

Finch thought quickly. Now what? There was no other choice. He would leave Hilo and return to the Americans. On his way, he would alert the farmers, just like he was supposed to do. He would return to Novacek's band with his mission completed and be in good standing with them. Kashii and Goto would doubtless send troops against the air base, but that could be blamed on something else. He knew he was clutching at straws, but that was all that was available. Damn! How could things have gotten so fucked up so quickly?

He would be in tremendous danger if the Americans got hold of Jap records and found out he'd been a spy. But that was a bridge to be crossed in the future. Right now, Charley Finch was concerned about staying alive for the next few days.

Maybe he could destroy the records. No, that was unlikely. Maybe he could convince the Americans that he was playing a double game and doing it for America.

Yeah. He grinned as he slipped off into the darkness and out of Hilo. That was it. He could still come out of this mess a hero.

AUGUST 1, 1942, had been an emotional drain for Colonel Omori. On his head rested the security of the island of Oahu during the visit by the fleet and Japan's dignitaries. He was exhausted by the need to keep his emotions under control. It wasn't every day that Japan annexed a new province and declared a new land to be a part of Nippon.

But it had happened, and the ceremony had gone off without a hitch. After hours of boring speeches, several thousand native Japanese and Hawaiians who had gathered for them had applauded tepidly and wandered off. Several hundred had been invited to a lavish reception that featured foods unseen on the islands for several months. Most showed up, but many others did not bother to attend, which disturbed both Omori and Admiral Iwabachi. Admiral Yamamoto, the guest of honor, apparently did not notice or chose to ignore the slight.

Toyoza and Akira Kaga attended, but Akira left early. He said his leg was bothering him, and this was accepted as an obvious truth. Before he left, Omori introduced the younger man to Admiral Yamamoto. Akira appeared properly awed, and the admiral was deferential to the maimed young warrior.

The reception was at a park in Honolulu, a place where the fleet could be clearly seen, and the view by the water's edge was particularly dramatic. The battleships and carriers were lit up in a vivid display. They were anchored so close to one another that they appeared as one solid, glowing mass.

"Impressive, isn't it?" said Toyoza Kaga.

"Incredible, absolutely incredible," Omori answered in a whisper. The sight was almost overwhelming.

"Will the lights be on all night? I do hope so," Toyoza said.

Omori chuckled. "Yamamoto has ordered a celebration to dwarf all other Hawaiian celebrations. Some of the ships may dim their lights, but the majority will keep them on." Then he laughed out loud. "They'll need to so the crews can find their way back."

Many of the fleet's officers along with a number of enlisted men had been granted shore leave and were celebrating hugely throughout the Honolulu area. Bars and dance halls were enjoying a business bonanza, and the sounds of the celebrations reached the official reception at the park. It was even louder than when the American fleet was in port because there were few restraints placed on the Japanese sailors. Many people, Omori thought, might have ignored the reception in order to protect their property and their women.

"There will be many monumental naval hangovers tomorrow," Kaga said with a smile. "I admit I am surprised that such activities are being permitted with the Americans always a threat."

Omori laughed again. He'd had several drinks. His new favorite beverage was Scotch whisky, and it was making him unsteady. "The Americans are not a threat, my friend," he said. "Their fleet is nowhere near the Pacific, much less Hawaii. We are as safe here as we would be in Tokyo harbor. Even so, we have planes aloft to watch the oceans as a precaution."

"But what about the Americans on Hawaii?" Toyoza persisted. "What if they try to disrupt things?"

"If they'd been able to, they would have done it before or during the ceremony. No, they are isolated on their island. Lieutenant Goto did inform me that they intend to do something against Hilo this weekend, but it will be feeble and it will be repulsed. After that, we will seek out and destroy them. That will put an end to their nonsense."

He had spoken more bitterly than he realized, and Toyoza noticed it. Omori must have been catching hell from Iwabachi and Yamamoto because of the continued presence of Americans on Hawaii. Too bad, he thought. Then he looked again at the Japanese fleet and its luminous presence. If they keep the lights on, a blind man could find them, he thought. He had news to signal to the Americans.

"I am an old man," Toyoza said with an exaggerated sigh. "I will leave you now and get some needed rest. I will sleep tonight secure in the knowledge that Japan is preeminent among nations."

Omori watched as the old man departed. Thank God there were a few people he could count on in these islands. Kaga might be a crook, but he fully understood where his future lay. Kaga was not an official member of the island's new government, but he was one of the most influential men on Oahu and one whose advice Omori would seek out even more in the future.

We need more men like Toyoza Kaga, Colonel Omori thought. Then he decided he needed another drink.

•

CHAPTER 22

At first awkwardly, but then with growing speed and grace, the giant flying boats sped down the lagoon that was their runway and lifted off into the sky. Colonel Jimmy Doolittle was in the first plane, and he banked it to see the others as they made it safely into the sky. Overloaded as they were with fuel and bombs, any crash landing would be a flaming disaster for plane and crew.

Once safely airborne, they formed a loose single line and headed toward the west and Hawaii. Doolittle was under no illusions. He was chasing the night so as to be at Oahu an hour or two before dawn. He was going to attempt the nearly impossible, a night attack on a small part of a small island in the middle of the ocean over two thousand miles away.

Fuel was not a problem, and they'd been over the navigation time and time again. The Americans on Hawaii would be sending out radio beeps that would help them find their way. If they followed the beeps, they would be only a few hundred miles off course.

Only.

A few-hundred-mile error would be disastrous. It would give the Japs time to spot them and attack. No, he had to keep the radio beacon to his left and home in on where his figures said Oahu was.

Tailwinds or headwinds could either speed him up or delay him without his knowing it in the bleak night, while crosswinds would blow him north or south. He and his crews had to stay awake and alert. The lead plane, his, would have primary responsibility for navigation, while the others would follow his taillight and check on his math. Between the five of them, it was hoped that they would find Oahu instead of Australia.

"What else is going to happen tonight?" Doolittle wondered. His copilot glanced at him and turned away. He wondered the same thing.

When the Japs had attacked Pearl Harbor, they'd apparently homed in on the sounds of a Honolulu radio station. Doolittle wondered if he would be so lucky. Surely, they wouldn't have kept the station on the air.

He also wondered just what impact his five planes, large though they were, could possibly have on the course of the war, even if they did find the Jap carriers in port.

"There has to be more than this," he said. "There has to be."

CORPORAL MATSUMOTO FUJI was as alert as he could be under the circumstances. Like most others in the Japanese garrison, he resented the fact that he was on guard duty at Wheeler Field while everybody else was celebrating and getting drunk, probably even laid. The fact that Wheeler was a virtual no-man's-land was not lost on them either. If the high command didn't think Wheeler was important, then why should they?

Thus, he and his comrades had felt little guilt when they'd had the opportunity to take a couple of drinks from revelers who'd passed by and offered them. After all, weren't they fellow Japanese who'd just been brought back to the bosom of the homeland? Fuji hiccuped and thought of other bosoms he'd rather be clasped to at the moment. The Hawaiian-Japanese had been good fellows and had done their best to make Fuji and the others on guard feel both wanted and good. As a result, Fuji and his companions were more than a little drunk.

Corporal Fuji was in charge of two four-man stations that guarded Wheeler Field's closely parked planes. He and one soldier in the other sandbagged bunker were the only regulars on duty. The remaining six were mechanics and laborers who, while in the military, knew next to nothing about their duties. He blamed the higher-ups who had decreed one squad was all that was necessary to protect Wheeler. Let additional bodies come from other sources, and that meant he shared tonight's duty watch with utter incompetents.

At least the long night would end in a few hours and he could get some rest. During the daylight hours, there were only four men protecting the planes, which Fuji definitely thought was inadequate.

"Someone's coming," one of the mechanics yelled.

The warning wasn't very military, but at least the oaf was paying some attention. Fuji blinked and tried to focus in the night. There were no lights on in the field, and he squinted through the gloom. A column of men was marching down the runway toward Fuji.

Corporal Fuji identified the newcomers as Japanese soldiers. This was a relief, although he wondered what they were up to. He nudged his companions, and they shifted their rifles to more aggressive positions, although one of them was having a difficult time standing. Fuji hoped the officer in charge of the approaching column wasn't a prick who'd write them up for celebrating on this day of special days.

Fuji signaled to the soldiers in the other bunker, who acknowledged that they too had seen the other soldiers. Who the hell were these guys and what was going on?

"Who goes there?" Fuji demanded. The column was scant yards away, and an officer was leading them.

"Your relief," replied the officer, a lieutenant, which meant that someone should go and wake Fuji's superior, the officer of the guard. That fool, an off-duty pilot, was drunker than anyone, and that was saying a lot. God help the empire if some of the pilots had to take off right away, Fuji thought.

Then it dawned on him. They were getting relieved. Wonderful. "What has happened, sir?"

The young lieutenant was almost up to Fuji, and the column was deploying around the other bunker as well as his. "Yamamoto's orders," he said stiffly, almost nervously, Fuji thought. "The revered admiral wants everyone to celebrate Japan's great achievement. Our turn was earlier, yours is now."

Fuji felt like hugging the lieutenant but thought better of the idea. He wondered why a full platoon was relieving his squad, but he knew better than to ask. Questions from inferiors often meant beatings from the superiors. He didn't need that on a night he was going to spend in Honolulu. He slung his rifle over his shoulder and waved his men out of the bunker. The whole thing was very informal, but, hell, he didn't care.

Then he noticed that the soldiers were carrying strange rifles. They were American Springfields. Fuji was about to say something when the stern-faced young lieutenant slashed a broad-bladed knife across his throat. The corporal tried to speak, but the gush of his blood stopped him. Before Fuji's misting eyes closed entirely, he saw the rest of his men being stabbed and butchered like him, and he realized that the same thing was happening to the other guards.

Only a few grunts and groans proclaimed the slaughter. A moment later, the "soldiers" fanned out in the dark and headed to their other targets. First on the list was the control tower, where two men waited for the return of the six planes that were the base's combat air patrol. Next came the pilots' ready room, where the relief group of pilots was preparing for their turn in the night skies.

They took no prisoners. Akira Kaga had told them they were too few to afford the luxury. Besides, it would soon be necessary for them to melt back into the Japanese-American population. They could not leave behind anyone who would recognize them.

When the base was secure, Akira was driven up in an old Ford. He got out awkwardly and looked down on the slaughtered soldiers.

He was about to speak when a burst of gunfire erupted from the enlisted men's barracks. Someone was awake and fighting. Two of Kaga's men ran from the building. One was wounded and had to be helped away.

"What went wrong?" Akira asked. He had known it would be impossible for the plan to work perfectly. Nothing ever did.

"No idea," the unhurt man said. "You want us to storm the place? There's only a couple of them in there."

It was tempting, but it would be a distraction and would entail taking casualties. "Later. Now just keep them pinned down while we do what we have to."

Akira placed a few soldiers so that they commanded the barracks and told them to shoot anything that moved. Other soldiers had already ripped out the phone lines, and he doubted that the men in the barracks had a radio. His force was safe for the time being.

"Take care of the planes," he ordered.

The destruction of the Japanese planes was simple and efficient. Some men opened gas caps and poured in a combination of dirt and sugar. Others took tools and ripped out spark plugs and smashed more sensitive equipment. The planes might fly again, but not for a very long while, and certainly not this night.

His men had taken over the control tower and called the combat air patrol. They didn't know the proper signal, so they made up a story that there was a power problem at Wheeler and that the patrol should land immediately.

When the lead pilot protested, he was told that the carriers would be in charge of patrolling and that two groups of planes in the air at the same time could cause confusion, even a collision. The pilot grudgingly agreed, and Akira saw the first of the Japanese planes lining up for a landing. The runway was unlit, but it was wide, well marked, and impossible to miss.

The Zeros landed one at a time. The bodies of the dead were hidden behind sandbags and in buildings. The intervals between planes were sufficiently long to permit the pilots to taxi to their normal places. As they started to climb out, "mechanics" ran up to them and killed them.

Just as the last plane was touching down, one of the real Japanese soldiers in the barracks opened fire on it. The pilot whipped the plane around and began to race down the runway.

"Shoot it," Akira yelled as he cursed the fact that one of the trapped Japanese knew how to think. Once the pilot was fully airborne, he would radio the fleet at Pearl.

The Zero gained distance as a hail of bullets chased it. As it lifted off the ground, a tongue of flame erupted from the tail. Seconds later, the tongue became a torch and the plane exploded.

It's true, Akira thought grimly. The Zeros do blow up easily.

The plane crashed a mile or so from the runway. Flames billowed from the spot, and fire engines would be on their way shortly, while civilians phoned about to find out what had occurred.

Their secret would be out in a very short while, but it could have been far worse. Akira ordered some of his men to take care of the runways while he sent others to set up roadblocks. In each case, they would use dynamite and TNT brought in by submarine to Novacek. With secrecy no longer necessary, he took personal command of a captured Japanese machine gun and pulverized the wooden barracks. There was no return fire.

Akira was content. He and his men had done their part. Now the skies over Oahu were empty. Who would claim them?

ERNIE MAGRUDER LED the first planes down the incline and toward the edge of the cliff. He was the loneliest man in the world even though he had just gotten best wishes from Captain Gustafson and Colonel Novacek. "Jesus, I hope this works," he said to himself.

The brave part of him had hoped that the mission would go off, while the sane part had hoped it would be canceled. The radio signal from Oahu had eliminated all choices, and Novacek had given the order to take off. Magruder had no idea what had transpired to make his chances of success now minimally acceptable, but someone must already have done something to the Japanese. This meant that persons unknown had stuck their necks out to ensure that he could attack. The least he could do was make the effort.

Then he was out in the air and flying free over the white-capped ocean below him. His two companions were beside him. He watched and waited while the other Wildcats flew into the sky.

There were no mishaps, and an elated Magruder whooped. Their radios were off. There was to be no chance of someone hearing a conversation in English and being warned.

Magruder's flock of geese formed up on his taillights. The night was partly cloudy, and the lights were a chance that had to be taken. He hoped that anyone seeing them would think they were stars or, better yet, not think at all. When he was satisfied that all was well, he turned and headed north. He would fly at a fuel-conserving height and speed. This would enable him to have as much fuel as possible left to complete his mission and get the hell away.

Get away? He laughed at the notion. If he was lucky, he might have an hour's worth of fuel left after his mission and be able to land on one of the islands. There was no way in hell he was leaving the territory of Hawaii this night.

He tuned his radio to the commercial Honolulu station. As always, it was on, and he began to follow its signal as if it were a homing beacon. He wondered if it was the same station the Japs had followed in last December.

Then he could see the dark bulk of Oahu against the silver of the sea, and the glow of the illuminated Japanese fleet below. He thought there was a bonfire out toward Wheeler Field, but he was too far away to be certain. Besides, who the hell would have a bonfire going on a night like this?

∎

LIEUTENANT COMMANDER TOM MEAGHER was almost distraught. Before the war, he had flown the giant flying boat to and from Hawaii a number of times and knew he could find the place, but this night he had lost his companions.

Doolittle had designated Meagher's plane "Tail-end Charlie" because of Meagher's experience with the plane and the route, and now he had fucked up royally.

Frank Tomanelli, his copilot and a young lieutenant j.g., looked at him nervously.

"We're not lost, are we, sir?"

"Of course not. I know exactly where we are. We're over the fucking Pacific. Can't you see?"

The attempt at humor was lost on Tomanelli, who was afraid of several things—Meagher, the Boeing 314, and the Japanese, in that order. Tomanelli was barely acceptable as a copilot of the giant plane, and this was his first lengthy flight in it. However, the lieutenant had volunteered for the mission, which made him a good guy.

The problem had been a minor mechanical glitch that had worked itself out. Meagher'd had to feather an engine and then restart. It was one of those things he'd never truly understand. Probably a piece of crud in the engine that had simply disappeared. It had been only a few minutes, but it had caused him to fall back, and now he couldn't distinguish the other four planes in the sea of stars and blackness ahead of him. This was getting seriously like the last time he'd flown the 314 from Hawaii. That was many months ago, when he'd ferried a number of high-ranking brass out of Pearl and even dropped off some soldiers on the Big Island. He sometimes wondered what became of them.

Meagher toyed with the idea of speeding up, but that carried the probability of passing the others and arriving over Honolulu too early. The thought of crashing into them was discounted as just too improbable, considering the vastness of the ocean.

"Where are the others, sir?" Tomanelli asked.

"Out there," Meagher said sharply, and Tomanelli shut up.

Meagher checked his fuel. By his calculations, they would arrive over Hawaii with more than half remaining. At least that part was going right. With his bombs gone, his return load would be much lighter.

Tomanelli had regained his courage. "What're we going to do now?"

"Lieutenant, we are going to do what we're supposed to. We're gonna fly to Hah-vah-ee and see if we can find us some Japs to plaster with all this crap the government has assigned to us."

Tomanelli gulped audibly. "Alone?"

Meagher looked at him in mock surprise. "Of course not, boy. We'll have our guardian angels with us."

SERGEANT CHARLEY FINCH HATED moving during the night through what he thought of as jungles. There was nothing to see, and, with his miserable tracking skills, he might turn around and be headed back to Hilo before he realized his mistake.

Something slapped at his leg, and he swore. It was only a branch, not a snake. He'd heard there were no snakes in Hawaii, but who the hell knew for certain? No, he could not return to Hilo, not after what he'd heard from Goto. He had to make peace with Novacek. Thank God the asshole colonel had no idea what he'd been up to.

Suddenly, Finch was flat on his face and spitting out dirt that had been forced into his mouth by the impact. Something heavy landed on his back, forcing his breath out in a whoosh while a sack was pulled over his head and tightened around his neck.

Hands and arms held him on the ground while his pack was taken from him. Finch's panic grew as his wrists were tied behind him. In an instant, he was helpless and blind. Nearby, but muffled, he could hear voices, and they were Japanese.

"And what do we have here?" a voice queried in heavily accented English. "An American guerrilla who's been visiting his friends? This is most fortunate."

Finch thought it was time to change sides again. "I'm a friend," he said through the thick cloth. "I'm on your side." He realized how foolish it sounded as soon as he said it. "Colonel Omori can vouch for me. So can Lieutenant Goto."

"Omori is gone," said the voice. "He was removed because he could not catch you people. I am his replacement in the *kempetei*,

Major Sendai. You are an American guerrilla, and, after I have questioned you thoroughly, I am going to let my men chop you into little pieces with their bayonets. Before you die, I will even make you eat your testicles so you do not go to hell on an empty stomach."

Finch writhed against his bonds as fear overwhelmed him. If only he could see. "No. I helped Omori. I can prove it."

The unseen Jap punched him hard, and he felt his nose crunch. Blood began to flow from his nostrils and into his mouth, sickening him.

"How?" asked the Jap. "And if I think you are lying, I will crush every bone in your body."

Finch spat out the blood. "You read his files on those guys on Lanai, didn't you?"

"Yes."

Finch saw a ray of hope in the darkness of the sack that covered his head. "I did that. I was sent in by Omori and got them to trust me. Then I led Goto to them and got them to surrender."

"What else?"

"Uh, there were some guys in the prison camp who ran a radio. I got them for Omori." He didn't add that he hadn't expected them to be executed. That would have made him sound soft. "Then I got the FBI agents Omori'd been looking for."

"If all that is true," Sendai said softly, "what were you doing here?"

More hope. Sendai was at least listening. "Omori sent me to work with Lieutenant Goto and get the American guerrillas. Look, I just warned him that there was going to be an attack on Hilo, and he's making preparations for it now. Why don't you take me to him and ask him?"

Finch was pushed to a sitting position and the sack pulled from his head. He blinked and found himself staring into the face of the devil incarnate, Lieutenant Sammy Brooks. The marine's face was a mask of mud and grease war paint that helped him blend into the night. The eyes, however, glowed with hatred.

"I don't think that'll be necessary," Brooks said with a Japanese accent. He'd been Sendai.

"Oh, Jesus," Finch moaned. He felt a wetness in his groin as his bladder emptied. "I can explain."

"Don't bother," said Brooks.

A shadow came from behind a tree. It was Alexa Sanderson, and she was similarly disguised. "Tell us about Melissa Wilson," she said. Finch was dimly aware of others with them.

"Who?"

"Melissa Wilson. The blond woman whose picture you're carrying and who you tried to tell me was your girlfriend. She was my neighbor and my best friend. She would never be a friend of yours."

Once again faint hope buoyed Finch. Maybe he had information he could bargain with. "Why should I tell you anything?"

Alexa knelt beside him, and Finch thought he'd never seen such feral hatred and contempt on a person's face. She slapped him across his broken nose, and he saw flashes of light through the sudden pain. "Because you are a traitor and you are going to die right now. It's your choice whether it's quick and painless or whether I let Brooks skin you alive. Maybe he'll even make you eat your balls, just like he said when he pretended to be a Jap."

Finch began to cry. "I told Omori I wanted a white woman, and he got her for me. I don't even think she ever told me her name. The picture was in her purse, and I found it on the floor after she left one time. She was drugged up all the time, and we just fucked. She was fucking Omori and all the Japanese officers. I don't know anything more, I swear it."

Alexa took a deep breath and tried to keep control of her emotions. What had happened to Melissa was what would have happened to her had she remained on Oahu. "What about her child?"

"What child? I don't know." Finch's voice was almost a shriek. Brooks held a wide-bladed knife in his hand. It was a skinning knife. "Please, I don't know anything about the woman or her child. Please don't let him hurt me."

Alexa acknowledged the sound of terrified honesty in his voice. If he'd had anything to tell, he would have. "Quickly," she said to Brooks and strode away. "I don't want it to be slow. That'd put us on the same level as him."

"Sergeant Finch," Brooks said, "Hawkins wanted to be here to do this because you disgraced the army you both serve in, and I'm a marine. But Novacek thought he was too important to come, so this is from him."

Brooks wrapped a length of wire around Finch's neck and paused.

"By the way, the info you gave Goto was all false. We planted it out there to tempt you, and you bit like the dumb fish you are. We're actually doing you a favor. We could've let Goto finish you when his raid on a nonexistent airfield turned into shit."

Finch could scarcely groan.

"You're a lucky bastard, Finch," Brooks said as he pulled on the wire with all his strength. "I really wanted to skin you and shove your balls down your cocksucking throat."

Finch couldn't answer. His neck was broken.

COLONEL OMORI HEARD the pounding through his sleep. When he was finally awake enough to think, the pounding continued, both on the door to his bedroom and in his tortured skull. He cursed himself for drinking as much as he had. He would have a terrible hangover. At least he could stop the noise from outside his quarters.

"Who is it?"

"Captain Mikura," came the reply. "I have an urgent message from Admiral Iwabachi."

Omori slid out of bed and put on his pants. Then he told the captain to come in. Mikura was a marine officer on Iwabachi's staff, and one of the brighter ones. Omori'd considered recruiting him for the *kempetei*.

"Sir," said Mikura, "one of our soldiers just showed up at a police station and said that our base at Wheeler was under attack by other Japanese soldiers."

"Really? And how drunk is this poor man?"

Mikura flushed. He wasn't used to sarcasm. "I was told he appears fairly sober and terrified. He said that several score men who were dressed as Japanese soldiers and who look Japanese have taken over the field, killed just about everyone there, and shot down at least one of our planes. He has no idea how all this was accomplished. He said he was in his barracks and had just finished cleaning his rifle when armed men burst in and started stabbing sleeping soldiers. He says he fired at them and thinks he hit one of them. He later fled out the back of the barracks and into the brush, where he watched as all this occurred."

It was far-fetched, but it contained the chilling germ of truth. However, the thought of Japanese soldiers perpetrating the attack was beyond belief. Something was terribly wrong.

"What have you done?"

"Sir, I immediately contacted the admiral and then attempted to raise Wheeler by phone. I could not get through. After that I contacted one of the carriers and asked them to try to raise the combat air patrol out of Wheeler, and they were unable to do so either."

Omori was now fully awake. "Then Admiral Iwabachi is aware of this?"

"Yes, sir. He directed me to awaken you. As we speak, a motorized column is being organized to drive up to Wheeler to investigate. It will take a while as we don't want to send a handful of men into an ambush if the soldier is telling the truth."

Which he probably is, Omori thought in dismay while he continued dressing. As his head cleared, he again wondered about the men who had attacked Wheeler. They could not have been Japanese. They must have been whites made up to look like Japanese. In the darkness and panic, the survivor must have been confused. Obviously, the raiders had worn what must have looked like Japanese uniforms, and the power of suggestion had resulted in the rest. The soldier would not be punished for his mistake. He had performed his duty under the circumstances.

"You've done well. Have Yamamoto or his staff been informed?"

"Admiral Iwabachi said he will wait until we confirm that something is truly wrong, and that it is a threat to the fleet."

Omori dismissed the captain and prepared to see Iwabachi. He would have to swallow the bitter pill of failure. Of course the soldier's reports were correct. He had thought the Americans incapable of a guerrilla raid on Oahu, and he'd been wrong. He would have to accept both the blame and the shame for his error in judgment.

This meant that Lieutenant Goto had failed as well. Again. He would send that stupid, spoiled child back to Japan no matter who he was related to. Whatever had just occurred at Wheeler must have had its origin with the Americans on the Big Island.

He would also wreak vengeance on the men who'd launched the traitorous attack. What they had done was unspeakably evil, and both they and their families would pay severely. Perhaps he would keep Goto around just long enough to do the interrogations.

But what was their purpose? A raid on a distant field was a minor thing. Why betray themselves for such a matter? It would be an embarrassment, but one that could be hidden from anyone outside of Oahu. In no way would it affect the fleet or change the course of events in Hawaii. The annexation had already taken place, so what was the reason?

Omori stepped outside. It was a couple of hours until dawn. He could see the fleet, and most of the ships were still illuminated. In the distance, he could hear the drone of planes. At least the fleet was well protected.

CHAPTER 23

It was a miracle, Magruder thought. The skies over Oahu were clear, and the ships below in Pearl Harbor were lit up like Christmas trees. No one had yet spotted his flight of planes, and he began to hope that he could make his attack without any interference.

It was not to be. A glowing finger of tracers lifted from a large ship—a cruiser or a battleship—as someone realized that the unexpected planes were hostile.

Magruder's eleven pilots were confused by the abundance of targets. Their orders had been to hit the carriers first and the fuel tanks second, but it almost seemed like there were more Jap carriers than Magruder had planes. This was something Magruder hadn't anticipated, and he ordered his pilots to spread out and attack several targets. He didn't want all eleven dropping their bombs on the same ship.

More antiaircraft batteries opened up, and the sky was alive with shells. Magruder screamed for them to attack, and the eleven planes began their dives.

And then there were ten as a Wildcat to the left exploded. Magruder homed in on a carrier. Guns were firing everywhere, and it dawned on him that they were just firing into the sky and hadn't really seen him in the darkness.

He pulled the release, and his two small bombs fell free and exploded on the flight deck. He banked away, and suddenly the largest ship in the world was in front of him, its antiaircraft guns blazing. Magruder fired his machine guns even though he knew doing so was like shooting spitballs at an elephant. Maybe he would hit some of the people shooting at him.

A fuel tank on a hill erupted like a volcano, and the concussion shook his plane. Or had he been hit? Magruder checked his gauges, and they were okay. He could keep on, but without bombs he was useless. He flew low over a destroyer and strafed it with some of his remaining ammo. As he flew away, he banked slightly and saw a fire on the destroyer's stern. Hot damn, he thought. A carrier and a destroyer! But how much damage had he actually done?

After only a few moments, the raid was over. Magruder flew out over the ocean, where a line of Japanese destroyer pickets was also firing at the moon. He again broke radio silence and called for his flock to gather on him.

Four of them found him—that was all. As they flew away from Pearl Harbor, Magruder tallied the cost. He had lost six of his eleven planes. But, judging from the fires he'd seen, they had caused immense damage to the Japanese fleet. There were still no Zeros in the sky, and this meant he stood a chance of getting to another island in safety.

To SORTIE or not to sortie, thought Admiral Yamamoto, that was the question. He was mimicking some of what he'd learned as an English language student at Harvard before the war while he waited for damage reports in what had been the offices of Admiral Kimmel. When he got them, he would consider his options, and sortieing the fleet was one of them.

The idea of anchoring the entire fleet in Pearl Harbor had been a good one. Had he anchored a good portion outside the defended confines of Pearl, those outside the harbor would have been at the mercy of American submarines, which were getting more and more aggressive. It occurred to him that a pell-mell exodus from Pearl might just lead him to a wolf pack of waiting submarines.

In order to stay out of the clutches of the submarines, those ships outside the harbor would have had to keep in motion, maneuvering to keep the tracking subs confused. That would use up precious fuel, which was to be expended while attacking Alaska and bombarding the American West Coast. The fuel storage tanks were less than half full; thus, he had no real fallback reserve.

But the appearance of American carrier planes had been a complete shock. Cursory examination of the wreckage of one had identified it as an F4F Wildcat.

So where was the carrier? Was there a carrier? Was there more than one carrier? Despite the chaos of the attack, Yamamoto was convinced that only a handful of planes had struck and then fled. Why only a handful? A shame he couldn't ask any of the pilots, but they'd either been killed or had not been found yet.

There was no carrier, he realized with a smile. Even a light carrier had many more fighters than had been thrown at his fleet. Thus, the planes had come from one of the other Hawaiian islands. Yamamoto concluded that they must have been hidden since before the invasion. The logical place was the Big Island of Hawaii, the only area where there was any American guerrilla activity. On such a large island, it wouldn't have been difficult to hide the planes, and he grudgingly admired both the bravery of the American pilots and their ingenuity.

Commander Watanabe approached him. "I have a damage summary, sir."

"Go on."

"No ships were sunk, and light damage was done to only a few. The *Akagi* was hit by one small bomb, but it did not penetrate her armored flight deck."

Yamamoto stifled a chuckle. Admiral Nagumo had been asleep on the *Akagi*. The sudden explosion must have shocked him considerably.

"The fuel fire is under control," Watanabe continued. "Only one tank was hit, and we were fortunate in that the ones beside it were empty. It may have been hit by one of our own antiaircraft shells and not an American bomb."

"Very good," Yamamoto said.

"Some other damage was also caused by wild antiaircraft firing. Falling shells struck several vessels and buildings, causing some spectacular-looking fires, including the fuel tank on the hill, but, again, no serious damage was done. No more than fifty of our men were killed or injured."

So, Yamamoto pondered, the attack had been a pinprick. No ships had been lost, and most of the precious fuel reserve was intact. But the Americans would trumpet it like a great victory. He could not deny that he'd been attacked, and the American propagandists would have a field day, while Japanese government officials would cringe with embarrassment. He would have to apologize for his failures.

"Do you plan to sortie the fleet?" Watanabe asked.

"No, although I may wish to send a carrier out in the morning. Inform Admiral Nagumo of my intent. I'm sure he's awake," he said drily. "I am almost totally convinced that there is not an American carrier nearby, but I do not wish to take chances. I also wish to speak with Admiral Iwabachi. Where the devil were his fighters? He had responsibility for protecting us, and he has failed. I want to know why."

Watanabe nodded. He too wondered how even a handful of American fighters had managed to slip in unnoticed until the last minute. The sharp-eyed lookout who had spotted them in the night would be commended. It occurred to Watanabe that he could hear no planes in the air. Were the skies over the fleet still empty of Japanese fighters? He would contact Admiral Iwabachi immediately.

GIANT ANTENNAE on hills near the California coast picked up even some of the most minor conversations and broadcasts emanating from Hawaii. The commercial radio stations had both reported explosions in the harbor before going off the air, doubtless at Japanese insistence. In the heat of battle, a number of military messages were broadcast in the clear; thus, Admiral Nimitz was able to stay apprised of events virtually as they transpired.

Nimitz turned and looked gloomily at the others. "Some success, but not enough. There is no indication of their fleet moving, nor is there any indication of serious damage to any of the ships or the fuel tanks."

Perhaps it had been a ridiculous idea, but what other choice had they? There were to have been three attacks at almost the same time. Yes, he'd accepted that such coordination over great distances was virtually impossible, but he'd hoped for better than this. Guerrillas had struck successfully at Wheeler, while fighters had attacked the fleet at anchor. The pilots would be trumpeting great victories, but experience had taught them all that these would be gross, albeit wellintended, exaggerations. Also, the pilots appeared to have attacked early. Someone in Nimitz's headquarters had misunderstood the difference in time zones, and Magruder's attack had been two hours too soon.

The third prong was Doolittle's flying boats, and where were they? By now the Japanese would be recovering from their shock and preparing their defenses. A handful of flying boats attacking later would not stampede them out of the harbor, and that was the essence of the plan. Pearl Harbor's Achilles' heel was the narrow channel that was both its entrance and its exit. The *Monkfish* was placed by the entrance for one purpose—to sink a large Japanese vessel in the channel and block it. With the Japanese fleet thus trapped, Spruance was to attack.

The plan was daring, convoluted, cockeyed, and crazy, but, if it had succeeded, a tremendous blow would have been delivered against Japan. Would have been, Nimitz thought sadly.

Jamie Priest stood quietly against a wall and tried not to stare at the admiral. He didn't envy Nimitz at all. The admiral's normally ruddy complexion was pale. People had died this night, and many more would die. High command was a terrible burden, and Jamie was glad he had none of it.

"What should we tell Admiral Spruance?" asked a more senior staff officer.

"Nothing. We'll let him wait until we're absolutely certain that this has failed. There'll be plenty of time to recall the fleet to California."

Off California, the smaller American fleet would have to confront Yamamoto in open battle, where they would be greatly outnumbered and outgunned. Defeat would be almost inevitable. Of course, he could save the fleet by holding it back and letting Yamamoto's ships bombard California's cities unopposed. What a helluva choice, Nimitz thought. He would have to tell Admiral King, who would have the pleasure of telling President Roosevelt. King had been worried about FDR's health, and this would not help.

Nimitz decided. He would save the fleet. They would not interfere with Japanese operations off California. It would likely be destroyed in any confrontation with the Japs and the West Coast bombarded anyhow. The civilians would have to watch out for themselves. In a perverse way, Admiral King might actually be pleased. He could use the attack as another lever to prod Roosevelt into sending more forces into the Pacific and not into Europe. Nimitz wondered if that was such a good idea. While he strongly desired to defeat Japan, he recognized that both Britain and Russia needed to be propped up or the United States would be fighting both Japan and Germany all by herself.

Damn it, he thought.

"Sir," ventured Jamie, "should we recall Colonel Doolittle?"

Damn. Why hadn't he remembered that sooner? Nimitz was about to give the order when he had second thoughts. Doolittle had wanted the opportunity, begged for it, and, besides, the American flying boats were probably making their runs right now. How late could they be?

"No," he said, "let Doolittle use his discretion. However, you may send a signal getting the *Monkfish* out of there." Then he paused. "But first wait until we hear from Doolittle."

Akira Kaga was one of the few remaining "Japanese" soldiers at Wheeler. Their task done, the others had been sent to their homes with orders to keep their mouths shut, bury the rifles, and destroy the Japanese uniforms. They all knew that if one of them was captured and talked, all of them would ultimately die horrible deaths at the hands of the *kempetei*.

"Here they come," said John Takura, one of the "sergeants."

They could see the headlights of a column of vehicles approaching the entrance to the base. Akira smiled. Whoever was in charge was being fairly prudent in bringing a large force but still didn't understand what had happened. A staff car led a number of trucks that easily contained a full company of infantry. With their lights on, they might as well have been driving in a moonlight parade.

"Now," Akira said, and John pushed the handle on a plunger. An instant later, the road where the staff car and the lead trucks had been erupted in a bright flash and the thunder of several explosions. Vehicle parts and bodies flew through the air until the dust and smoke swallowed them.

Akira nodded again, and a second plunger was pushed. A series of larger but distant explosions rocked the air. Immense clouds showed where Wheeler's runways, now cratered, had been. A series of smaller bangs, and the parked planes, already sabotaged, were obliterated. This last part was a luxury. Akira hadn't thought they'd have time to do any more than ruin the engines.

Akira surveyed the ruined column of vehicles. Screams and shouts could be heard, but no one had begun a move toward the base. He must have beheaded their leadership. Akira nodded to his companions and allowed himself a smile. "I think we've done pretty well. Now let's go to our homes and forget we ever knew each other."

■

ADMIRAL YAMAMOTO WAS LIVID. Iwabachi had not kept him properly informed. There were no fighters flying over the fleet, and none were available. Wheeler's runways had been cratered, and all the planes there had been blown up. It was now even more imperative that a carrier and its escorts be situated outside the confines of Pearl Harbor.

For the moment, aerial surveillance was being performed by the handful of floatplanes attached to the cruisers and battleships. As these were lightly armed at best, they could hardly be considered a combat air patrol. But at least they could watch the area outside the islands, and they had confirmed that no enemy warships were in the vicinity.

The floatplanes had limited range, however, and Yamamoto had ordered the larger seaplanes recalled from Hilo and elsewhere for longer patrols.

Colonel Omori and Commander Watanabe walked outside Admiral Yamamoto's Pearl Harbor headquarters for a cigarette. Inside, Iwabachi was getting thoroughly chastised for letting the attacks occur, and neither man wanted to be present at the other's humiliation.

Omori, who was not in as much disfavor with Yamamoto as was Iwabachi, was puzzled. "Forgive my ignorance of naval matters, Watanabe, but why can't you use the planes on the carriers?"

The naval commander flipped his cigarette butt onto the sidewalk and ground it with his heel. His frustration was obvious. "Because carrier planes must be launched into the wind and from a moving vessel. The combined wind and ship speeds are needed so a plane can get enough lift to get airborne. With the carriers anchored in Pearl, no planes can take off. The floatplanes are launched by catapults from the battleships and cruisers, so they don't need the wind as much."

Now Omori understood the need to get a carrier out to sea, although he wondered why catapults couldn't be developed for use on a carrier. Getting a carrier out of the harbor would not happen until dawn at the earliest. Yamamoto did not want to risk a ship going aground in the narrow channel and blocking it, and there was no arguing with his logic. With no enemy fleet, or even additional planes, there was urgency but no need to do something rash. It was getting lighter with each passing moment, and the designated force had steam up and was almost ready to proceed.

An additional problem was the way the ships were anchored. The sunken American warships in the harbor had compounded the crowding, and the carrier *Akagi,* not one of the escorting cruisers, as would normally be the case, would be the first ship out. The *Akagi* was anchored closest to the entrance, and it was impractical even to attempt to maneuver the cruisers past her bulk. Ships could not be shuttled around like cars in a parking lot. Yamamoto was not happy with the situation, but he accepted the reality.

The large carrier's decks were full of planes ready to take off and protect the remainder of the fleet, and many of her officers who had been celebrating in Honolulu had been located and returned. Even so, the *Akagi* would depart significantly shorthanded, and with pilots whose heads must be bursting from hangovers.

Watanabe walked by the water, and Omori followed him. "At least this crisis will be over shortly," Watanabe said. "It is incredible that not only are there no usable planes on Oahu but there are no usable fields. It will take only a day or two to repair the damaged airstrips at Wheeler, but, until then, we are naked. I am confident the fields at Hickam and Ford Island will also be put into service in a matter of hours."

In the dark blue sky that preceded dawn, Omori saw motion. Planes were approaching. For a moment he puzzled over their odd shape, and then he identified them. "Ah, I see the flying boats from Hilo are arriving."

Watanabe was puzzled. "Why? What are they doing here? They are supposed to be patrolling." Then a look of horror crossed his face.

As THE DARK and mountainous islands grew closer and the dawn began to rise, Colonel Jimmy Doolittle saw fingers of smoke arising from several places in the harbor.

"Damn it," he muttered, "they've already been attacked. So much for coordination." He didn't add that headwinds had slowed his flight, making them later than planned.

Captain Haskins, his copilot, chuckled grimly. "What'd you expect?

Just a typical navy fuckup. At least we were able to find Hawaii. Too bad we seem to have lost Meagher's plane."

Doolittle wasn't inclined to argue. As they approached, the two men searched the sky for fighters and found none. At least that part was going right.

But where was Meagher? With him gone and radio silence still unbroken, the five planes were now four. A 20 percent reduction in their small force and nothing had happened yet. He had no idea where Meagher was, but they couldn't wait for him. Any second now and they'd be spotted and Zeros would be all over their butts. No, Meagher would have to take care of himself. Maybe he'd had an engine malfunction and had turned back? It didn't matter. They were going to go straight in, drop their bombs, and fly out the back door.

The four planes went in side by side, low and as fast as they could, which caused the surface to race by. Finally, puffs of smoke in the air said that antiaircraft gunners had spotted them. Uncertain exactly which Japanese ships were where in the harbor, Doolittle's planes broke in pairs, with two on each side of Ford Island. South of Ford Island, along Battleship Row, where so many American battleships had been sunk, six carriers were anchored. Doolittle noted that one of them seemed to be making for the entrance, while smoke came from another.

North of the island were the battleships and heavy cruisers, and a couple of the cruisers were moving as well. Other, smaller ships were parked like trucks in a motor pool in the East and Middle Loch around Pearl City. They didn't concern him. He wanted the carriers and the fuel tanks.

Doolittle broke radio silence and ordered the two planes north of Ford to ignore the giant battlewagons and swing south to attack either the carriers or the fuel.

There was a tremendous flash to Doolittle's right. "What the hell was that?"

"Miller's plane," answered Floyd, one of his side gunners. His voice was shaky and difficult to hear over the chatter of the machine gun. The side and tail gunners were using their guns on anything in sight, and the din had become almost deafening. It might not have been useful, but damn, it felt good.

"It's blowing up like the Fourth of July," Floyd added.

Doolittle swallowed. With so many incendiaries and so much fuel onboard, a direct hit could turn them into a flying Roman candle like Miller's.

The plane rocked from near misses, and debris from exploded shells rattled against the hull. They were so low, only five hundred feet, that the Japanese gunners were having a hard time tracking them. Then they were over a carrier, and the plane shuddered as the bomb load was released. They had done their job.

"Let's go home," Doolittle yelled. Another of his planes was burning and heading for the deck. She would not make it to California or anywhere else. Doolittle watched in horror as antiaircraft guns concentrated on the cripple, blowing hundreds of little pieces off her. Her only chance was a landing in the waters just outside Pearl. He prayed that some of her crew would survive.

At least, Doolittle thought grimly, she was distracting Jap guns from him.

The plane lurched violently. "What the hell?" he blurted out. They'd been hit. Haskins ran back to check on it. Seconds later, he reported over the intercom that the side gunner, Floyd, was dead and two others were wounded.

"Can we fly?" Doolittle asked.

Haskins's voice trembled. "God, Colonel, Floyd's all over the place. It's awful."

"But can we fly?" Doolittle repeated.

Haskins paused. This time his voice was a little firmer. "Yes, if you don't mind a large hole in the fuselage. I would recommend flying slowly and at low altitude."

"Okay," Doolittle said gently, "now you take care of the wounded as best you can."

"Yes, sir."

Doolittle ordered his other surviving plane to head directly back to California. She too had been hit a number of times, and he wondered if she would make it. Then he gained altitude for a look at the damage they'd wrought and was dismayed. There were no large fires, and no explosions. There were several small ones, but they looked like they could be contained. He may have added a little to what damage had been done earlier, but it was hard to tell.

It was bravely done, he thought, but was it worth it? Assuming he made it home, he would get his brigadier's star, but for what? He'd slapped the Japs across the face, but that was all.

"For Christ's sake," said Haskins through the intercom. "Will you look at that?"

Doolittle turned and looked out over the harbor. Meagher's plane had arrived and was beginning its run. But he was high, much too high.

WITHOUT THE OTHERS to guide him, Meagher had flown at a higher altitude than planned. This, he'd hoped, would make it easier to find the islands by widening his scope of vision. That and good navigation had worked. Oahu was dead ahead.

As he put the plane in a gentle dive toward optimum bombing height, he noted the absence of serious smoke and fire, the total lack of Japanese aircraft and antiaircraft fire. For a fleeting second he wondered if his was the first plane, but then he saw a few small fires burning and knew that the others had preceded him. They didn't appear to have accomplished a lot, he thought.

But he wasn't late by much, he exulted. And all the Jap gunners were tracking the two flying boats he could now see off in the distance. Nobody was looking for Tail-end Charlie.

"Pick a target," he yelled at Tomanelli.

His copilot swallowed and tried to control his terror. The entire Jap navy was on review before them. "That carrier on the move," he said. "Its decks are full of planes."

"Good thinking," Meagher responded. Most of the others had only a few planes on their decks, while this one was loaded for bear.

Meagher lined up his plane. He would cross the carrier on a stern-to-bow run and then fly out over the ocean and to safety.

Then the Jap gunners saw them and opened fire. The plane shuddered from minor hits and near misses as the Japanese frantically tried to get them in their sights.

Meagher was just about to order bombs away when a four-inch shell from a destroyer ripped through the front of the pilot's cabin and blew him to bloody pieces before it exited the top of the plane.

Tomanelli was knocked unconscious by the blast and the impact of

Meagher's body parts striking him. The copilot's body slumped forward on the controls, and the plane dropped more sharply as it rapidly approached the carrier.

At first, it looked like the crippled flying boat would pass over the *Akagi,* but then it dropped more quickly and fell onto the flight deck, about a hundred feet from the stern. To the astonished Japanese, it looked like the flying boat had attempted a landing on the carrier.

Still moving forward, the massive Boeing plowed through the parked planes, knocking several of them overboard like they were toys. The flying boat was slowed by the wreckage and finally stopped as its massive wing collided with the carrier's superstructure. For a second, it sat there, a dead plane on the flight deck of a Japanese carrier. Then the fuel exploded, and, an instant later, that set off the bombs still in its hull. The crash landing on the *Akagi* had ruptured fuel tanks on the Japanese planes, and they too exploded almost immediately. In seconds, the carrier's entire flight deck and superstructure were engulfed in a cloud of flames that was punctuated by explosions as Japanese bombs and shells were lit off.

The *Akagi* was now a moving torch, with torrents of flame dripping down her sides and crewmen hurling themselves off her and into the safety of the harbor. Without apparent guidance, she continued inexorably on in the last direction that had been ordered. There was no one alive on her decks or on the bridge to order a change of course as she headed toward the side of the channel.

THE OFFICERS AND MEN in the *Monkfish* had spent a restless night. The explosions in the harbor resonated through the water and caused the sub to vibrate. Despite the obvious danger, Lieutenant Commander Fargo had recognized the necessity to keep the air changed and the electric engines charged. Thus, they had spent a good deal of the night with the conning tower barely visible.

The sub's crew were gaunt, unshaven, and filthy, and those not actually on duty were condemned to spend their time in their bunks as a means of conserving energy and oxygen.

While on the surface, they caught the tail end of the fireworks display that had marked Magruder's attack on the fleet. By the time

Doolittle's planes had arrived, the sub was snugly back under the water. Fargo was confident that Japanese radar was crummy and their sonar even worse, but there was nothing wrong with their eyeballs.

Now, as gunfire reverberated for the second time, the men were at their battle stations, where they tried to pretend they weren't scared to death.

"This is it," Fargo proclaimed unnecessarily. Even the village idiot knew that tonight was the reason they'd waited so long in the Pearl Harbor channel.

His chief of boats announced that he thought he could hear screws approaching through the clutter. Fargo accepted the assessment. It was said that the chief could hear a mouse pissing ten miles away. If Flannery said a ship was coming, it was coming.

Fargo peered through the binoculars at where the channel turned slightly. At first there was nothing, and then the bulk of a large ship came into view.

"Carrier," he said, and then incredulously, "and she's burning. Oh my God."

The ship that filled his view was aflame from bow to stern, and he saw people jumping off the crippled vessel from wherever they could. For a moment Fargo wondered, if this ship was already badly damaged, should he wait for another one?

Then he realized that the carrier was out of control. With a lurch, the ship ground into the side of the channel and began to swing away as her screws continued to churn up the water. In a few seconds, she would be broadside to him, and Fargo fully understood what he had to do.

"Fire one," he ordered, and the sub vibrated as the torpedo sped on its way. It was virtually point-blank range. The enemy ship was so close, there had been only the need to point the sub and shoot. Nor had there been any thought of firing under the ship and using her magnetic field to detonate the torpedoes. These would be impact hits. "Fire two. Fire three. Fire four."

The men of the *Monkfish* held their breath and waited for Fargo's report. Seconds passed, and there was nothing. The first torpedo had been a dud.

"Damn it," snarled Fargo. As he said it, the second torpedo struck the side of the carrier and exploded, sending a column of water high above the burning flight deck, but not as high as the flames that billowed from it.

Torpedoes three and four exploded seconds later, and the crew exulted. While the forward tubes were being reloaded, Fargo carefully turned the ship around so that the stern tubes faced the stricken carrier. These were fired, and both exploded against the hull of the dying carrier.

It was time to go. If the carrier survived five hits and the fire, she deserved to live. He ordered the *Monkfish* out into the open sea. Still at periscope depth, he searched for Japanese destroyers and saw a pair of them several miles to his port side. Incredibly, they were cruising away from him! He had no idea what had distracted them from the channel, but he didn't care.

Swiveling the periscope back to the channel, Fargo saw a sight that stunned him. The carrier, torn apart by the five hits and other explosions, had taken on a definite and fatal list to port. Burning debris had begun to fall off the flight deck and into the sea as the ship slowly capsized.

"We got us a carrier," he announced to his cheering crew. "And, if we're damned lucky and the creek don't rise, we got us a chance of getting the hell out of here."

And maybe, he thought, just maybe, they had blocked the fucking channel.

∎

CHAPTER 24

Jake Novacek carefully and quietly aimed his Springfield. The Japanese scout was barely visible in the tree about two hundred yards away. Jake had a dilemma. To fire and shoot the scout would alert the other Japanese soldiers in the area, but it was highly likely that the soldier would see Hawkins and his companions as they moved to a new firing position. Damned if I do and damned if I don't, Jake thought.

The Japanese response to the American attack on Pearl Harbor had been so immediate and so savage that the Americans had been thrown off balance. The Japanese at Hilo had become a whirlwind of brutal activity.

Jake estimated that three of the four companies of marine infantry stationed at Hilo had exploded out toward where they thought the Americans were hiding. He cursed himself for not anticipating the savagery of their response; as a result of his failure, his small force was reeling and disintegrating.

The Japanese had extracted information regarding the Americans from a civilian population that surrendered the knowledge as an alternative to seeing their loved ones raped, burned, mutilated, and chopped to living pieces before their eyes by Lieutenant Goto. In very short order, trucks full of Japanese soldiers had closed in on Jake's sanctuary. The Japanese weren't very good soldiers, which made it fairly easy for Lieutenant Brooks and his marines to ambush them and inflict a disproportionate number of casualties.

But the marines were only a handful, and the Japanese learned quickly. Brooks was dead and the other marines either dead or scattered after their last known position had been overrun. Brooks had bought them a little time, however. It had enabled Jake to dismantle the facilities and move Gustafson and some of the others by fishing boat to Maui, where Ernie Magruder and two of his companions had managed to land. A fourth plane was rumored to have landed on Molokai.

Alexa had gone with Gustafson, which took a big load off of Jake's mind. Their parting embrace had been tearful, with her not wanting to leave, but Jake had been adamant. On Maui, she might just survive, while he would not have been able to think had she remained on Hawaii. On Hawaii, she and the others would have been hunted down like dogs. Survival, he reminded her, was their primary goal. If everyone couldn't make it, that was too bad. Once again, she should do everything she had to in order to live.

In the long term, Jake thought that time was on his and Alexa's side. Only thing, the Japanese soldiers were just a few hundred yards away. If the radio reports were to be believed, the Japanese at Pearl Harbor had been clobbered and were continuing to be pounded. This meant that liberation was imminent, possibly in only a few weeks.

But, he thought grimly, first I have to live through this day.

The Hawaiians and others in his contingent had been dispersed, to return to their families and try to blend into the surroundings. Again, he felt they would make it long enough for help to come. So that left him and the Japanese scout in his sights. He didn't think the Jap saw him, but Hawkins and the others were impossible for the Jap to miss. Either way, he thought, the Jap was going to send for his little yellow brothers to help him.

"Fuck it," Jake snarled and pulled the trigger. A second later, the scout tumbled from the tree.

THERE WAS PANDEMONIUM in Admiral Nimitz's San Diego command center for the Pacific Ocean Area. Just when they had written off the entire operation as a noble failure, Doolittle had radioed the word that a carrier had been sunk in the channel.

This, coupled with overheard Japanese messages, confirmed that a degree of victory had just been snatched from disaster. Doolittle had mentioned something about the American pilot intentionally crashing his plane on the carrier, which he identified as the *Akagi*. If that were true, it was agreed that the still unnamed pilot was due one helluva medal. Sadly, it looked like it would be posthumous.

Only one question now remained—what to do about Spruance?

While there was a strong consensus that he should be unleashed on the trapped Japanese, a vocal minority led by Vice Admiral Robert Ghormley felt there should be more assurances that the channel was actually blocked.

"It's too big a risk," Ghormley said. "It may look blocked, but we won't know until the Japs try to get out. Give it a day, maybe two, and let's verify it."

The vice admiral's voice carried weight. He had been responsible for planning the operation and knew more about its details than anyone else. However, Ghormley had a reputation for caution. Hardly a sin, Nimitz thought, but was it time to be reckless or time to go for the jugular?

Nimitz decided. "Send Spruance. The longer we wait and it is blocked, the more time the Japs'll have to solve their problem."

Jamie Priest was the runner who relayed the information to the radio center. Moments later, he was back in Nimitz's conference room, exhilarated and fascinated by what was happening.

"Spruance acknowledged?" Nimitz asked.

"Yes, sir. No doubt about it."

Nimitz nodded, then looked at Jamie with a curious smile. "Tell me, did the radio people note anything unusual with the transmission of his confirmation?"

Jamie was puzzled. "Sir?"

"Commander, did the signal come from where it was expected, or elsewhere?"

It was impossible to tell distance, but a good operator could get a feel for the direction of a signal. "Admiral, the operator said it came from a good deal farther north than he expected it to."

Nimitz shook his head, then he grinned. "I'll be damned. Ray Spruance left early," he said, thinking of his admonition to Spruance to be careful. Then he laughed. "He'll be there before the Japs can do a thing." And, Nimitz thought, here's to everyone who thought Spruance was too scholarly and indecisive for the command thrust upon him because of Halsey's illness.

■

MORE THAN A DOZEN OFFICERS crowded into the office that over-looked Pearl Harbor. Admiral Yamamoto was the only one seated, while the others clustered around him. He saw no point in returning to the flagship *Yamato*. Neither it nor the remainder of the Japanese fleet was going anywhere for a while.

Yamamoto's mouth was a grim slash, and he looked ashen. What had been an aggravating pinprick operation by the Americans had be-come a disaster. No matter how he tried to rationalize what had hap-pened, he could not escape the fact that Japan had suffered its first significant naval loss in almost a century. The question of who had won or lost the battle in the Coral Sea had just become moot. Japan had definitely lost the second battle of Pearl Harbor with the sinking of the *Akagi*.

How the Americans had come up with such a resourceful and dar-ing plan was almost irrelevant. Japan had lost a battle and, even more humiliating, had done so in front of many thousands of civilians. It would be Yamamoto's responsibility to apologize to the emperor for his failure. He would do it and offer to retire.

But first he had to get his fleet out of its unwelcome anchorage. He noticed Commander Fuchida easing his way into the room. Fuchida was on crutches and had released himself from the hospital. He had broken his leg leaping from the burning *Akagi* and was lucky to be alive. He'd been pulled out of the oil-covered and flaming water only seconds before he would have been burned alive. Yamamoto ordered a second chair brought in, and Fuchida accepted it gratefully.

Admiral Nagumo would not be there. He had been on the bridge of the *Akagi* and was presumed incinerated. So too were the ma-jority of the carrier's pilots and crew. Fuchida had been lucky. Only a couple of hundred had survived the catastrophe, and many of those were severely burned. Maybe Nagumo had been lucky too, Yama-moto thought. He would not have to confront the results of the defeat.

"Is there good news?" the admiral asked.

"Only a little," Commander Watanabe responded. "With the ex-ception of the *Akagi* and some slight bomb damage to the *Ryujo,* we are in good shape. Our floatplanes and seaplanes continue their patrolling, and there is no sign of any American ships or planes—"

"However," Yamamoto interrupted, "we have only a few of those virtually unarmed planes, and most of them have very limited range."

"True," Watanabe said.

"Then it is imperative that we get out of this harbor. What is the situation with the *Akagi*?"

Watanabe grimaced, and there was a distinct shuffling in the room. The *Akagi* lay on its side in the channel. A sizable portion of it remained above the water, and that part still burned fiercely. Oil and gasoline continued to spill out and burn on the water.

"The engineers say it will be sometime tomorrow before the fires are out. After that, the hulk must cool down sufficiently for the damage to be assessed. It is now confirmed that the *Akagi* was torpedoed as well as bombed. Several survivors, including Commander Fuchida," he said and gestured to the commander, "have reported seeing torpedo tracks and explosions against her port hull."

"And where is the sub?" Yamamoto asked.

"Gone. She escaped when our picket destroyers all went after the wreckage of the American flying boat that landed near the coast."

Fools, Yamamoto thought, but the damage had been done. "What about other subs? Where there was one, there might be many."

"The destroyers are back on station, Admiral. Their captains are properly chastened and are vigilant. No other submarines have been sighted."

"Very well. Back to the *Akagi*. Can any ships leave, and when can she be moved?"

"With her still burning, it's hard to tell. There may be room for destroyers to squeeze by, but not anything larger. As to moving her, the engineers are not optimistic. Traditionally, the holes in her hull would be plugged and then she would be righted as the water was pumped out. But this is a process that could take months under normal conditions for a ship her size."

"No!" Yamamoto said harshly. "If we are here for more than a few days, the Americans will gather like wolves and savage us. If they figure out that we cannot move or launch planes, even their ships in the Atlantic will be steaming here. Tow her out."

Watanabe was confused. "Sir, we don't have any tugs strong

enough to do that. The *Akagi* is not just aground. Her hull is full of water, and towing her in that condition will require a massive effort."

Yamamoto glared at him and then at the others. "But we do have some of the most powerful warships in the world. Use the battleships as tugs. Attach lines to the *Akagi* and haul her off. Use every ship in the fleet if you have to. If the fires are out tomorrow, I want the lines attached as soon as possible. We must get our carriers out of here!"

Yamamoto took a deep breath and calmed himself. Then he turned to Fuchida. "I must presume that the effort will take time. While that is being done, I want planes to be taken off at least one of our carriers and be able to use the field on Ford Island. Can it be done?"

Fuchida thought quickly. The field on Ford was in bad shape, but that would be relatively easy to fix with plows and shovels. The planes were a different matter. They could not be flown off a carrier. They would have to be unloaded by crane and would quite likely have to have their wings removed. He thought there were cranes available on the shore, but he wasn't certain. But, even if there were, had they been damaged in the earlier fighting?

Regardless, once the planes were on the ground, the wings would be reattached and the planes could either taxi or be pulled by truck to the field, from where they could begin to patrol and fight. But not until then. What an incredible mess.

"Can it be done?" Yamamoto repeated.

"Yes," Fuchida replied cautiously.

The admiral understood his hesitation. He trusted Fuchida's judgment. "How long will it take?"

The commander shook his head. The pain in his leg was increasing. "A week."

Yamamoto nodded. In a week, either the *Akagi* would have been cleared from the channel or he would have planes flying from Ford Island. In a week he would be able to defend himself. In the meantime, the Japanese fleet was almost defenseless.

Colonel Omori had eased in and caught the end of the conversation. "Admiral," he said, "I understand that some of the American flyers have been picked up. I wish to interrogate them in order to find out just how the Americans knew that we were going to be here in sufficient time to plan the attacks."

Yamamoto looked at him with scarcely concealed disdain. Four badly wounded survivors from the crashed flying boat had been picked up and were being held only a few feet away. They were all enlisted men.

"Tell me, Colonel," he said sarcastically, "do you really think that Roosevelt or Nimitz entrusted such important information to men of such low rank?"

Omori bowed deeply to hide his embarrassment. "Of course not, sir."

"Leave the prisoners where they are. Do not waste your time on them." Yamamoto continued, "Concentrate on finding those who attacked Wheeler. You have confirmed that they were indeed Japanese, haven't you?"

A second survivor had been located. He had been left for dead by the attackers and had revived sufficiently to confirm what the first soldier had said. The men who had murdered his corporal and nearly killed him had indeed been of Japanese descent. Since all those of Japanese descent in Hawaii had always been considered Japanese citizens by Tokyo, even before the annexation, the act was one of treason and not of war.

"It is confirmed," Omori said and heard shocked hissing in the room.

"Then you will find those who have betrayed Japan. I will defend the fleet. You search for the traitors. I doubt you will have far to look. Unless, of course, they have joined their brethren so skillfully hiding from you on the other island."

Flushed with shame, Omori left the room. He understood full well that the attack on Wheeler had been the cause of the problem and remained the main problem. Because of the attack on Wheeler, there had been no planes to defend against even a small American force. Because of the attack on Wheeler, the fleet was bottled up in Pearl Harbor. And it was his fault that the attack had taken place. Omori's *kempetei* were responsible for the security of the islands, and through his failures the attack on Wheeler had taken place.

Omori lit a cigarette and walked to where his car and driver waited. Someone in the Japanese community knew about this and would pay dearly, as would the Americans on Hawaii. He would talk to Toyoza Kaga and see if he had heard anything about disaffected young Japanese who would strike against their homeland.

■

COMMANDER BOSHIRO PEERED through the periscope of the *I-74* and cursed silently. A large force of warships, American by their silhouettes, was in his view. He pivoted and saw two carriers and at least one battleship. Other, smaller vessels ringed the larger ships, and they were on a direct course for Hawaii. It was also possible, even likely, that additional ships were out of his limited view.

Boshiro had a dilemma. He was submerged in relative safety, and planned on remaining that way until dark. Then he could surface and cruise faster, possibly close in on some of the enemy ships. Then he would attack. That would be prudent. Surfacing in daylight would make the *I-74* as visible to the Americans as they were to him.

But he was fairly certain that Admiral Yamamoto in Pearl Harbor was unaware of the force creeping up on him. Thus, he had to warn the admiral immediately, and that meant surfacing so that a radio message could be sent off.

Surfacing would be tantamount to suicide. Additional American ships were coming into view, and they confirmed his suspicions about the size of the American forces.

They also made his decision simple. Regardless of the cost, Yamamoto had to be warned. "Surface," he ordered.

ADMIRAL RAYMOND SPRUANCE PACED the bridge of his flagship, the carrier *Enterprise*. A little while earlier, the sound of explosions had resonated in the distance.

"Well?"

Captain Mitscher had taken it on himself to find out. "Damndest thing, but a Jap sub came up just about right under a couple of our planes. After the pilots got over their shock, they began strafing and bombing. Those were the explosions we heard."

Spruance nodded. It was bound to happen sooner or later. It was too much to hope they would never be seen. "Did they get the sub?"

"Confirmed. Both pilots reported seeing her break in half and sink. A destroyer is just about there and has spotted large pieces of wreckage and a couple of bodies. She's not on the bottom and pretending to be dead; that sub is gone."

"There was only one reason for her to surface like that," Spruance said. "She'd seen us and was going to signal her friends. Did she get off a message?"

Mitscher shrugged. "We don't know. It all happened so fast, no one was listening."

"Then we must assume she did," Spruance said thoughtfully, "and react accordingly."

The admiral continued pacing. "We must assume that she gave Yamamoto a full description of the fleet, its direction and speed. Yamamoto will be able to do the calculations and recognize that we can attack just after first light. He will have all his defenses prepared for us."

He stopped and stared up at the sky. "Then we must weigh that fact against our instructions, which were explicit: We were not to take any undue risks with the fleet."

Mitscher was aghast at the implication. "Jesus, you're not thinking of pulling back, are you? Not after we've come this far!"

Spruance smiled benignly. "Hell no. Of course we're not pulling back. We'll just speed up and attack a little sooner."

THE AIRCRAFT CARRIER *HIRYU* had been moved as close to Ford Island as was possible, but she was still about a hundred yards off. The darkness and the presence of wrecked American ships made moving closer in to shore dangerous, and the availability of barges made it unnecessary.

A large crane had been set up on the *Hiryu*'s flight deck. It had been dismantled from a shore facility and moved to the carrier, where it had been reassembled and buttressed to stand the weight of an airplane. Despite its looking jury-rigged, the engineers were confident it would work.

While this work was going on, several Zeros had been disassembled and were ready to lift into the barge. There would be one plane per barge, and it would take almost an hour to raise and lower the plane onto the vessel. From there, it was an extremely short trip to the island, where another winch would remove the plane and set it on dry land. Trucks would then tow it to the airfield, which was already almost ready for planes to take off and land as literally hundreds of men had been filling the cratered runways all day and night.

Commander Fuchida estimated that his disassembly-assembly line would begin within minutes, and, once the first plane was at Ford Island, at midday, Zeros would be ready for combat at the rate of one per hour. He had moved to the island, where he would watch the carrier and oversee the other part of the operation. He did not consider basing himself on the carrier. His leg would not permit him to move about. As it was, he was in a wheelchair.

He was pleased, as was Commander Watanabe, who stood beside him, visibly impressed. If everything went according to their improvised schedule, the *Hiryu*'s sixty-plus planes would all be patrolling Oahu's skies in a little more than two days, and not the originally estimated one week. A smaller number of planes would be ready by nightfall.

Day and *night* were somewhat irrelevant terms. Floodlights bathed the *Hiryu* in an unnatural glow and permitted work to be done on her. Other ships were similarly lit as repair crews worked through the night, and, in the channel, the *Akagi* still burned, although not as brightly.

The emphasis on speed had come as the result of a garbled and incomplete message received from a Japanese submarine. Watanabe had relayed the information to Fuchida. "The sub had just begun to identify herself when she went off the air. We have no idea what her message was going to be, except that there was sufficient reason for her to surface and try to send. We presume she was sighted and sunk," he said.

Fuchida had nodded grimly. If the sub had been sunk, it meant the Americans were nearby. But in what strength? Yamamoto had been adamant that the main body of the American navy was in Icelandic waters. Of course they could be racing toward Hawaii, but that trip would take weeks.

Both men had concluded that the likeliest threat came from American submarines. The unfortunate Japanese submarine must have spotted a large American wolf pack heading this way and had died sending the message.

Yamamoto had responded by urging haste with Fuchida's project.

It was deemed far more likely to succeed in the short run than towing the *Akagi* from the channel. The *Hiryu*'s planes must be ready to attack the American subs and protect the fleet when it finally did emerge from Pearl Harbor.

Both men, however, were still extremely disturbed by the lack of air cover. Since it was night and the Japanese floatplanes lacked radar, most had been recalled so the planes could get some maintenance and the pilots get a little rest. Many of the remainder of the men of the fleet were also resting and preparing for the day. Yamamoto had determined that there was no point in all of them working themselves to exhaustion. Men were not machines. They were flesh and blood that had to eat and rest.

"Please tell me, Commander, precisely how many planes are in the air at this moment?"

Watanabe grimaced. "Two, and neither of them fighters."

"Tomorrow night I'll give you a dozen," Fuchida promised.

Watanabe laughed. "It is a gift I'll accept gladly. Then you can get back to the hospital, so your leg can heal."

Fuchida wished Watanabe hadn't reminded him about his wound. With all his activities, he had almost forgotten it. He had to stay seated most of the time with his leg propped up, but he could still command.

A distant growl caught their attention. It was hard to identify over the sounds of voices and clattering machinery emanating from the *Hiryu*.

"Planes," Fuchida said, puzzled.

"Can't be," said Watanabe. Then he looked ill. "No, can't be."

Out of the darkness they dropped. The dive-bombers from the American carriers had easily eluded the Japanese search planes and, like moths attracted to light, had homed in on the lights illuminating the Japanese ships.

An American plane completed its dive and roared over Fuchida's head. Seconds later, the bomb exploded on the *Hiryu*'s flight deck. The commander watched in dismay and horror as the crane flew into the air and tumbled into the barge beside the ship.

More bombs struck the *Hiryu*, and, like her sister the *Akagi,* she was soon engulfed in flames.

Fuchida steeled himself to count the planes as they swirled by and back into the dark. He stopped at thirty. This was no raid by older-model land-based planes left over from the initial battles for Hawaii. This was a carrier attack, and the attackers were newer-model Grummans.

More bombs ripped the *Hiryu,* and other ships began to take hits. Japanese antiaircraft guns filled the sky with glowing tracers, but they seemed to do little harm. As before, they couldn't shoot what they couldn't see until the last minute.

As the attack thundered on, the Japanese gunnery did get better, and American planes started to fall in flames from the lightening sky. Several Americans attacked the *Yamato,* which, despite being protected by nearly 150 antiaircraft guns, had several bombs explode against her superstructure.

And then it was over. Fuchida stood on his crutches and wept. The *Hiryu* was a burning ruin, and so were his hopes of protecting the fleet with her planes. The *Kaga* and *Soryu* were also burning, although not as badly as the *Hiryu.*

Fuchida was about to say something to Watanabe when a tremendous explosion ripped through the *Hiryu,* sending a shock wave over the area and ripping all around her with metal debris.

Fuchida found himself lying on the ground several feet from where he had been sitting. Much of his uniform had been blown off, and now his other leg hurt like the devil. He saw a piece of bone sticking through the skin of his thigh.

Watanabe lay beside him, but Watanabe was dead. A piece of debris had decapitated him, and his head was nowhere to be seen.

Fuchida attempted to focus his dimming vision on the remains of the *Hiryu.* She had broken in half, and both ends were sinking toward the middle.

He tried to rise and felt hands pushing him back. "Be still, sir. Let us take care of you."

The commander was helpless. Both his legs were broken, and he was having trouble both seeing and hearing. He gave in to the darkness that was engulfing him. "Poor Japan," he murmured. "What have we done?"

ACROSS THE HARBOR and through the flames and clouds of smoke, Admiral Yamamoto watched the destruction of his dreams and the future of his nation. For a brief moment, he contemplated going off to some solitary place where he could commit suicide in accordance with the code of *bushido*. But the thought passed as he realized that intentional death was the coward's way out. No, he had an obligation to his men and his nation to retrieve as much as he could from the debacle swirling about him.

Thus focused, he concentrated on the options yet available to him. First, it was appallingly obvious that Fuchida's task of lifting planes from carriers and onto the land was doomed. The *Hiryu* was sinking, and at least two other carriers were damaged. While they might still be able to off-load a handful of planes, it would take too much time, which meant that this was no longer the solution. The fleet had to move out of the harbor through the channel, and that meant concentrating on towing out the hulk of the *Akagi*.

And he no longer had days in which to solve the problem. Instead, he had hours.

Judging from the sheer number of American planes in the most recent attack, there were at least two carriers, possibly more, in the vicinity of Oahu. Identification of the carriers they were from might come from interrogating shot-down pilots if any had survived, but it was almost irrelevant. Such knowledge would not come from Japanese floatplanes and flying boats. They were patrolling, but they were vulnerable and would be shot down by the next wave of attackers.

Yamamoto still had two carriers and the rest of the surface fleet intact. Several of those ships had sustained hits, but nothing severe. In particular, the *Yamato* had been struck by a pair of bombs and seemed to have brushed off the damage. If the remaining portion of the fleet could sortie out and do battle with the Americans, at least some of the shame could be washed away.

The attempt to remove the *Akagi* must be accelerated, despite the risks. The Americans would be returning to their floating bases to refuel and rearm. They would be back in the harbor in a matter of hours. Japanese gunners would put up a stout defense, but it was a given that bombers would get through to the ships if there were no planes to impede them. Thus, it was also true that each ship damaged or sunk reduced the number of Japanese guns, which made it easier for the attackers to get through the next time. It was, he mused, a spiral into hell. It had to be broken before the rest of the Japanese fleet was pounded to pieces.

But how had the American carriers appeared off Oahu at this precise time? Was German intelligence so slipshod as to mistake the presence of the Americans off Iceland? Or had the Germans betrayed their Asian allies to their white counterparts? Yamamoto decided he would write down his thoughts and have the message sent to Tokyo.

And how had the Americans known so far in advance as to be able to place their ships and planes in such an advantageous position? There were only three options: Treason, espionage, and the breaking of the Japanese codes. Of the three, he considered espionage the most likely. There were far too many people in Hawaii who had known in advance of his arrival. The information could have been stolen from them and sent to the United States via those damned guerrillas on Hawaii. That a Japanese citizen could have betrayed his country in favor of the Americans was unthinkable. So too was the idea that the Japanese codes had been broken.

At least the Americans on the Big Island would be eliminated. Colonel Omori had given his assurances in that regard.

■

CHAPTER 25

*L*ieutenant Goto was exhausted. It had been a long time since he'd been out in the field, and he was definitely out of shape. But at last they were driving the Americans before them like the animals they were.

Goto heard a noise and turned around. Captain Kashii had hacked the head off an American corpse. Kashii took the head and put it on the hood of his truck.

"Interesting hood ornament, isn't it?" the captain asked with a cackle. "Not as exquisite as a Rolls-Royce's, but it satisfies me."

"Indeed," said Goto. Kashii's action confirmed Goto's opinion that the disaster at Pearl Harbor had deranged the captain. Instead of being aggressive, Kashii's actions had been wild and irrational. For instance, why did he insist on the troops returning to the trucks even for small advances? They had been ambushed while in such vulnerable columns, although the attacks seemed to have stopped since the last couple of marines had been killed.

The American marine Kashii had beheaded had been captured barely alive but had died while Goto was trying to extract information from him. From his papers, they learned that he'd been an officer. A shame he hadn't told them anything.

They'd been able to get information from the local population fairly easily. The short trail from Hilo was littered with scores of dead and dying Hawaiians, whose agonies had motivated others to talk freely. Several villages, swollen with people who'd fled Hilo, were nearby, and the occupants had been easy to terrorize. As a result, they were closing in on the handful of Americans who remained on the loose. There weren't more than a dozen left, and there were still more than three hundred Japanese chasing them. The end was inevitable. He only hoped that this Novacek would be captured alive, along with the woman who had so angered Colonel Omori.

Of course, some of the guerrillas would have scattered, but they would be found in short order. When it was over, Goto and Kashii could return to Hilo, although Goto wondered just what they'd be returning to. If the bad news coming from Pearl was even remotely correct, Japan was in danger of losing the Hawaiian Islands.

Goto thought this was almost beyond credibility. Japan did not go to war to be defeated. What had happened? It had to be betrayal, and it had to have come from the Americans they were chasing. If Japan was forced to quit Hawaii for a short while, it would not be the fault of the military.

Gunfire in the distance grabbed Goto's attention. "We've caught them," Kashii shrieked and waved his bloody sword in a circle around his head. "Back to the trucks, we'll circle behind them."

Goto wondered at the logic of the move. The Americans were only a mile or two away. They should be pressed by men on the ground, not by soldiers in trucks driving over harsh terrain that caused the column to stretch out at times and pile up at others. On the land they were traversing, men in trucks moved more slowly than men on foot. Using trucks for the pursuit would give the small American force a chance to squeeze away and delay the inevitable.

But then Goto saw the irrational glint in Kashii's eyes. No, the lieutenant decided, he would not attempt to discuss tactical or logistical matters with a lunatic waving a sword.

IN THE TWO DAYS since the first American attacks, wave upon wave of fighters and dive-bombers had hurled themselves at the bottled-up Japanese fleet. American bombs and bullets found a wealth of targets trapped in the harbor and unable to maneuver. And they steadily destroyed both ships and the antiaircraft defenses that remained. Thus, with each succeeding attack, the Japanese navy had less with which to defend itself.

In a frenzy, Admiral Yamamoto focused everything on moving the hulk of the *Akagi*. In only a short while, there would be nothing left of his fleet. He had waited too long, and now all six of his carriers were lying in the mud of Pearl Harbor. Fortunately, he thought with some irony, two had sunk upright in shallow water, which deceived the Americans into thinking they were still afloat. As a result, he still had two of his four battleships, the *Yamato* and the *Kongo,* while the Americans concentrated on resinking the dead carriers.

The old battleship *Haruna* had been sunk, and the *Yamato*'s sister ship, the *Musashi,* had suffered a truly ignominious fate. In an effort to pull the *Akagi* out of the channel, she had been used as a tug, and the exertions, combined with an inexperienced crew, had resulted in a blown engine plant. If and when the remainder of the Japanese fleet managed to sortie, the *Musashi* would be scuttled. In the meantime, she would function as a floating battery.

Along with the two battleships, there remained four heavy cruisers, two light cruisers, and a dozen destroyers. All of the ships were damaged but seaworthy and would put up a fight. All he had to do was get them out of Pearl Harbor before they too were destroyed.

The fighting had not been totally one-sided. There were far fewer American planes in the air; Japanese gunners had exacted a heavy price before being destroyed.

The eighteen-inch guns of the *Yamato* and the immobile *Musashi* had fired over land and into the approaching American fleet. They had all gained a measure of satisfaction when the *Musashi* sank a Brooklyn-class light cruiser that had ventured too close. However, it did not stop the American battleships and heavy cruisers from steaming close in at night and lofting shells into the harbor as their damned planes dropped flares and called the fall of shot.

The drawn-out battle reminded Yamamoto of a prizefight where both boxers were exhausted but only one had the strength to hurl punches and the other had no means of resistance. Both had been bloodied, but only one would soon be standing.

He had been informed that there would be no attempt at relief. The decoy fleet off Australia was both too small and too far away. The Japanese in Pearl Harbor had to escape or die.

There was a knock on his office door. He was still ashore as he saw no point in being aboard his flagship, which was under frequent attack.

"Come in."

Commander Shigura Fujii, his chief of intelligence, entered hesitantly. It should have been his friend Watanabe, Yamamoto thought, but Watanabe's ashes were in a box awaiting shipment to Japan. That is, he thought wryly, if we are able to get out of our prison. Even if they did, the ashes of the dead trailed behind the living as a priority for escape.

"What is it?" the admiral asked.

"Some good news," Fujii said. "At last the channel's clear."

Yamamoto took a deep breath. Why hadn't this happened earlier? The towing had managed to move the *Akagi* a little ways, and the final clearing effort had used explosives. A few hours before, engineers had blown her to pieces. They had waited only for confirmation that some giant piece of the carrier hadn't shifted and blocked a different part of the channel. Several engineers had died trying to jam the carrier with explosives, because hot spots still existed and there had been several small, premature detonations.

"We will sortie immediately," Yamamoto said grimly. "What are the Americans doing?"

"Waiting for us," Fujii answered. "Their planes have been watching, and their ships are poised to pounce on us as we emerge from the channel. The American carriers are out of sight, but we can see four battleships and at least as many heavy cruisers. There are numerous light cruisers and destroyers as well. They will be waiting to cross our T."

Of course, Yamamoto thought. Crossing the T was the classic naval maneuver that every naval commander attempted to perform. In it, all of one fleet's guns could be brought to bear on the head of an enemy column, which could use only a portion of its own guns. The fleet that crossed the other's T was almost always victorious.

The Americans would cross his T, and there was nothing he could do about it. His ships had to exit the channel in a single line, into the teeth of the American guns and torpedoes. Fujii had neglected to mention the likelihood of American submarines.

"The destroyers will lead," Yamamoto said, repeating what had already been decided. "They will attack the Americans with torpedoes and scatter them. Then the battle line will emerge, with the *Yamato* leading and the others following. As the *Yamato*'s guns destroy the

American ships, the cruisers will search out and destroy the American carriers. Give Admiral Abe my congratulations on the great victory that he will win. I will wait here for his return."

Fujii gasped. It was a death sentence for Abe and his ships. "Yes, Admiral."

Yamamoto waited until he was alone again before burying his head in his hands. One or two ships might fight their way through, but the whole effort was what the British called a forlorn hope, an effort virtually destined for failure.

Yamamoto would not be waiting for their return. A submarine was positioned just off Honolulu, and, during the distraction of the battle, he and a handful of others would be rowed out and taken aboard for their escape to Japan. A transport ship also waited off Honolulu for the opportunity to escape with the irreplaceable remaining carrier pilots. The highly skilled pilots had never fought, and, with the exception of those lost on the *Akagi* and a few others, all were alive. With them, the handful of new carriers Japan was building could be staffed. Without them, the carrier planes would be flown by untrained personnel who would be slaughtered by the more experienced and increasingly skilled Americans. The sortie of the *Yamato* and the others was nothing more than a giant distraction. The pilots had to be saved.

JAKE NOVACEK STIFLED A SCREAM as he dragged Hawkins into the brush while his handful of other survivors covered them. It had been only a small Japanese probe, but it had been enough. Hawkins had taken a bullet in the leg that had smashed the bone, and Jake had been hit in the chest by a bullet that first ricocheted off a rock. If it had hit him squarely, he would have been dead. As it was, he had several broken ribs. Hawkins's leg was strapped to a rough splint made out of a tree branch.

With agonizing slowness, they reached the crest of the ridge and looked down into the narrow valley. "Shit," Jake muttered.

"That good, huh?" Hawkins managed through clenched teeth.

"Yeah," Jake said. "Out-fucking-standing."

A thousand yards away, a long column of Japanese trucks wound slowly down a rough path. They were bunched up, but, slow as they were, they were moving behind Jake's force. In a few minutes, they would be in position. Hundreds of Japanese soldiers would then disgorge from the trucks and climb the hill.

Hawkins had clawed himself upright by grasping a tree. "Damn, there are a lot of them. I guess it's over, ain't it, Colonel Jake?"

"Sure looks like it, Captain Hawk," Jake said. They could fall back the way they'd come, but doing so would put them back where that Japanese patrol waited for them to come running. Or, in his and Hawkins's case, come crawling.

"I guess we should stay here, then. No point in chasing around anymore, is there?" Hawkins said.

None of the Americans had any intention of being taken prisoner. After all they'd done, the Japanese would make their suffering long and horrible. They'd all decided to do what was done in the bad cowboy and Indian movies—save a last bullet for themselves.

"Colonel, if I can't manage it, will you shoot me?" Hawkins asked.

"Only if you'll do the same for me."

"Deal. Christ, I wonder if this is what Custer felt like?"

"Fuck Custer," Jake said. "I'm just glad we hurt the bastards and saved some of our people."

THE DESTROYERS WERE the first Japanese ships out of the channel. Twelve had entered it, but only eight emerged. The other four had been pulverized by swarming American dive-bombers. The sinking destroyers did manage to avoid blocking the channel by beaching themselves.

When the remaining destroyers emerged, they found themselves in range of a double line of American destroyers and light cruisers, along with a half dozen submarines and still another swarm of planes. Behind them was another line of battleships and heavy cruisers, all firing on the head of the column.

Japanese torpedoes were vastly superior to their American counterparts, but only a handful of destroyers managed to launch any before they were overwhelmed by concentrated American firepower. Even so, one American destroyer and a light cruiser were hit and sunk.

After the destroyers came the battleships *Yamato* and the *Kongo,* with the remaining Japanese light and heavy cruisers trailing. The *Yamato* was so huge she made the other Japanese battleship look like a toy. Overhead, newly promoted Rear Admiral Marc Mitscher watched from his seat behind the pilot of a Grumman TBF Avenger. It was his job to choreograph the deadly dance unfolding below. The U.S. Navy had total air superiority, but they'd lost about a third of their aircraft to Japanese gunners. Mitscher had to ensure that the remainder were utilized properly.

The size of the *Yamato* caught his breath. He'd seen her in the harbor, even watched as planes attacked her, but this was different. Now she approached the American battle line with her eighteen-inch guns blazing.

As the *Yamato* plowed through the sea, swarms of American planes flew about her. From his perch, Mitscher thought they looked like gnats around an angry bull elephant.

For the first time, American torpedo bombers were able to unleash their weapons while dive-bombers plunged from the sky. The *Yamato* took hit after hit, sometimes appearing to shudder, but she continued on.

Then the sixteen-inch shells from the *North Carolina* and the *Washington* raised mountainous splashes as they sought the range. These were quickly followed by shells from the older *Colorado* and *Maryland*. The *Maryland* had been damaged at Pearl Harbor, and her presence in the battle line was an inspiration to the crews of the other ships. Mitscher ordered the planes away lest they be hit or knocked down by the concussion from American shells.

Hit after hit struck the *Yamato,* and flames could be seen coming from her pagodalike superstructure. One of her forward turrets was knocked out, and the other seemed damaged, with one of the great guns askew. The *Yamato* turned so her rear turrets could be brought to bear on her American tormentors. This meant it was impossible for her to close with her adversaries, but that no longer seemed her task.

"Good God," said Mitscher, "won't anything stop her?"

The *Yamato* had endured more punishment than could be imagined, much less survived. He wondered what kind of hell was going on within her. So far, nothing had touched the giant battleship's power plant, but, one by one, her guns were put out of action and she became a flaming wreck. Admiral Oldendorf commanded the battle line, and he sent the *Maryland* and the light cruisers to finish off the

Yamato with torpedoes. The *Colorado* had been hit by the *Yamato* and was burning and dead in the water.

The *North Carolina* and the *Washington,* along with the heavy cruisers, soon bracketed the *Kongo* with their shells and killed her. While this went on, Mitscher's planes continued to savage the remaining Japanese ships until there were none.

Mitscher looked for the *Yamato.* American ships continued to fire shells and torpedoes at almost point-blank range, and the Japanese ship was listing to starboard. Finally, the beast was dead and sinking.

"That's for the boys on the *Pennsylvania,*" Mitscher said, and his pilot laughed harshly. Both had friends who'd died on the *Pennsylvania.*

It was over. The ocean outside the entrance to Pearl Harbor was littered with the smoking ruins of dead ships. Mitscher wondered how much fuel remained in their plane and was astonished at the amount. He checked his watch. The battle had taken less than an hour.

LIEUTENANT GOTO nearly embarrassed himself as he half jumped and half fell out of the front of the truck. His sword had gotten tangled up in his legs, nearly causing him to land in the soft dirt by the side of the miserable road.

Behind him, the other trucks disgorged their passengers. It would take but a few moments for Captain Kashii to organize the men and begin their climb up the hill. Goto was confident it would be all over quickly. Then he could get back to the relative comforts of Hilo. He never thought he'd actually long to return to that squalid and abandoned town.

With the noise of the trucks and the shouting of his troops drowning out everything else, Goto's first realization that something was dreadfully wrong came when the trucks behind his began to explode and the men started to scream.

Another ambush, he thought, and a major one. Then a dark shadow swooped overhead, and it was followed by another and another. "Planes," he shrieked, and dived into the bush. Others in Kashii's command had already beaten him to what they hoped was safety.

The ground around Goto was churned by bullets as another plane swept by. He glanced skyward and saw the Americans who'd already struck turning and preparing for another attack while others strafed and bombed at will.

There was a deafening explosion as a bomb ripped through just behind him, sending pieces of vehicles and soldiers flying into the sky. Within moments, every truck in the column was burning and bodies lay everywhere. The Americans understood where the surviving Japanese were attempting to hide and strafed the ground to either side of the trucks. Goto fought back his fear as bullets impacted within a few feet of him, showering him with dirt.

Then it was over. The planes were gone. Almost disbelieving, Goto realized he was unhurt. Oh, a few bumps and scratches, but nothing serious. He stood, and several others did as well, but few had been as fortunate as he. A soldier stood by Goto. One of his arms had been ripped off, and he was bleeding profusely. He groped for assistance with his remaining arm, and Goto pushed him away. The soldier fell over a legless corpse and didn't get up.

"Where's Kashii?" Goto yelled. At first, no one seemed to notice or care. Then a soldier gestured, and Goto lurched over on legs unsteady from fear. Kashii lay just outside his truck. He had caught several bullets in the chest, which was a bloody mass of red meat and white bone.

"What do we do, Lieutenant?" It was a young corporal, and Goto realized he was now in command of the decimated column. He doubted he had one in five unhurt, and even many of those were in shock from the suddenness of the assault. The corporal who'd asked the question was literally shaking with shock and fear. These were garrison soldiers, not shock troops, and they'd never been subjected to anything like what had happened to them.

"Gather everyone," Goto said. "We will return to Hilo." He did not think that the code of *bushido* required him to die this day. Japanese forces were permitted to retreat so they could fight again, and that was what he planned to do.

Goto noticed people moving through the rear of the shattered column. What the hell? he wondered. Then he realized. They were Hawaiians from the nearby villages and camps. Some had guns, and they methodically shot any Japanese who was standing. He watched in shock as axes and clubs were brought down on the wounded Japanese, while other Hawaiians picked up fallen rifles and turned them on the men who'd been their tormentors just a short while ago.

Goto turned to flee. He had gotten only a few steps when he was overwhelmed by a half dozen Hawaiians who pinned him to the ground. They relieved him of his sword and pistol and stripped him naked. He heard a voice and tried to turn his head. He recognized a woman he'd interrogated the day before. There was a bandage where he'd slashed one of her eyes after raping her.

The woman said something, and the men around her yanked Goto to his feet. The woman approached him and spat in his face. A man grabbed Goto's face as others steadied him with his arms held outright. They tied a rope around each of his arms, and he wondered why. The ropes were so tight he was in pain.

Then he realized. He screamed as they hacked off his hands with his own sword. The ropes would function as tourniquets and keep him from bleeding to death. Numb with pain and fear, he watched as a Hawaiian tied a string at the base of his penis and scrotum.

The woman appeared in front of him with a knife. With one smooth motion, she sliced off his testicles, and his screams reached an even higher crescendo.

Goto's body was a sea of red agony, and he could barely comprehend what was happening to him. When would they kill him? A rope was looped around his neck, and he thought they were going to hang him. A cloth bag was put over his head, and he heard laughter as someone jerked on the rope, pulling him forward.

After a few halting, lurching steps, he realized he wasn't going to die, at least not yet.

WILL HAWKINS LOOKED in disbelief at the carnage in the valley, the pain in his leg momentarily forgotten as a result of the sudden change in events. Only a handful of Japanese remained, and they were being run to ground. "Colonel Jake, did you know that was going to happen?"

"Not entirely," Jake said. "At least I wasn't confident enough that I thought I should tell you."

"Uh, you gonna tell me now?"

"Sure. Magruder landed on Maui with two other planes. All three were nearly out of fuel and had no bombs or ammo. Gustafson siphoned what remained out of the other two and put it into Magruder's, along with some stuff they found at a farmer's personal strip. Magruder contacted our carriers by radio, and he flew out to them with enough fuel to land.

"It was a helluva thing to do, because Magruder really wasn't certain where the carriers were. He had one chance to find them and one pass to land; otherwise, he'd have been lucky to be picked up by anyone anytime. Anyhow, we'd agreed by radio that I'd pull us back to this hill and that Magruder would lead planes to it. The whole thing was a little shaky. After all, Magruder'd never flown over here and only hoped he could find this hill among all the others. He had coordinates and all that, but this is still a small hill on a big island full of small hills."

"Shit," Hawkins said softly. "Shaky, my ass. What if he didn't find the carriers or couldn't land? What if he couldn't convince the carrier jocks to send the cavalry? Then what if he couldn't find this fucking hill? I'm glad you didn't tell me. I would've said you were crazy."

Jake smiled. "A fella's gotta take chances sometimes, although it sure helped when the Jap patrols stuck with the trucks. They stood out like a sore thumb, I'll bet." And it had worked, he thought. "Of course, I had no idea the local population would rise up like they have. That's frosting on the cake."

"What do we do now?" Hawkins asked.

Behind the hill, the surge of Hawaiian civilians was routing the small patrol that had been waiting for Jake and his handful of men to be chased back to them. Jake wondered how the Japs liked being the hunted instead of the hunters.

The woman with the bandaged eye approached him. Now what the hell did she want?

THE WOMAN WAS NAMED LANI, and she was of native Hawaiian ancestry. She told Jake that Kashii and Goto's thugs had taken a number of prisoners, including her husband and brother. They were now lodged in Hilo, in a bay-front store that served as Kashii's headquarters. Hilo was not an incorporated city, but it was the county seat. It had government buildings, including a federal building, but Kashii had avoided using them.

"We saved you, now you save them," she said simply. She admitted she had no idea if her family was alive, but she had to rescue them if she possibly could. How to do it was the only question.

"We had a choice," she added. "We could try to save our people while Kashii and Goto were out chasing you, but if we did, they would have returned and destroyed this little force, along with our families and others in and around Hilo. We decided to help you by ambushing Kashii and Goto and then imploring you to help us. I have to admit, we had no idea there were so few of you. Still, you must help us. You owe us."

"Agreed," Jake said, and others nodded.

Jake did not like planning operations on the fly, but this was an exception. To the best of Lani's knowledge, no Japanese soldiers had escaped her people's attack; thus, whatever garrison remained in Hilo was ignorant of events.

The American planes had done almost too good a job on the Japanese vehicles. Only three of the trucks were drivable. On the plus side, they were able to find a number of Japanese uniforms.

Jake's ribs had been taped but still hurt like the devil. Hawkins would come along, but his broken leg needed expert care. He would lie prone on the back of a truck, although he insisted he could move with crutches.

Thus, a column of Japanese trucks returning to Hilo and carrying Japanese soldiers would likely be taken at face value by the handful of Japanese soldiers who remained at Kashii's combination police station, military headquarters, and jail. They had to hit the place before the Japanese realized that Kashii and Goto were dead or captured, along with the vast majority of Hilo's garrison. They were about fifty miles from Hilo, and it was late afternoon. With luck, they would arrive when light was fading.

Lani permitted her bandage to be removed. The eye hadn't been gouged out, but it was bloodied and the flesh around it badly sliced. One of Jake's surviving soldiers was a medic, and he told Lani that she might not see out of that eye again. She sat still while the medic stitched her cuts and replaced the filthy rag with a clean bandage.

"Another reason to kill them," she spat.

"Hasn't there been enough killing?" Jake said.

Lani stared at him. "Not quite."

In a short while, the three trucks were rolling down the road toward Hilo. A handful of civilian vehicles followed. Hawaiians in Japanese uniforms rode the trucks along with Jake and a couple of other American soldiers. The Americans were lightly trussed to the truck and, to the casual observer, appeared to be prisoners of the triumphant Japanese. Jake had traded his rifle for a submachine gun now hidden under the seat, and the other Americans were similarly armed. The Hawaiians carried Japanese rifles, and Jake wondered how many knew how to use them.

As they drove, Jake had several fears. First, that there would be roadblocks, which would either delay or stop them; second, that Japanese warships would be off Hilo; and, last, that they'd be too late.

Luck was with them. There were no roadblocks. However, they could hear loud explosions coming from the bay. As they approached Hilo, now slowly and cautiously, they saw a Japanese destroyer moving away as fast as it could. One of her turrets was burning, and she was listing to starboard. In the distance, they could make out American fighter planes also leaving.

They stopped, and Hawkins was helped into the bed of Jake's truck. "Y'know," he said, "our planes might have mistook us for real Japs and killed us."

"Timing is real important," Jake said solemnly. "So are copious quantities of luck."

They approached the Japanese headquarters cautiously. It was late in the afternoon, and Jake hoped the fading light would hide their real identities for a few moments.

Very few of the city's remaining civilian population were to be seen, and these quickly disappeared at the sight of what appeared to be a Japanese column rumbling down their clean, neat streets. Only a handful of soldiers were visible at Kashii's headquarters, and they were busy watching the damaged destroyer. Clusters of civilians were gathered just outside the compound.

Finally, one soldier turned and gestured excitedly at the approaching trucks. Seeing what they thought was a victorious return, the soldiers began to wave and cheer until a noncom yelled at them. He snapped orders, and they started to fall into line.

"Some sergeants are real pricks," Hawkins said as they drove closer. The "prisoners" gathered their weapons, careful to keep them out of sight. The trucks drove quickly to the headquarters and through the formation, causing the Japanese soldiers to scatter. The noncom looked at them, puzzled. They braked sharply, and the American soldiers and Hawaiians inside jumped down, firing rapidly and killing Japanese at close range. Only a couple of Japanese soldiers managed to fire their weapons, but they were quickly eliminated. Jake jumped down, and the impact sent waves of pain from his ribs, nearly causing him to black out.

"The jail," he gasped. Only seconds had elapsed, and all the Japanese outside were dead or dying.

Jake led the surge into the jail. Another Japanese NCO stood behind a desk, a look of shock was on his face, and he was drawing his pistol. Jake cut him down with a burst from his Thompson. Two more soldiers emerged from the cell area and were gunned down by others who'd followed Jake.

There were no more Japanese, and silence was sudden. The Americans moved gingerly into the prison area. A handful of gaunt and bloody specters stared at them, disbelief on their faces. They were naked and chained to the bars, their bodies covered with burns and scabs.

Lani pushed her way through. She screamed when she saw her husband and brother. They had been horribly brutalized, but they were alive. Freed from their shackles, they were barely able to walk. Helping hands took them and the others out into the sunshine.

Jake looked around. In the distance, the damaged Japanese destroyer was disappearing over the horizon, black smoke pointing the way for more American planes to find and kill her.

Armed men pushed the civilians who'd been gathered around the Japanese HQ toward him. Lani had an ancient revolver in her hand and waved it. "They are collaborators. We are going to kill them."

Jake limped up and calmly took the pistol from her hand. "No," he said. "Enough. You told me the killing wasn't over, but now it is."

Lani glared at him, then softened. The fire went out of her eyes. "You're right. It is enough."

Jake continued. "First, we're going to investigate, and then we'll punish the truly guilty, and not just somebody who sold groceries to the Japs and would have been shot if they hadn't."

Lani nodded reluctantly and turned away. The suspected collaborators ran. It didn't matter what they did. They had nowhere to go.

Jake shook his head. He was so sick and tired of the fighting and the killing. When Lani was truly calmed down, she could begin interrogating the so-called collaborators.

Hawkins hobbled over. "What now?" he asked.

Jake took a deep breath. Was it over? Was it all truly over? His ribs hurt, and he had a host of other bruises to contend with.

"Captain Hawk, we're gonna wait up here for things to settle down. Then we get you and the other wounded taken care of by our new best friends down here in beautiful Hilo. After that, I'm going to radio Nimitz and tell him we've taken the town and I've declared myself the military governor of the island of Hawaii. Then we'll see what we can do about driving out any other Japs running around in the countryside. Can't be too many of them left, and they're leaderless and probably scared shitless. I'll bet I can get some planes to help root them out. Sound good?"

"Sounds great, Colonel. After that, can we go home?"

"Yeah," Jake said. Only thing, he wondered just what and where home was, and what part of it included Alexa. Did she really want her life to include him?

WITH ONLY ONE TORPEDO LEFT, Lieutenant Commander Fargo had considered taking the *Monkfish* back to California. However, he decided to wait a couple of days in case a good target turned up. A good submarine never returned with unspent ammo.

But no target did show up, and he was about to head east when he picked up a distant shape through his periscope. He waited as it drew closer and identified it as a typical merchant ship, one of hundreds like her. But she was Japanese and heading away from Hawaii, toward Japan. She was fair game, and he had one torpedo left.

"The hell with it," he said and ordered a firing plot. If the torpedo worked, they might sink her. If it didn't, they'd head for home with nothing lost.

At just under a mile, he fired. At just the right time, the torpedo exploded against the hull of the transport. Not bad, Fargo thought. He chuckled as he realized he was getting blasé. What fun was it to sink a transport in an open ocean after having braved the narrow channel of Pearl Harbor to sink a carrier?

Something strange was happening on the transport, though. She was belching people. What the hell? Fargo thought. She was definitely sinking, there were literally hundreds of people trying to get off her, and it quickly became apparent that there were nowhere near enough lifeboats or rafts. Shades of the *Titanic,* he thought, and fuck the Japs for not planning ahead.

But were these civilians or military personnel? When submarine warfare had started, a sub had been expected to give a ship a fair amount of time to disembark those aboard before torpedoing, or even to radio in the location of the sinking. Nobody did that anymore, of course. It was just too dangerous.

But he was curious. Still submerged, he eased the *Monkfish* to where he could see the dying transport better. Now most of her human cargo was in the water, and few would last more than a little while.

The ship was going down by the bow, with her stern high in the air. Fargo was able to read her name: the *Wichita Maru.* Hell, he thought. Why did the Japs name a ship after a town in Kansas? He noted it in the log and wondered just who was on the *Wichita Maru.*

CHAPTER 26

■

Jake Novacek sat in the high-back chair in the sparsely furnished anteroom and waited his turn to speak to the great man. Other colonels and even generals looked in at him and wondered just who Jake was and what he was doing in the partially completed Pentagon.

It had been more than four months since the battle on the hill and the liberation of Hilo, and so many things had happened.

The agony of Hawaii had been far from over. Even though abandoned, Admiral Iwabachi had gathered several thousand Imperial marines and other naval personnel and then unleashed a reign of terror over Oahu and Honolulu. In a spasm of fury, he'd slaughtered thousands of civilians, even continuing when the American 24th Infantry Division landed under the command of Major General Joe Collins. Iwabachi had retreated to Honolulu and forced the 24th to take the city street by street and house by house. The admiral and the remnants of his army had finally taken refuge in the brick building and dock where the Lurline liners had once brought smiling tourists from California to the islands.

It had been a mistake. Naval guns had flattened the dock at point-blank range. No survivors had been pulled from the rubble. However, Honolulu was virtually destroyed.

While the fighting had raged, Toyoza Kaga had been executed by Iwabachi for what the Japanese said was treason. Akira Kaga had survived and begun to pick up the pieces of his father's commercial empire.

No trace had been found of Melissa Wilson, but her son had been located in the care of a Japanese family who were very glad to give him back to the Americans.

Will Hawkins was in a hospital in San Francisco, while Ernie Magruder and Karl Gustafson had returned to other duties.

Jake and Alexa had been reunited quickly and flown to San Diego as soon as conditions permitted. While they waited, they found a place to stay, made love, and tried not to think about the future.

In San Diego, Jake had been greeted warmly by Admiral Nimitz, and both he and Alexa had been pleasantly surprised to see Jamie Priest. Their presence solved a small problem for Jamie; both Jake and Alexa stood up for him and Suzy Dunnigan at their wedding. Suzy was pregnant as a house and had been discharged from the WAVES, who, according to her, didn't have a sense of humor about pregnant sailors. She said that, while she had wanted to honor her dead father by serving in the navy, perhaps it was a greater honor to give him a grandchild.

Since Jake was privy to the existence of Magic, Jamie got Nimitz's permission to give him an update. Admiral Yamamoto had made it by sub to Japan, where he was calling for a negotiated end to a war that Japan could not win. This call had split Japan's government down the middle, with hawks and doves fighting for supremacy. In short, there was chaos in Tokyo.

Colonel Omori's whereabouts were unknown. Feeding the fishes was Jake's thought. At least Lieutenant Goto was dead. The Hawaiians who'd captured him had finally put him out of his misery a week after taking him.

But then Jamie had dropped the bombshell. "The Japs have been screaming on their radio about the whereabouts of a ship called the *Wichita Maru*. Jackass name for a ship, but it is or was a freighter that left Honolulu at night just before the Japanese attempted their breakout and hasn't been heard from.

"We all wondered just what the hell was so important about the *Wichita Maru,* and then we found out what her cargo was. She was carrying all the remaining Japanese pilots from the sunken carriers. We've checked submarine reports, and we're reasonably certain she was sunk with all hands by one of our boats. Jake, the Jap pilots are even more important to them than the carriers. Ships you can replace, but the Japs do not have a system for replacing their pilots. Jake, they're fucked."

Jamie also told him that the late Toyoza Kaga was being hailed as the man who had headed up a spy ring in Honolulu and provided the United States with all the information regarding Japanese plans. Included in his ring were the colored staff at the various officers' clubs, who, it was said, had overheard many Japanese talking about those plans, and could not imagine a Negro understanding Japanese. According to Magic intercepts, the Japanese had accepted the story as gospel; thus, the existence of Magic was still a secret.

Jake and Alexa left San Diego by rail and arrived in Washington, D.C., a week and a half later. The trip gave them a chance to find out more about themselves and the world about them. The invasion of North Africa under Eisenhower had occurred, and both England and Russia appeared to be holding out. Jamie had told them this meant the fleet would be returning to the Pacific, where Admiral Spruance and a rejuvenated Bull Halsey would lead attacks against a pair of lightly defended islands off the coast of Japan—Okinawa and Iwo Jima. With little in the way of a Japanese navy left, the Americans could roam the Pacific at will, and the two islands would be set up as bombing stations for attacks against Japan. General MacArthur was steamed because he wanted the Philippines liberated first, but the navy's star was ascendant, and the Philippines would wait for a little while.

In Washington, Jake met Alexa's uncle and thought that, under different circumstances, the short, stubby congressman could have been a ridiculous little man. However, he exuded a genuine fondness for Alexa that was reciprocated and that meant he was Jake's friend.

Jake's thoughts were interrupted by a very sharply dressed captain who told him he could go into the inner sanctum. Jake still wore the eagles of a full colonel, although he wondered what his real rank might be. The next few minutes would tell as he stepped into the office.

Jake started to come to attention, but General George C. Marshall stopped him, rose from behind his desk, and shook his hand. "You did a great job in Hawaii, Colonel, a great job."

"Thank you, sir."

Marshall gestured for him to be seated. "How did your meeting with Roosevelt go?"

"Very good, sir. He seemed almost exuberantly happy." Jake smiled at the recent memory. "He even made me a martini."

Marshall smiled inwardly. The overwhelming victory in the Pacific had purged Roosevelt of the demons that had been plaguing him. There was no longer any serious worry about the president's health. Henry Wallace would not be the next President of the United States.

"Good. Now let me get to the point of this meeting, which is, of course, your future. By the way, Admiral Nimitz wrote me and said you could transfer to the navy anytime. King endorsed it."

"Uh, I'll pass, sir." Jake hoped it was a joke.

"Wise decision," Marshall said with the barest flicker of a smile. "Colonel, it is rumored that I keep a list of officers who I think can accomplish things. That rumor is true, and it is also true that your name was not on it. It is now. You have conclusively proven that you are a wartime officer, and we are in a war that will last for some time. Sadly, the beginning of any war requires the weeding out of men who appeared qualified in peacetime but who fail to live up to expectations when the shooting starts."

Jake understood that Marshall was talking about people like Admiral Kimmel and General Short. Both had been honest, decent men who'd failed the test of battle. There had been many others; even division and corps commanders were sacked for being unable to function in the face of a real enemy.

"First of all, Colonel, you will keep your rank. It's now permanent, and you deserve it."

"Thank you, sir." A year ago Jake had been an overage captain. Now he was a full colonel, with prospects for additional advancement.

"I wish you to work here in the Pentagon for about six months, providing us with as much insight as you can regarding the Japanese way of war. After that, you will be sent to England to serve with those who are planning future actions against the Nazis. It is most likely that you will be serving in an intelligence and security capacity. Because of your knowledge of Magic, you will not be given a combat command."

Jake was slightly surprised, but not disappointed, at not getting a combat command. He'd had his fill of fighting. "Then I will not be returning to the Pacific?"

"No. The land war portion of the Pacific campaign will belong to the marines and General MacArthur, with the marines probably bearing the brunt of it. Your penchant for honest evaluations and assess-

ments would not serve you well there. MacArthur's staff includes officers who tell him what he wishes to hear. They would destroy you.
Eisenhower is probably going to command in England. He is an honest man who can handle bad tidings. He doesn't like them any more
than the next man, but he can deal with them."

"Yes, sir."

Marshall stood. The interview was over. "Take a couple of weeks'
leave time, Colonel. You deserve it, and that's an order."

Jake grinned. "Thank you, sir."

"Oh, and you're going to get a medal. No one's decided which one
yet, but a Silver Star is very likely."

Jake found it difficult to speak. "Thank you, sir," he finally managed.

In the hallway, Alexa took his arm. She was wearing a blue dress
that must have been several years old since it covered much of her
magnificent legs.

"How did it go?" she asked.

"I have two weeks off, six months here, and a future. Oh yeah, I'm
getting a medal."

She squeezed his arm. "Excellent summary. I can see why the military likes you. Take me to dinner and fill me in on the details."

"All right."

"Here's a summary of my own. You have two weeks. Marry me."

Jake took a deep breath. He loved her, and they'd discussed marriage a number of times, although without coming to any conclu-
sions. "Are you sure?"

"You're a colonel with medals, and that'll dazzle my relatives. Soon
you'll be a general, and that will knock them on their elegant cans. Besides, my dearest Jake, I love you very much, and, after all we've been
through, do you think I give a shit? I want to be called Mrs. Novacek,
and I want to have a little Jake on the way before you go to England."

Jake laughed. How the hell had she known he was going to England? Magic?

ACKNOWLEDGMENTS

This is my fourth alternate history novel, and all have been published by Random House's Ballantine division. The people at Ballantine realize that alternate history is a growing and very intriguing niche in the world of historical fiction. And, for a writer, it is intellectually stimulating and just great good fun to tweak or twist history and make it come out plausibly and logically.

Along with being grateful for my wife, Diane; my daughter, Maura; and all the friends who have supported me, I'd like to thank Ryan Doherty and Fleetwood Robbins of Ballantine for all their assistance and advice.